Another Word for Help

K. E. Marlow

K. E. Marlow Publishing
author@kemarlow.com

ISBN 978-1-953937-00-1 (Paperback) • ISBN 978-1-
953937-01-8 (e-book) • ISBN 978-1-953937-02-5
(alternative e-book)
Genres: Contemporary Fiction • Young Adult
Subgenres: Coming of Age • Disability Lit • LGBT Lit

For more information on K. E. Marlow's past, present,
and future works please visit www.kemarlow.com
where you can also ask questions or follow her on
social media for the latest news.

Thanks to my loving family, consisting of my mom, dad, sisters, husband-to-be, and my cats. Especially the cats, because they aren't already entitled enough.

PROLOGUE

"I just don't think you should take this job."

Keith tried to hide his annoyance. He really did. He must have failed though because he could feel the tension forming in his forehead as his eyes narrowed slightly. For the past week he'd been hearing the same thing over and over again, and if he was being honest he was one-hundred percent done arguing about it.

"It's too late," he stated. The look of shock on his Person's face was ignored. "I already signed the paperwork when I went over for my final interview last night. I start in August."

"You signed right away? Why would you go and do that?"

"Because I wanted the job, Will!" He shot back with an equal amount of attitude. Instantly a wave of regret washed over him, and he sighed at the familiar feeling of guilt. Keith hated raising his voice at anyone, let alone his friend and Person (the person he was currently assisting). "Sorry. I just… it's going to be different, but it's not like I won't get the hang of it. I've been helping you and Jordan for almost three years. I'll be fine."

Will's mouth was set in a thin line. He appeared to be thinking about what he wanted to say, one hand messing with the controls on his power chair as he did so.

"Something's just not right about those people," Will finally said. He'd stopped fidgeting in exchange for curling one hand around the joystick of his chair. "Your new

Person's disability isn't a cognitive one. He should be able to make decisions without his mother's approval, but from what I gathered when I gave her your verbal recommendation she rules over every aspect of that guy's life. There's no way in hell I ever would have let my mother do what that woman does for her son. He passes out; he's not an invalid. There's no reason other than either the guy being lazy or his mom being completely domineering for his lack of involvement in finding his own PAs."

"That guy has a name you know."

"I forgot what it was, so..."

He sighed. "*Brandon* is going into his last and eighth year of school to get his master's degree in history. It makes sense his mom would be taking care of finding personal assistants for him since he is halfway through the process of writing a one-hundred-plus page paper."

"Maybe, but from what you said Brandon has never dealt with any of the hirings since he's been here. It's going on eight years, Keith. Doesn't that seem a bit strange to you?"

"Not really. I think his mother just really cares and wants to do what she can to help her son. If he doesn't mind his mom taking care of the complicated stuff then who am I to judge?"

"I don't know. Something about his mother just rubbed me the wrong way when we spoke on the phone. She seemed critical of my questions and was offended when I displayed surprise over how much she assists her son. His disability is different than mine, she said. That much is obvious; however, I still know from experience with other people with the same disability that none of the job descriptions have been as high maintenance as this one. It's... concerning. That's why I didn't want you to take the job. What if you find out you hate it? You said that the contract is legally binding, didn't you? You'll have to help for two semesters now."

"That's right. And I'm well aware of your feelings on the matter," he began tersely, "but as much as your concerns are valid I *need* this job. Hate it or not I won't be able to afford this last year of college without it."

"You've gotten through the last three years fine, Keith. Why not one more?"

"I only got through the first year because my dad took out money from his retirement fund, and the last two years I managed to get the student loans I needed as well as made enough money from my three jobs to pay off the difference. As it is I won't be getting the loans I need to pay off my last two semesters, which is why this job being an in house thing makes the ten thousand dollar room and board charge disappear. I need it to disappear if I don't want to risk dropping out."

"I get that, but—"

"This job gets me free housing, food, PA experience, and even pays me on top of all that. This is basically my dream job. Why can't you just be happy for me, Will?"

Nothing could stop the hurt look from crossing over Will's face. Keith almost felt bad, but after days of being talked down to like a child again and again he was losing his patience. As much as he was going to miss being Will's PA the stubborn guy was getting on his nerves. Keith refused to keep listening to this during the last two weeks on the job.

"I'll stop bringing it up then," Will said curtly. He turned his power chair on and made his way to his desk, seemingly pulling up his latest homework assignment. "I just don't understand this Brandon guy. If he is twenty-five years old then why is his mom the one making all of the choices for him? As soon as I was eighteen I kicked my mom off any form I could. I might have cerebral palsy but that didn't make her any more qualified to take care of me than myself. I interviewed my PAs, I handled figuring out my room and board. My family has money but even I wouldn't have allowed my parents to buy a freaking house for me to stay in while I went to college. It's strange to me, alright? And I'm worried about you."

Now Keith felt like a jerk for being so defensive. He'd been listening to his friend's concerns, but he hadn't really been *listening* to him.

His eyes softened. "I know you're worried, Will, but I'm not the same freshman that started here three years ago. Brandon's mom is off-putting, I'll admit. She's only going to be there to train us for a week though, okay? After that it'll be me, Brandon, and the other two PAs. I'm going to be okay. I'll just miss you a lot is all."

"You could always come to visit me in New Jersey," the other joked while spinning his chair around to face Keith. The tension between them was finally dissolving. "I'd be happy to host you. Maybe you could come up when Jordan comes to visit sometime. You know she likes to make frequent visits."

"Sooner or later she's going to be moving out there," he punched Will's shoulder lightly. "You guys have been engaged for what, like two years?"

"One year and seven months, stupid. The wedding won't be for a while though. We both have things we need to finish up in our hometowns, and then we need to decide where we'll be settling down, and then comes the wedding planning so— you're distracting me!"

"Sorry! I'm just curious. Anyway, I might have to take you up on that offer if I ever make it to the east coast. We could go to a Dave & Buster's and drown in a ball pit again."

"That was one time, and it was so totally worth it."

"It took two people to get you out, and three others to laugh at me falling in."

"But it was so *fun*."

"You nearly gave your mom and I heart attacks."

"Still worth it!" He sang, making them both devolve into laughter. After a couple of moments Will reached an arm out, his hand curved slightly inward but his fingers stretching out as far as his muscles would allow until he grasped Keith's shirt. "I'm going to miss you too, man. You are one of my best PAs. Brandon will be lucky to have you."

Keith leaned down, hugging the Person he'd been bathing, feeding, helping go to the bathroom, putting to bed, taking to the movies, escorting to class (rain or shine), cleaning up after he came back with his girlfriend absolutely hammered, helping get into sexual positions, and so on for the first three years of his college experience.

Nobody would ever replace his first Person, but that didn't mean he wouldn't form a relationship just as unique with Brandon too.

CHAPTER ONE

As they pulled into the driveway Keith felt the knot in his stomach tightening. During the ride over he'd expected to feel some nervousness; however, while he'd always been an anxious guy when it came to transitioning this bout of unease was particularly strong. Usually changing dormitories was enough to unsettle him. It wasn't until his belongings were put away and his bed was set up to his liking that he'd fully relax. Why was this move so different?

Seeing as he was moving into a home with three more or less strangers probably made the anxiety he'd felt in the past pale in comparison to what he was feeling now. At least in previous years he'd known his roommates before moving in. As it was he had only interacted with his new Person for a grand total of ten minutes, not to mention he didn't even know the names of his other roommates. All he had to go by were the initials on the schedule that had been sent out a month in advance.

Not very helpful when trying to dig information up on his new roommates and coworkers on Facebook.

The prospect of having every meal for the next week with his new Person's parents for training purposes only put him further on edge. It's not that he didn't look forward to getting to know them. The meals he'd had with Will's mother and step-father were happy memories. On the other hand, in those cases he had neither been the one working nor had he felt any pressure to conduct himself diligently in front of his Person's family.

The Thompsons had… higher expectations. What else could he call it when reading a thirty-plus page contract with twenty-five pages of expectations on how he should behave as well as step-by-step instructions on how to do the tasks explicitly expected of him daily and weekly?

Yeah, higher expectations sounded like a good way of summarizing that up.

Despite how daunting the instructions had seemed at first glance Keith knew he could handle it. Truth be told he was a good actor; it was what made him so good at customer service as well as in his field of working with people in a more health-oriented setting. It meant plenty of smiling, nodding, and feigning confidence at something he wasn't particularly sure how to accomplish. An agenda book to help keep track of his different jobs and tasks helped too.

One thing that did worry Keith was the prospect of constantly being around his coworkers. He liked to conduct himself in a certain way when working. He always remained calm, patient, attentive, respectful, and absorbent of information; living in his workplace was going to be a challenge because it meant always being "on". If his perfected mask of professionalism fell off, then there was a chance they wouldn't see him as capable anymore. Not to mention what would happen if Brandon thought he was weird. Keith knew from experience it was hard to work as a personal assistant when the Person they worked for didn't "click" with them or vice versa. The constant strains of silence were awkward as hell.

It won't be awkward. I can do this, he told himself as he hopped out of the car. Once his parents were done admiring the house he would be living in they came out of the vehicle too. *Remember how hard it was to pick up Will when I first started? I kept hurting my back because I wasn't lifting with my legs, and I felt so strange to be taking care of someone I didn't meld personalities with that at first I almost gave up. I was about to quit, remember? But what did I do? I kept working at it and soon enough became one of the best PAs he had. This is that awkward beginning all over again. Whatever happens I can do this!*

"Keith, are they expecting us or should we knock?" His mother asked as they approached the back door of the house.

"Also shouldn't we be going to the front?" His father added.

He shook his head. "They don't use their front entrance because they don't want to mess up the veneer in the doorway. They said to use the back door for everything, especially move in since it's by the driveway anyway. Moving boxes into the house and upstairs will be easier. And yeah, mom, just knock. They're probably waiting for us in the kitchen, which is just a couple feet from the back door."

"Okay."

True enough upon knocking Brandon's mother was at the door in seconds.

She had longer hair than any adult he'd ever seen, the yellow color of straw which stood out like a sore thumb in a family where everyone else's hair was black. Her height was above average, and as she ushered everyone inside with a quick "Welcome!" he noticed that like every time he'd visited before her tanning-bed tan skin was covered by dress pants, a fancy top, and dress flats as if she was attending some sort of business meeting. It struck him as odd when he noticed her husband dressed far more casually, but he guessed it was either because she wanted to make a nice first impression on his parents or she just liked dressing up.

"It's so nice to meet you," she directed at Keith's parents after everyone was seated at the kitchen table. Her husband, who was wearing jeans and a T-shirt, sat beside her silently. "My name is Jacqueline Thompson, and this is my husband Larry."

"Hello," Larry greeted politely, an awkward smile on his face. Perhaps he was shy?

"My son Brandon is upstairs with his full-time PA at the moment," Jacqueline resumed, "but you'll be able to meet him when we bring you upstairs for the tour. I assume you'll want to see the place your son will be living in for the next year?"

"We get to see your room?" Keith's father was all excitement and a teasing grin.

"Dad," his son whined.

"What? This is such a lovely house. I can't wait to see what your room looks like."

Jacqueline smiled at the compliment. "I'm glad you find the house appealing. We bought it after Brandon was done with undergrad since rent and food for him and his PAs ended up being cheaper than university housing anyway. We've been keeping it clean and trying to prevent damage so we can sell it after he finishes up his master's program this year."

"Well you've done a great job," Keith's mother said. "I'm Colleen Sloan by the way."

"And I'm Michael."

The husbands reached out to shake hands while Jacqueline got up from her spot at the table. "Would any of you like something to drink?"

No one took her up on her offer. When she came back a moment later with a glass of water for herself she launched into some details about the job.

"From what Keith has told me," she spoke mainly to Keith's parents, "you've seen him work with his last student, William, in the past. While William was an individual with cerebral palsy and more often spent time in a power chair, my son does not use a wheelchair unless he does not have a PA. He also does not need help eating, bathing, or going to the bathroom. Brandon has an impairment that causes him to more or less pass out. He does not have seizures. He does however have these fainting spells, or episodes, two to nine times a week. When it happens it is completely random; however, when he is stressed out emotionally or physically ill the number of episodes he has usually goes up to three or more a day. This means he more or less loses complete muscle control for a moment which causes him to faint for anywhere between five seconds to a full minute. Keith, along with the other PAs, will be preventing Brandon from getting hurt from the falls he'll be experiencing."

"Oh wow. Is it genetic? Is it caused by something in the brain? Or the nerves between the brain and the body?" Colleen asked. She didn't know much about disabilities as it was, so she was interested.

Jacqueline shook her head solemnly. "Yes and no. Unfortunately, he was born with a genetic mutation that randomly acted up when he was a few years old. It affects his blood cell count and makes it fluctuate erratically for no reason. When his cell counts get low it causes a complete body shutdown. It's a blunder of the signals in his body going haywire for no reason at all. The doctors are baffled. There is no pattern; it just acts up as it pleases."

"And there's no way to stop it from doing that?" Michael questioned dumbly.

Keith elbowed him, frowning.

"Dad!" He hissed.

"What?" The man whispered back. "I just want to know."

The woman across from them took a sip of her water, noticing the exchange with some amusement.

"Brandon is on some medications that help stop counts from rising or declining too quickly, but there's nothing else anyone can do for him. We could put him through annual bone marrow transplants; however, not only would it be counter-intuitive to his overall health to do it almost yearly, there would be the constant struggle of finding donors. Not to mention the expenses."

Colleen winced. "That sounds like a lot of money. Still, if the condition is so dangerous to Brandon anyway wouldn't it be worth trying it out at least once? He might find it's worth the trouble after all."

"Seeing as you've purchased multiple houses it can't be that unrealistically expensive either, right?" Michael added in only for his wife to glare at him. "What? Keith had to document how much he makes a year before getting the job. It's only right I did some research of my own."

The blonde laughed, which was strange considering the topic.

"Isn't he in good hands? I admit we do own three properties as well as a portion of the company Larry works for, but we don't have that much money." She waved the prospect off like it was a crazy notion. "When my mother-in-law passed away not too long ago she left us quite a bit; however, even with insurance Brandon's medical bills add up over time. We have to make sure not to spend it fruitlessly in case something bad happens and we need the money at hand. We get some money from the state to help us out as it is."

Keith could tell his father was doubtful about this family "not having a lot of money". They knew people who had a lot of money to spend, but not even those people purchased a six-bedroom three-bathroom house with the works outright.

"Anyway," she continued, "there's no guarantee the treatments would help long enough to truly benefit him anyhow. He would still have blood irregularities in a less severe fashion, not to mention the fact he wouldn't be able to live a fulfilling life in and out of the hospital. We didn't want him to be in pain or get left behind in school."

This much Keith hadn't known. His heart went out to

the Thompsons as he listened to his parents offer their apologies for asking and regrets at possibly upsetting them.

"It's quite alright. I have to go over this with just about everyone who winds up interacting with my son. Medical officials, professors, strangers; you name it. If I had a dollar for every time Brandon passed out in public, which as you can imagine draws a lot of attention as well as a helpful Harry or two, then we would be rich. I also used to be a health teacher, so I'm a bit more impartial about explaining his condition than your average parent. That being said would you like a tour of the house now before Larry and I bring the boxes upstairs?"

She smiled politely, one hand gesturing toward the other side of the house while the other held her glass of water. Something about the way she spoke and the way she held herself suddenly felt plastic. Despite her saying the questions hadn't upset her, the unyielding aura she exuded screamed otherwise.

Keith shrugged off his observations. He was always a bit too quick at reading people, and oftentimes he jumped to conclusions. He needed to get to know the Thompsons better before letting his gut feeling overwhelm his opinions on them.

"We can bring up the boxes," Michael proposed after accepting their offer. He was already standing up and stretching lightly. "There's no need for you to go through the trouble of doing it. Keith and I can handle it."

"Actually, I would prefer my husband and me to take care of it. We used to allow the PAs or their families to help bring luggage or boxes upstairs, but at one point a banister got scratched because someone slipped and something got dropped onto it."

"Someone fell?"

"The wooden steps can be slippery," Jacqueline reiterated. "If you're wearing socks and are going down them in a rush it's pretty easy to take a tumble. Honestly it's a safety hazard at this point. When we're done with the tour you can bring the boxes up to the front door though, and we'll take them from there."

Unlike his parents Keith had already known the Thompsons would be the ones taking care of his luggage. He'd read it in the booklet of rules he'd been given that moving anything bigger than a laundry basket or heavier than a full backpack technically needed to be handled by someone in the Thompson family. It had seemed silly to him at first, but after rereading the thirty-page document of rules and finding out he could get in big trouble for violating it he shrugged it off. It meant less work for him to do. He couldn't complain.

Part of him did wonder how his parents would react if they knew it was actually against his contract to bring a box up the stairs.

He pushed the thought away. There was no need for him to be petty right now; he had a tour to go on.

The tour was solely for the benefit of his parents, but that didn't mean Keith wasn't paying attention. If he was being truthful he had been too worried over making a good impression during his last three visits to take the "minor details" in.

They began in the kitchen, a lovely marble-topped space with stainless steel appliances, a dark wooden floor and cabinets to match, and two separate dining rooms that put any kitchen he'd ever been in to shame. The fridge was so wide it would take his entire wingspan to encompass it, and it still towered a foot over him. There were also more cabinets than he could count on both hands.

I guess with four guys they need a lot of space for food, he mused as his family walked past a bathroom and into the front room of the house.

The living room wasn't exactly new to Keith seeing as it was the room he'd had his interviews in, but as Jacqueline pointed out the couches arranged around a glass coffee table, flat-screen television, a rocking chair sat next to a fireplace, and harmonium stationed purely for decoration purposes only his parents were blown away.

What was new was the trip to the basement, which was so large it could fit four college students comfortably. In it was just really laundry room type stuff, the washer, dryer, racks with towels and cleaning implements on them, and so on. There was an entirely separate room used as what seemed to be a bedroom, but it only really had a bed and a small table with a lamp in it.

"That room," Jacqueline pointed at the very place he was looking at, "is where either my husband and I will stay. There's just a queen size bed there. Unlike the rest of the house which will be cleaned by the part-time PAs every weekend either my husband or I take care of cleaning it. It's not used much save for during training and when we pay the occasional visit."

There were also designated areas for vacuums (yes there were three) and lawn care items, in addition to the floor to ceiling shoe rack that was somehow already half full.

"Oh, most of those are my son's dress shoes. His regular shoes are in the rack in his closet. Feel free to use the space as you'd like too, Keith."

He nodded at Jacqueline's words, the question of why a guy would own so many shoes lost in thought as they made their way up the stairs and another flight to the second floor.

"There are four rooms on this floor," she continued as they surveyed each room. "The master bedroom is for my son. The door is closed at the moment which means he's probably in the bathroom. He'll be out shortly I'm sure. While we wait, the second largest room is for the full-time PA since he will be working the most hours. He's already moved in as you can see."

The bedroom was rather spacious, white and gold-colored furniture not taking up a lot of room in comparison to the bed stationed in the middle of the wall. There was only one window which was blocked by a tree.

It probably gets pretty dark, he thought as they left the room. *No wonder there are like four lamps in here. It's not even overkill; they're just that necessary.*

"This one is the other part-time PA's room."

Slightly smaller than the last, this room had ebony furniture as well as a lot of metal racks and large fuzzy rugs. It got a lot more natural light than the other one though that was for sure.

"And finally this is your room, Keith."

He suddenly remembered why he'd liked his room way more than the other ones.

Firstly, he could appreciate the obnoxious number of windows that gave him a view of the street below. He needed the sunlight to get him up in the morning when possible or he would just sleep the day away. Secondly, the room was big yet small enough that it wouldn't feel empty when he unpacked. He also admired the maroon red paint, which was in stark contrast to the white and gray of the rooms prior. The wicker bed, dresser, bedside tables, and wardrobe also looked nice. Not as nice as the ebony furniture of the second room, maybe, but better than what was in the other part-time PAs room.

"This looks very comfortable," Michael commented as he gazed at the carpet which took up most of the floor space in the room.

"It does," Colleen agreed. "I love the wicker furniture you guys got. Did you find it all separately, or did you purchase it as a package?"

The women were five minutes into a discussion about shopping for furniture when the door to Brandon's room opened.

Two people stepped out, one face being the familiar face of Brandon while the other one must have been one of the PAs. Brandon had somewhat long black hair that grew past his ears, murky greenish-brown eyes, and freckles that stood out on his boyish cheeks. His nose was a bit bigger than his face complimented though, and his smile looked a bit lopsided. This made him seem a tad awkward at first glance.

As for the other male holding onto Brandon with one arm, this one was far less expressive. His hair was short and dark, his eyes a more vibrant green than the male beside him. He was olive-skinned and taller than Keith, but still an inch short of Brandon who was nearing six feet. There wasn't much emotion on his face as he took in the people before him. Either he was focusing on his job completely, or he wasn't too excited about the number of people standing in the hall. Something made Keith guess it was the latter case.

"Great, you two are done! Now you can introduce yourselves to one another. Keith, why don't you introduce your family first?" Jacqueline instructed.

"Oh, um, sure." He said oh-so smoothly. "These are my parents. I'm Keith, one of the part-time PAs."

"I'm Brandon," the boy greeted more eloquently. He held out a hand for his parents to shake, which was more than Keith would have offered. It felt a bit too formal or business-like in his opinion. "It's a pleasure to meet you!"

Lastly, the PA holding onto Brandon nodded in greeting. "Hello. My name is Isaac, and I'll be working full-time."

"So you're not a student then?" Colleen asked.

"Not here. I've been taking a couple of online classes, but it's slow work. College is ridiculously expensive."

"We're well aware of that," she agreed with an understanding smile before glancing back at her son.

Keith wanted to say something more, perhaps ask Isaac about his prior personal assistant experience or voice his agreement with school's expensiveness, but Jacqueline launched into another bout of explanation.

"Oh, one last thing! If you hadn't noticed there is one other door in this hall. This one," she motioned to the door between Brandon and Isaac's room, "is to the bathroom the PAs will be sharing. Brandon has a bathroom in his own room."

"Anyway," she said while heading back down the stairs with Larry at her heels, "now that the tour is over why don't we bring in your stuff?"

After waving goodbye to Brandon and Isaac, Keith followed the adults down the stairs. While the Thompsons worked on propping the doorway and disabling the security system Keith helped his dad bring the boxes and suitcases to the door for Larry to take. The black-haired man muttered a quiet thank you every time he was handed a box, which seemed sort of excessive after the every one. After several minutes of merely watching the man grab his belongings the car was empty.

"That went smoothly!" Jacqueline smiled as she stood outside with Keith and his parents. "Keith, are you going to head upstairs to unpack right away? You and Elijah, the other part-time PA, have training with Brandon and Isaac at seven tomorrow morning. He'll be here later tonight to drop his belongings off, which isn't ideal since you'll both have to be up so early, but it can't be helped. I just want to make sure you get settled before it gets too late."

"I'm going to go out to dinner with my parents before they have to drive back home," he responded. "I'll be back in an hour though, so I can unpack when I get back tonight."

"You're leaving now? We haven't had time to teach you how to use the security system yet. I suppose I can give you the house key, but without knowing how to disable the security system it might notify the police."

"If it's too much trouble we can skip dinner," Colleen offered much to Keith's dismay. He was looking forward to spending time with his family while he could.

Jacqueline shook her head. He could tell she was unhappy about their plans not corresponding with hers, but he could also tell she was trying to hide it by flashing a smile at his mother.

"Oh, I couldn't stop you all from having a nice family dinner! I'll teach him how to use it tomorrow I suppose. As for right now I'll give you the key," she directed at Keith, "but perhaps when you're back you can text me so I can disable the alarm. Then I'll teach you how to do it."

"Sounds good to me. See you later, Mrs. Thompson."

His parents said goodbye to Jacqueline and Larry, joining Keith in the car after a couple of minutes of conversation he hadn't overheard. Once the trio was on the road, however, Michael turned around in his seat to look at his son.

"I have a question. You're not going to be living in that house with the boy's parents there too, are you?"

The confusion was plain on Keith's face. "No. They'll be here for the next week for training purposes, but after that they should be going back to their own house upstate. Why?"

His father turned back in his seat looking relieved. "I just wanted to make sure. They seem a little uppity for my taste. They also act kind of strange, don't they?"

"Yeah, they're a little weird." His mother agreed, throwing Keith for a loop.

"What are you guys talking about? They have a lot of money, sure, but they aren't that weird."

"They want you to deep clean the entire house every weekend. Isn't that a bit excessive?"

"It's what I'm getting paid to do though. And I'm only going to be cleaning half of the house every weekend, not the entire thing. The other part-time PA cleans the other half."

"Isn't it still going to take a long time? You mentioned

a four-page list on how to clean each specific piece of furniture and room."

"She estimated three hours to clean each floor, so it's not that bad."

"Perhaps, but you have to cook dinner three nights a week as well, right? Then you have to completely clean the kitchen after every meal, and—"

"I knew I shouldn't have told you anything about the job." He cut in. "It's going to be fine, alright? I can handle it."

Colleen let out a sigh. "Sweetie, we're just worried. You tend to overwork yourself. Didn't you say you were still going to be working at that restaurant and the library twice a week on top of the twenty-five hours you'll be working there? You're at the maximum number of credit hours for this semester too, aren't you?"

"I need to do the maximum if I want to graduate on time."

"Making up that one failed math class from your freshman year has set you back way too much," his father complained. "The fact one class has made it to where you need to load yourself up on courses for the rest of your college career is asinine."

"I switched majors too, dad. I'm lucky biology was close enough requirement-wise to make switching to kinesiology feasible. I won't have to take an extra semester if I get the rest of the credits I need this year. Trust me; I mapped out my schedule super well so it shouldn't be that overwhelming."

"Do you really need all three jobs though?"

"Mom, you know that even with three jobs I still might not be able to pay off school on time to get my degree when I graduate."

"We'll figure something out," Michael intervened. "We always do."

Keith frowned, suddenly annoyed. "I don't want to wait

until the last second, dad! We always do that and it makes me sick to my stomach. I'm doing what I need to make sure I can finish school without owing more money out of pocket than I already do. I'm lucky enough that my loans will be in the thirty-thousands as it is."

"I'm sorry we can't help you out more, sweetie."

"Mom, it's fine. You both have already helped me out enough."

"But we haven't. If we did you wouldn't be working so hard. Three jobs on top of eighteen credit hours is a lot for a twenty-one-year-old."

"I know someone a year older that has seven jobs on top of school. I can always work harder."

"You shouldn't have to. I don't want you working yourself ragged, Keith. You're supposed to have fun during your senior year."

"I'll still have time to have fun," he pressed. "Can't we stop talking about this? I just want to enjoy a nice dinner with the two of you before you have to go. I'm not going to be able to go home until November for Thanksgiving break, so it's going to be a while until I get to see you guys again. Unless you visit me."

His mother pouted. "Three months is too long for us to go without visiting you. We'll try to visit you for your birthday, okay?"

"Sounds good to me," he said. A thought occurred to him after a moment though, making him pause. "Wait. What about grandma? I know grandpa is fine in the home, but Kassie can't come if she's watching her."

Wincing, his father let out a long sigh. "Honestly, she's deteriorating fast. We're getting her into hospice care any day now if the insurance approval would just hurry the hell up."

"That's good, I guess. You guys can't handle taking care of her as it is." Fault Keith for being detached, but years in the PA field can mess with one's natural levels of empathy and apathy. There was also the fact that he barely knew his grandparents. They were fundamentally strangers to him since they lived so far apart for the greater part of his life, so he felt sadder about his father's pain than he did about his grandparents reaching the end of their lives. "Kassie shouldn't have to babysit her own grandma either; she's thirteen. With how violent grandma's been getting it isn't safe. She doesn't even know who we are anymore."

"I know, Keith. She's been gone for a long time. I just thought it would have been quicker. The game we've been playing the last seven months has been horrible. It's sick to watch your parent's health go downhill, to watch her slowly lose her mind. It would have been less painful for everyone involved if she'd passed away before this point."

Colleen put a hand on her husband's shoulder as she drove.

"There was nothing you could have done, dear. Your parents are stubborn and never bothered to take care of themselves, but not even they could win against aging."

"I know... It just sucks. Anyway, Keith, if she passes away sometime in the next couple of weeks you don't have to come up for the funeral. My brothers probably won't even be able to make it, and I don't have the money to spend on anything other than cremation like she wanted when she was in her right mind."

"Oh. Okay then." There was a heavy silence before he broke it once more. "I'm sorry, dad."

"There you go again apologizing for things you have no control over. I thought college would help you break that habit."

"Nope."

Michael sighed. "It's not healthy to— well, you've heard that rant before. Let's just focus on dinner now, okay? We might not get to see you for a while and we're going to miss you."

Keith nodded slowly. "Alright. Where are we going

anyway?"

"Your favorite restaurant. A place where kids are king," his mother answered jovially, trying to lift the mood.

He managed a wide smile. His parents knew exactly how to cheer him up.

CHAPTER TWO

The sky was beginning to brighten when his alarm went off. Instantly awake, Keith reached over to press the "dismiss" button on his phone. After some time passed with him just lying there he grabbed his phone again, this time scrolling through social media for about five more minutes. It was only when he heard another alarm go off down the hall that he shot up out of bed, hurrying to the bathroom before the other PA could beat him to it first.

Minutes later he was back in his room, the other PA's door still closed across the hall. As he closed his door he took in how nice his room looked. It had taken him almost the entire week of training to unpack, but now that he had his room was a lot homier.

The bed was decked out in a *Pokémon* bedspread courtesy of his mother. Random knickknacks collected from free college events and craft nights decorated his wardrobe, his backpack resting in the beanbag chair he'd set in the corner of the room. His clothes were all put away either inside the wardrobe or dresser. He had so much room he only utilized the top halves of both storage spaces; he didn't have a lot of clothes as it was. His two pairs of shoes and his flip flops were the only things that took up the entire space that was his walk-in closet.

Maybe I should put the beanbag in there, he mused as he walked over to his dresser to grab some clothes for the day. *Then I can talk on the phone with Elizabeth with less of a chance at being overheard. The walls in this house are paper thin I swear.*

Over his dresser a large picture frame sat propped up against the wall. It held images of his close friends and family, not to mention a photo of his girlfriend he had taken some years prior. There were a few smaller prints pinned to the cork center of the frame as well, mostly pictures of his cats back home, as well as some cringe-worthy photo booth shots that captured way too much detail.

In front of the picture frame sat his wallet, house keys, and work contract folded to the page that began detailing how to clean the house. With a sigh he grabbed the folded sheets of paper. Eyes skimming the small text of the page with disdain, Keith tried to tell himself cleaning wouldn't be so bad. The other part-time PA and he would be watching Jacqueline clean today for a riveting six hours anyway in order to have visuals of the complicated notes they were otherwise left with. He wouldn't be doing a lot of it. They'd just be observing.

Somehow watching someone clean for half a dozen hours made him feel almost more miserable.

"Keith?" A light tapping on his door drew his attention. It was Elijah, the younger boy's voice sounding thick with sleep. "Jacqueline said she's ready to go when you are."

"Sorry! I'm ready too."

"Cool."

He walked over to the door, opening it with a polite smile aimed at the other part-time PA. "You ready to clean house?"

Elijah raised an eyebrow as if the amount of energy Keith had this early in the morning was strange. Guessing by how the other's light blue dyed-hair (a little bit of bleached blonde sticking out) was almost always arranged in classic bedhead in the morning he did probably think Keith was the weird one of the two. He didn't know that Keith was used to getting up this early for the past three years, or else his own mop of dark hair would've been a mess too.

Nevertheless, Keith smiled politely. He knew the whole personal assistant thing was newer to Elijah than himself. The only experience the transfer student had working with people with disabilities was in a nursing home. It helped, sure, but even case by case working with the elderly for a few hours a week was a lot different than working with a full-fledged doctoral student five to six days a week. Honestly just looking at the number of hours Elijah would be working each week made Keith cringe. He would be working almost as many as the full-time PA, which in comparison to the twelve Keith would be working was almost tripling that.

"I'm focusing on school and work this semester," he'd stated last night when they were going over the schedule one last time with Jacqueline. *"I'm only taking three classes, so working thirty-two hours a week will be fine."*

"Are you sure?" Jacqueline seemed unconvinced it was a good idea but was willing to let him have the hours anyway. "Because the schedule you pick now is final until next semester."

"I'm sure."

Keith had pushed his concerns away after remembering the amount of free time they'd have while working. During the interviews it was stressed time and time again that they could work on homework or read while keeping an eye on Brandon. This meant they could kill two birds with one stone, getting schoolwork done on the clock as to let them use their off time for themselves.

With two other jobs and five classes Keith was counting on that.

"I guess I'm ready? I just want this finished as soon as possible. I hate cleaning," Elijah said.

"Yeah," he nodded while checking to see where Jacqueline was. When he didn't see her he continued. "Me too. It'd be one thing if we just had to clean our rooms, but deep cleaning the entire house every weekend seems a bit extreme if you ask me. I'd ask if we could do it maybe every other week or once a month."

"I already tried the other day. She went on a twenty-minute rant about the immaculate state of the house and how it needs to be perfect if they want to sell it." Elijah's voice was dripping with annoyance, his eyes darting to the stairs that led down to where Jacqueline must have gone back down for something. "I think she thinks I'm stupid now for proposing such an idea. Honestly, I wouldn't deep clean at all if we weren't specifically paid to; all the different cleaning supplies and specific ways to wipe stuff down is overkill if you ask me."

"I get that. Back at my house we vacuumed, swept, and wiped stuff down if we had guests coming over, but that was it."

"Exactly! And having us clean the entire kitchen and dining room after every meal? With the hour cooking time they expect us to be here for, and all of the cleanings we have to do, we'll be at dinner for at least two or three hours."

Keith hadn't thought about that yet. He remembered the food sheets they'd had to fill out before their first day; they were basically spreadsheets with different time calculations based on what items of the meal would take what amount of time so that they would know when exactly to start each part of the meal. It was the most ridiculous thing he'd ever filled out as he was used to cooking dinner without having to worry about perfectly timing the food so everything was done at the exact same moment. So what if the veggies were done a few minutes after the main dish? So what if the main dish was running late and the other food might have to sit for a little bit? Jacqueline had talked about eating lukewarm food as if she'd never been more affronted in her life. Well, if he didn't count the face she'd made when he asked about if they stored leftovers.

"You can store and eat leftovers if you wish, but Brandon won't be having it. Fresh food is the healthiest option."

Her opinion about how unappetizing leftovers were wasn't hard to guess after she commented that reheating food was "primitive".

"Maybe things won't take as long as we think?" He tried.

Elijah raised an eyebrow. "Dude, you weren't here for dinner at all this week."

"Jacqueline said we only had to be here for training, so I was getting in hours at the restaurant before school starts in a couple of days. I get free food with every shift anyway."

"Keith, they eat their meals in courses. *Courses.* You should've been here. It takes them like fifteen minutes to eat a salad, half an hour to get through their actual meal, and another ten minutes to eat whatever dessert they decide they want that night. Meanwhile every lunch is just sandwiches, chips, and cookies. And don't even get me started on their opinion of leftovers."

He was about to respond, yet the sound of footsteps coming from downstairs told him to resume the conversation later.

"I apologize for the wait!" Jacqueline stated loudly, wearing yet another combination of dress clothes that were far too nice to be cleaning in. "Good morning, Keith. Did you sleep well?"

"I did. Thanks for asking."

"That's lovely! Now, let's all go to the basement so I can explain what cleaning supplies you'll need and how to carry everything upstairs in just three trips."

The moment she turned around Elijah and Keith's eyes met in mutual exasperation.

And so began the most riveting six and a half hours of Keith's life.

"Okay boys, you have the next couple of hours off. I'll need you both back here for your food preparation lesson at five though, so don't be gone for long if you decide to go out."

Said boys responded with a polite "okay" before trudging up the stairs tiredly, which was impressive considering they hadn't actually completed all of the cleanings they would be expected to do normally.

"That was… fun." Keith stated dryly.

Elijah gave him a pointed look over his shoulder.

"If you call being shown how to use five different vacuum settings throughout the house fun, then sure."

"C'mon, you didn't find mopping the entire house using a rag enjoyable?"

"As enjoyable as the lesson on how to wipe down wooden surfaces going along the grain, not against it."

Trying to lighten the mood, he nudged Elijah with his elbow playfully. It had turned out spending nearly seven hours together doing less than desirable tasks had made them fast friends.

"It wasn't that bad," he tried. "At least she did a lot of the cleaning for us. Next time we'll have to do it all on our own."

"I suppose you're right. Plus, we both learned something incredibly important today."

"What? The ideal leaf blowing route around the house, or how to fluff a couch cushion?"

"No. Patience."

They both were silent for a moment before Keith started laughing, Elijah joining in slowly a couple of seconds later. After all, the younger part-time PA had a valid point. It would have been easier to ask what they *hadn't* learned today. The most important thing they'd learned wasn't any one of the twenty dozen ways to make one's home look brand new either; it was patience.

Definitely patience.

Because after being given a step by step tutorial on how to dust a room efficiently one could only have oodles of the stuff.

They learned how to clean marble and glass surfaces with a plethora of different cleaning foams and sprays until it was spotless. They learned how to carefully clean lampshades and antique picture frames like pros. They learned how to polish the porcelain that made up the toilets in the house, scrub the sides of Brandon's bathtub, lightly wipe the insides of the sinks (enough to clean them but not enough to scratch them mind you), and polish the faucets for good measure. They learned how to wash down everything inside the refrigerator which required them to take everything out first, as well as how to deice the freezer with a hairdryer because "it's the most accurate way". They learned how to get to all eight gutters around the house so they could get all the leaves out of them, as well as polish every wooden chair in the house to keep them looking nice; there were twelve of them by the way.

Honestly they could probably write a ten-page paper on the techniques they were shown today, but fortunately for them it already existed as their contract's cleaning stipulations.

Once they'd calmed down, the junior by transfer credits gave Keith a small wave. "Well I'll see you later for dinner."

"Yep. See ya," Keith said before going to his room.

The first thing he did was pull out his phone, closing the door behind him as he went to his recent calls. As he pulled up his most recent call he grabbed the beanbag from the corner of his room and tossed it into his closet. He was sitting down on it and closing the closet door just as his phone started calling his girlfriend.

Elizabeth answered on the second ring.

"Keithy-pie!"

He smiled broadly at the high-pitched screech that assaulted his ear.

"Hey, sweetie."

"I missed you!"

"I missed you too."

"How was learning how to clean?"

"Just like you'd expect. They're so particular about every little thing here. It's strange."

"Rich people, Keithy. What can you do? At least they're paying you well."

"Technically they aren't the ones paying me. The government is who pays me for working as their state-approved PA."

"Maybe, but the food and housing costs are coming out of their pockets."

"I guess. Enough about work though; are you back in town yet?"

"My parents just got done dropping me off," she answered happily. "I was about to text you that I was free when you were. Want to get food? I had a snack before we went on the road but my parents didn't have time to stick around to eat. I'm starving."

"Me too! Jacqueline made everyone a single sandwich for lunch, so I'm still hungry especially after cleaning all morning."

"I thought you were only supposed to watch her clean today?"

"That's how she made it sound, but it was more like her showing us how to do something and then having Elijah and I do what she started to show us. It sucked having to mop the floors with a rag."

"All that money and they can't afford a mop?"

"She said a rag is more accurate and also hurts the wood less than a mop."

"Hurt the wood? They make mops that are made to not scratch all sorts of surfaces, yet they still had you use rags?

That's stupid. Wood doesn't even have feelings that can get hurt!"

"Yeah… but whatever. It's not that bad. Anyway, where do you want to eat?"

"Something fast. McDonald's?"

"Fine with me. Let me call you back when I get out of the house. I'll only be a few minutes."

"That's fine. I need to go to the bathroom before I leave the dorm anyway. Call me back in five mins?"

"Of course. Love you!"

"Love you too!"

With that he hung up, getting up from his beanbag chair and exiting the closet. He made sure to grab his wallet and keys before heading to the bathroom and then downstairs a minute later. Just as he was about to walk through the kitchen, however, the sound of raised voices made him grind to a halt. In a moment of uncertainty he stepped back quietly, hiding his form around the corner of the staircase.

"I'm not saying he's doing a bad job, but I think he was dishonest to say he didn't have dietary restrictions during the hiring process. This is going to make preparing meals for everyone so much more troublesome."

"Honey, it's not a big deal. Isaac isn't vegetarian or vegan; he just prefers to not eat certain meat. The other boys aren't going to mind eating dishes more oriented away from beef or pork. It's not that big of a deal."

"But Brandon enjoys red meat! Our son shouldn't be robbed of something he enjoys because one person doesn't wish to eat a particular food. Back in our day we ate what we were given. Between Keith not liking any fish or crustacean and Isaac not eating dishes with beef or pork all they're going to eat is chicken. Why can't they just eat what they're given? Kids these days are spoiled brats compared to how it was back then."

Larry could be heard trying to placate her. "It's going to be fine. Keith is only here for dinner during the nights he cooks, so that's a non-issue most nights. Isaac won't be eating dinner Friday through Sunday so there will be two days a week he can have whatever meat he wants."

"I suppose you're right. It's just annoying these boys are so picky."

Keith's heart rate spiked slightly, hearing what he felt an unwarranted amount of venom in Jacqueline's voice as she spat out the last word. Why was she getting so worked up over this?

Honestly he wished he could evade them by going out the front door, but he would get into trouble if he did that. The only way out of the house was to go through the kitchen and use the back door there.

I don't want to interrupt them, but if I don't I might never get out of here.

"Calm down, dear. This is why Brandon schedules meals weekly. There's an endless amount of combinations he can come up with, so worrying about him not getting what he wants is a bit silly. Not to mention the fact there are easily microwavable things in the freezer anyone can microwave if they don't want what's for dinner."

"I don't want them to have to rely on that though. They'll get lazy if they do. I don't want Brandon eating frozen pizza or something he can throw in the oven just because the PAs don't want to spend an hour cooking."

"No one said they wouldn't be cooking. Listen, Jackie, honey—"

It was at this moment Keith walked out into the kitchen like he hadn't been eavesdropping around the corner.

Immediately he noticed Jacqueline's entire demeanor change. Her shoulders lifted just as she smoothed a plastic smile over the previous frown on her face. When she spoke her voice had a lighter lilt to it as if she hadn't just been complaining about her son's PAs behind their backs.

"Oh, Keith. Are you heading out?"

"Yeah. I'm going to hang out with my girlfriend for a

bit."

"That's lovely," the blonde said despite her eyes telling a different story. "You'll be back before dinner to learn how to prep meals, right?"

"Yep."

"Great. Have fun then!"

"Thanks!"

He flashed a friendly grin at them while he made his way past the kitchen table and around the corner, dropping the corners of his mouth as soon as they were out of sight. Just as he was descending the handful of steps that led to the back door a shout stopped him.

"Sorry, Keith, but can you poke your head back in here for just a second?"

Confused, he spun around before stepping back into the kitchen as Jacqueline wanted.

"Yes?"

"I just wanted to make sure you're aware of the part of the contract that pertains to significant others." She looked at him expectantly like she already knew the answer to her own question, which made him wonder why she was even asking him in the first place.

Keith held himself back from raising an eyebrow; instead he nodded politely. "I read everything in the contract. It states that they're not allowed in the house without having met Brandon outside of it first and that they can't go on the second floor in any circumstances. Why?"

"We just wanted to make sure you knew. We've had past PAs overlook this, or sneak their girlfriends over in a few cases, and since that's directly prohibited in the contract we had to not only fire them but bring them to court as well. I don't want something like that happening to you is all."

"It won't. Elizabeth already knows she can't come in. Her roommate doesn't mind though, so I'll probably just spend most of my free time there."

"Lovely! That's all I wanted to confirm. Don't let us keep you any longer," she made a "carry on" motion with one of her hands.

With a small wave Keith retreated down the stairs to the back door. He slipped his shoes on quickly before entering the code to deactivate the alarm system temporarily. Once the beeping began he ran out the door and closed it, locking the door with his key with half a minute to spare before the locking system could check his work.

Walking down the driveway, he pulled out his phone and called Elizabeth.

"Keith," she whined. From the sound of cars in the background she was already outside. "It's been like ten minutes, not five. What took so long?"

"Brandon's parents were complaining about one of the PAs in the kitchen, which I have to walk through in order to get to the back door. I was trying to wait until they stopped talking but they just kept going."

"Ugh, that's awkward. Which one were they complaining about?"

"Isaac. Supposedly he doesn't like eating pork or red meat, and Jacqueline was mad about it."

"He's the full-time PA, right?"

"Yeah."

"He's only eating there four days a week then. And it's not like it's hard to make a dish with or without meat. Spaghetti? Just do the meatballs on the side. Stir fry? Just add the meat last after setting some aside. And honestly with how things are nowadays, it's not like she can choose not to hire someone over their diet anyway."

"I know, but his mom was getting super worked up about it. She complained about me not liking seafood too but to a lesser extent. Yet when I walked into the kitchen she acted like nothing was wrong."

"Damn. This woman is two-faced."

No more than me, he thought to himself. He knew he

was an actor of sorts; it came with working in the customer service industry for too long. Still, despite seeming hypocritical something about Jacqueline's behavior worried him. Unless he eavesdropped on her again how would he ever know what she was truly thinking?

"A bit, yeah." He ultimately said. "She also reminded me that you're not allowed in the house. She brought up how PAs in the past have tried to sneak their girlfriends in and not only got fired but were brought to court for breaking the contract."

A long whistle came in over the other line. "You've got to be kidding me. There's no way they brought someone to court over that; maybe fired, but c'mon now. What would they gain? You already told me they're loaded." The sound of cars cut off abruptly, letting him know she was inside now.

"They told my parents most of the money comes from the state or a deceased relative. They tried passing it off as using it wisely, but they own two houses. Two! It's not like they're cheap ones either. And who in this day of age can afford to buy an entire house, let alone two?"

"People with money? Wow. And here my family can barely afford monthly rent for one house."

"Tell me about it. They're not just small crappy houses either. During my second interview Brandon showed me a picture of the house they own upstate and I swear to you I heard his dad say it was 'just' three-hundred thousand. The house I'm staying in now is worth over two-hundred thousand. I don't know how much money someone needs to be classified as well off, but I think they're above that."

"And they can't exactly use disability checks to help pay for all that housing," he continued as he crossed the street and made a b-line across one of the four quads of campus. "From what I've learned in school and from what Will has told me the checks would go straight to Brandon since he's an independent. He could use them to pay for the house he's staying in here on campus, I guess, but even then the government is pretty strict with how much people get and how they use said money."

"So they're lying about not having money. That's dumb."

"More like weird, but they're weird on so many levels, Elizabeth. They do laundry at least three times a day. Once in the morning to wash Brandon's dirty clothes from the day before, once in the afternoon to wash all the bathroom towels in the house, and once at night to wash all the rags used to clean up the kitchen."

"That is a lot of laundry."

"I know! Like, they could just wash them all together, but I guess Jacqueline doesn't want anything from the kitchen or bathroom getting on Brandon's clothes."

"But they're all getting washed. You know, with hot water and detergent?"

"I don't get it either. They also have this thing where we need to sign up for TV time slots if we want to use the TV in the living room."

"TV time slots? You mean like sign up for when someone can use the TV?"

"Yeah. I won't be watching TV anyway because Netflix and the internet, but it is kind of strange. I don't know. I'll just be happy when Brandon's parents leave tomorrow night. I think Brandon is a pretty chill guy; it's just his parents and all the rules that kind of make the atmosphere of the house tense. Anyway, you're already at the union, right?"

"Yep! I'm waiting for you at the northern end. Right now I'm sitting on a couch by the fish tanks; there aren't many other people here. It's pretty dead seeing as it's day one of move-in weekend. Students are either busy moving in or aren't even here yet."

He made a noise of affirmation before responding. "I'll be there in a couple of minutes. I just got to the main quad.

Looks like they've already got the tables set out for Club Day tomorrow, huh?"

"I saw! I am so excited to grab a bunch of free stuff again. We gotta make sure we get all of the T-shirts and the little toys the bus people always give out."

He laughed, passing by another building. "We will. I work until two tomorrow, so I'll be able to catch the second half of Club Day. Are you volunteering to work for the church's booth at all?"

"I help set up and work for the first two hours, so it works out fine. Anyway, I've been getting a couple of texts so I'm going to let you go so I can answer them. You're almost here?"

"Yep."

"Awesome! See you soon then, sweetie."

True to his word he was walking past the fish tanks that decorated the front entrance hall of the union roughly sixty seconds later. His eyes swam over the mostly unoccupied couches until he spotted a brown-haired figure slouching down in one. She was so focused on her phone that she didn't realize he was sneaking up on her until he said her name in greeting. Upon hearing her name though, she nearly vaulted off the couch in excitement.

"Keith!"

She quickly turned off the screen of her phone and slid it into her pocket, standing up and hugging him tightly a moment later. It was only after squeezing the air out of his lungs that she released him. Her hazel eyes stared into his own leaden green ones, exhilaration obvious in the way they bore into him.

"I missed you," she continued, jumping up and down happily. "One week feels so long after spending the entire summer living together."

"It does." He agreed, a hand grabbing hers tightly. Then he frowned. "Lizzy, it's nearly eighty degrees outside right now. Why is your hand freezing? I could use this," he held up her hand, "as an icepack."

She groaned. "I know, right? It's only seventy degrees inside and you know my body can't hold in heat for crap, but somehow my hands are colder than the freaking temperature around me."

Keith sighed, tugging her in the direction of the door. "Let's go outside then so you can warm up. You're hungry anyway so we can start walking to McDonald's."

"It's only a two-minute walk though. My hands won't even register the heat in that time."

"Then hold my hand, silly. You know I give off heat like a furnace."

She did so, grinning all the while. "Wow. I'd say you're smooth, but we're already dating. That would be a great pick up line for other guys though…"

"Once again, you're silly." He said with amusement.

"Well you're dating me, so who's sillier? Huh?"

CHAPTER THREE

After eating lunch and spending the next hour walking around campus playing *Pokémon Go* it was time to say goodbye.

"I'll see you after two tomorrow then?" Elizabeth said as they waited at the bus stop. It was visible just down the road, meaning after it finally made its way past the busy crosswalks she would be off. "You'll call me before bed though, right?"

"Of course. I'll let you know how dinner goes. It'll be the first one where everyone is together, so I'm a little anxious."

"Isaac will be there too? I thought he didn't work weekend evenings."

"He does today and tomorrow because of training. Anyway," he rushed as the bus pulled up, "I love you and I'll talk to you later tonight."

"Love you too!"

She gave him a quick peck on the lips before making her way onto the bus behind a couple of other students. He waited a few seconds to watch the bus close its doors and pull away before walking down the sidewalk towards his new living arrangement.

What do I even call the place? It's not my home, he mused. *It belongs to Brandon and his parents. I wonder if the other PAs think of it as our house. I feel like a total stranger in it, but still. I'm living and working there. I have free range to use the kitchen, be in the living room, watch*

TV, and so on, yet it feels like I'm an intruder.

I'll get over it eventually though, I'm sure. I only just moved in. I'll start feeling more comfortable once training is over and our regular routines start. Not to mention Brandon's parents finally leave tomorrow. Maybe with just Brandon and the other PAs it'll become home.

Feeling hopeful, Keith's steps quickened. He needed to take a page from his girlfriend's book and start being a little more optimistic.

"No matter how bad things get it'll always work out in the end!"

He smiled as he remembered Elizabeth's words. She was seriously the more positive one between the two of them, which was honestly hilarious considering she was a computer engineering student and made constant jokes about hating her life or regretting her choice in a major. Despite knowing that statement was not true by any means she stuck to the belief that believing things would work out often led to better outcomes than if she were pessimistic about it. At first he thought that logic to be a bit childish, but after learning about the placebo effect in every single class he took within his own major her hopefulness grew on him.

A lot of new things in his life threw him off balance; however, he would be okay. He just needed to believe that to be true.

Unable to stop himself from humming a song, Keith finished walked the last two blocks home with a spring in his step. He quickly stopped, though, when he got to the bottom of the driveway. He saw a very angry Jacqueline blocking the doorway as she gesticulated wildly and talked to someone on her cell phone with a surprising amount of fury.

"What do you mean the price went up? Our cable bill has been the same for the past twelve months and now you're telling me it's suddenly going to be forty dollars more a month?" A pause. "I don't understand. When we switched to using you guys I was told a rate of forty-five dollars a month for as long as we need the services." Another pause. "Well, I don't think your associate informed me that the rate I've been paying was only for the first twelve months of use. I shouldn't have to pay more because I was told the wrong information." Yet another pause. "Oh, so now you're telling me to either pay you more or get another provider? I'll have you know that this house belongs to my disabled son and his assistants. Paying over ninety dollars a month for television is ridiculous. He has a hard enough time as it is managing everything else in his life and you—"

Someone on the other line cut her off. She listened with a clenched fist, affronted at being interrupted. A moment later though the disdain on her features shifted to a triumphant grin. "Why thank you! I'm so glad you can make an exception due to the circumstances. Brandon will be so happy to hear that." Another pause. "No, thank you. You've been very helpful as it is. You have a nice day now. Bye-bye."

She hung up and slipped inside the house without noticing Keith awkwardly inspecting the bushes near the end of the driveway.

What the hell was that? Did she just use her son's disability to extort a cheaper cable bill of all things?

Something sour made its way into Keith's mouth. Will had done a few similar things throughout the years, but they were usually minor things like skipping the wait in line at the school's cafeteria or getting better seating at the union's movie nights. Most of the time he wouldn't even take people up on said offers since he didn't like to be treated differently due to his disability. If Keith told him what he'd just overheard Brandon's mother say, then he would surely go on a rant about how that's exactly what people with disabilities don't need toxifying their culture.

At least she doesn't know I overheard, he told himself as he made his way to the door.

Pushing down the wrongness he felt, he waited a minute before entering the house just in case the security system was still locking down from when Jacqueline went inside. Upon entering he heard someone moving around in the kitchen.

He checked his watch. There were fifteen minutes until he had to be in the kitchen for training, which meant he had time to get some homework done.

"Keith? Is that you?"

The sound of Jacqueline's voice through the front wall startled him. Luckily he was out of sight, so she didn't see the frown that donned his face at her call.

"Yeah, it's me." He replied. Making his way up the landing and into the kitchen, he saw the older woman sitting at the dining room table by herself with various papers, binders, and pens spread out.

"You're back early; wonderful! I've got the meal sheets Elijah and you submitted over the summer for us to review. The past week Larry and I have been making the meals, but from now on you'll be using these. There are a lot of changes to make though seeing as many of your ideas were the same. We'll also need to make some changes on account of dietary restrictions, but we'll get through it!" Her bubbly voice had a forced lilt to it towards the end.

"Oh. Okay," he responded dumbly. He wasn't sure what she wanted him to say.

"Anyway," she continued despite inching towards the staircase to his room, "since you're already here why don't you look over the changes I made to some of your meal sheets?"

Resignation washing over him, he gave her his best customer service smile. "Sure!" He took a seat and set to reading them one by one at a leisurely pace if only to make sure she didn't ask anything else of him before Elijah joined them. He planned to remain silent for the remaining ten minutes, but as he read her comments on his meal sheets it made that plan very hard to keep.

What does she mean burgers and chicken sandwiches aren't viable options? Just because they eat turkey or ham and cheese sandwiches for lunch doesn't mean we can't have sandwiches for dinner. Homemade fries aren't healthy enough? They don't eat canned vegetables? I love peas and creamed corn though. If I want them does that mean I have to buy them myself? Why can't I just make some for myself then? Are you kidding me; pork chops are too unrefined for Brandon to eat? That doesn't even make sense. Bacon is too fatty, casseroles are too messy, and instant mashed potatoes are fake, but making them homemade takes too much time? It's my time I'd be taking up anyway. Now suddenly she cares?

Keith tried very hard to keep the confusion off of his face as he kept reading. The more comments he saw the more dread he felt. He loved eating a variety of foods, and much of what he liked was, according to Jacqueline, too messy, unhealthy, or did not suit Brandon's palate. When he took the job had no idea he'd need to change his diet too.

He was so wrapped up in his frustration that he hadn't noticed the sound of Elijah coming down the stairs. The younger man greeted both of them as he took a seat next to Keith, a concerned look growing on his face as he took note of Keith's frown.

"What're you reading?"

Looking up, instantly wiping the frown away, Keith tried to respond when Jacqueline beat him to it.

"Just the amended versions of your meal sheets," she stated, handing Elijah his papers. "Now that you're both here I can explain how meal prepping works. Every Saturday Brandon will choose what the meals will be for the next upcoming week. Based on what appetizer, main dish, sides, and desserts he wants you will have to fill out the time sheets accordingly some time beforehand to ensure all of the food will be ready promptly at dinner time. Salad will be the appetizer on most days, which is something you can get done while other things are cooking. We also do slow cooker meals often which are mostly prep and less work right before dinner."

She pushed a binder across the table, flipping it open and turning to the table of contents.

"This has meal combinations from the past few years. Brandon will choose what you'll all be eating out of here, and this is also where I'll be adding your amended meal plans."

"I have a question."

"Yes, Elijah?"

"You wrote on my paper that we can't do sandwiches for dinner because Brandon always has sandwiches for lunch. Most of the school week we probably won't even be here around noon because we'll be in classes, so does this mean Isaac and Brandon will be making burgers, meatball subs, sloppy Joe, and stuff without us for lunch most days? Because unless they are I don't really get why we can't have those things for dinner from time to time."

"Brandon and Isaac will be sticking to sandwiches using the lunch meat and cheese in the fridge since that is easier for Isaac to prepare while also keeping an eye on Brandon. You're both welcome to pack a similar lunch to bring while you're out and about too. Anyway, there are so many meal options that are healthier than a burger or chicken sandwich that I don't want him to have more sandwiches for dinner. You understand how a nice fresh stir fry or stew is better than a fat-filled meat patty or sub made from frozen meat, right?"

The blue-haired boy nodded hesitantly, but Keith could tell by the side glance he received once Jacqueline looked away from them that he thought her logic was bull.

And he definitely agreed.

Part of him wanted to speak up as Elijah had. The whole meal situation seemed unfair. Just because Brandon wouldn't want something, despite the part in the contract stating he would eat anything except for a few choice items, they wouldn't be able to have it. From all of the red marks on his and Elijah's meal plans it seemed Brandon was far more limited in diet than anyone else in the household. Whether that was by his choice or his mother's was yet to be seen.

"One last thing before we begin prepping tonight's dinner," she said. "Both of you strongly put that breakfast for dinner would be a good idea, which is something I get every single year. What I want to explain is that if Brandon wants to do that, then it will consist of oven-baked sausages and hash browns, as well as fruit and either toast or pancakes using a toaster. Making fresh pancakes is a mess and it takes too much focus to flip them while managing the other food. Bacon is also a no go due to how fatty it is, and the grease would make a big mess in the kitchen that would be challenging to clean up. I don't want anything stained seeing as we'll be selling this house next summer."

"So we can't cook bacon at all is what you're saying?" Elijah asked.

"I'd prefer you didn't, yes."

"Is there anything else you don't want us cooking?"

Keith supposed it was a rhetorical question, but to his dismay Jacqueline rifled through some papers before pulling out a sheet with at least two dozen bullet points on it. He only got a glimpse of "cabbage, as it smells absolutely atrocious when cooked" before she was handing it to the boy beside him.

"You can both look this over when you have the time, but it will be in the dinner binder if you need to review it at a later date. As it is we only have an hour before dinner."

She got out a blank meal sheet with the excel tables

blank save for the labels reading "food item, prep time, oven temp, cooking time, serving time, and total time". A pen was handed to Keith as she instructed Elijah to grab the items they would need to cook. Once he'd set out the chicken thighs, asparagus, lettuce, salad vegetables, and a bag of frozen fries she ushered him to sit back down.

Looking at them both with her telltale plaster smile, she began going over how to fill out the meal sheets properly.

"So what you first need to do is fill out the food item section. Next, the easiest thing to do is fill out the cooking time accordingly with what I've written down in the food binder. For example," she demonstrated, opening the binder up to the sides section and flipping to asparagus, "I've already written down that it takes about eight minutes in the microwave to steam the asparagus correctly. If we flip to entrees and find thawed chicken we can see it will take about half an hour to cook as well as what temperature the chicken should be at. The bag of fries has the oven temp on it already so you won't find it in the binder. Salad isn't in it either just because all they require is chopping up tomato and mushrooms, adding croutons to the romaine lettuce mix we'll keep in the fridge. Keith, if you could fill out the sheet using this binder I'll start showing Elijah how to prep the barbeque chicken we'll be having tonight."

"Okay."

With that he set to putting numbers on the appropriate boxes. Occasionally he'd stop to glance at Elijah, who seemed to be hiding his frustration as Jacqueline showed him how to pour barbeque sauce over the chicken like he was too foolish to figure it out himself. When Keith was done plugging numbers in he asked what he could do to help if only to give Elijah a break.

Jacqueline handed him a cutting board and knife.

"Do you know how to dice a tomato?"

Keith blinked stupidly. "Yes. I've cut up vegetables before."

"Wonderful! Let's see how you do then."

She handed him a tomato, eyes watching his every move like he was holding a bomb. He made sure to rinse it before setting it on its side and chopping the stem end off. He flipped it onto the side he'd just chopped off, preparing to slice vertically when an audible "tsk" made him stop.

A second later Jacqueline was taking the knife from his hand and gently instructing him to watch what she did. Instead of chopping it vertically, then into strips, then into cubes like he usually did she went down the tomato and chopped them into slices. Only after that was done did she cut them into tiny triangles. Once a small pile was made on the edge of the cutting board she called Elijah over from portioning the fries to watch her cut up the mushrooms next.

"You always want to chop them in half first, and then…"

Keith and Elijah watched in silence. A moment later when Jacqueline went to the cupboards to get the croutons the older of the two nudged the younger before putting his hands together in a mock praying motion. Elijah stifled a grin. Several minutes later, once the asparagus was properly cut and seasoned with the olive oil paste she'd shown them how to make, he made the same praying motion back at Keith while she was putting the fries in the oven.

God give us patience, he thought. *And please make this night go by faster.*

"Okay boys, now while we wait for everything to finish cooking I'm going to show you the diagram for setting the table. Always always always set it the same way each time. No matter what meal we make every person gets a regular fork, a salad fork, a knife, a dinner plate, a smaller plate for whatever appetizer you make, a dessert plate for after dinner, a napkin, and their glass of whatever drink they want. It seems like a lot to remember at first but I'm confident after setting the table a couple of times you'll both be able to do it from memory. Keith, why don't you start by…"

Everyone sat in assigned chairs around the dining table. At the head was Jacqueline, followed clockwise by Larry, Brandon, Isaac, Elijah, and then Keith.

"You forgot to give yourself a salad plate and fork," Brandon pointed out. His parents turned to Keith in concern like he'd just committed a taboo.

He shook his head. "Oh, I didn't forget. It's just I don't care for salad. Cold, crunchy vegetables aren't really my thing."

Larry frowned. "Do you want anything else to snack on during the appetizer then? There's applesauce in the fridge, and there's the fruit in the fruit bowl too."

"No thank you. I'm fine as is, don't worry." He reassured.

The older man nodded, unperturbed, yet Keith couldn't help but shrink in slightly at the disappointed look Jacqueline shot at him for just a split second. It was gone before anyone else could notice though. Instead the woman merely put her hands together, asking everyone save Isaac, who was watched over Brandon, to bow their heads as she prayed over the meal.

Once that was over, everyone save Keith dug in.

"So," Larry started conversationally, "Elijah. Jacqueline tells me you play soccer."

"Yes I do. I've been playing for fun since I was young, and I started playing competitively in high school. I want to join a club here if they have it since they don't have an official team."

"Cool! I used to play in high school myself, but never found time to play afterward. Do you tend to play offense or defense?"

"Oh, definitely defense. I'm good at stealing the ball

away from the other team.”

“You must be pretty quick on your feet then. I was always better as a go-between if I remember correctly.”

Keith listened to them talk, occasionally taking a sip of water if only to abate the awkwardness of not having anything to eat while they ate. He was genuinely interested in the conversation after listening to Elijah talk about what he did in his free time. Then Larry turned to him.

“What about you, Keith? Do you play any sports?”

“No. I did marching band for seven years before college, which counted as a spring sport, but other than that I never did anything else competitively. I did tumbling when I was younger? By the time I got to middle school I wanted to focus more on my studies and band though, so I gave it up. Marching band was more manageable anyway.”

“Smart young man,” he commented.

Jacqueline made a noise of agreement. “He played the saxophone too, such a tasteful instrument.”

Tasteful? Okay then…

“I don’t know about that. I was average when it came to playing the alto sax. My girlfriend on the other hand was first chair in her concert band and third chair when she got moved up into symphonic. She played the trumpet.”

Brandon’s eyes lit up in interest. He leaned forward, forgetting his salad momentarily. It was the first time Keith saw him looking so animated over something he’d said.

“I love the trumpet!” He exclaimed, his voice a tad louder than the otherwise silent dining room warranted. “That, violin, and harmonium music pieces are my favorite.”

Clearing her throat, Jacqueline cut in before taking a large bite of her salad.

“Sit up straighter, sweetie. Slouching ruins your back.”

“Yes, mother.”

“Speaking of your girlfriend,” she continued a second later as she turned to Keith, “why don’t you tell us a little about her? I'm sure your roommates are curious."

Elijah did seem pretty interested, same with Brandon, but Isaac just kept his eyes on their Person. Other than focused it was hard to tell what Isaac was feeling. Maybe indifference? Keith wasn't sure.

"Well, Elizabeth and I met online through a mutual friend in high school. After a couple of months, we started dating long distance. I would only get to see her once or twice a year since we live five hours apart and neither of our families could afford to make a trip that far too often, but since we chose the same college we get to see each other all the time. We've been dating for nearly six years now."

"Six years?" Brandon gaped.

Elijah whistled. "Wow, dude. That's impressive. You must be about ready to pop the question, right?"

Keith fought off a blush. Of course they would bring up marriage. It's all anyone asked him once he told them how long he and Elizabeth had been dating. In all honesty it was beginning to stress him out. How was he supposed to surprise her with a marriage proposal when everyone around him was constantly hounding him to do it already?

"We agreed to wait until at least after we both graduate before worrying about getting married. There's also the fact we need to make sure we can support ourselves financially, which means I need to get a stable job. Preferably with benefits. Hopefully once she's finished with her degree we won't have to worry about not being able to pay off our loans or any bills we'll have in the future."

"What's her major?"

"She's in computer engineering," he answered his Person's question.

"That is one of the most profitable fields to be in right now," Jacqueline said. "Our daughter Chelsee is a hydraulic engineer herself. She's studying abroad at the moment. The field is very good right now despite how much it actually costs to get a good education in it. She wanted to get an apprenticeship to help her pay for her degree, but there simply wasn't enough to go around, although honestly I think it's because female engineers are still marginalized in comparison to male ones."

If he had more confidence Keith would have burst out laughing, surprising everyone at the table. Instead he gave a half-hearted smile as he tilted his glass and watched the water move around in it.

"I, uh, really don't think that's it." He ventured like he was walking over a field of burning coal. "At least from what I know about how it works here, I mean. It's like the exact opposite here. Elizabeth is paying her way through undergrad because several gender-specific scholarships reserved only for females in engineering, seeing as there is a far lower number of them. She's even getting a full ride for her masters here due to winning a grant through her work, which strives to bring more girls into the STEM field all around, from the university that can only be granted to her *because* she's a girl. Her boss even said that if she were male she wouldn't have gotten it, since the college sets more money aside for gender and race-specific scholarships than general ones as it is."

To his surprise Isaac spoke up. The dark-haired boy was louder by comparison, his cool voice more sure of himself than Keith's had been.

"That's how it works at a lot of the top state colleges. It's all about statistics and making up for the lack of enrollment of minorities. My cousin got a full ride a few years ago to a top ten university because she applied to industrial design and less than five percent of who make up the major are women. She didn't even have amazing grades." He shrugged.

"Chelsee was probably unlucky is all," Keith tried to lift the mood of the room after such a borderline heavy conversation. He didn't like bragging about Elizabeth's good fortune. She was smart and deserved the scholarships and grants she was getting. Still, he didn't feel right letting Jacqueline bad mouth the male gender even if engineering was a male-dominated field. Coming from a guy in kinesiology, a predominantly female-populated field, he knew what it was like to be sort of the odd one out.

"Excuse me, but is everyone ready for the main course? I've been smelling that chicken cook for a while now and I'm ready to dig into it." Larry cut in jovially, placing a hand on Jacqueline's shoulder.

She turned her unreadable stare away from Keith and Isaac. First instructing Elijah and Keith to help collect the salad plates before grabbing the bigger plates herself, she told them to put the same amount of food on each plate.

A minute later they were all seated at the table again, this time with Keith eating along with them.

"Is anyone else in a relationship?" Keith tried to instigate more small talk. The atmosphere at the table was tense without it. The constant clanking of everyone's metal forks on their ceramic plates somehow set Keith's nerves on edge. It was like they were robots, simply functioning instead of eating.

Isaac nodded with a mouthful of asparagus. "There's a girl I met back home in Italy two years ago. We only started dating some months back, because she learned she would be able to get a work visa next year to come to the U.S. once she finishes up school."

"Dude, that's awesome!" Elijah responded. After a long drink of water he kept going. "I'm honestly jealous of both of you. I've been in three relationships and all of them ended after a few months, some even weeks. I told myself after transferring here I would focus on my education more instead of trying to find love."

Jacqueline smiled brightly at that.

"That's smart of you, Elijah! Brandon is doing the same thing. There was a girl he liked when he first started here, but she kept trying to bring him into situations that would have been too dangerous due to his condition, so he let her go."

"Yeah," Brandon rolled his eyes, "she really wanted us to go swimming, remember mother? Seriously. What if I passed out while in the pool? I could've drowned."

"Not to mention she didn't pay you much attention once she met me and realized I wasn't going to let you put yourself in danger by going along with her silly ideas." She smirked as if she'd won a game against a novice opponent, but was so conceited it felt like a grand victory. "I honestly don't think she liked you anyway though, sweetie. We need to be realistic. She probably wanted to hang out with you because of our money. I told you buying her all those gifts wasn't a good idea."

"I know now." Brandon groaned. "It'll never happen again."

"I know it won't. With your disability you'll be hard-pressed to find someone who can put up with the shortcomings it comes with. It'd be best just not to get your hopes up. We'll be taking care of you for as long as we can once you graduate anyway, won't we, Larry?"

Keith stilled in his seat, his eyes nonchalantly meeting the eyes of the other PAs at the table. Isaac's face hid a barely concealed horror at what Jacqueline had just said while Elijah looked completely gobsmacked.

There was no way the three of them had just heard their Person's own mother basically say he wouldn't find love because he was disabled.

To their bewilderment, however, her husband merely smiled in support.

Brandon even nodded acceptingly as if he'd already known this was his fate. "Yeah, I know. I love you guys more than I ever could anyone else anyway."

Keith was utterly confused.

What the hell? He chanced a look around the table

again, not believing the things he was hearing. His stomach churned with nausea at the very thought of any of his friends with disabilities being told that with a clean conscience. *How can he just accept that when it's not true? Everyone deserves love. For his own mother to tell him no one will love him because of his disability is just... wrong.*

Part of him hoped Isaac or Elijah would speak up, but to his dismay they both kept eating their dinner with their eyes not meeting anyone else's at the table but their own.

If I'm the only one to say something this could get ugly and awkward faster than when Elijah had touched the thermostat. But I can't just brush that off. Right?

He had to say something. Anything.

"You can't go swimming?"

Not that you idiot! He screamed at himself mentally.

Brandon raised an eyebrow. "Of course not. It's too dangerous for me to even stand up in a pool," he answered like he was dealing with a child. "I have never been swimming."

It was too late now. Keith had to finish what he'd started.

"That's no fun," he began. He tried to speak nonchalantly as if to not sound standoffish. "Did you know the recreational pools on campus have chairs that lower into the water with straps attached so the person sitting in them can't fall out? They also have ones that roll into the water so people who can't stand can go in the pools and hot tubs. I brought Will and his girlfriend swimming several times since I've been here."

"Who's Will?" Isaac asked.

"Oh, Will was the student I assisted for the last three years. He graduated with his degree in Sports and Recreation just last May; he coached the wheelchair basketball teams on campus while he was here too. Anyway, Will has cerebral palsy and still stood up in the water alongside me and another trusted PA whenever we visited the indoor pools on campus, so I think we could make it safe for you to go in a pool yourself." He spoke to Brandon specifically before speaking to the entire table. "Maybe we can all go to the pool sometime? Then there'd be no chance of you being in danger even if you did pass out while in it."

"Maybe," Brandon said. However, when Keith glanced at his face he noticed the sheer disbelief in his gaze.

Did he truly believe something as simple an activity as swimming was lost to him?

Maybe Keith was being arrogant, but after working as a personal assistant for three years he felt there were a lot of things people with disabilities could do if they just had the right people helping them. Take the trip to Dave and Buster's he'd taken with his Person, their respective significant others, and parents. He'd promised Will he'd get him in and out of that ball pit safely and he had (albeit with the help of his Person's dad as well). The happiness Will had expressed at sliding into it with a protective Keith making sure his head and neck hadn't got agitated in the ride down was heartwarming.

"No one has ever offered to do that with me before," Will explained the next time Keith was getting him ready for bed. They had just gotten out of the shower (Will having been the one to actually get cleaned but Keith still ending up with wet shoes, shorts, and arms since the shower sprayer was a dysfunctional little ass pickle) and were picking out Will's usual nightclothes. "I always wanted to go in a ball pit though, because when I was a kid my brother always got to play in the one at McDonald's while I sat and ate with my mom. She said I couldn't go in because I might get stuck in there and she didn't want to cause a scene."

"Well," Keith responded as he lifted Will up with his legs and arm while the other arm pulled his shorts on, "we're adults and I don't really care if we cause a scene.

Which I admit we almost did because of your huge ass sliding further down into the pit when I specifically told you to stop moving around."

"I was pretending to swim! Also the plastic felt nice on my hands."

"I get that, but it took me and your dad to lift you out of the pit while your mom and our girlfriends laughed at us."

"You're right. Elizabeth should have been helping us, but the video she got of me elbowing you back into the pit was so worth it."

"Very funny. Wait, what video?"

"Uh, nothing."

"Will!"

Experience aside, Keith had always learned in his disability courses not to think in terms of things someone can't do but be creative to figure out how they can do anything else people without disabilities can do. After learning Will skied competitively every winter, managed the wheelchair basketball team, and participated in marathons he knew to assume what people can and can't do was for the ignorant.

Everyone ate in silence while Larry talked about his day tending to the greenery around the house. Keith tried to pay attention to what he was saying, but his mind kept wandering elsewhere.

He realized he didn't like the Thompsons. This was bad because after he made a judgment about whether he liked a person or not he usually stuck to it. He was stubborn that way. Not that he wasn't having mixed feelings about Brandon, which he was, but something told him having parents who were about as ableist as the Spartans (and about as entitled as the Athenians) would make becoming friends with him somewhat challenging.

I can't just give up though, he thought as he lay in bed that night. *Brandon might act differently when his parents aren't in the picture. Once that happens I need to be ready to be impartial. Just because I don't care for his parents doesn't mean I should shy away from being his friend. He's my new Person now. Being just his personal assistant isn't going to work for me; we'll be friends in a week. I'm sure of it.*

CHAPTER FOUR

"You're wearing that to church?"

Keith looked down at his *Haikyu!!* shirt and black jeans while Brandon pulled on his finest slacks and button-up behind him. He was sitting on his bed as he got dressed to avoid injury if he had an episode, not liking other people seeing him naked. The PA merely stared at the door waiting until his Person told him to turn back around.

"Should I change?" He asked, confused. "Jacqueline said last night we didn't have to dress up. I don't usually when I go to my church, but if most people at yours do then I can go put something else—"

"No, don't worry about it. Plenty of students wear what you're wearing. You can look now, by the way."

At his word Keith turned around, walking to Brandon's side and offering an arm automatically. He grabbed the arm and stood up, letting Keith lead him to the bathroom before getting onto his knees.

"Close the door and wait outside until I'm done. I'll get you when I'm ready to wash my hands."

"Okay. Should I still ask if you're okay every thirty seconds like when you're in the shower, or just listen?"

"Just listen. What my mom showed you and Elijah last night was a bit over the top. If you can hear me moving around you know I'm not passed out on the floor."

"Ah, okay."

The rest of the morning was about as strained. Keith tried to instigate small talk, but Brandon's curt one word

58

answers told him to give it up. At breakfast he listened to his Person talk more to his parents than either him or Elijah; Isaac was sleeping in upstairs since today was his day off. The two PAs attempted to talk to each other between bites of cereal, but they quickly stopped trying when the Thompsons kept speaking over them without notice.

Walking to church lifted his spirits a bit. The weather outside was beautiful, warm enough to wear shorts but cool enough to get away with pants and without breaking a sweat. A gusty breeze picked up about halfway during their walk, which felt just as nice as the sun's rays on his skin. If Keith wasn't working he would have loved to simply walk outside listening to music in this weather. With many of the students still sleeping or on their return trip to school there were very few people out and about which made the atmosphere even more peaceful.

"Remember, make sure to always have him walk on the side of the sidewalk with grass or with fewer objects for him to fall onto in the event you don't catch him."

Jacqueline's voice drew him out of his thoughts, and he answered her with a quick "yes" out of habit. His eyes scanned the path before them as he noticed several trees to their left and brick columns on their right. Seamlessly switching over to Brandon's right side, Keith made sure to slot his left arm under Brandon's right. That way if he suddenly were to fall Keith would be able to help him slowly and safely to the ground.

"Good judgment. Brandon is also aware of what routes have the most greenspace for him to cross, so he will lead you more often than not. Elijah, since you'll be bringing Brandon to music class on Tuesday nights it would be good for you to know where the music building is. The music library is also attached to it on the other side."

She pointed in the opposite direction of where they were currently heading. While she explained to him which building was which and what entrance to use Keith remained hyper-aware of their environment.

He had to admit this job took a lot more focus than his previous one. While Will could maneuver himself in his power chair Keith had still taken to mapping which sidewalks were the smoothest if only to have a more pleasant commute. Walking with Brandon, however, was a whole other story.

First, there was physical contact. If Keith and Brandon were at least friends it would have been easier, but because they were still on the PA and Person stage of their relationship it made him feel a little awkward. Isaac had taken to escorting Brandon arm-in-arm well because his family was large and expressed themselves physically so often it didn't bother him in the slightest. Elijah had still seemed a bit rigid last night when he walked Brandon upstairs and around his room during his bedtime routine, but that had been his first time working without Jacqueline breathing down his neck. He was also probably nervous. Keith, while more vigilant than self-conscious, still felt a little weird merely serving as functional arm candy.

It'll be easier once we're closer, he reasoned as they walked into the biggest Catholic Church on campus.

The service lasted about an hour and a half. The homily sermon itself wasn't bad, and the priest was someone Keith could get behind. There was also an inviting smell of incense wafting through the air. Stain glass windows rose up two stories on either side of the pews; Keith thought they added a lot of beauty, yet the crowdedness of the building along with the constant call and response wasn't his cup of tea. They also didn't indicate what songs the choir was singing in any way. He found himself unable to sing along with the Thompsons and the rest of those around him, which just served to make him feel even more out of place. His church had a projection screen with the lyrics to whatever they sang. He found himself missing it.

Once church service was over the five of them waited until the pews were more or less empty before heading out.

"It's easier to maneuver with fewer people around," Jacqueline said for the umpteenth time that week.

Brandon's arm wrapped around Keith's and the PA assisted him past the aisles of pews to the front entrance with ease. He managed to open the door for both of them without much trouble either. His vigilance increased as they went down the steps of the entrance though, his muscle locking tight in case his Person was to have an episode on the steps. The last thing he wanted was for both of them to topple down the stairs.

Once they reached the bottom Keith let out an internal sigh of relief.

"Great job," Larry said, suddenly appearing at the PA's side. "You're very good at focusing on his safety. I heard you've been doing a great job all week. I'm glad. Knowing Brandon's in safe hands will help Jacqueline and I not worry as much."

At the praise Keith allowed a genuine smile. While he still thought Larry was a bit odd the man was someone he could talk to without feeling like he was being looked down on.

"Thank you, Mr. Thompson."

Larry opened his mouth to say more when Keith felt the slightest tug on his arm.

Bending his knees slightly, he braced his arm for the dead weight that he was feeling pulling him down. It didn't help much though seeing as he landed hard on one knee before he could stop himself. After catching himself though he carefully dropped onto his other knee, using his free arm to gently direct Brandon's limp body onto the ground. Before his shoulder could touch the ground Keith made sure to use his hand to cradle Brandon's head. Once his head was secure Keith untangled the arm he'd had wrapped around Brandon's own and used it to check the time.

Twelve fifty-seven, he noted as he saw a couple of people staring at them from his peripheral vision.

"Nice work getting him on the ground safely without injury."

The sound of Jacqueline's voice nearly made him turn around, but he kept his attention on Brandon. He counted silently in his head even as he overheard her, her husband, and Elijah explain to several concerned passersby that this was a normal occurrence and that there was no need for them to call an ambulance. He ignored the drool getting on his wrist as he held his Person's head in his hand too.

Finally, after nearly fifty seconds, Brandon began to mumble.

"What is it? I have to..." Each word was airy and dropped off in a huffed breath.

"You're okay," Keith stated. He repeated this a few times as the older boy lifted his head off the ground. "You're okay; I've got you."

His Person made a few noises similar to groans as he pushed himself up, but when he went to stand Keith stopped him from doing more than sitting.

"Brandon, let's wait for a minute. You just fell and we need to make sure you're not going to pass out again. I want you to be safe, okay?"

The black-haired boy seemed confused, his eyes unfocused for several more seconds until his brain caught up with what must have happened.

"How long was I out?"

"About fifty-five seconds. It happened at twelve fifty-seven."

He pulled out his phone to note it in his log, seeing as he kept track of every occurrence for medical purposes. Not long after his parents and Elijah got those crowding them to move on from the scene.

"Are you okay?" Jacqueline questioned.

Brandon nodded, his eyes on his phone. "It wasn't that

disorienting of an episode. I also don't even feel like I fell."

Elijah squatted on the sidewalk next to Keith, his eyes wide and in awe.

"Nice job, man! He hasn't passed out while I've been on duty, so I haven't been through that yet. You handled it really well."

Keith rubbed the back of his neck sheepishly.

"It was actually my first time dealing with it too. My heart was pounding, but I managed to make sure he didn't get hurt and to time it accordingly."

"That's awesome."

It's our job, he wanted to say. Instead Jacqueline came over and told Brandon he'd been sitting around long enough. She instructed Keith to grab onto his arm again so they could be on their way, to which he did without a fuss.

"It's so troublesome when strangers try to help," she expressed as they walked. "The average person thinks they have good intentions, wanting to help someone they see as needing help, but they often don't take lightly to not having their help reciprocated. I've had to fight people on my knowledge of my son's condition numerous times. Why am I not calling nine-one-one, they'll ask. Do I even care about my child? As if these strangers know more about his condition than his own mother.

"In those cases though, please inform them you are not just a personal assistant. If you inform anyone who sees you tending to Brandon then please use the term trained professional. Not only will strangers take you more seriously, but they will understand that you are familiar with these cases and would help more by allowing you to do your job."

The PAs responded in kind, letting her know they understood.

Keith in particular was well-versed in what Jacqueline was talking about.

He believed most people were naturally good. Nine

times out of ten if someone saw a person collapse on the sidewalk he or she would go check to see if that person was alright. If someone sneezed, then a decent person would say bless you. Unless you were heartless seeing a lost child would send anyone into a protective panic to find said child's parents. It was just that simple. Helping a stranger in need was a common human decency everyone was born with, he thought.

Not that it always stayed, he had to admit. He knew as people experienced the world the harder it was to help each other. When he was a child he wouldn't have second-guessed giving homeless people money; now he knew that some horrible people masqueraded as beggars for personal gain, or pretended to need money for a bus only to demand cash when a kind-hearted person offered to buy the ticket for them. When he was young he wouldn't have been scared to walk up to a less fortunate person and give them any extra food he had; now he was too socially anxious to even talk to his classmates, let alone approach a stranger who might speak back to him.

Despite how learning facts about life and experiencing the world can widely mess with someone's general disposition, Keith was sure people more often than not offered their help out of the goodness of their hearts. And if not, even the most selfish hypocrisy was still a deed done to benefit another regardless of what drove it. This meant a person's ulterior motives mattered not to him.

If someone was trying to help, then their actions would be good even if the intent wasn't.

Those offering to call an ambulance for Brandon shouldn't be completely shut down, especially since they were probably genuinely concerned for another person's safety. Telling them it wasn't necessary, yet letting them know their offer was appreciated helped his conscience rest a bit easier. He didn't want to make anyone think offering help was a bad thing. Sometimes help was necessary; he wanted people to know that.

He'd elaborated on such in the past while working with Will and his girlfriend. He was always grateful for whatever assistance was offered even if he turned it down most of the time, because the times he did need help he was lucky to have it.

"Keith? Are you listening?"

Said PA blinked, his focus having been on swapping which sides of Brandon he was on in case he had a follow-up episode.

"No, sorry." He apologized to a now pouting Elijah. "What were you saying?"

"I was asking if you could get me some stuff from Club Day since I'll be working the rest of the afternoon. You said they give out a bunch of coupons for the bookstore and restaurants on campus, right?"

"I can do that, yeah." He instantly agreed. "I'm going to grab everything I can like I do every year, so I'll probably have a bag of stuff by the time Club Day is over. I'll make sure to grab you a map of campus as well as the booklets the bus company gives out. They have all of the information on bus routes and times of operation, which is probably something you'll need to know."

"Thanks!"

The blue-haired boy flashed an excited grin as he fell into step next to Keith for the time being. Every so often he wound up next to Brandon since Keith would need to switch sides to make sure Brandon was on the less dangerous one. Behind the college students the elder Thompsons chatted about something involving their church's music group policies, something he was sure he and Elijah tuned out.

Not too much later they were all home and enjoying a pleasant lunch which consisted of chips and turkey sandwiches.

"So Keith," Jacqueline started after some idle chatter

between her and her husband, "according to your schedule you'll be working six hours at the library, as well as two nights at the restaurant a week."

"That's right."

Brandon raised an eyebrow, yet the PA couldn't decipher if it was in astonishment, awe, or just judgment.

"You're at eighteen credit hours too though, aren't you? How are you going to have time to do homework and study for all those classes on top of working here too?"

Keith shrugged.

"I've always worked three jobs since attending here," he stated in between eating a handful of chips. He'd finished his sandwich almost immediately after it had been placed in front of him. "It's not a big deal. The art of time management is something I've mastered since my first year."

Larry whistled. "Wow. That's pretty impressive for someone your age."

The PA was almost embarrassed by the man's continuous praise. Could he be any more flattering?

"I wouldn't say that, but thank you. I know of a few people who work more jobs than me. Trust me, I could be working harder."

"Perhaps, but you need to take care of yourself too," Jacqueline commented. "You have that fitness class two mornings a week too, don't you? You'll have to be up pretty early for that."

He felt tired just thinking about it.

"Yeah. I'll need to get up around six-fifteen in the morning, so I have time to get dressed and walk over to the gym."

"Whoa, that is early," Elijah said. "I'd hate getting up at that time just to exercise."

"It's not too bad. The sessions have been doing wonders for me since I started going to them last semester. I teach a stretch class which starts at seven sharp, and after that I help out with the strength class and sometimes balance class too."

"How many people do you teach?"

"There are usually around thirty to forty people. It depends on the day though. I think Wednesdays are busier than Mondays, but either way everyone is pretty good at coming in. The only time people don't come in is if they're sick or are on vacation. Well, sometimes they're watching their grandkids so they have to skip, but—"

"Wait, grandkids? Who are you teaching again?"

"Oh, I teach for a group of retired educators. All of the members are at least fifty years old. Our oldest members are in their eighties."

"That's crazy. They must be in good shape then, yeah?"

"Amazing shape. All of them can hold a plank longer than me, and I can hold it for about a minute before my abs give out. It's pretty awesome what consistent exercise can do for someone. These guys have been exercising their entire lives; I'm hoping I can keep it up too."

Brandon seemed skeptical.

"None of them have gotten hurt during these classes? That's surprising."

"We do adaptive exercise, so what we do can be toned down either by using less weight or by using a different movement entirely. They know what they can and can't handle. A lot of them come because they had an injury that is being… healed for lack of a better term because of their exercise regimen. Rotator cuff surgery, for instance. I developed an exercise plan for strengthening the shoulder, arm, and back muscles to help specifically with rehabilitation after such a surgery. It's been doing wonders for the two I prescribed it to."

He said this with an air of confidence, feeling a sense of pride in his work. While teaching a fitness class had been scary at first since he got quite anxious when standing or speaking in front of a large group of people he'd warmed up to it rather quickly. There was something relaxing about just stretching to music for thirty minutes. It allowed him to think while also doing his body wonders.

To be fair he wasn't fat per se. He was on the shorter side of most guys his age though, which made him seem a little wider by comparison. The real issue was that he didn't have much muscle on him. He was carrying around unnecessary fat that made him feel chubby despite Elizabeth telling him he looked fine.

Now I finally have some sort of muscle definition, he thought proudly. He'd come a long way in just five months.

"I wish I could exercise," Brandon said, the emotion in his eyes finally discernable as sadness.

"Why don't you?"

"I'm disabled, Keith."

"And?"

"It's not safe for someone like me to exercise."

"He's right," Jacqueline agreed. "It would be foolish to take such silly risks when he's already in good health from his diet as is."

Keith could feel himself becoming physically upset. Who taught this family that people with disabilities were handicapped?

"Maybe, but you do realize many people with disabilities exercise or go to some kind of physical therapy, right? Will exercised four hours a week both in and out of his power chair, and his girlfriend Jordan did too despite having nearly zero ability to move her arms and legs. There are ways to adapt exercise to virtually anyone."

"Gyms are too dangerous," his Person shot back. "Too much equipment that would lead to me getting seriously injured if I had an episode."

"You don't have to use equipment to exercise."

"Really? Then what would I use, huh?"

"There's yourself for one. You can do plenty with your own body weight on a mat," Keith explained. "Heck, even stretching for ten minutes a day would be better than doing nothing at all. Sedentary behavior can lead to all sorts of problems, you know. The risk of heart attacks, back problems, and so many other medical issues are much higher for people who don't get at least three to five hours of light exercise in a week. Maybe we could go for walks together? You only leave the house when you walk to and from classes, so walking for an extra half hour every few days a week could be fun."

Brandon seemed to be considering it.

"That does sound nice," he admitted. "Getting out of the house would help for the days I have online classes. Otherwise I stay in the house all day."

"Awesome! Let me know when you're free to—"

"That's enough."

Jacqueline's razor-sharp voice cut between the PA and her son so suddenly both of them flinched out of shock. Beside her Larry looked down at his dish while across the table Elijah shot an affronted glance at her.

"Keith, I appreciate your concern for my son; however, it is rude to push your opinions on others who have different ones than your own."

Opinions? I was stating facts.

Part of him wanted so badly to speak up, yet he couldn't find the courage to do so. If he did say something it was possible he would upset the Thompsons more. Not only would it look bad on him to argue with them hours before they left for home, but there was a chance they wouldn't trust him to do the job well and would stay until he fell into line.

The last thing he wanted was Mrs. Thompson staying there any longer, so he kept his mouth shut.

"And stop slouching, Brandon. How many times do I have to remind you? It's bad for your back."

"Yes, mother."

Everyone who was still eating went back to doing so

while Keith silently burned with embarrassment from being scolded. All he'd been trying to do was explain to Brandon why he was wrong about not being able to exercise.

Okay, maybe I could have been less pushy, but he is wrong. He thinks he can't do all these things because of his condition and that's just not true! Why does his own mother want him to believe such lies? Why doesn't his father speak up? It's obvious he has differing opinions, but he won't disagree with his wife. Ugh. It's not right.

What if they're both scared of her? It wouldn't be that hard to imagine. She's sort of a tyrant if this last week painted any sort of picture. What if Brandon just needs help? Perhaps without her around he'll open up more. Maybe he acts completely different. Maybe I'll be able to show him all the things he can do if he just has a little help. We can go swimming, work out, watch a movie, go to dinner—

But that's not your job, another part of him reminded. *You're just a PA. You're paid to do what is outlined in the contract and nothing more. Just let it go. Brandon doesn't care for you anyway, so why should you care if he's missing out on things? He's old enough to stand up for himself. If he's unhappy, then he can speak up to his mother. He's not helpless. He's not being abused. He's probably fine and you're just making a bigger deal out of it than it is.*

Maybe.

As they finished lunch and got the cookies out he listened to Jacqueline chastise Brandon about taking more than the recommended serving size on the box.

"It says two, Brandon. Taking three wouldn't be healthy."

"I'll put it back then. Sorry."

"It's too late now. You already touched it. Just eat the damn thing."

"Okay. Sorry, mother."

She didn't seem impressed by his apology.

"Whatever. Anyway, Elijah, after lunch you need to make sure Brandon gets in his required five hours of violin practice. Isaac is familiar with this, but to keep up his skills from…"

As she carried on Keith noticed how the corners of Brandon's lips seemed heavy. His eyes spoke of frustration and resignation, yet he kept quiet.

This was a common occurrence, but he had brushed it off as not understanding how things worked in their family. Now he was paying attention to it. It was like he was hyper-aware of every little thing that seemed off about them.

Something was definitely wrong with the Thompsons. Jacqueline was too controlling, Larry was a pushover, and Brandon was being held back. None of them seemed particularly happy; especially Brandon.

I'm going to help you, he decided as he stared at his Person. *I'll show you you're just like everyone else. Someone taught you the world was a dangerous place, that someone like you shouldn't be a part of it just because of a disability, but I'll teach you that they were wrong. Just watch me.*

CHAPTER FIVE

"The first mini-project is due next Friday, Keith. I'm already so done with this class I can't even—" Elizabeth cut herself off with an exaggerated scream of frustration. "I'm not going to have any time this weekend to watch my YouTube videos which means I'm going to get behind again! I just spent all summer getting caught up. I hate electrical engineering. I hate it. I just want to program, but no; I need to learn how electrons at really small scales can just go through barriers like they're not even there, which pisses me off because it makes it basically impossible to design very small transistors. Like how am I supposed to stop them from passing through? I can't. Freaking electrons. Think they're so great 'cause they're so small and can do whatever the hell they want. They're like bugs. Invading my house like they don't even care that there are walls there!"

He just let her rant over the phone as he walked. Telling her he didn't really understand what she was talking about would have just made the rant longer, as she would attempt to explain things to him that she too would only forget once this class was over, so he just agreed with her every once in a while. Seeing as it was just past nine on a Friday night this meant also ignoring the loud conversations of drunk students on his walk home from the restaurant.

"Hey, Keith?"

"Yeah, sweetie?"

"Why can't you come over to my dorm tonight? I

thought you didn't work until seven tomorrow morning."

"Elijah texted me during work and said he and Isaac were going out after he put Brandon to bed at ten. One of the three of us has to be home when Brandon's in bed in case he has an episode or needs anything during the night, so I need to get home before they head out."

"I get that, but they could have given you more notice. We already had plans."

"I know. I mean, I can text them and tell them I have to work until eleven instead of nine thirty? They don't need to go out."

A sigh on the other end of the line conveyed her annoyance.

"They don't, but I also don't want you to have to lie to them or stop them from having fun. Elijah and Isaac have had a tough first week from what you've told me."

"Isaac has been working eleven hours a day the entire week. Elijah is overwhelmed with all of the different groups on campus as well as his classes, so he's more stressed than I am. I've done this for the past three years. Neither of them is used to working this much while taking classes."

"Not even Isaac? I thought he's done this before."

"He's taken online classes while working as a live-in PA, yes, but they didn't have him working over sixty hours a week. Jacqueline also said in the interview that we could get schoolwork done while watching over Brandon; however, Brandon has made it clear that if we don't have our undivided attention on him he could get hurt. The most we can do is read or scroll through social media while working with him. Getting too focused on schoolwork, watching TV, or listening to music will make Brandon all snappy with us. It's sort of annoying. I can barely take notes from a textbook without him asking me if I'm still watching him."

"That's stupid. You shouldn't have to put up with that,

especially if they told you during the interview you would have time to study while working."

"Yeah. It sounded like the dream job when it was offered, but now it's sort of a pain in the ass. At least I'm getting free housing and food, as well as payment on top of it," he rationalized. "I can do this every week until we graduate as long as it means getting my degree. I also want to help Brandon experience some new things even if we're rubbing each other the wrong way right now."

A bark of laughter came from Elizabeth before he realized how the sentence had sounded out loud.

"Lizzy, no. You know I don't swing that way."

"Yes you do. You swing both ways."

"Okay, but I'm not leaving you for some guy I just met. Not at this point. If I did I'd go for Jose, not Brandon."

"Jose is a handsome guy," she agreed between giggles. "Smart and funny too. Honestly, he's pretty much the perfect person."

"You're right. Maybe we should ask him if he's open to polyamory."

"No way! I'm not sharing you with anyone."

"It's fine. I don't think we'd be good enough for him anyway."

They laughed a bit at that before Elizabeth sobered up enough to continue their conversation.

"Sorry. Back to Brandon I'm honestly amazed you want to help him despite how he's been brushing you off these past few weeks. I'm also really proud of you enduring all this work on top of school so you can get what you want. You're amazing, Keith."

He blushed. "You're more amazing," he replied without a second thought.

"I wish you'd stop arguing with me about this all the time. You're the most amazing!"

"Well you're the mosterest amazing, so ha!"

"Keith!"

"Lizzy!"

"You're a brat," she whined.

He smiled. "Maybe, but I'm your brat. And you love me anyway."

"Yes I do." A small sigh, and then: "I just wish you had more free time. I really wanted to see you tonight."

"I know, and I'm sorry. You'll have more time to work on homework without me distracting you at least."

"I guess, but we're already barely going to see each other all year."

The sadness in her voice made his heart ache in response, leaving him feeling a bit heavier than he had throughout the week.

"We're meeting up tomorrow afternoon, aren't we? I'll be finished cleaning by eleven. We can meet somewhere for lunch and then head back to your dorm until I have to be back in the evening to cook dinner?"

"Can we cuddle?"

"Duh."

The smile on the other end of the phone was audible. It made the corners of his lips lift into a smile too.

"Good. I guess I'll work to get a bunch of progress made tonight so I won't have as much to worry about tomorrow. I gotta spend time with you when I can," she vowed.

He was about a block away from the house at this point, so he began slowing down just so he could be on the phone just a little bit longer. He ended up pacing outside the front driveway for another twenty minutes until Elizabeth realized it was almost ten.

"You were walking the block again, weren't you?"

"No, I was pacing out front until I had to go in. I told you the walls inside are uncomfortably thin, didn't I? When Brandon's mom was still here I could hear her complaining about Elijah from her room on the third floor. Not to mention I can hear Brandon whenever he talks to his sister on speakerphone in his room some nights. That's why I usually hide in the closet when I talk to you." This time he caught his words before she could react. "Lizzy, no, I'm not—"

"You're still in the closet, huh? Any chance Jose can coerce you out of there?"

"Just because he has fantastic hair, dresses well, is intelligent, and is a decent human being doesn't mean I'd leave you for him."

"I don't know. Blonde Sarah is the female version of Jose and I would date her," she joked.

"She has a boyfriend."

"For now."

"*You* have a boyfriend."

"That is a much more valid point."

He rolled his eyes. "Anyway," he said while checking his watch again, "I do need to go though. I'll text you when I'm done cleaning tomorrow to make sure you're awake for lunch. You have a nice night, okay? I love you."

"I love you too. Don't stay up too late reading, okay?"

"I won't…"

"Somehow I don't believe you." He could hear her smile. "Have a nice night, sweetie. See you tomorrow."

"See you tomorrow. Bye."

"Buh-bye."

With that he hung up, placing his phone in his pocket as he got out his house key. A few moments later he was reactivating the alarm, kicking off his shoes, and noticing that he'd shown up a little late.

Hoping his roommates weren't mad at him, he walked through the kitchen and up the stairs. When he got to the second floor he took note of Brandon's closed door. Since the light was also off it seemed like their Person was already ready for bed. He peered into Elijah's room since his door was wide open, but no one was there. Finally he turned to Isaac's room to where the door was cracked open a few inches. The sound of chatter reached his ears.

I should let them know I'm home. The alarm is hard to hear from the second floor.

He made his way to Isaac's door quietly as to not disturb Brandon who was only a room away. Just as he raised his hand to gently push the door open and make his presence known, he discerned the sound of Isaac's strained voice.

"I can't do this all year," he said to who Keith could only assume was Elijah. "They have me working nearly sixty hours a week. They said full-time when I applied, but I didn't think to read the fine print on one of the pages stating full-time fifty-five hours. It clearly said forty on the page for working hours throughout the state in general. I didn't freaking know it was different for just me."

Even as Elijah replied Keith found himself frowning.

I thought Isaac has been working so much because he wanted to. Sixty hours is a lot when he's taking two online courses, but surely he's fine working so much if he's getting paid well? He can get homework done while working too. Still, the part-timer thought, *if what he said is true the Thompsons are crooked.*

"That's messed up," the youngest PA barely kept his voice down. "I'm pretty sure full-time for the state is forty hours, it's just their contract decides full-time staff here work fifty-five hours. Just tell them you can't work as much as you did this week."

"I'm going to, Eli. I'm just worried. Jacqueline is so much more petty than you realize. Did you know she went through the trouble to get this house marked as historical just so a local gas station chain wouldn't buy it and tear it down in a year? She told me she didn't care about the house, but that she had a bad experience with one of the representatives asking to buy the house, so she did it just to make sure they couldn't buy it."

"What the hell?"

"She was so proud of herself," he continued, "telling me how livid they were with her for getting the county board to agree with her by telling them her son loved this place so much that the voters took pity on her and went with her proposal."

"Of course she mentioned his disability too…"

That's like her favorite pastime, Keith thought in agreement. Part of him wanted to join in their conversation, but another part of him worried they would blow him off as soon as he walked in. It was sort of their thing to do that to him now.

"She had to have. It's like second nature to her to tell everyone she meets about him."

"I know!" Elijah exclaimed a bit louder than he'd probably meant to since his volume dropped sharply a second later. "When she brought me to the grocery store last week she told the cashier of all people that we were out buying supplies for her son's PAs, which turned into storytime about her struggles raising 'her disabled son' as she calls him."

"It's really annoying."

"It is! Like I haven't been a PA for people our age before, but it doesn't seem right to treat him like she does. She's constantly telling him he can't do things. And neither Brandon nor her husband care."

"She's really cruel to Brandon," Isaac stated darkly. "During the day when he's playing the violin she would interrupt every couple minutes to tell him what to do to make it sound better. I asked Brandon if she knew how to play too, but she doesn't. She just nitpicks everything he does."

"She was always telling him how much to eat too."

"Yeah, and then she makes those little comments about our eating habits too. Ugh, remember what she said about him not ever finding love? I almost lost it."

"You almost lost it? I feel like Keith was about to quit

right then and there.”

“He did look completely done with the situation, which I get because he’s worked with people with disabilities longer than either of us. I could also tell he switched to using his passive demeanor when dealing with Jacqueline and Larry for the remainder of their stay here. I think he was trying not to say something he’d regret.”

Keith was surprised. *Did they notice my customer service mode? I’m impressed. Most of the customers just think I’m happy and approachable all of the time; they must have worked in retail or food before too,* he decided.

Elijah made a noise that could only be described as a cross between a sigh and a whine.

“I wish I had his patience. I’m not sure if I could have stayed quiet any longer than we did, honestly. I was so glad after Brandon’s parents left. It was like I could breathe again.”

“I get what you mean. Jacqueline’s presence was so suffocating. It was like she was breathing down our necks whenever she was around.”

“I know. She was constantly commenting on every single thing we did, and never stopped complaining. I don’t know how Larry deals with her. He’s such a nice guy; I don’t get why he lets her walk all over him.”

“There is such a thing as being too nice. Combined with how emotional and manipulative Jacqueline is it’s no wonder he’s such a pushover.”

There was rustling coming from the room, and a moment later Keith found himself knocking on the door lightly in panic. He didn’t want to get caught being nosy. He would just pretend he hadn’t overheard, instead of apologizing for being late and letting them know he was going to go to bed.

When he did this he wasn’t surprised when neither Elijah nor Isaac mentioned anything they were previously talking about.

"Thanks for being here tonight," Isaac said.

"Yeah!" Elijah grinned. "I'm excited to check out campus town. There are a ton of bars over there as well as one that does karaoke. We'll be gone for at least a couple of hours."

Keith forced himself to return his roommate's enthusiasm.

"Sounds like fun! Be safe though, alright? Some of the students here are intense when they're drunk."

"We'll be careful. See ya!"

That was all Keith got from them before they began talking about something else as they made their way down the stairs.

It was normal, he supposed. They rarely had much to say to him anymore. When the three of them were together they often acted like nothing was wrong, pleasantly talking to one another while Keith merely listened. Either of the two only ever talked to him when the other wasn't around, which was pretty rare with how busy he was juggling school and other jobs.

Maybe that was why Keith didn't care when they completely pulled away from him.

At first it had upset Keith to notice the other PAs becoming best friends. It only took a couple of days for the two of them to hit it off, talking to each other at all times of the day despite one of them usually working as they did so. Even when Brandon needed quiet time to practice the violin or study one PA was usually texting the other. At dinner they always sat next to one another, having a conversation amongst themselves whenever Keith tried to strike up a conversation with Brandon. No effort was made to even look at Keith unless they had to, but he doubted they were conscious of this. It's not like they were super close to begin with.

I thought we were friends, Keith thought as he shed his uniform in favor of a nightshirt and shorts. *Elijah and I bonded during the first couple of days and then when we cleaned. What happened? I know Isaac was always a bit distant with me and Brandon, but we got along. I've been nothing but kind to them too. Why is it they can talk to each other honestly, yet leave me out of it? I have as much to complain about regarding this job as they do.*

What got Keith feeling a bit left out was how they would blatantly ignore everyone else around them when they talked, making plans with each other during the few times Keith worked as a PA during the week. While it was true they all couldn't hang out at the same time unless Brandon came with (which would never happen) it occurred to Keith how neither of them ever tried to hang out with him since making such good friends with each other. He was a busy guy, sure, but he'd offered to show them fun spots around campus during his free time on multiple occasions. Why did they always turn him down?

If someone asked him if he cared, he'd say no. Part of him truly didn't mind that they didn't want to be his friend. He had plenty of other people in his life that were far more important to him. Even on campus he had his girlfriend, two friends from high school (Jose and Blonde Sarah), and some special people he'd met during his first few years here. If he wanted to hang out with someone he had his options.

However, part of him felt a bit betrayed. Coming in he'd wished for a pleasant relationship between his roommates. Instead all he got was a Person who didn't respect him save for his ability to do his job, and two roommates who brushed him off at nearly every interaction. He couldn't help but feel a tendril of isolation when he thought about it.

It wasn't like he could just invite Elizabeth or his friends over either. Brandon had to approve of their visit, as well as be present during it, and have met said friends at least twice before allowing them in the house. There was also the fact Brandon had yet to show any interest in meeting Elizabeth, whom Keith had asked about the three of them going to the movies or getting dinner with twice already. Each time Brandon had said he'd think about it, yet one week in without Jacqueline or Larry around he still hadn't made up his mind.

Oh well. It's not like being friends is necessary. It would make the job easier, yeah, but I can deal with things staying as they are for two semesters. I'm still going to try and get closer to Brandon. It's his last year here; he deserves to have a little fun. Elijah and Isaac can do whatever they want though. As long as they get their jobs done I have nothing to complain about.

He tried telling himself this as he lied down in bed. Instead of pulling up fanfiction like he usually did before he was tired enough to sleep he shot a message into the group chat his friends from high school had. They were going on five weeks since their last group call, and the pang of loneliness in Keith's chest had him asking his friends if they were free to talk.

Several minutes went by without a response. Some of his friends had read the message, but no one had come forward seconding his idea.

It is a Friday night. They're probably all busy, he reasoned.

Feeling a bit silly for asking his friends to talk at such a bad time he opened a tab on his phone and began filtering some high-quality content out of the trashier works on the site. He was two chapters into a particularly fluff-filled story when someone on the group chat finally responded. Soon after that, two more messages of interest popped up, and suddenly Keith's fan fiction was replaced with a live video chat consisting of three of his friends.

"Hello everybody," a trying too hard to be suave Puerto Rican greeted, "sorry I'm late. I got done with a five-mile jog and had to shower."

"Of course you were exercising. You don't do anything else." Another voice replied.

"Joel, what did I do to earn such hostility?"

"Exist."

"I see. You're just jealous because I haven't taken care of you in a couple weeks. Don't worry; next time you visit I'll seduce those cross country shorts right off your ass before—"

"Jesus, shut the hell up."

Keith laughed as Jose played with the filters on his screen, turning his face into a panda, a strawberry, and several other things as Joel and Jesus continued to make fun of each other. After a few minutes Jesus finally noticed what Jose was doing and began messing with the filters himself.

When he did this Joel breathed a sigh of relief. "Anyway," he said as he rolled over in bed, his phone following his movements. "How's senior year going for everyone?"

"My first exam is next week," Jose stated.

"But this was the first week of class for you, wasn't it?"

"Yeah."

"Oh. Well that sucks for you, man."

Jose dramatically pretended to burst into tears as Jesus asked Keith how he was doing.

"You got a new job assisting another student with a disability, is that right? How's that going?"

"Okay, I guess. I don't think he likes me," he admitted. "He's so sheltered and rich that I don't think he respects me much since I can't really relate to him. I think I keep making him annoyed because I want to hang out with him."

"Ouch. I'd just let him hang then, boy. He's not worth your time if he's brushing you off like that. What about your other roomies?"

"They're fine. I get along with both of them pretty well, but they're more friends with each other than either of them are with me. Not that it matters since I use all the free time I have to be with Elizabeth. It honestly works out pretty well since she has such a difficult workload this semester. We're both busy."

"That's good. I've been pretty busy too," Jesus said while making his face look like a cheetah. "Working at the golf course and trying to finish up my associates, y' know."

"You'd have it by now if you weren't taking only two classes a semester," Joel pointed out.

"I know, but I'm not in a rush. Working forty hours a week while taking a few classes works better for me than being a student full-time."

"Whatever floats your boat, I guess."

"How are your classes going?" Keith asked Joel since he'd yet to answer his own question.

"Fine. Half of the classes I'll be taking this and next semester are just the useless gen-eds I'm required to take to graduate. I just need to get a D or higher in order to pass, but the ones I'm taking are pretty easy as it is. The other classes are the ones I need to actually try in."

"The ones in your major, you mean?"

"Yep. Honestly I could have graduated a semester early if not for the year and a half of gen-eds the school makes me take. I only need three more classes in my major to get my degree."

Keith could resonate with that. He'd finished getting all of the required classes in his major done in three years, which left him to spend his senior year either taking classes for fun to get up to degree hours or because they were required gen-eds. He was even getting a minor he didn't originally plan on since he had the time to do so. It felt like a waste of time and money to spend an entire year (which was roughly thirty-five thousand dollars) on classes he'd never utilize the knowledge for his future endeavors.

Japanese history? He loved Japanese culture but listening to an uninterested lecturer go over PowerPoint slides three hours a week paled in comparison to watching the history channel or YouTube videos on the subject.

Healthcare in the U.S.? Elizabeth knew more from reading online news articles on the subject than what he'd learned in class. While he'd learned some important or interesting things it wasn't knowledge he couldn't learn by using Google or going to his brother-in-law, a registered nurse who'd worked as a healthcare provider customer service agent for two years.

Scandinavian literature? Reading was a passion of his, so he had honestly enjoyed the class. The professor had been amazing too; however, knowing he could have been taking a class related to his field of study instead of having to write a twenty-page paper on the symbolism in *The Ice Castle* made him wish gen-eds weren't a requirement. Coupled with the fact so much time and money went into taking classes that weren't necessary for his future dream careers made the debt he gathered while taking said classes that much heavier.

"That's why I'm focusing on work instead of going to college," Jesus said. "Taking some classes online to get a degree is so much less expensive and time-consuming than devoting four years of my life to studying at a physical university. That and I can still put that I got a degree in my resume while building up money and work experience."

"Sure, but I've made a lot of connections here at college. Not just with businesses doing internships. I've made a couple of good friends here too," Joel replied. "The same goes for Jose and Keith."

"Our school does have great connections. I've done so much hands-on research since coming here it's insane compared to what people coming from other schools get. Not to mention being at an accredited university helps with job recruitment. I've already received a couple of offers for work after college, albeit in other states."

"What Jose said," Keith agreed. "Still, I wish I'd done

what you did before coming here, Jesus. If I'd gotten my gen-eds out of the way before coming here I could have saved up money for college and skipped an entire year's worth of classes."

Jose nodded slowly as if reluctant to agree. "Same."

All of a sudden another window popped onto their phone's screen revealing a grinning Dante.

"What's up assholes?"

Keith rolled his eyes as their prior conversation devolved into general gossip about people in their home town and them complaining about their various jobs.

"Did you hear Hunter got another girl pregnant? He's already paying child support for two other kids. You think he'd have realized not to sleep with someone just because they will."

"Ha! What a dumbass."

"You think he's stupid? I had a man fresh off the interstate order a chocolate soda the other day."

"A chocolate soda? Like chocolate ice cream with soda poured into it?"

"No. He wanted me to add a crap ton of chocolate syrup to a cup of carbonated water and blend it together."

"What in God's name…"

"That sounds disgusting."

"I know. He also got angry when I told him we didn't have carbonated water in the first place. I was like: this is Dairy Queen, not Baskin Robins."

Sometime after that Jesus started jokingly flirting with Dante, Joel ignoring them to pull out his 3DS and play *Pokémon* as Jose involved himself in the banter as well. This left Keith to listen to his friends talk while interjecting with a comment every now and then.

After over an hour of this, however, the consensus was to end the group call due to Joel and Jesus having to work out early the next morning.

"Good night fellas," Dante said in farewell before

dropping off the call.

"Night!" Keith stated tiredly, the other guys responding the same. After an awkward moment while half of them struggled to find the button to exit the call he was left lying back in bed feeling happier than he had in a while.

He loved talking to his friends. They were the most important people in his life, on par with his parents and little sister. There were seldom things he wouldn't tell them, and even fewer things he wouldn't do for them. They meant the world to him.

I'll have to plan a get-together for fall break, he mused as he rolled over to lie on his side to sleep. *I miss them a lot. The same goes for my family, and it's only been two weeks since I've last seen them. If only I wasn't such a workaholic.*

Thinking of the next time he'd be able to travel back home, Keith fell asleep to the thoughts of what he would do with his friends and family next he saw them.

Saturday had been a good day for Keith.

Cleaning in the morning had gone much more smoothly without Jacqueline watching his every movement, lunch with Elizabeth had been fast food at the park since it was such a beautiful day, and even dinner had gone well between the PAs and Brandon with them talking about their favorite movies. That evening Keith even convinced his Person to watch an anime about music that he ended up falling in love with due to some of Brandon's favorite pieces being featured in the first couple episodes. To say Keith was pleased with this development would have been an understatement.

On Saturday, everything had been great.

As for Sunday, well, it had started out fine. Until the four guys eating lunch in the dining room heard the back door unlock.

"Is anyone home?" Jacqueline's voice carried over the

sound of the alarm system's beeping. Brandon called back a confused "yeah" while she disarmed the alarm. A minute later she was up the steps and swinging around the corner so fast those at the table flinched.

"Mother?" Brandon's back straightened in unease at his mother's sudden appearance. All around him the PAs stopped eating their lunch as the tension on the house skyrocketed. Naturally, her presence had that effect. "What are you doing here? It's only been a week since school started; you usually wait a couple of weeks until checking in."

Jacqueline smiled her sickly sweet smile. She knew something they didn't. None of them had any idea what that was, which only put them more on edge.

"I just thought I'd stay a few days to make sure your last year is going as well as it can be. Your father and I want you to finish up strong."

"Oh. Thank you." Brandon responded despite his obvious confusion. "You could have told me when you were coming through beforehand. I would have had someone prepare lunch for you."

She waved the notion off with a flap of her hand.

"I can take care of myself, sweetie. Don't worry. I had plenty to eat before the bus ride." While she spoke she surveyed the kitchen, eyes sharp like she was zooming in on every countertop or surface. Finally her eyes ran over the sink area.

"Whose turn was it to clean downstairs yesterday?"

"Mine," Elijah answered reluctantly. "Why?"

Jacqueline clicked her tongue before lacing her tone with disappointment. "I can see streaks on the stainless steel of the upper part of the sink. You remember what I taught you about spraying the stainless steel cleaner and then gently rubbing it with the grain, not against it, right? It shouldn't look like this unless you forgot to scrub with the grain all the way around and didn't rinse the sink out afterward."

"But I did. I followed the directions exactly."

"Maybe you think you did, but I know for a fact that—"

"Excuse me, sorry, but I think the streaks in there are from when I did the dishes yesterday." Keith interrupted. "I used the rag to get the little pieces of food off the sides of the sink before using the sprayer to rinse them down the drain. The marks you're seeing are probably from that."

Embarrassment seemed to flood the older woman's face for a moment before it was quickly replaced with annoyance.

"I see. Well, next time make sure to wipe the sinks down correctly. It doesn't look good for the sink to have streaks on it."

Why does it even matter? It just means it's been cleaned; it's not like anyone here is going to care if the sink isn't spotless.

"Okay."

He went back to eating his sandwich, because he thought the conversation was over with, but to his and the other PA's dismay she turned to the microwave and squinted. A moment later she opened her mouth to speak again.

"There are little marks in the inside of the microwave. Keith, did you make these too?"

"No. I didn't use the microwave for dinner last night."

"Well then, Elijah, do you remember what you cleaned this with yesterday?"

"A wet rag followed up with a paper towel?"

The shake of her head was enough to tell he'd messed up. "That's the problem. You need to use the spray I showed you first, then a wet rag, and then..."

Keith shrunk down in his seat as he tried to ignore her condescending voice. The sandwich on his plate began to seem less appetizing the more she talked, so after taking a few more bites he moved onto munching on a handful of chips instead. They weren't too flavorful either, not like they'd been the afternoon prior, but it was an improvement.

"Oh, Isaac." She stated at the same time she grabbed her suitcase and walked to the doorway that led upstairs. "I received your email yesterday. When you're free after lunch please come find me in the living room so we can discuss it."

The Italian nodded. Keith wondered if it was about what he'd overheard on Friday night, especially when he detected the worry on the other male's face.

I hope the conversation goes well, he wished him luck mentally. Since he would be talking to Jacqueline he'd surely need it.

CHAPTER SIX

Keith wanted to kick himself. How could he have been so stupid? He should have seen the signs; Elijah had, and yet he'd been so oblivious. Denial-colored glasses weren't even a good excuse. The clues had just flown right over his head because he hadn't considered the idea that one of them would ever be fired.

Sunday afternoon, for example, was the first sign that something had been wrong.

There were tears in Isaac's eyes as he came up the stairs. Keith grew alarmed, heart-clenching in his chest as he left the bathroom to see his roommate in such a state. He did his best not to stare if only to not embarrass the taller boy.

"Hey, um, are you okay?"

It was a stupid question. Keith knew that, yet he needed to know if there was any way for him to help. He wouldn't know unless he asked.

Apparently, now wasn't the best time though. The dark-haired man's face twisted in anger for a split second, a typhoon of harsh words ready to break free from his lips as he opened his mouth. But that wouldn't happen. A moment later his fury was replaced with sorrow and frustration as it swept over his face, the shift in emotions childishly easy to read.

"I can't talk to you about it," he settled on. "Or I might get sued."

Their shoulders brushed as he walked past him, and the

younger of the two could only stare as the other slammed his door shut. Part of him wanted to knock on Isaac's door and demand an explanation. What could Jacqueline have said to him to make him act like that?

The part that told him it wasn't his business won out in the end. He figured he'd find out what was going on at dinner that night.

Of course no one mentioned a thing. The PAs were too busy listening to Jacqueline gripe about the state of the house after one week of her being gone for anything else to come up in conversation All Keith knew was that Isaac and Elijah were shutting everyone at the table out far more than usual. That worried him.

Next, there was Monday's "hint".

"Hey, you mentioned you worked at a restaurant, right?"

Isaac's question caused Keith to perk up. It was the first time since he'd been actively approached by the guy in over a week.

"Yeah. Why? Do you want me to get you a discount?"

"No, nothing like that. I just wanted to know if you could get me some boxes."

Keith smiled, completely ignorant of why he'd be needing boxes.

"Of course! Tuesday is a big order morning. I'll text my now manager to set some aside for me and I can bring them over here tomorrow after class."

"Thanks man. You're a lifesaver."

"No problem, Isaac."

Then, Tuesday:

It was late at night when Keith had a chance to empty the dishwasher. After putting the ceramic dishes and silverware away painstakingly slow as to not make much noise, he headed upstairs for bed. Making a quick pit stop to the bathroom he noticed the sounds of shuffling coming from Isaac's room. He seemed to be moving around a lot.

Why he was up so late Keith wasn't sure, but he didn't pay much mind to it as he passed out in bed seconds later. If he'd taken just a minute longer putting the dishes away he would have seen Isaac open his door to reveal a room devoid of any of his belongings. All he would have taken in would have been the sight of boxes stacked upon boxes, and an emotional Elijah. Alarm bells would have surely gone off at that, right?

Wednesday, however, Keith was just trusting that someone would tell him Isaac was leaving. Until someone did why should he worry?

"Why is Larry here?" He asked Elijah that morning before classes. Despite the young adult looking like he wasn't in a good mood he'd taken the chance to strike up a conversation. Besides, he was curious. He was pretty sure Larry worked during the week writing news articles or something for some big-name company. Why had he driven here on a Wednesday morning then?

Honestly some sort of connection should have been made. Crying Isaac? Boxes? Larry's appearance (as the only person allowed to carry boxes up and down the stairs)?

The usually laid back male was furious at his question. His reaction startled Keith so bad he felt anxiety curling in his gut. He hadn't meant to make him mad!

"Are you an idiot?" Elijah bit out.

"Huh?" Keith blinked. Had he missed something?

Elijah scoffed at him. "Whatever. You'll realize later tonight."

With that the other PA left the house in a mad rush. This left Keith's question to go unanswered until later that night.

"I'm sorry to say it, but Isaac is no longer with us."

Jacqueline's words sat heavily upon his ears.

"What?" Keith asked, thrown for a loop that no one had bothered to share this information with him until now. It hurt that Isaac hadn't even said goodbye to him. "Why?"

Later, when he thought back on the last few days, he would realize he might have been rejecting the reality about what had been going on with the full-time PA.

The woman across from him, her hands folding tightly together as if she were trying to present herself in a regal light, gave him a look of almost calculated sympathy.

"It seems like he couldn't handle the workload as a full-time PA."

"But he was doing a great job, wasn't he? Why couldn't you just cut his hours down a little bit?" He broke in before he realized he'd just cut her off. "I'm sure Elijah and I could have taken some of his hours so he wasn't working sixty hours a week."

"It's what he agreed to when he signed the contract, Keith. And as sure as I am about you and Elijah being able to cover some hours he wasn't doing a great job anyway." She spoke flippantly in front of Brandon and Larry. Since Larry was here he offered to take care of dinner duty for tonight, leading to Elijah skipping dinner in favor of going to a soccer club meeting or something, which Keith was glad for. The blue-haired boy wouldn't have been happy hearing their boss talk bad about Isaac. "He would text while Brandon was in the bathtub instead of focusing all of his attention on listening to make sure he was okay. I caught him doing it three times during the week of training alone. Who knows how much he did it when I wasn't around? Not to mention he never truly acted like he cared about my son."

"He didn't show much emotion to anyone other than Elijah," Brandon put in hesitantly before turning a hopeful smile on Keith. "But you're different. You actually care about me. I think Elijah just tries to get along with me because he has to, but you want to be friends. It means a lot to me."

Larry nodded. "It means a lot to all of us."

Keith wasn't sure what to think. On one hand they were praising him for doing more than just his job, which was nice because that meant Brandon was finally getting that Keith cared about his happiness and well-being. On the other hand, the whole situation filled him with panic.

How were they going to manage without a full-time PA?

"Thank you, but who's going to replace Isaac? Do you already have a replacement?"

"Not yet, but we started looking online yesterday. We got the university to put up an advertisement on the job board this morning. I've also sent an email to the individuals that applied last summer, so there should be someone within a week here to replace Isaac. Hopefully after a couple of phone interviews whoever it is will be able to move in as soon as possible."

He nodded, understanding the situation but still completely worried underneath his façade.

"Maybe it would have been better to just cut his hours," he stated. "Isaac wasn't doing a horrible job, right? He could have been working at least half the hours he had been while looking for a replacement. Are you going to be taking care of Brandon during the day until then? I thought you said you couldn't on account of your knee pain."

The blonde pursed her lips. "There were other… complications that made it to where moving him out today was the best solution we could have hoped for with him. Anyway, I will be taking care of my son temporarily because there is no other option, but I was hoping you would be able to work a little more as well. Perhaps you could take the week off working at that restaurant so you can work on Friday night?"

"I'm not sure if I can find a sub on such short notice," he answered honestly.

"That's a shame. We pay you more for working here as it is, and it is a far easier job isn't it? Honestly I'm not sure why you stay employed at such a place when you could make more money here. It's not like manager experience will help you more than adding to your personal assistance experience. As it is I could use extra help during the days you have downtime then too. I'm trying to see if a past PA we hired can do a chunk of hours here and there in the meantime, but he's not very reliable. We'd prefer it if you could take on more hours instead."

"Oh."

He could feel his stress levels rising already. Was she implying he quit one of his other jobs to compensate for the fact they fired Isaac? She didn't know anything about his other jobs. He wasn't working at either of them for the money. He genuinely enjoyed the staff and the regulars he assisted at the library; at the restaurant the free food alone was another reason in itself.

On another note, she also wanted him to work more hours. Even if he gave up his two nights a week at the restaurant working any other time would make it nearly impossible to go out during the day or in the evening to visit Elizabeth. How was he supposed to find time to spend with his girlfriend if he was working more than he already was? He couldn't go a week without seeing her.

She'd be so sad, his heart ached at the thought. *And I wouldn't get my cuddle fix. God that sounds weirder in my head than it actually is.*

He was a man who liked cuddling. Sue him.

"I might be able to do that," he finally settled on. There was no way he was just going to agree right away. "I'd need to see if someone could take my shift on Friday and if they're slow enough not to have me work my shifts next week too. It also depends on how much homework I have."

"You know you can do homework while watching Brandon," Jacqueline put in helpfully.

He hadn't forgotten. Keith looked away awkwardly. "That's true, but some of my homework requires a lot of focus and some of my quizzes are timed. I can't do those while working without putting Brandon at risk. There's also the fact that I need to watch a lot of videos in order to take notes for one of my classes, and we're not allowed to watch videos while working. If you sent me a calendar of the time you need to be filled I can get back to you on when I can help out?"

Jacqueline agreed, but he could tell she wasn't happy with his answer. What was she expecting him to do though? He couldn't just drop everything for Brandon. Part of him didn't want to even ask his other employer about giving up his shifts because he knew he'd feel less miserable there than he would at the house now that Jacqueline would be there indefinitely. It wasn't his fault Isaac was no longer working. For Keith to have to step up to help out wasn't something he was required to do.

After dinner Keith slipped into his room. Not even ten seconds later was he on his phone calling Elizabeth while resting in the safety of his closet. With two doors between him and the rest of the upstairs he wouldn't have to worry about anyone overhearing their conversation.

"Keith?" She sounded surprised at the spontaneous call. "You said you'd call me later tonight because you had homework you needed to work on after dinner. I was just about to go to the dining hall."

He winced. "Sorry! I was just being impatient. Can you call me back after you eat?"

"I can wait a little longer, silly. The dining hall is open for another hour."

"I know, but they start to run out of food towards the end of the night. You should go now. I can do homework in the meantime."

"Are you sure?" She sounded concerned as he stretched his spine in the beanbag chair he was sitting in.

"I'm sure. We can talk about it after you get some food. I know how you get when you're hungry," he teased.

"Food is important to me, okay? I love it almost as much as I love you."

"You love me more than chicken nuggets?"

"Even chicken nuggets."

He made some mock crying noises over the phone that had her scoffing.

"Stop that! Anyway, sweetie, I'll call you back in half an hour okay? They're having turkey cheddar bake tonight and I am beyond excited."

"You do love turkey and cheddar."

"I do! Anyway, love you! Bye-bye!"

"Make sure to get seconds, Lizzy. I love you too! Bye."

With that she hung up, leaving Keith in a strange state.

Usually he felt happy and without much worry after talking to Elizabeth, yet the same feeling he'd felt downstairs when surrounded by the Thompsons sat heavily on his chest. Could it be that he was still anxious about having to work more hours? He could just say no. He didn't have to ask his other boss to have someone else cover his shift either.

But then what about Brandon? Guilt surfaced ominously like a shark fin in dark waters. *It's not his fault that he has no one to help him out now. And knowing he's going to have to do everything with his mom for however long it takes to get a replacement worries me. Jacqueline is too harsh on him. He's going to be miserable even just practicing the violin with her around.*

It's not entirely my job to care though, part of him reasoned.

I can't just not care, a stronger part shot back. *He's my friend and if I can stop him from being unhappy I should do it. All I need to give him is my time. Surely that's not too much?*

I can't give him all of it though. I need time for myself too. There's no way for me to get all my work done without having an hour to myself every day.

Keith was a naturally indecisive person. It was more his style to let others choose things for him, as he could not bring himself to have a preference. The hours he worked at all three of his jobs were scheduled however it worked best for his employers after taking his class schedule into account. He would make whatever they needed work regardless. Adding several more hours to his week to help out a boss who was honestly the most garbage human being he knew? At the cost of helping our Brandon, someone who didn't have much control over his situation, maybe.

He needed to talk to Elizabeth.

"Don't let them pressure you into doing something you don't want to."

Elizabeth's words rang through his head repeatedly like the steady beating of a gong. After their conversation last night Keith was more confident about not doing anything he didn't want to do. He didn't want to lower his hours at the library or restaurant, but he did want to help out now and then with watching over Brandon while a new PA was being hired.

He looked over his schedule critically.

If I change clothes at the gym after exercise classes on Monday and Wednesday then I'll have an hour to hang out with Elizabeth those mornings before we both have class, and I can still meet her for lunch on Wednesdays. On Thursday mornings I don't have class until one in the afternoon, so I could work from seven until noon without interrupting anything since she has class all morning on Thursdays.

I can rearrange some stuff so I can work Saturday afternoon once I'm done cleaning, I suppose. If I do homework on Tuesdays and Thursdays in between classes when Elizabeth is also busy, or if I work on my stuff late at night after Brandon is in bed, then I can get it done and just take notes when I work the extra hours. That way I don't need to worry about the timed quizzes.

But what about our Saturday afternoons together? I guess we can just hang out Saturday night, yet having to be up at work again from seven the next morning to noon is such a pain. I could just sleep over at her place otherwise since Elijah will have to stay home at night more often now.

Keith felt bad for Elijah. He really did. After Isaac's sudden firing the blue-haired boy was never in quite a good mood. It teetered on malcontent and snappish, perhaps forced disinterest when he was working with Brandon.

Said disinterest and lack of emotion only made living with Brandon and his mother more awkward by the day though.

Dinner that Saturday night, for example.

"You should try not to frown," Jacqueline commented as she bit into a stuffed tortellini noodle. "Your face looks ugly drawn in such a manner."

Keith had been convinced Elijah would have gotten up and left the room if he wasn't working.

"Oh, Keith, thank you for taking on more hours in Isaac's absence."

The older of the two PAs gave a barely perceivable nod.

"I try."

He didn't want to say anything else, already having noticed the stink eye he was getting from his once mellow roommate. Ever since Elijah had snapped at him three mornings ago they hadn't so much as spoken to each other outside dinner if only to keep Jacqueline from going on and on about how minorities were, evidently, stealing teaching jobs away from white people.

"They're hiring based on race and ethnicity instead of intelligence," she went on for the second night since she'd been back. "All these black and foreign teachers who get hired are never as smart as those that come from private schools here in America. Having a quota on diversity in the workplace is the stupidest thing. When I was a girl…"

Neither Keith nor Elijah could bear to listen to this exact rant a third time. Why were they even sitting here listening to her again?

Right. Because they signed a contract. Maybe Keith could just pretend to do badly at his job so they'd fire him too?

I need the money, he reminded himself while Jacqueline told the PAs once again not to touch the thermostat. He knew it was Elijah touching it since he said he got cold at night, but Keith wasn't going to say anything. Jacqueline was a jerk to him enough anyway.

"Keith?"

He nearly jumped, his mind elsewhere rather than the conversation going on at the table around him.

"Yes?"

"Your birthday is coming up next week, isn't it?"

He was honestly surprised Brandon had remembered. The last time he'd mentioned it had been in a passing comment a week ago while he was helping him get ready for bed. He'd just assumed the other boy hadn't been listening.

"It is. I asked off for work that night from both of my other jobs so Elizabeth and I could spend the evening together. She'd kill me if I didn't do anything for my birthday."

"That sounds sweet," Jacqueline commented. "Did you have any plans in mind?"

"I think we're going to watch a movie with some of our friends on campus, and the two of us are going to eat out or get ice cream or something beforehand."

"What movie?"

"We're not sure yet, but probably something animated. I love the soundtracks on the Disney movies, so maybe we'll rent *Moana.* I haven't seen that one yet. We'll find something regardless."

The woman nodded appreciatively. "That sounds nice. I hope you have a fun time."

"Me too."

There were several beats of chewing as they continued to eat until Brandon's eyes widened in sudden remembrance.

"Wait, Keith, didn't you need to ask my mom about going home next weekend? I thought you wanted to see your grandma."

He nearly choked on his food. He'd told his girlfriend about his plans on asking his employers about taking time off for an impromptu visit back home, but he was sure that he hadn't mentioned it in front of Brandon.

He must have overheard me talking to her last night, he thought. It had been the one time he'd chanced talking while lying in bed instead of holding himself up in the closet since he'd been particularly upset. After getting a call from his parents about the state of his father's mother he was debating putting life on hold to make sure his father was okay. He needed all the support he could get.

The fact Brandon just brought up something he wasn't supposed to hear made him draw his shoulders inwards. He'd need to be more careful on the phone from now on.

"Oh, did something happen to her?" Jacqueline asked, seeming genuinely concerned.

"Sort of."

"If I recall correctly she was being relocated to hospice care around the time you moved in. Your parents were having a bit of trouble getting the insurance to agree on which one to use, is that right?"

"Yeah. She's not doing well. I mean, she was getting bad regardless, but her health has declined rapidly over the past few days. The doctors say she'll be gone by the end of the month, so I was going to ask about maybe visiting her before she passed. I haven't seen her for months."

The blonde woman nodded. "I understand. We'll move

your cleaning to another day of the week, and I can cover your Saturday dinner shift and Sunday morning shift if need be."

He smiled, grateful that he could get the time off if need be.

"Thank you, but it's fine. It was just something I was mulling over. She can't remember anyone anyway, so I don't think it matters if I visit. After everything with not having a full-time PA it doesn't seem as important either."

Brandon frowned, voice rising in distress.

"But your grandma is dying! You have to go see her."

"I don't think that's your call," Elijah suddenly interjected.

Keith was glad for the support.

"She's been gone mentally for nearly a year," he told Brandon. "What's the point?"

"You might regret not seeing her for one last time before she passes away. Even if she doesn't know who you are you know who she is."

"I know, but even if I do go she's just going to be unbearable. Ever since the beginning o summer she's been mean to everyone she interacts with and has been getting violent. I'd rather not get screamed at by the hollow shell of who my grandma once was. It's hard enough remembering the last time I saw her as it is. The only reason I would go is to support my father, but he would rather me wait until the funeral since she's looking so terrible."

It seemed like Brandon wished to debate this further, but Jacqueline stepped in.

"Sweetie, it is Keith's decision. If he wants to go home next weekend, then he can. We're not going to make him go."

"Fine…"

"I apologize for his behavior," she told Keith while getting up to pour herself more water. "He was very close to and beloved by his grandparents. It's hard for him to hear you must not have had a close relationship with your own."

Keith raised an eyebrow. He supposed he understood, but now he felt defensive like she was implying it was his fault that he wasn't close to his grandma or grandpa.

"I didn't see them much growing up. They lived a state away from us my entire life until their health problems forced my parents to take them in, so I never really had a chance to get to know them other than seeing them once a year for Christmas. My grandpa was also mean to me as a kid, and my grandma had a habit of stealing things, which upset me when I was a preteen. I never felt much of a connection with them."

"Even after they moved in with you?" Brandon ventured.

"They only moved in after my dad discovered his father had been keeping my grandma's escalating health problems a secret. We noticed she was starting to forget people two Christmas's ago, and she got lost on the way to a store she usually walks to. They didn't have many friends or family in the area they lived in. No one noticed anything was wrong until there were major problems, although my dad is upset with his siblings for not being present in their lives. They live halfway across the country, but they have a lot of money. They also know their mom is going to pass away soon and they would rather visit for the funeral instead of seeing her while she's still alive. They haven't seen her in years. I get that she doesn't remember me, but she still remembers her sons. If anyone needs to visit her it's them."

"That's so sad." A pause, like she was about to continue, and then suddenly she was whirling on her son. "Brandon, what did I say about playing with your food? Hurry the hell up and eat or else I'll take your plate right now."

"Yes, mother."

Elijah shot a look at Keith, the younger boy's eyes

clearing indicating a message. He wanted Keith to get Jacqueline's attention off Brandon.

"Um, sorry for unloading that on all of you," the older PA went on like he wasn't unnerved by the treatment of her son. "It's a stressful situation. I do appreciate your concern though, Brandon. It means a lot that you care."

As soon as he said that Brandon beamed. Keith had never seen him that happy before, and the fact that only a few words made him brighten so much brought a smile to his own face. Sitting adjacent to them, Elijah seemed pleased. He was looking less combative for the first time since Isaac had left.

Maybe we can interact like proper roommates now, the elder PA thought as Jacqueline began relaying the story of her father's days in hospice care for the fourth time. *It'd be nice to hang out sometime too. Perhaps he, Brandon, and I could go to one of the free movies the school puts on? This weekend is a good one too.*

When there was a break in conversation Keith brought up his idea. Brandon seemed psyched to go see a movie that was still in theaters for free, Elijah appeared at least mildly interested, and even the usually stoic Jacqueline was mulling around the idea.

"We'll see how his practicing goes this week, and if he's not behind he can see the seven o'clock showing on Friday."

"Awesome!" Brandon grinned, turning to look at Keith with something resembling gratitude.

Keith was still a bit irked his Person had brought up the situation with his grandma. Still, despite those wishy-washy feelings churning in his gut, he managed a smile in return.

I guess I just need to be more careful from now on. I don't want anyone overhearing something they shouldn't.

CHAPTER SEVEN

"They think you're at work?"

"Yep," Keith replied without a hint of remorse. "I got both days off from the restaurant without any trouble at all. Turns out another coworker wanted more hours anyway."

"Great! You needed this time to relax."

"I really did."

He glanced over to where their friends Tucker and Jared were talking on the other side of the hot tub. The brothers were in the middle of talking about a new video game they recently downloaded, leaving Elizabeth and Keith to talk without having to feel pressed to include them.

"I'm still working for them Friday night. Brandon is finally starting to warm up to me, so I want to spend more time with him without his mom hovering over us to get to know him better. It'll make him happy, I think," he continued after a brief period. As he began talking again Elizabeth scooped some of the bubbles from off the top of the water and arranged them on his face to look like a beard, causing him to grab a pile of bubbles and give his girlfriend a mustache. "I thought you said you didn't like me with facial hair?"

"I don't. You look lame."

"Well then!" With a dramatic noise he flung the remaining bubbles off his face and pointed a finger at the girl next to him. "Your mustache is lame too."

She giggled as he threw a tiny bit of water at her face,

her eyes already closed since she'd seen it coming. After a few seconds she began fidgeting with the bubbles around them again and tried to make a mountain out of them.

"I hope she lets Brandon go to the movie on Friday," she wished aloud. "I still haven't gotten to meet the guy."

"You just don't want to have to see the movie with only Tucker."

"Can you blame me? He's a little brat."

From three feet away Tucker glowered at Elizabeth.

"I heard that."

"Trust me, I know."

"Rude."

"You always laugh at all the sad scenes whenever we watch a movie! That and you never stop complaining about what the protagonist could have done better."

"If it's a good movie then there will be nothing I can complain about," he shot back.

"So help me I'm going to come over this weekend and put on some movie where the dog dies just to get you to shut up."

"You wouldn't dare."

She grinned cruelly.

"But I would."

Jared broke in with hands raised in the air like he was God about to lay down a sermon about respecting thy neighbor.

"Now now children, I got this Friday off too. If anything I will be able to stop you," he motioned to his brother "from complaining and stop you," he gestured to Elizabeth, "from giving away the entire plot of the movie before it happens."

"That only happened like three times!" She protested.

"I've only watched a total of three movies with you, Elizabeth."

The brunette crossed her arms angrily. "I don't see your point."

After a few more minutes in the hot tub, the four of them entered the pool. Since they were the only ones there at the moment this meant getting free-range in the section that contained a volleyball net. Once Jared acquired a ball from the far side of the pool a game of water volleyball ensued.

"Brothers versus couple," Keith stated dramatically. "Who will win?"

"Me! I mean us!" Elizabeth screamed before throwing the ball into the air and hitting it with all the strength she could muster. When it hit the net she made a peculiar face before pretending to drown herself under the water.

"Hey," he called before pulling her up and messing up her already chlorine-saturated hair, "as funny as that was you're supposed to hit it over the net."

She narrowed her eyes at him. "I know that…"

"Heads up!"

Suddenly they were turning to see Tucker hitting the ball clean over the net to the open area beside them. Keith tried to leap forward in the water to hit it back, but with his movement slowed the ball plopped heavily into the water without resistance.

"Ha! Take that, losers!" Jared gloated before high fiving his brother. "Our brotherly love will never lose!"

"Stop calling it that." Tucker deadpanned.

"But bro, what about the power of our bond?"

"Please stop. It's embarrassing being in public with you as it is."

In the end the brothers did win. It didn't help that neither Keith nor Elizabeth were any good at volleyball to begin with. Keith could hit it over the net, but maneuvering through the water was a hassle. Elizabeth could move in the water faster, but she was extremely uncoordinated. Even if she managed to hit the ball it would either go behind them or spiral right back into their side of the net.

"Oh, let's see how many times we can go down the

water slide before we get tired."

Keith raised an eyebrow at his girlfriend.

"I'll go down the slide once. That's it."

Jared stretched his arms behind his head, looking uninterested. Tucker on the other hand…

"I bet I can go down more times than you."

"You're on, Tuck Tuck."

Keith and Jared resigned to sitting back down in the hot tub after a couple of minutes. Once they'd had their fill of sliding down the slide and watching Tucker and Elizabeth race up said slide for the fifth time they knew they would be there for a while.

"I'd hate to say this, but Tucker will probably win." The PA noted.

"What makes you say that?"

"As fit as she looks Lizzy is far from being in shape. Going up those stairs to the slide is bound to kill her after a dozen or so times."

"Tucker doesn't exercise either."

"No, but he at least walks everywhere on campus. And as excitable as she is she crashes hard. She'll call it quits before twenty."

Jared laughed. "Well, I'm glad she can bring out Tuck's competitive side. God knows the boy needs to de-stress. He keeps switching majors semester after semester and finding out he doesn't enjoy anything he's doing. I'm worried he's going to drop out without his degree."

"I'm sure he'll figure something out eventually. There's no rush."

"Yeah, I suppose. I just want him to be happy though, you know?"

"I know, Jared. I know."

They stared at the bottom of the slide where Elizabeth landed in the water with a splash. A couple of seconds later Tucker landed as well. Then back up the duo went for their ninth (tenth?) trip up.

"Anyway, how's the job going?" The nuclear engineering student asked as he stood up and made his way over to the side of the hot tub to hit the large red button there.

Keith hummed when the jets activated once more, bubbles rushing to the surface as the multiple tiny underwater air cannons did their job.

"It's… going." He settled on.

"You seem stressed."

"Maybe. There are so many rules to follow and now that Brandon's mother is there even walking through the kitchen feels like walking on eggshells."

"Why?" His friend was genuinely concerned.

"I'm not sure how to explain it. It's like when I leave my room it gets harder to breathe. I'm constantly listening for Brandon's mother, Jacqueline, because whenever we cross paths she forces me into a conversation. It's not like I'm in a rush to go to most places, but the things she starts ranting me about are usually so negative or drop my mood entirely. She'll start ranting about the potential PAs she's been interviewing and make fun of different things they do, wear, or say. Or she'll tell me something horrible she just read about on the news 'just to keep me informed'. It's like thanks for telling me about how a man set fire to his house after killing his wife, children, and dog! That's horrifying! I have to go to class now okay bye."

"That's… interesting."

"Interesting? Tell me about it. When she's not talking to me she's usually driving her son nuts. I can't tell you how many times I hear her berating him for not playing the violin well enough for her despite her never learning how to play one herself. And she gets so mean, Jared. Like she will full-on scream at him if he makes too many mistakes."

"Huh. Does she stop when someone else is around though?"

"If she knows Elijah or I are there she acts completely

different. She's all cheery and encouraging like she wasn't just calling her son a dumbass. And don't even get me started on how she treats him outside of music practice. If I had a dollar for every time she's told him to sit with his legs closed, sit up straighter, stop frowning, stop slouching, and so on I'd have at least a grand." His eyes darkened as he made to impersonate the woman. "I can't stand your voice! Would you just shut up? Don't wear this; wear this or you'll look like an idiot!" He shook his head. "She has no idea what volume control is either. That's why I hear all this from upstairs. I'm sure Elijah has heard the same."

"That's, uh," Jared tried to find his words, but Keith beat him to them.

"Messed up? Well with the full-time PA gone here's something even crazier; since Jacqueline has a knee injury from her teaching days she can't assist Brandon in getting around anywhere. That means when Elijah and I aren't there she makes him crawl around on the floor to get where he's going."

"What the heck? That doesn't make any sense. Are you sure he can't just walk by himself?"

"That'd be too dangerous, I guess. He could fall and hurt himself. And yet his mother is fine with him crawling up the stairs like an animal."

"I hope he doesn't bruise his hands or knees," his friend worried out loud before clearing his throat. "I mean, Keith, my man— that sounds almost like abuse. Not physical, unless he does end up getting bruised from crawling around his house all day, but verbal or mental of some sort."

The PA felt his fingers curling to form fists.

"I was thinking that too. I can't tell though," he admitted shamefully. "Maybe this is just how some families are?"

"Dude, no one I know has had their mom make them crawl around the house. And getting constantly screamed at or having their every action controlled is as unhealthy an environment for someone in their late twenties as it is for a child under eighteen."

"You have a point. Elizabeth told me I should report what's been going on anonamously just to scare Brandon's mother into cleaning up her act, but we're both worried about making things harder for him. That and she might use his handicap to her advantage."

Jared winced. "You're in a sticky situation then my friend. I don't know what else to tell you other than we're all here for you if you need us. If you need help I'll be there for sure. You can't quit without legal repercussions though, so persevering might be the only thing you're able to do."

"I guess. I just wish I could do something, you know? Not that I want to be a hero or anything, but I want to do something to get Jacqueline to stop acting so mean to him. That or getting Brandon to realize that he's not being treated like he should be. It's so hard though. He thinks it's normal to be treated how he is. He'll be like: 'she's only cross with me because she cares', or 'she's not yelling; she just talks loud'. It's driving me crazy."

"Hey, buddy, do you want a hug? I think you could use a hug."

Without waiting for an answer Jared waded forward in the water and embraced Keith lightly. Getting a hug from the graduate student wasn't out of the ordinary since he was a pretty touchy person overall, but with them being both shirtless and wet Keith cut the action shorter than usual.

The hug still meant a lot though.

"Thanks, Jared. I needed that."

"Anytime, man. Anytime. Now," he stated while standing up and surveying the water slide, "it looks like Elizabeth gave up."

Seeing his girlfriend floating on her back in the middle of the pool while Tucker continued to race up the stairs to the slide made him roll his eyes in exasperation.

"I wonder how many times they made it up."

The answer was seventeen times. Nineteen for Tucker, because winning by one was quote-unquote "too easy".

"I'm hungry!" Elizabeth wailed as soon as they were done changing out of their bathing suits.

Keith poked her on the nose, but his voice was affectionate.

"We were already planning on going out to dinner, silly."

"I know, but we never decided *where*."

"This is always the hardest part with us," Tucker complained. "You guys think half of what we suggest is too expensive, and Elizabeth is too picky when it comes to food."

"Am not!"

"I'm sorry, Lizzy, but you are," Jared said. "You don't like most things."

"Name five."

"Fish, salad, most vegetables, Indian food, sushi, bacon, mushrooms, peanut butter, cheesecake, vanilla anything, spicy food, red grapes—"

"Grapes aren't like people! They don't all taste the same on the inside! The green ones are superior, okay? Purple and red just aren't as good! Also that was like ten things."

"I can come up with a couple dozen more examples if you want: sour cream, shellfish, watermelon, most sweets that aren't chocolate flavored."

She pouted. "Whatever… How about the diner down by the biology buildings? We could get ice cream or milkshakes afterward."

Surprisingly, a phenomenon that happened only once in a blue moon, they all were happy with the first suggestion offered.

I wonder if it'll be this easy to pick what we want to order when we get there, he wondered as the four of them piled into Jared's car and made their way to their next destination. Despite it only being a five-minute drive to the diner Tucker turned on the radio to the classic rock station if only to subject those in the back to Jared's over the top singing. Still, as Keith sat in the back listening to Elizabeth sing along with the driver, he couldn't help but feel extremely happy. He hadn't hung out with his friends like this since the new PA job started.

He'd really missed it.

Later that evening Keith and Elizabeth curled up in her bed. After all the exercise they'd gotten playing water volleyball (and one of them running up a flight of stairs seventeen times) along with the large dinner they'd eaten shortly after their bodies felt heavy. With her roommate at dance practice for a couple of hours this meant it was the perfect time to take a nap. Combined with the food coma that had set in the two were more than happy to cuddle the hours they had together away.

"I love you," Elizabeth mumbled. Her voice was soft from sleep, having just woken up due to Keith's shifting. Where her face was half pressed into her boyfriend's shoulder she continued to talk quietly. "I love you so much."

Keith smiled, his eyes still closed. Those words never got old.

"I love you too, sweetie."

"A lot?"

"More than you can imagine."

Silence, and then a more mischievous: "Enough to tell me what you want for your birthday?"

"Of course," he responded just as coyly. "The thing I want the most is your love and affection."

"Keith."

"That is my name."

"Keith," she whined again. Her voice went from soft to its regular volume. "You never tell me anything you want for your birthday, our anniversary, Christmas, or Valentine's day. It's not fair."

"We're already watching a movie and eating food together that night, so what's more to ask for?"

"Monetary possessions."

"There's nothing I need right now."

"But there are things you want, right? Anime merch? Books? A new video game?"

"Of course there are things I want, silly. But you don't need to buy any of them."

"But I want to! You get me stuff all the time; it's not fair that you won't let me even get you a birthday gift. It's not like we both don't have a little extra money we can use to spend on things for ourselves."

"I know, but why spend money on things I don't need? Why buy me presents when I can have your presence instead," he joked.

Elizabeth groaned, lifting her head so she could glare at her boyfriend. In the low light that was the dorm room being lit up by only an always turned on computer screen she could barely make out the shape of his shit-eating grin.

"You're a brat."

"You know, you call me that an awful lot."

"Because it's the truth!"

Before he could respond her lips were on his, feather-light yet malleable as she became more persistent. Even as she deepened the kiss, sliding a leg over his own in order to tease him further, he put up little resistance knowing she was much better at playing him than he was at playing her.

At first it had been embarrassing. He hadn't been with any other girl his entire life, and from what other guys said in high school he thought he was supposed to be the dominant one in a relationship. Many things he read in books, saw in the movies, and read in online articles gave him a similar impression; however, instead of allowing those outside influences to make him insecure he quickly realized "most people" were missing out.

They were so wrong it was laughable. At least the first season of *Game of Thrones* got something right; guys were missing out if they didn't consent to allow their girlfriend to… have the top bunk.

It was heaven.

"Hey," he managed to get out once she came up for air. "I thought you just wanted to cuddle tonight?"

"Did I say that?"

"You also said you were tired."

Keith thought he could see her raising an eyebrow in the darkness.

"It's been at least a week and a half since we've had real alone time."

"Uh-huh."

His feigned innocence would get him nowhere. Not when her hands were approaching places that would turn him into putty in her hands.

"Now who's being mean?" He tried as she all but crawled on top of him.

She laughed. "Probably me, but you deserve it."

"Do I?"

A rough kiss had him shutting up for some time after. He had other important things to do with his mouth anyway.

In stark contrast to the near-perfect evening, early the following morning Keith noticed his mother had called him at seven-thirty during his exercise class. He felt his stomach twist uncomfortably. He knew the only reason she would be calling so early in the day before his birthday. Part of him was relieved though; it would have been awkward for his grandma to die on his golden birthday.

"How's dad?" was the first thing he asked when his mother answered the phone.

She sounded so tired when she responded.

"I thought you'd figure out what happened without me telling you. She passed away in her sleep. The home called us at nearly four in the morning to inform us, but I didn't want to wake you up."

"I appreciate it." He was barely getting four to five hours of sleep as it was. "So there was no pain?"

"Not any more pain than she was already in with all those tubes and medications going into her. From what your dad was told it was the most peaceful way for her to go," she explained. "He called his brothers about an hour ago and told them both since their names weren't on any of the medical forms; he also has to do some paperwork before she gets cremated since he had the power of attorney."

"Does he have to identify the body too?"

"We're going to do that now. We're driving there as I speak."

"Mom, you're not supposed to be talking on the phone while driving!"

"I know, but I needed to answer the phone since your father is busy arguing with his brothers over text."

"Why does it keep changing the word when I'm trying to type?"

The frustrated voice of his father getting angry with autocorrect would have usually made Keith laugh. Right now though he just wanted to go home to make sure his parents were as "okay" as they seemed.

"Well since you guys are both busy and I'll have to go to class after a while is it okay if I call you back later tonight? I want to talk to dad then too."

"Sure thing, sweetie. We'll probably know more about the funeral as well too. It'll probably end up being this Saturday or Sunday afternoon, but we'll see."

"Okay. Try to hang in there, I guess?" Honestly he wasn't sure what to say or how to feel. His grandparents had never been close to him. He had cared about his grandma to an extent, but not even her passing could make him cry when he barely knew the woman past seeing her for a couple of hours a year back when she was in her right mind.

He knew he'd regret their lack of a relationship one day. Today, however, he just wanted to lessen his parents' pain.

"We will, Keith. Focus on your classes for now. Talk to you later tonight; love you!"

"Love you too," he replied before dropping the call.

The rest of the walk home was somber. He was debating if he should text Elizabeth the news or wait until later in the afternoon when she was out of class to tell her, ultimately deciding to go with the latter option, when he reached the driveway of his current abode.

I hope they already finished breakfast, he thought as he unlocked the door. He quickly ran inside to disable the alarm system. It was when the beeping stopped that he heard the telltale sound of a metal spoon hitting a ceramic bowl and he resisted the urge to groan. Of course they were in the kitchen. The only way up to his room was through there, which meant he'd have to talk to them or be considered rude for rushing past them.

He really didn't want to play that game today.

"Keith, is that you?"

Jacqueline's constantly loud voice wafted around the corner and down the steps to him like an unpleasant odor. Her voice honestly made him nauseous.

"Yeah, it's me."

With that he made his way to the kitchen with the tiniest smile he could manage. He didn't feel like smiling, but he knew if he didn't they would ask him if something was wrong. If they did that there was no way he would be getting out of there anytime soon; they didn't like it when he tried to brush them off. It only made them more judgmental.

"We're just finishing up breakfast," the woman motioned to the near-empty bowls before them. "I can still get out a bowl if you'd like to join us."

"No thank you. I had a snack earlier this morning, and I have some things I need to get done before class."

"Oh, I see." There was a moment of silence and for a split second Keith was baffled that she had actually gotten the hint that he didn't want to talk. And then: "How did your exercise class go this morning?"

It was like she hadn't even heard him. Or noticed him inching towards the doorway to the upstairs.

"It was fine. Same as usual, but I got out a bit late because someone asked for exercises and stretches to help with her shoulder. She recently finished up physical therapy after getting rotator cuff surgery and—"

"That sounds like you did a very nice thing for her! You're such a sweet boy."

Keith might have thanked her had he gotten the chance to talk, but as it was Brandon did what he usually did and, despite his noble intent, asked all the wrong questions.

"Hey, Keith, how's your grandma? Are you going home this weekend to see her after all?"

To see her ashes, maybe. He resisted the urge to bite back. Brandon had no idea of the news he'd received after all; it wasn't fair to be annoyed with him. Keith was pretty sure he just genuinely cared.

"She's not in any pain," was what he chose to say for now. That way he wasn't outright lying. "I'm going to call my parents tonight to talk about visiting this weekend. It depends on some factors." *Like if the funeral is this weekend or next weekend. My family can wait however long they want since all everyone will see is an urn.* "We're still fine to go to the movie on Friday night, right?"

Brandon turned to look at his mother hopefully. The way Jacqueline side-eyed the two of them like they were asking permission to go to some wild party made Keith want to roll his eyes. The woman thought standing up was too dangerous for her son. Who was he kidding thinking that going to the movies was any safer?

An average human being perhaps.

"I suppose as long as he's still having a productive week by Friday evening he can go. It's been a while since you've been out of the house with friends after all. You could use some fun." She smiled like she was giving him a great gift to the twenty-five-year-old. "I trust Keith to keep you safe. He hasn't made a mistake yet," she gloated before whispering something sour about Elijah under her breath.

At her words he couldn't help but feel a stab of pressure. He was doing great at catching Brandon during any falls; however, this only made everyone else think he was flawless at his job. The belief that he wouldn't make any mistakes in the future stressed him out. It meant high expectations from Brandon and Jacqueline. It also meant the moment he screwed up they'd be tackling him straight off the pedestal they put him on. He didn't want to disappoint anyone.

The last thing he wanted to lose was their trust or confidence in him. He just wished they understood that he was going to mess up sometimes.

And I thought just knowing someone had barely any faith in me felt bad. Someone having too much faith in me feels just as uncomfortable.

CHAPTER EIGHT

Once the stars were visible in the sky and all the phone calls had been made, Keith mentally prepared himself to walk downstairs to talk to Jacqueline.

He assumed she would react strongly, as she usually did to any sort of negative news; however, he forgot how much she liked to talk. What started with him informing her that his grandma's funeral would be next weekend and that he would need that one-off instead of the upcoming weekend soon led to an hour-long conversation of her telling him the story about her friend's passing several years prior. Part of him wondered if she brought up the story as her way of being empathetic, or if she just wanted to talk about herself again. When her story veered off into other less desirable topics he had to cut her off. As riveting of a tale of injustice was Elizabeth had been texting him like crazy. She wanted to hear his voice before she went to bed.

"Sorry," he'd apologized to her once he's finally gotten away from his boss. "I was being held hostage, I swear."

"What?" Elizabeth questioned with a yawn.

"I meant to just ask Jacqueline about getting next weekend off for the funeral, but it turned into storytime with her telling me about when one of her friend's father died. That conversation led to one about how much she hated hospice care and the personnel who take care of the elderly on their deathbeds. Then she started going on about some coworkers she used to work with back when she was a teacher, which I honestly couldn't care less about, and led her to the topic of racial inequality…"

He was met with a hum of understanding.

"Sounds like a fun time, sweetie. You're fine though. I was just getting sleepy," she explained with another yawn. "I have that test tomorrow I need to study for, so I'm going to get up early to do that since I stayed up way too late last night."

"And whose fault was that?"

"What're you talking about? I let you go well before midnight so you could get sleep before your fitness classes."

"Yes, and then you did your homework afterward instead of going to bed and doing it in the morning like you should have."

"My roommate was up until almost two in the morning anyway. I wasn't going to fall asleep with her tapping away on her keyboard with all the lights in the room on."

"You've slept through it before," he countered.

"Maybe, but it's easier to fall asleep once she's gone to sleep. I was super productive too. I finished one of the hardest mini-projects we've been assigned this semester. My code might not be concise, but it gets the job done."

"Good job sweetie; now go to bed."

"I'm gonna, I'm gonna. My roommate will be out of the shower any minute now anyway, and you know she hates it when I'm on the phone when she's trying to sleep."

"Yet she keeps you awake by not only leaving her light on but requiring your side of the room to be lit up too? I'd stay on the phone just to annoy her."

"I am tired though. But before I go, are you sure you're okay after today?"

He felt his lips quirk into a small smile.

"Yeah, I'm fine. Is that wrong?"

"No."

"My grandma died today, and I haven't shed a single tear. I'm more sad thinking about how my dad must be feeling. It feels like I'm letting them both down. What kind of grandson doesn't cry when their grandparent dies?"

"Just wait until the funeral," she advised. "Going to even a stranger's funeral is bound to make anyone cry. Sometimes it's not about how much you know the person who passed away. Sometimes it's hearing from those people he or she left behind and crying because they are crying. Trust me, sweetie, you're not abnormal. It's just not time yet."

That made him feel better, which was strange considering how downtrodden the mood should have become from that topic.

"Thanks, Lizzy. I'll see you tomorrow after classes and work for dinner and the movie, okay?"

"Uh-huh. Wait, have you decided what movie we're watching?"

"Actually, I was thinking we could watch *The Rise of the Guardians*? I haven't seen it in a while. I was going to suggest *How to Train Your Dragon*, but I think that's best saved for a time we can watch the entire trilogy."

"Sounds good to me. Jared, Tucker, both Sarahs, Jose, and I are taking care of the food, by the way. Whenever you're done with dinner over there call me and we'll send someone to drive you over."

"I can't wait. But don't go too overboard, okay? Remember I'm fine with a birthday cake made of chicken nuggets."

"I know."

"Uh-huh, but somehow no matter how many reminders I give you I feel like you're not going to listen."

She yawned again, but he could tell she was smiling. That meant she was planning something. "Whatever you say, sweetie. I'm going to go to bed now, okay?"

"Okay. Sweet dreams."

"You too, Keith. Happy birthday."

He looked at the clock on his phone. It was a minute

after midnight.

"Thanks, Lizzy. I love you!"

Much like he'd hoped, his birthday kept going by blessedly smooth.

It was off to a surprisingly great start when he slipped out of the house without being noticed by any of its inhabitants, which was rare. If it wasn't because Elijah was awake trying to make a silent escape just like him it was because Jacqueline was making a racket forcing Brandon to crawl down the stairs. On mornings like those Keith would stop whatever he was doing to get up and help the guy down the stairs if only because he was a decent human being. Sadly, it always led to him helping out for far longer than he'd meant to, either making him nearly late to class or just putting him in a bad mood at Jacqueline's satisfied smile.

I'm not going to let myself get annoyed today, he reminded himself as he walked to class. *Not today. If not for myself, because Elizabeth will be sad to know I was upset on my birthday.*

With that thought he powered through his anatomy lab and four hours at the library with surprising ease.

It wasn't hard for four hours at the library to go by fast. He kept himself busy by assisting other students or faculty members, which was second nature to him after working as a desk clerk for three semesters prior. He enjoyed greeting people who walked in the library even if it was just to check if the study room in the back was open. It meant the library was a valuable space regardless if books, movies, video games, and other various forms of entertainment they carried weren't their main selling point.

There was also the fact that when someone came in to get a book half of the time he assisted him or her in finding said book. This led to him being able to show off his knowledge of the Dewey Decimal System which was such an underrated skill in a library that carried thousands upon thousands of books

And he wasn't even working at the main library. That one held at least a million books if not twice that amount. Throw in the other dozen or so libraries on campus, or even their book exchange program with the other public schools in the state, and one was looking at over a billion books at his or her disposal.

Sue him for getting excited when someone was checking out a book that he'd read. The chances of it happening were slim in a sea of texts he would never have the time to read.

He enjoyed it when someone asked him for a recommendation. With so many options he had several go-to suggestions for every genre or topic, and he had to physically stop himself from going on about one book for too long lest he give away spoilers. It made him even happier when someone took to one of his suggestions, and he would smile for days if someone came back to talk to him about it.

Along with assisting library patrons, Keith also had other tasks to complete every week. One was a book or audiobook display that required him to explain the plot with just pictures. He loved spending time doodling in eraser marker for that one. The other task was simply choosing a CD, movie, video game, magazine, board game, or loanable technology to spotlight. It was the library director's idea to spotlight a non-book item if only to show passersby what else they had to offer.

And when there was nothing left to be done he read fanfiction. He was not allowed to read books or magazines in their collection when he was clocked in because it was against policy. Reading stuff on the internet as long as he was aware of patrons somehow wasn't.

Elizabeth was jealous of that job sometimes. If she wasn't getting paid twenty-five dollars an hour to do cool tech things with kids he would almost feel bad.

He did have to admit it was one of his cushier jobs. The university paid him more to be a library clerk than the restaurant did to be a phone associate, and even when he subbed a few manager shifts at the restaurant he was still being paid a quarter less to run an entire restaurant than he was to read on the job.

He wouldn't complain though. That pizza place had hired him on the spot when he'd needed the hours over the summer to make his tuition payment. He'd met some interesting people and made friends with a couple of his coworkers. Not to mention the free food and tip money he'd gotten over the summer which helped keep him and Elizabeth alive for a good part of the summer as well.

Anyway, work had gone by quickly. It was a nice follow-up to the productive three-hour anatomy lab that had somehow flown by without stressing him out. His group's mink, the animal they were dissecting and being tested on, usually annoyed the hell out of his group because it was so fatty. He and his lab partners often wanted to hurl the dead thing at a wall because picking the fat off without destroying the tissue they would be tested on was nearly impossible.

Luckily, they'd been pleased to find out that this week's lab focused on the intestines. Everyone in his group had taken human anatomy and physiology last year, which led to their group being the first to finish with all of the mink's tiny organs pinned and labeled.

They were even allowed to leave early! Keith could've cried, because this meant instead of sprinting for a bus he could leisurely walk and listen to music on the way to work.

Happy birthday to me, he thought with a content grin. Even as he remembered the dinner he didn't want to cook at the house before going to join his friends for their plans he couldn't help but smile. He was going to enjoy the day no matter what.

"Happy birthday!"

Keith blinked in surprise, a strange feeling of embarrassment and gratitude squeezing his heart as Jacqueline held up a beautiful strawberry shortcake. After the delicious stir-fry they'd eaten he was expecting to have to get the cookies or ice cream out like normal. It hadn't crossed his mind that his boss would make him something.

"Brandon told me you liked strawberry," she went on to explain as she set it down. While she talked she grabbed a trio of forks and plates. Brandon sat at the table carefully cutting the cake into slices. "I made sure not to make it overly sweet since I know you are picky about overly sweet things. It's a shame Elijah was busy tonight." She mused as if it were an afterthought.

He found himself wringing his hands underneath the table. For some reason he felt guilty.

"You didn't have to do that," the words popped out before he could manage to thank her.

She shook her head as she put a slice on all three plates. "Nonsense, Keith. While I'm well aware you have plans with your friends tonight that is no reason for us to not celebrate your birthday here. If your parents were here they would probably take you out to a fancy dinner or something, right?"

No, he thought truthfully, but didn't contradict her. His mom usually made him homemade food for his birthday because he preferred it to restaurant food.

"Anyway, making a cake was the least I could do. It was also nice to bake again. I've been so busy looking for another personal assistant I have little time for anything else. There is some good news though. One of his old assistants, a young man just a little older than you by the name of Chandler, is doing a couple of hours tomorrow night. He can only work once a week temporarily. Not a great help, but it's something."

Keith opened his mouth to say thank you for the dessert as well as something optimistic about getting some help, but before he could speak Brandon cut him off.

"Oh, mom, you should tell him the other good news!"

"It's a little early to be celebrating, Brandon. He might not take the position."

"I think he will."

"I'm not so sure about that. Even with our compromise on the hours he was being a bit finicky on some terms."

"They can be worked out. As long as I have someone to get me up in the mornings on weekdays I can deal with a couple of nights having to crawl up the stairs."

"You shouldn't have to. He should have just taken the position as is instead of complaining about the hours. I only negotiated with him because my back has been killing me accompanying you around the house and campus as it is. That and I hate how people stare at me when I push you in the wheelchair."

"I hate having to be in the wheelchair," Brandon countered. "It's embarrassing."

The newly twenty-two-year-old absentmindedly started eating his cake as they went back and forth. All he could think about is how flip-flopped their priorities were. Jacqueline cared more about her own health and image than her son's health and having proper care. Brandon was somehow embarrassed to be pushed around in a wheelchair on a campus where they are as common a mode of transportation as bikes. Keith tried not to let that bother him as much though. Brandon wasn't used to being in a wheelchair his entire life like Will, so of course transitioning from being able to walk freely to having to be pushed was difficult.

At least it seems like he won't have to use it that much longer, he thought as they talked of the soon to be hired full-time PA.

"Wait, you found another PA?" He suddenly spoke up when he finally registered the conversation.

Jacqueline ate a bite of her cake before replying.

"Well one is in the final stages of our hiring process. We sent him a revised offer letter and if he accepts we can get the background test done and he can start in a matter of days. It all depends on him. If he rejects it we're back to square one again. Also, Brandon, would you stop slouching already? That's the third time this week and I'm sick of reminding you to not do that."

"Sorry, mother." He said while straightening himself. As he did so his mother's sharp eyes followed him like a hawk, full of cold annoyance before warming slightly once she took her eyes off him. "I still think he'll take the job."

"He is a lot older than we'd prefer as well," Jacqueline confessed. "He's in his fifties, but he has been a caregiver for decades. This job will be nothing for him especially since he's in great shape for his age."

"It's going to be awkward having him hold me up though. He's so much older than me people might stare."

His mother rolled her eyes, her tone souring. "You're just going to have to deal with it, Brandon. It's either feel awkward and be able to walk or feel embarrassed and get pushed around in a wheelchair."

"I wasn't complaining."

"It sure sounded like it."

"Sorry, mother."

"I know." With that she turned to Keith, eyes much kinder than they had while talking to her son. "So how's the cake?"

Jose rolled up to the house with *Taylor Swift* blasting from the speakers of his Cadillac.

"Get it?" He shouted as Keith climbed into the passenger seat of the car laughing. "Because you're twenty-two now?"

"I get it, Jose."

"But are you *feeling* it?" He asked, extending a hand and gripping his shoulder dramatically.

"I'm feeling something," was the suave retort.

"Something romantic?"

"Something along those lines."

Jose grinned devilishly. "Good, because you'll be feeling *someone* tonight. That someone being me. And then tomorrow you'll be feeling sore but oh so satisfied."

"Bring it, *Mi Amor*."

Keith kept a straight face long enough to wink at the Hispanic before both of them burst out laughing. God he loved his friends.

Several minutes later they were pulling into a metered parking spot near Jared and Tucker's apartment. Being a block away from the university's buildings meant finding parking was always a hassle, and even when one found parking it was almost always metered or a tow-away zone.

"Dang parking fees," Jose grumbled dramatically as he inserted a few quarters into the meter.

Keith squinted at the machine before surveying the other machines along the road. It was with a sigh that he walked up to Jose and told him to stop putting money in it.

"Why?"

"Because it's free after five, Jose."

Said car-owner looked more closely at the meter before scrunching up his face.

"Damn it."

"You didn't pay for parking earlier too, right? You came over at like five-thirty."

"Double damn it."

Keith patted his friend on the shoulder as they walked to the apartment complex and messaged Tucker to buzz them up. "Sorry, man, but you need to pay more attention to the details. Isn't that why you got your car towed from downtown last winter?"

"No."

He was met with a pointed look.

"Okay, maybe. I didn't realize that street was a snow zone in March too."

"It is. Probably because it snows until April in the Midwest."

"I hate the cold. Boo," he stated casually just as they reached their friend's apartment. "Anyway, we have arrived."

"I can see that," Keith replied with a smile. Just when Jose was about to open the door for them, however, it was torn open by an excited Elizabeth.

"Happy birthday, Keith!"

Her scream was joined by the just slightly less enthusiastic voices of the brothers and both Sarahs. Jose awkwardly stood there for a moment before saying the same thing in monotone, saying they didn't tell him the plan.

"I'm pretty sure I did," the blonde Sarah countered.

"Well then I wasn't listening."

"It's fine guys," Tall Sarah broke in. "Jared, Elizabeth, and I have the food ready. Everyone sit down so we can set the food out and dig in."

"She's starving," Jared added helpfully.

She nodded. "What he said."

He surveyed Elizabeth bustling around the kitchen grabbing all sorts of sauces and dips to go along with their chicken nugget dinner.

"Can I help with anything?" Keith asked.

Even busy she shut him down immediately.

"Nope. What would you like to drink though?"

"Water is fine."

Since she wouldn't let him help her with the food Keith helped Tucker get the computer chairs from their bedrooms. After playing musical chairs they finally figured out a set up that would let six of them sit at the table while the remaining person got the couch next to the table.

"I call the couch!" Jose screamed before jumping onto it and nearly falling off.

"If you break our couch we're deporting you," Tucker called from across the room.

Jose stuck out his tongue in the other's general direction. "You can try, but I'm legal!"

"And I know a Jewish lawyer."

"Well fudge. I'll have to buy myself a shovel."

"Why a shovel?"

"To dig under Señor Trump's wall of course. Oh, or I could learn to pole-vault."

Those listening either sighed or rolled their eyes at their antics. There was no reason to stop them unless Jose got Tucker talking about Hitler, in which Jared would stop the conversation before his brother's "admiration" for the man was made too obvious. Even if it was an inside joke Blonde Sarah wasn't aware of that yet and no one wanted to explain it was one of Tucker's attention-seeking tendencies.

"Everyone sit down!"

At Elizabeth's command everyone except for the taller of the two Sarah's found their spots. A moment later she was setting bottles and packets of condiments like ketchup, barbeque sauce, mustard, ranch, and honey mustard on the table along with a pile of napkins. When she followed up by bringing a platter that held a giant assembly of chicken nuggets formed into the shape of a cake Keith grinned. They had gone all out.

There seemed to be at least seven layers of chicken nuggets, every layer from a different fast food chain. Each layer had to have at least forty chicken nuggets. Such a giant cake would have been way too big for the two of them but considering there were seven hungry college students eagerly waiting to dig in it was perfect.

A giant bowl was the last thing she set down. It contained a mountain of French fries, to at which Jose would have gagged until Sarah slipped him a tiny plate of onion rings.

"I made sure to get you some because I know how much you hate potatoes," Elizabeth stated while she took a picture of their feast.

Jared made a face at Jose as he took a fry from the bowl. "How can you not like potatoes? Fries are amazing."

"They're starchy and gross."

"You're starchy and gross."

Jose fake gasped.

"It's because I'm brown, isn't it?"

"What?"

"He does sort of look like a potato. Maybe he's worried about cannibalism?" Blonde Sarah joked.

"How does he look like a potato?" Keith questioned.

Just as Tucker went to say "they're both brown" Blonde Sarah cut him off by saying "they're both round" just a bit louder.

"I'll have you know I'm a healthy weight!" Jose cried out before dramatically stuffing his face with onion rings. "And Sarah is more brown than I am!"

Tall Sarah thought for a moment before staring at her light caramel-colored skin. "Well, technically I'm half *black*, not half brown, so you're still browner than me."

"Yeah," Jared agreed. "If I had a potato it would look a lot more similar to you than Sarah. She's more of a beanstalk."

"Jared, I am as sweet as a cinnamon stick and look like one too. You don't need to lie. Also, I see you dipping your nuggets in hot sauce. You know your white ass can't handle that."

"Hey, that hot sauce is mine to begin with," Tucker trailed off while grabbing a hand full of fries and dumping them onto his plate. He ignored the giggles that ensued when Jared passed the saucer holding extra spicy buffalo sauce over to him, the true spice-lover of the two. "Jared, you disappoint me. You're perpetuating the stereotype."

"Me perpetuate a stereotype? Bro, you literally have a printout of a dog Hitler painted hung up in your bedroom."

"It's called being funny, Jared. Also, I like dogs."

"We're *Polish*."

"Your point? If anything I'm going against the stereotype by appreciating German culture."

"He was Austrian!"

Elizabeth soon ignored the conversation completely, instead watching Keith load up his plate with chicken nuggets and French fries before making pools of ketchup and barbeque along the side. His eyes were wide with excitement as he debated trying all seven different types of chicken right away to guess what restaurants she went to.

After some time they managed to finish dinner Jared having almost and decided to play a couple of card games before starting the movie. It was only after Blonde Sarah and Jose dominated every round of *Cards Against Humanity* and *Funemployed* that the group rage quit, getting ice cream and chocolate cake for dessert and putting in Keith's preferred animated movie in favor of most of letting the two aforementioned winning streaks continue.

"Keith?"

Elizabeth's whisper had him leaning down slightly so he could better hear her. It also helped him to talk to her since everyone else was watching the two characters on screen face off for the first time with rapt attention.

"Yes, sweetie?"

"Did you have fun?"

His fingers squeezed the smaller hand they were wrapped around comfortingly.

"I had a lot of fun. You went a little overboard on the chicken nugget cake and the desserts, but I expected it and am glad you didn't do anything else."

"I was going to but Jared and Tucker stopped me," she complained halfheartedly. The wry smile on her face gave her away. "I'm just glad you enjoyed tonight. I didn't get you any real gifts because I wasn't sure what to get you, so…"

"Lizzy, this is a 'real' gift. All I wanted was to spend time with you and our friends while also eating a crap ton of unhealthy food. And we did that, so I'm happy. You know even if we hadn't done all this just being with you would have been enough."

Elizabeth gave him a full smile. It was the sort of close-eyed smile that made her dimples visible, and the kind that made happiness contagious.

Honestly he couldn't have asked for a better birthday.

CHAPTER NINE

Keith could tell there was some drama going on around the house. How could he tell? Other than the fact that Jacqueline's booming voice could carry clear across the house when she was upset, it was obvious by the tense argument going on outside his door.

Literally. They were standing right outside his door like the hallway was a good place to have a semi-heated not-quite screaming match.

Thankfully he had it closed, so at least they couldn't put the fault on him for listening in.

"What did I tell you about touching the thermostat?" Jacqueline demanded. "Honestly, Elijah, it's like our rules are just suggestions to you. You have to be reminded continuously like a child. I half expect you don't even know what they are." Keith imagined her gesturing to said thermostat wildly as if Elijah didn't know where or what a thermostat was.

"I know what it says in the contract. It says not to touch it," he answered her in the most apathetic voice he could manage.

"Then why did you turn the temperature up?"

"Because my room gets cold at night."

"Then you should have emailed me about it."

"At one in the morning? What was I going to do? 'Oh, I'm sure she'll be up to read my email at three in the morning.' Seriously?"

"I don't think I like your tone."

A moment of silence, which was most likely Elijah making a face or attempting to control himself from responding with "I don't think I like you."

Finally, he responded in a more controlled manner.

"Why email you about turning it up when the thermostat is literally inches away from my door?"

"Because the contract states that you will not adjust the temperature of the house without Larry, Brandon, or I doing so to make sure the humidity doesn't drastically change. If it does it might ruin the harmonium downstairs."

There was a short breath, and then: "Okay, then I apologize for not realizing how dire of an action it was to turn the upstairs temperature up by two degrees. I have been getting pretty cold at night despite all my blankets. Sixty-eight degrees is a little low; I'm used to homes being at least seventy degrees."

"I'm sorry to hear that. I'll see what I can do about making your room more comfortable, like perhaps getting your room, in particular, a heater."

"I don't need a—"

"Whatever you do, do not open your window on humid nights. I'll have to remind Keith of this too. If you do it could affect the entire house and I don't want the wood of Brandon's violin or the harmonium downstairs swelling. If it were to get ruined it would cost a lot to get new ones. It costs roughly…"

It was at about this moment that Keith grew bored with the conversation. As he relocated himself and his laptop into his closet, sitting down on the beanbag and closing the door so he could barely hear those in the hallway, he sighed. Sometimes he was almost happy with his job. More often than not, however, Jacqueline did something to stress him out. Getting after Elijah for nearly everything he did was one thing. Bringing up the contract to make both of them fall in line was another.

Of course it would have been one thing if it were a

friendly reminder. "Remember to get your laundry done once every other week" instead of "Remember the contract states you have to do your laundry at least once every two weeks. The upstairs is starting to smell because some of you are slacking."

Sorry, Jacqueline, but it's hard to get laundry done with you running your own three times a day.

He tried to focus on studying instead of getting worked up about what he'd just overheard. After ten minutes he ended up closing his laptop, his mind stuck in a vicious cycle of complaints about living in this house. It honestly drove him crazy that he became fixated on those things. Living here wasn't the end of the world. So many more people were less fortunate than him, and while Lillian, Brandon, and the stupid contract made him feel lousier as the weeks went on he needed to just get over it.

I can't ignore my feelings like other guys do. Everything rubs me the wrong way. I'm stressed, anxious, and constantly on edge. I hate not being happy when I'm here. What is wrong with me?

An alarm going off on his phone snapped him out of his thoughts. It was almost time for him to start cooking dinner.

Steeling himself, he took a deep breath before getting up and leaving the closet. He needed to keep positive. The last couple of days, excluding his grandmother's death, had been relatively great. Maybe it was because he worked less. Maybe it was because he had taken more time to hang out with his friends. Either way, just because those he lived with kept getting in bad moods or were driving him crazy with rule upon rule didn't mean he should let that get to him.

He could try to just stop caring. Maybe then he'd be less stressed out, which would help make the remaining months working as Brandon's PA pass more smoothly.

Be optimistic, he reminded himself as he set out to

starting dinner. They were having Korean noodles and potstickers tonight. *Two months down, eight more to go! I'm already a quarter of the way finished with this job. Nothing will come from letting them get to me before it's over.*

If only staying positive was as easy as it sounded. Unlike some of his friends, he'd had growing up who explained being able to "shut off their feelings" he found that task to be impossible. How could someone just detach from themselves like that? Wouldn't that do more harm than good in the long run?

He didn't get it. When he felt an emotion he felt it strongly. There was no dampening it, much less shutting it off.

Maybe what Elizabeth mentioned about people in my major tending to be empaths wasn't that far off.

He remembered skimming over the online article he'd been sent with unbelieving eyes. He hadn't known what an empath was or if feeling in such a way was realistic; however, sometimes he wondered.

He did tend to feel more strongly than other guys his age, or at least he thought so. It surprised him how many of his friends would say they just didn't cry. Even when a pet died or a really sad scene in a movie played they just didn't get upset enough to shed tears. He was the complete opposite. He didn't cry over every little thing, but certain songs, movies, books, and interactions with people just pulled on his heartstrings. Crying seemed like a fine way of helping his emotions reset.

Tucker called him overly sensitive. Maybe he was.

As Elizabeth had pointed out years prior he was also affected by the emotions of others. Take a person's happiness, anger, or sadness for example. If someone else nearby was radiating sunshine he often found himself smiling for no reason. In contrast, just being in a room where people were arguing amongst one another made him anxious or irritated. Watching someone else cry was enough to sober his own mood or depress him entirely. Sometimes it even overwhelmed him completely, giving him headaches or making his chest feel tight. That happened in crowded places as well as places where the noise levels were way too loud or in situations like on the bus where there were too many people brushing up against him. Having too busy of a day threw him off too. Even if it were a day filled with friends and fun there would be a point where he just found it exhausting.

Jared found that strange, as he was an extrovert by all meanings of the word, but Elizabeth understood the feeling well. She was just as introverted as him.

There was also the fact that he'd been called a great listener by countless people. From college acquaintances to close friends he would patiently listen to someone's story, which he found odd because in other situations he could go from occupied to bored out of his mind in a matter of seconds. However, when it came to people, his attention drew towards them like a magnet.

Perhaps this was why he made friends with so many narcissistic people. Perhaps this was why strangers to friends to relatives dumped their life stories and problems on him, often seeking him for advice. Perhaps this is why he let them come to him with their pain and angst because his heart was too big to turn someone away.

Perhaps... this was why he let people walk all over him.

Well not anymore! I'm going to start putting myself first by saying no to anyone (but Elizabeth) when it comes to doing something I don't want to do. I'm twenty-two years old. I'm an adult. It's about time I started acting like one!

Halfway through cooking dinner, however, he heard a piercing scream.

His heart began to pound.

He dropped a potsticker into the oil on accident, making

several drops of oil splatter across the stovetop and his uncovered arm. His skin stung. The scream sounded like it was coming from downstairs, and the only one in the house who could contort her voice to such an octave was Jacqueline.

What's going on? He tried to calm himself. *Should I forget the food and go downstairs to see if she's okay? Did she just see a spider or something? She can be really dramatic some days. What if she's hurt?*

Just as he was reasoning with himself about the pros and cons of abandoning the potstickers, the sound of heavy footfalls started. Running up the stairs Jacqueline burst through the doorway to the kitchen crying profusely.

Her makeup was a mess, and her ever expensive outfit was a tad wrinkled, but her blonde hair was as well-kempt as ever.

She immediately noticed him simply standing there and staring at her. Accusatory eyes just like her son's pinned him in place.

Keith's muscles locked. What should he say? What should he do?

They held three seconds of eye contact before she brushed past him to grab the car key. As she snatched it off of the key holder, a far too expensive piece of art that matched the rest of the vanity present around the house, she left venomous words in her wake.

"Brandon got hurt on the way back from class. Chandler let Brandon's arm land under him when he fell on the concrete, and now his arm is turning purple. You and Elijah can eat dinner by yourself. I'm driving Brandon to the emergency room and making that goddamn PA go with us for as long as it takes to get this issue sorted out. Then I'll have to fire him. Anyway, we'll be gone for a couple of hours. I'm sure the arm is broken."

"Oh no," he stuttered in surprise. "I'm sorry."

Jacqueline looked like she could kill.

"Is there anything I can—"

"No. I'll see you later tonight or tomorrow. Goodbye."

With that he could hear her pounding the buttons on the security system so she could race out the door to the car. Screeching tires made him wince, the beeps from the security monitor not even having finished the thirty-second timer before she had driven off.

That was scary, he thought as he quickly finished fixing up dinner. Some of the potstickers were burnt. *I wonder if Elijah heard the commotion.*

The other part-time PA made his appearance only minutes later.

"Keith?" Blonde and blue hairs could be seen from Keith's periphery. "I was in the shower and heard a scream. Unless you were a countertenor in high school choir I'm assuming it was Jacqueline?

"Yep," he answered coolly despite the frown on his face.

"What happened?"

"An accident, I guess? Chandler, a former PA who was helping them out starting today, apparently didn't catch Brandon or something. He hit the ground and might have broken an arm?"

Elijah made a low whistle. "That's crazy."

"Yeah. I'm pretty sure they're not going to let him work anymore now."

"I'd believe that. Hey, is she bringing him to the emergency room?"

"Jacqueline said something about that, yeah. He was bruising a lot, so either he broke or sprained something in his arm when he hit the ground? I don't know, but either way they won't be back for dinner. It's just us two tonight."

"Thank God. I don't think I could have put up with that woman again tonight."

The older of the two turned to look at the other incredulously.

"And Brandon?"

"Oh I feel bad for the guy don't get me wrong; I'm just happy Jacqueline won't be here for a while. She's been getting after me for every little thing lately and it's driving me nuts." His face scrunched up as he went on. "She saw me with a box of dye for my hair yesterday and flipped out on me about how I can't dye my hair in the house because of the mess and fumes. Then, just an hour ago, she yells at me for turning the temperature up. Can you believe it?"

"Yep."

"She was like telling me to email her about being cold instead of me just touching the freaking thermostat. I only bumped it up like two degrees, man. It's not going to ruin her harmonium or violin."

He hummed in agreement. "It is a bit chilly up there."

"I know right? Now she wants to buy me a space heater and it's just like… why the hell is everything here made so much more complicated? They take the word 'particular' to a whole new level."

"They're a strange family, I'll admit."

Elijah gave him a peculiar stare. "That's a nice way of putting it."

Keith shrugged, turning back to the skillet and turning the stovetop off.

"I could say some other things about them, but it won't change them or make me feel any better. Anyway, dinner is done if you want to help yourself. I'm going to put the extra dishes I set out away since they're not going to be here."

"You're not going to serve me or have us eat in courses?" The younger fake gasped as he helped himself to some salad and then put the rest in the refrigerator. He knew Keith wouldn't want any. "You deviant."

Rolling his eyes, Keith told Elijah to fend for himself or starve.

"I see how it is. Well, since they're not going to be here

for a while, I'm going to eat in the living room then."

"You know we're not supposed to do that."

"Are you going to rat me out?"

"Not if you put on cartoons."

Elijah pointed a finger gun at him, nodding his head all the while.

"You've got a deal, dude. I'll see if SpongeBob is on."

"Hell yeah!"

It was much later in the evening when Jacqueline and Brandon got home. Honestly it was so late in the night Keith wondered if the hospital had done something to help Brandon. Maybe they gave him a splint? He wasn't sure, but he knew they would have to see someone to get a cast of some sort. He also knew that sometimes hospitals would do temporary fixes since it was late around the time the accident had occurred, so there was a chance that Brandon would have to see a doctor again the next day.

As he heard the mother and son clamoring around downstairs he debated going down to greet them. He wanted to know if Brandon was okay.

If I go down though there's a chance they'll stick me with putting Brandon to bed. Or worse, Jacqueline won't let me come back up here and I won't be able to finish this homework. Surely Brandon is okay if he's here, right? If something really bad happened she would have emailed us about it.

This time only a flash of guilt surfaced when he resigned himself to wait until the next day or an email to hear about what happened with his Person. Part of him hated himself for being more worried about his own wellbeing than the person he was supposed to be taking care of, but another part of him reasoned he had no obligation to listen to a rant or assist Brandon because his parents fired a PA. This just was not his shift.

Stop letting people walk all over you. A voice he often

squandered roared at him, indignant. *You do this all the time. You're too nice! You give and give and give until your head is bursting at the seams and your heart is faltering under the pressure. The moment you stop giving people notice, they will label you as selfish. They take advantage of your kindness. And you never learn.*

I learn! Part of him argued back, but his words were feeble. He knew he was lying.

No, you don't. You walk around making decisions about people after a brief interaction, because you know if you think the best of everyone around you like you want half of those you don't perceive as a threat will betray you. It's happened before. Remember Don? He played you like a fiddle. Found a new best friend in a psycho that treated you like shit.

That wasn't— I don't think it's fair to…

To bring it up? You tried hanging on to your relationship for so long just because you were friends since elementary school despite knowing it was a lost cause. He chose to be surrounded by assholes instead of you. That wasn't your fault. It was him. You reached out and he slapped away your hand. You blame yourself for not being a better friend when there was nothing you could have done to change his mind. But we're getting off-topic. You need to grow a backbone. You will not let these people walk all over you.

They aren't.

His chest felt tight. He knew he was in denial.

Not walking all over you? What do you call Jacqueline griping about how you should quit your other jobs to help them out more? A helpful suggestion? She praises you time and time again just to butter you up before demanding something of you. She has no regard for your time and doesn't show an inkling of affection for her son. He's like an object to her and you know it. You've seen it.

This was true. The only times he had witnessed

Jacqueline showing any display of love towards her son were the rare times after yelling at him that she smiled in his general direction. And even then it wasn't a tender smile. It was something along the lines of one admiring a trophy or medal falling perfectly into place on a display.

It made Keith almost physically ill to think about. A mother who only saw her child as a possession or prize. Or a burden.

She has some compassion in her though, he mulled over. *I mean, she did bake me a birthday cake. She didn't have to do that.*

Anyone is capable of an act of kindness. That doesn't mean she doesn't make her son crawl around the house on his hands and knees, or yell at him over trivial things. That doesn't mean she doesn't degrade her husband verbally every chance she gets, on the phone or in person. That doesn't mean she doesn't talk bad about other people when they aren't present or use her son's disability for personal gain. Just because she is good at pretending doesn't make her less of a garbage person. It also doesn't make her any better of a boss.

His spiraling thoughts were rudely interrupted at that moment, sharp words loud enough for him to hear as the mother and son ascended the stairs.

"Can't you go any faster?"

Keith swung off his bed in a flash, frantically turning the light off in his room as he heard them reaching the top of the stairs. He made sure his door was securely closed just before the stomping made its way into the hall outside his room.

"I'm crawling as fast as I can. Sorry."

"Sure you are," was the disgruntled response. "You know I've had a stressful day playing damage control after Chandler's screw up, and tomorrow I'm going to have to pull you out of classes so we can take another trip to the hospital tomorrow." She swore profusely for a moment before seemingly composing herself. "I'm going to have to pay thousands in medical bills *again*."

Brandon's meek voice: "I'm sorry, mother."

"Telling me sorry over and over again won't fix anything, Brandon. It's not like you're trying to be an inconvenience; you just naturally are. Now hurry up so we can get some rest tonight. After I get you in bed I need to make sure Keith cleaned up the kitchen properly. He's been doing a shit job of wiping the stove off as of late. Still, he's not as horrible as Elijah."

"Sor— I mean, I'll hurry."

Sounds of hands slapping on the thin wooden surface of the hall started again. After a long moment Keith heard the click of a door shutting, most likely Jacqueline closing her son's door after entering his room to get him to put him to bed.

The second the door closed Keith let out a breath. He hadn't even realized he'd been holding it.

That's what characters in books mean? I didn't even realize I stopped breathing. That's... scary.

Panic prickled in his chest like the beginnings of pneumonia. Between having overheard his boss force Brandon to crawl around on the floor like a dog and rate his cleaning performance as S for shitty his eyes burned with unshed tears. How could she be so mean? The way she talked about him when he wasn't around was rude, but calling her son an inconvenience to his face was unfathomable.

I can't imagine how Brandon must be feeling. If he was ever insecure about being a burden to his parents, then Jacqueline would have confirmed his fears. That's not right. And why is she so comfortable badmouthing Elijah and I right outside our rooms? Surely she knows how late the two of us stay up. Did she want us to hear her? She could confront us directly, or send us an email like she usually does when she decides ranting to us in person is harder than sending a three-page article on hygiene.

There was now an odd feeling fluttering around in his gut as well as his chest. He wasn't exactly sure what it was, but it was something that felt so utterly wrong that when he lied back down in bed he was wishing it would go away. After several minutes he was hoping his chest would loosen up, but instead it slowly became tighter and tighter like he was beginning to lose oxygen. That couldn't be it though. Why would he be losing oxygen right now? He was breathing. He was breathing a lot, much quicker than he usually did.

Except that hyperventilating wasn't doing his lungs a huge favor either. Even as he opened his mouth to get in more air the dysphoria grew. After a minute he was forced to sit up, practically choking on nothing while his vision danced with spots.

What's happening? Why can't I breathe?

Hysteria ran through his veins like a drug, which didn't help the situation.

Is... is this what a panic attack feels like? That can't be right.

He'd only read about them in books or seen them in movies and television shows. They always looked terrifying for the person experiencing them. Such a loss of control that could either cause a person to just shut down or devolve into a crying, blubbering mess; it looked exhausting, embarrassing, and pity-inducing no matter how much fictional literature or media attempted to glorify them from time to time. He wouldn't wish one upon anybody, and he certainly never wanted to experience one.

He *couldn't* be having one at this very moment, could he?

Keith vehemently denied it, trying desperately to calm himself down; however, this only proved to make his blood roar louder in his ears.

Stars stood in his eyes and hands clasped around his

throat. He surged across the room and threw the window open. Such an action would have made him look ridiculous, but the only light coming into the room at this time of night was from the streetlamp. No one outside could see possibly him.

Knowing he was alone in his misery helped him calm down faster. Gradually, his vision cleared up and his chest began to unwind in the crisp October air. He kneeled on the floor by his window for what seemed like hours but couldn't have been more than twenty minutes. However long, it was enough to make his legs feel like they were on fire when he finally decided to stand up. The pain in his legs was a nice distraction from the unwanted thoughts he was having though.

He crawled back into bed properly this time, forgoing whatever homework he had planned on working on.

Something is wrong with me.

There was something shameful about losing control as he had. The feeling of his consciousness drifting just out of reach, an invisible monster sucking the breath from his lungs to the point he could see the night sky with his eyes closed, was also terrifying. It made him think back to the times when he had night terrors as a child. He'd wake up screaming his throat raw before choking due to not taking in enough air. Somehow freaking out like he had instilled more worry in his heart now than when he was a child. Back then he tried his best to get used to it, knowing it was just something that would happen. There had been nothing to do other than hope he would grow out of it. Which he had.

What if this one panic attack was just the beginning?

He pulled his blanket around him tightly, shoving his head down into his pillow as he heard Jacqueline exit Brandon's room. After listening to her trudge down the steps toward her room in the basement he set an alarm on his phone for six the next morning. Minutes passed and just as he began drifting off to sleep the sound of Jacqueline chattering away on her phone in the basement started.

Keith frowned heavily, his knuckles pale as he lifted his pillow and put it over his head. The last thing he wanted to do was lose sleep because Jacqueline was ranting loudly to her husband over the phone. It still irked him how thin the walls were, although the sounds from the basement were most likely coming from the vent in the corner of his room. Either way, he wished he could just mentally block out the disjointed words he caught from her. The snippets he caught caused him more anxiety than he liked to admit.

"He's got… and temporary splint…"

That didn't sound good.

"…tomorrow his elbow… about potential setback…"

That sounded even worse.

"I fired Chandler on the spot. Incompetent…"

The curse words that surrounded the old PAs name made Keith wince. He imagined the fall had been an accident with him being out of practice, so to be talked about with such hatred made his heart go out to the poor guy.

"…to Elijah and Keith tomorrow. This… their fault, because… Are a couple more damn hours so hard to ask for? Poor Brandon… selfish PAs…"

Suddenly, Keith found himself struggling not to cry in frustration. Again. After the stress of the panic attack he'd just had along with his boss's apparent blaming of him for what happened to Brandon his emotions were fluctuating between embittered, guilty, indignant, and just plain depressed.

It wasn't my fault. I was scheduled to make dinner tonight, so there was no way I would have been able to help out. Elijah might have been able to, but he works enough hours as it is.

Were they truly being selfish by not working even more than they already were?

You're not selfish, he reassured himself. Elizabeth told him this over and over again when it came to people asking too much of him. *You're just selfless to a fault. And people often confuse not getting what they want after never being denied it as a personal attack. They aren't used to you saying no to them. That's not entirely your fault, but that just means when the time comes to stop saying yes you better stick to it!*

Even as he drifted off into a fitful slumber, the constant barks of malicious words making his head sink into an even darker place, he tried reminding himself Elizabeth was right. He wasn't selfish. He was a kind person.

And he couldn't let Jacqueline walk all over him anymore.

CHAPTER TEN

He didn't see Jacqueline, Brandon, or Elijah the next morning. It seemed no one else was in the house by the time he got out of bed for class. He wasn't complaining, as this made having a nice breakfast of cereal and toast by his lonesome one of the most pleasant mornings he'd had since moving in. No pressure to hold a conversation. No pressure not to clink his spoon on the ceramic bowls in fear of being passive-aggressively told he was being too noisy so early in the morning. It was just a nice, relaxed morning meal.

By the time he went to class and worked a few hours at the library he had stopped thinking about the cruel words he'd overheard the night before. Instead he texted his friends about the movie they were going to see tonight. He didn't even feel bad when he thought about how there was no way Jacqueline was going to let Brandon out of the house. He was still going out tonight regardless. He wouldn't bail on his friends.

However, a text from Jacqueline just as he was getting out of work made the dreadful feelings from the night before resurface.

Dinner meeting tonight to discuss the incident from yesterday.

No email? It must be urgent.

It was common for her to send emails regarding what would be going on in Brandon's life each week. Often she sent emails simply reminding the PAs of house rules when she noticed them not being followed, followed by her verbally reminding said employees of those rules. Once in awhile Larry sent the email instead, but it was obvious the email signature was the only thing that belonged to him. The verbiage used in every email was uniquely Jacqueline.

Seconds later another text came in.

All PAs are REQUIRED to be there. From your schedules there should be no work or class conflicts. If there is something more important you must be doing at six tonight, then give me a call.

The way she worded it rubbed Keith the wrong way. He was confident Elijah and he weren't dogs, which is what he felt like when she treated them like they had to answer her every beck and call. Tonight was supposed to be his night off. What authority did she have to "require" him to be there? If she had just asked politely then maybe it wouldn't have bothered him so much.

Nevertheless, Keith had already planned on being home for dinner anyway. Elijah was cooking something he liked tonight, which was rare when Brandon and his mother usually picked out their favorite meals for the week. Keith ended up eating vegetables and bread rolls half of the time because all they ever seemed to want was fish, shrimp, or sausage dishes. He could choke down a few bites of sausage, sure, but any sort of seafood made him sick.

Not that they cared to add more variety to meal rotations. Jacqueline had told him once to make a sandwich if he didn't like what was being served and that was that.

Keith went to the undergraduate library on campus after work to study all the same. Taking the chance that Jacqueline and Brandon were home was something he wasn't willing to take because he knew he wouldn't be able to focus on getting his work done when *someone* was screaming over the sound of a violin.

A couple of hours passed in blessed productivity. All of his coursework for the weekend was finished save for studying for a biology test taking place in class next week.

This meant he could enjoy his weekend without having to worry about getting any assignments done, which was a huge lift of pressure off his shoulders. He disliked going out to have fun when he knew he had work to do because there was always a nagging voice that kept reminding him he hadn't completed it yet. It made it hard to enjoy anything when that happened.

Thankfully, with his homework done he was able to head home without having that constant worry in his head. Now the only thing making him anxious was the dinner meeting they were having tonight. He knew he shouldn't be worried over anything, but for some reason he found himself wary of it anyhow.

I need to stop psyching myself out, he mentally berated himself. *You're just eating dinner while listening to Jacqueline tell a story like normal. Brandon is okay if he's going to be there tonight, so there's no reason to be concerned about him either.*

In an attempt to stop himself from thinking too much he put his headphones in as he walked home. Listening to music proved to have the desired effect as he spent the rest of the trip singing along in his head.

"Would you please sit down?" Her voice raised in pitch as she spoke, whine evident in the last word of her statements. "I'd like to have this discussion over before the food is cold, thank you!"

Keith sat still as a rock as Elijah stopped pouring his drink halfway to hurriedly sit down at the table. The younger PA didn't try to hide his annoyance as he gave his undivided attention to his boss. Beside him, Larry motioned for his wife to begin.

"As you were both made aware, Brandon fell yesterday evening while being escorted from class by Chandler. Chandler has been taken off of any future scheduling and will not be working with my son again. Brandon's arm hit the ground wrong during the fall, which is unacceptable of a PA with his experience level."

Beside her Brandon nodded, the minuscule movement of his head barely noticeable.

Jacqueline placed a perfectly manicured hand on his shoulder as she continued, her eyes not straying from where they alternated focusing on the PAs.

"Anyway, I drove Brandon to the emergency room after picking them up. The hospital got him in relatively quickly because of the state of his arm. It was turning purple at the elbow. After a quick X-ray they decided to put a temporary splint and wrap over it as you can see." Cue both PAs instinctively looking at their Person only for Brandon to look away embarrassed. "As for his arm there is a clear fracture in the head of his radius. We are going back to the hospital today to get him fitted for a hard cast."

"Unfortunately, unless I can convince them to not wrap his hand with the hard casting he will have a very hard time practicing his instrument the next few weeks. Even with a rushed treatment they wouldn't be able to get the cast off of him for three or so weeks, so after some discussion Larry and I deemed it best for us to spend the weekend, Monday, and Tuesday at home. That way Brandon can relax after the ordeal and get some work done before getting a second opinion from another doctor. This means we'll be heading out shortly after dinner and leaving you two alone until late Tuesday night. I'm telling you when we're coming home now because I trust you not to break any rules while we're gone. No friends or girls in the house while we're away. The deep cleaning still needs to be done as usual, although the time of day doesn't matter as much. You can decide whether or not you want to cook each other dinner or just fend for yourselves. No adjusting the temperature," she side-eyed Elijah. "Do I make myself clear?"

The PAs both nodded, but Jacqueline only frowned.

"I would like a verbal confirmation."

Keith and Elijah glanced at one another before answering with a quiet "yes" so she was satisfied. Sadly, she didn't look much happier even after they verbally agreed. This made the atmosphere of the room pretty awkward as she finally gave them all permission to dig into their salads. Meanwhile Keith nibbled on a bread roll, eyes keeping track of Brandon despite not working tonight.

Once the appetizers were finished, the younger part-time PA served dinner without talking much. Only a curt "Is this enough?" every once and a while until all four of them were seated once more.

The tension in the room only grew from there.

There was a gnat flying around the kitchen table at one point, and for some reason it made Jacqueline visibly furious. It had migrated from its origin, the bowl of fruit that was rarely touched on the windowsill on the other end of the dining room, and was currently roaming around above where the food was laid out. Keith wasn't bothered by it; he was too focused on breathing, eating, and paying attention to Brandon to care. Everyone knew Jacqueline was in a foul mood tonight, and it made Keith's heart race as the meal went on.

Was it fear he was feeling? Or was it just extreme discomfort? He wasn't sure. All he knew for certain was that he wanted to be done with the meal as soon as possible.

He gazed at Brandon, curious if he felt off-put either by his ordeal or his mother's mood. To his surprise Brandon seemed to be completely unaware of the short words and harsh undertones being used by his parents as they spoke about Chandler, the hospital, the doctor, and so on. Even as Jacqueline and Larry's voices rose in volume the older boy showed no signs of unease. He just stared at his food like it was the most interesting thing in the room.

Is he spacing out? It's like he isn't even listening to anything around him anymore.

A part of Keith was worried. Brandon seemed to almost be dissociating, which would explain why his mother's cruel comments or griping never got to him.

That can't be healthy, right? Maybe I can ask him about—

"Die, you damn bug!"

The rage-filled shout and slamming of a ceramic plate completely took Keith, Elijah, and Brandon by surprise, making Keith flinch back violently while Brandon's hand rushed to his chest to calm his shuddering heart. Elijah was simply frozen. The trio brought their equally terrified gazes to the center of the table where Jacqueline had used a small dessert plate to kill the gnat that had been flying around.

"Honey, calm down. It was just a bug."

Larry's monotone voice proved to make his wife even more upset, her eyebrows narrowing and her mouth twisting into something similar to a snarl.

"I'm not going to calm down, dear." Her words were clipped, each one of them dripping with disdain. "That bug was pissing me off. We can't sit here and have a nice dinner with one of those damn things buzzing around our food, can we?"

"It didn't cause too much of a distraction, did it? The boys didn't seem too bothered by it."

Faster than Keith can recompose himself Jacqueline's blonde hair is whipping around with her head.

"You think it's annoying, don't you, Brandon? Keith? Elijah?"

No one was sure how to respond. If Keith responded with complete honestly, then she might be furious with him. If he were to lie, then he would feel crappy for lying as well as not having Larry's back. The poor guy was ganged up on by his wife and son enough as it was.

Just as he began to open his mouth, a bit too caught off guard to do anything further than stuttering an unsure "um", Elijah let out a long breath.

"Honestly the gnat didn't bother me one bit. It was more annoying to have to listen to a plate get smashed against a table to kill it; that scared the crap out of me."

Jacqueline's mouth formed into an "o" shape at Elijah's blunt response. Mentally Keith was cheering. What the other PA said was exactly what he'd been thinking. The only thing he would have added was that she was overreacting getting so upset over a tiny bug.

As it was, Keith slowly agreed with an inclination of his head.

"It was kind of a harsh reaction," he said. He made sure to keep his eyes on his Person rather than his boss as he said this. The hellfire in her eyes could be felt on him regardless, but he didn't want to see it. That would only make him feel more anxious.

A moment passed without anybody speaking. Elijah and Jacqueline were staring at each other intensely, Keith's own eyes darting to every single person at the table while Larry watched his wife and Brandon's gaze flickered between his plate and his mother.

The tension in the air was oppressive before, but now it was just unbearable.

Why is this even happening? He groaned internally. *I hate being put in these situations. Why can't we have, I don't know, one meal that doesn't lead to me feeling horrified to know these people?*

Suddenly, Jacqueline was closing her eyes and putting on that picture-perfect smile that made chills run up Keith's spine.

"I see how it is," she said with closed eyes. A moment later her smile fell and her eyes opened to reveal orbs narrowed in fury. "After all I provide you boys with you would agree with a moron like Larry? Completely ridiculous."

"Jacqueline, dear, take a deep breath." Said "moron" tried to intervene.

"Shut up, Larry."

"Dear—"

"No!" She stood up then, blonde hair flying around her slowly reddening face. As she shouted her eyes roved from one face to another, making everyone at the table lean back in either fear or surprise at her outburst. "None of you care about how I feel. You all think I'm annoying just because I'm trying to keep this house flawless in order for us to sell it! The rules I've spent years implementing are getting tossed out the window. Then there's the fact I'm here in the first place. One PA had to be fired and another one hurt my son. I have to take up the slack for it now! Why? Because you two," she glared at the PAs, "are too goddamn lazy to help out in your free time! When do *I* get to relax, huh?"

At that Elijah finally found his words.

"That's not fair," he argued. Frustration was evident in his voice, and under the table his fists were clenched. "We work the hours we were hired to work. Keith is already taking time off from one of his two other jobs to help you out as it is. Talk about ungrateful."

Oh God why are they talking about me?

"It's not that I'm not grateful, but it is idiotic to stay working at a lowly Italian restaurant that pays four dollars less than we do just because he likes the people there."

Maybe if I stay quiet enough they won't notice I'm here. I'll be more or less invisible, and then I can slip upstairs unnoticed...

There was no way Keith was getting involved in this argument. Not in a million years.

"It's not idiotic! Don't you understand that money is not the only decider of what people do in life? He works there because they gave him a job when he needed one. You'd know that if you actually listened to us when we talk about ourselves. Instead you only care about yourself."

"Are you calling me selfish?"

"I don't know. Is the definition of selfish 'only caring

about one's self"? If it is, then yeah I am."

"That is no way to speak to your boss."

"Oh please," the blue-haired PA rolled his eyes. Keith had no idea where he was getting this courage from, but was it amazing to watch? Yes. "This is casual compared to how you talk to Brandon and Larry. You think we can't hear you screaming at Brandon while he's playing the violin, or when you're calling Larry every degrading word in the dictionary from downstairs when you think we're all asleep? The walls in this house are thin, Jacqueline."

"You do not get to tell me how I talk to my own family."

"That's fair, but as employees we should be able to voice our concerns about how you treat your family in the house we're supposed to be living in."

"I'm not even supposed to be here," she hissed. "You think I want to waste my time dealing with grown children when I could be at home with my husband? You think I want to get gawked at by strangers when I push my child around in a wheelchair because the people here lack manners?"

Elijah let out a laugh.

"Well it's not our fault you call time with your child *wasted*. And it's not our fault you fired Isaac."

"He was a shit PA and you know it. No wonder the two of you got along so well."

That was the wrong thing to say, because if Jacqueline had been listening to what Keith said a couple of nights ago at dinner she would know that Isaac and Elijah still hang out together outside of work.

"You know what? Fine." The younger PA's voice lost any trace of emotion as he continued, his tone growing more calm yet frigid. "Maybe I'm not as good as a PA as Keith here. He has more experience than me, and I know that. Maybe I am a shit PA. But I'd rather be a shit PA than a shit mother who uses her son's disability for her own gain."

Keith paled dramatically. The situation had been escalating for several minutes, but now he wasn't sure how Elijah was going to come back from this. The elder PA was sure the younger would be fired for such a comment. It was a serious accusation even if it were true (which it was).

Before he could think about the possible outcomes of this conversation, one of the unused ceramic coasters on the table was flying onto the floor of the kitchen. It shattered upon contact. Several pieces slid across the floor as Brandon nearly seized up at the sound.

"How dare you?" She screamed, anger scraping her voice raw. "*How dare you?* I should fire you right now for accusing me of something so immoral! It's slander!"

"It's not slander if it's true, and I have Keith here to back me up on that. Honestly with the way you're acting right now getting fired would be a blessing. This job doesn't pay us near enough to have to listen to you verbally abuse everyone all day long."

The two kept going at it for another minute or so until Keith caught something falling out of the corner of his vision.

Except it wasn't something that was falling; it was a someone.

Crap. The stress must have been too much for him.

Because Larry was too focused on trying to deescalate the already too far gone situation, Keith was the first one to notice Brandon's body beginning to slip downwards. He was scooting over next to his Person and grabbing him tightly if only to stop the guy from falling underneath the table. Once Brandon was stable enough to not fall in any direction, the PA adjusted the position of the older boy's head so it wasn't at such an awkward angle. It was during that stage of his help that Jacqueline finally realized what had happened, and she let out an ear-piercing screech.

"Do you see what you did?" She accused Elijah. "His

chances of having an anemic episode go up when he's sick or stressed, and I'm sure he just passed out now because of your rotten attitude and horrid words!"

"Rotten attitude? You slammed a plate onto the table and broke a coaster while throwing a tantrum like a six-year-old kid."

Larry tried to speak up.

"Hey, both of you, how is continuing this argument possibly going to—"

"Shut up, Larry!" His wife seethed at him. "As always you're no help at all when it comes to backing me up. Why don't you make yourself useful and put the bags I packed earlier in the car so we can get on the road? I can't stand being here right now. That's not too hard for you, is it?"

Elijah groaned and gestured at the two adults in exasperation. "This is what I'm talking about! You're so mean to him, and he doesn't deserve it."

"He's my husband, so mind your own business."

"It is my business when you two are living here. Neither of you was supposed to even be here. It was supposed to be Brandon, Keith, Isaac, and me; however, you ruined everything when you fired Isaac. Now everything is going to shit and you're blaming everyone around you while treating them like garbage. That is not okay!"

"What's not okay is the way you're speaking to—"

"Would you both shut the hell up?"

At Keith's outburst all eyes in the room swung to him, even the half-lidded eyes of Brandon who was still mostly limp against the chair and his PA.

"Seriously," he continued, outraged at the entire situation, "if any of you cared about Brandon you would stop your arguing for a single second to make sure he's okay. None of you were paying attention though, were you? His episode lasted for forty seconds before stopping. Then he had another one that lasted a little over twenty seconds. Maybe instead of screaming over the dining room table like children you two could talk this out in another room like full-fledged adults? Away from Brandon who is already stressed enough with the PA problem and the arm thing, perhaps?"

Elijah opened his mouth, his entire demeanor screaming guilt, but whatever he was going to say was cut off by Jacqueline's stern voice.

"Crudely spoken, but you're right. We were all acting a bit childish. Brandon, how are you feeling, sweetie?"

Keith scowled at the woman. Brandon was still too disoriented to speak.

"He's too out of it to talk." He expressed with a deflated sigh. "Honestly I shouldn't have had to catch him though. It was your job to watch Brandon at dinner tonight, wasn't it? You should have been the one to drop everything when he started falling. Not me. I—"

"I appreciate—"

"And can you please stop interrupting me?" He broke her off before she could say more than a couple of words. She seemed offended that he would do such a thing, which was so hypocritical Keith almost laughed. Instead his voice was wobbling like he was holding back tears. "You do it all the time and it's a bit upsetting to say the least. I know you hate it when people interrupt you, so could you treat us with the same respect and not do it to us? Thank you. And I'm sorry for being so blunt, but I guess now is the time for everyone to say what they're thinking."

He took a deep breath. "I think you, Larry, and Brandon should go. Take the weekend and Monday to relax or whatever, because it's obvious tensions are too high and the stress is getting to everyone. It's neither good for a work environment nor any of us in general. And I'm sorry for yelling earlier. I just couldn't stand it anymore."

"Sorry, Keith." Elijah apologized once a few seconds of silence ticked past.

By this point Brandon was sitting up on his own and taking turns staring at both Elijah and Keith in awe.

As soon as Keith noticed this a wave of anxiety swept over him. It took all of the anger he'd been feeling away leaving him with instant regret.

Oh my God. What did we just do? We shouldn't have spoken to Jacqueline like that no matter how mad we were. What if she hates me now? I mean, she doesn't think too highly of Elijah, but he doesn't care what she thinks. What if she fires him? Will I get fired too? They're short-handed, so I doubt it, but still. What if? I won't have anywhere to go. I'd be homeless. Okay, so maybe I could crash with Jared and Tucker. Maybe. Ugh, I can't believe I yelled like that. This isn't my house. I can't act like a brat just because they were too.

Feeling nauseous, Keith politely excused himself and calmly walked up the stairs. Elijah half-heartedly mentioned he would store the uneaten food on Keith's plate, which was most of it since his nerves had caused him to eat slowly, which the elder PA appreciated.

He would appreciate it even more after dumping out the contents in his stomach into the porcelain bowl of the toilet.

Ew. Well, that sucked. I haven't thrown up out of anxiety in years.

That fact made him all the more worried about his health. Maybe four days without work or the Thompsons around would make him feel better.

After puking his gut outs, he checked the time on his phone and sent a quick text to Elizabeth. He grabbed his keys, wallet, and flip-flops before making his way down the stairs carefully. He could make out the sound of people talking in the kitchen still, and after what had just happened there was no way he was going through them to get to the back door. Instead, he used the front door knowing Jacqueline didn't like it when they messed with the ornate entrance.

Too bad, Jacqueline. I'm using the entrance for what it was made for.

No one called for him as he deactivated and reactivated the alarm. Even as he walked down the front steps he didn't get a single text message from either of the Thompson parents telling him to come back in the house (which tended to happen from time to time).

Instead, he was left alone. Blessedly alone.

A familiar ringtone broke through the sounds of nature that surrounded him. Like a lifeline Keith answered the phone in an instant, a breath of relief flowing through him all the while.

"Keith?" Elizabeth's concerned voice came from the other end of the line. "I got your text and called in exactly five minutes. What's up?"

"A lot of things. You're at your dorm, right?"

"Yeah."

"Cool. I'll be there in less than twenty."

"Okay, but we need to leave for the movie pretty soon after you get here. Jared, Tucker, Jose, and Blonde Sarah are meeting us at the campus union at six-thirty. Tall Sarah is going out with her boyfriend to celebrate one of their mutual friend's birthday tonight though, so she can't make it."

"She said during the party she thought she was busy tonight."

"Yeah, I told her it was no big deal. Anyway, sweetie, are you sure everything is okay? You sound stressed and I'm pretty sure dinner at that house usually runs longer than this. Did something happen? Is it something to do with the accident from yesterday?"

Keith hesitated. After the altercation that had just occurred, he didn't want to have to describe it in detail for Elizabeth right now. It would only bring down their moods.

"Some stuff happened that I can tell you about tomorrow. Long story short everyone but Elijah and I will be gone until Tuesday night though," he said with a smile.

"Really?" Elizabeth was almost screaming. "That means you can sleep over here! My roommate will be gone all weekend; this worked out perfectly."

He laughed at her enthusiasm. "I can come back to grab some stuff after the movie. I have to get some cleaning done tomorrow morning though, and then we'll have the rest of the weekend to ourselves."

"I. Am. So. Excited!" She squealed.

"Me too, Lizzy. Me too."

CHAPTER ELEVEN

Much to Elizabeth's surprise, Keith suggested they use the second half of Saturday and the entire day Sunday to visit her parents. She would have thought he'd want to relax or get something to eat after having spent hours cleaning. Instead he'd called her about taking an impromptu train trip south, to which she pleasantly accepted.

Still, she was heavily suspicious.

"You hate going to my house," she brought up despite them already being on the train. "My parents end up driving you crazy."

"Sometimes."

"They always make us help them around the house when we're there."

"True."

"Every time we eat dinner together they bring up politics, which leads to an argument between my mom and dad which stresses you out."

"Most certainly."

"Then why buy tickets to see them?"

"Because you miss them."

She wasn't fooled. "I know you love me, but not even that can explain why you'd subject yourself to dealing with them. Let's say for a moment you weren't lying about why you wanted to take this trip. Even if I do miss them a little you don't get time off that often as it is, so for us to be doing this right now is a bit unfair to you. We could be visiting your parents who live so much further away."

"We're going to visit my parents this next weekend coming up though, aren't we?"

"For a funeral, Keith. That's different."

He sighed, taking his eyes off of the window and instead turned to Elizabeth.

"I wanted to get away from everyone and everything for a bit, okay? We had a lot of time to hang out with friends this week, so instead of trying to figure out what to do with ourselves today and tomorrow I thought we could mix things up and go to your house. Being in the country for a day will do us both some good, won't it?"

"I suppose," she stated slowly. "I mean, like I said earlier I do miss my parents. And my cats. I like being able to cook at home too. I'm still surprised you wanted to visit though."

"One night can't possibly end horribly, right?" Keith asked optimistically.

The resulting look he got from Elizabeth made him wince.

"Babe, I love you, but I can tell you right now you will regret the decision to get away from the stress on campus by visiting my parents whose auras exude constantly anxious pheromones."

"Well it won't be the first decision I regret, and definitely not the last."

He tried his hardest not to let his voice become pessimistic; however, his girlfriend always picked up on his feelings.

Elizabeth frowned thoughtfully. A second later she was scooting closer to him until she was practically draped on his side, her presence reassuring. She followed this by slipping her hand into his and humming in concern.

"Keith, what exactly happened last night?" Her words started measured and tactful before picking up as her worry pervaded her voice. "You didn't want to talk about it yesterday, which is fine, but you'll have to tell me eventually. It must have been bad to make you want to leave campus entirely."

"It wasn't that big of a deal."

"You say that, but…"

"But you don't believe it?"

"No. There's obviously something bothering you, sweetie. I just want to help you. I can't do that if you don't tell me what happened, or if you keep everything bottled up."

"Technically I'm not supposed to talk about anything negative that happens in the house to anyone."

Elizabeth rolled her eyes. "That's a shitty rule and you know it! Just like the rule about not saying anything bad about any of the Thompsons or the one about not being able to make a doctor's appointment without informing Jacqueline why. That's a total breach in patient-doctor confidentiality by the way. There's no way they can legally do that."

"I know, I know. God, between all the rules, arguments, and overbearing negativity in the house I'm going crazy. Yesterday was just all of it finally hitting the fan."

"What happened?"

"Jacqueline lost it on Elijah, Larry, and I during dinner." He explained, the rest coming out all at once like air from a popped balloon. "She freaking threw a coaster onto the floor during her screaming match with Elijah, making a dangerous mess on the floor where Brandon almost slipped onto because no one was paying attention to him having an episode during the entire ordeal. I got so angry about it I basically told her that she should leave because everyone needed time to themselves to chill out. They were already leaving for four days though. I shouldn't have said anything, but she made me so mad."

When he didn't continue Elizabeth squeezed his hand comfortingly.

"I doubt you'll get in trouble for pointing out the obvious like that."

"Probably," he sighed, "but it just annoys me that I lost my cool. I got overwhelmed so fast…"

"In such a situation that's understandable."

"I guess. I still would like to be better than that."

"That's one of the things I love about you, you know."

"Hmm?"

"Your desire to improve; I love that about you. You're already an amazing person to me. You're patient, kind, passionate, and so much more, but you see yourself as imperfect so you strive to be better. No one will ever be free of faults, yet you try to learn from them and not repeat past mistakes. It's a bit silly, honestly," she smiled while trying to think of the words she wanted to use. "Many people don't put much effort into bettering themselves like you. You admit your mistakes instead of excusing them outright. I wish I could be like that."

"No you don't."

"Huh?"

"I don't want to be a better person because I'm consciously telling myself I need to be better. It's a complete involuntary feeling of just needing to *not* mess up," he admitted. "Like, my anxiety sucks as it is but when I make a mistake it just overtakes me. It makes my skin burn and my chest hurt. Everything inside me screams that I'm a massive screw up."

"Sweetie, I—"

"I *hate* feeling like that, so I try my hardest to never do anything wrong so it doesn't happen again. It scares me to loathe myself so much when I'm trying so hard to love myself like I love you. But it's difficult. I'm much more selfish and cruel than you realize. Sometimes I feel like Charlotte and I have more in common with each other than I'd like to admit."

"Your crazy sister? She sold her child's medication for

drug money, Keith; you are not anything like her."

"I am though. I have greedy thoughts, and I think about hateful things I could say to people if I had the backbone to say them. Most of them are passing thoughts and desires but they still run through my head."

"But you're not acting on them," she argued, always the optimist.

"I'm not, but isn't thinking them just as bad as acting on them?"

"What do you mean?"

"Like, with that guy you work with at your tech office."

"Oh, what's his face with the degenerate yet somehow captivating personality? What about him?"

He gave his girlfriend a look. Of all the ways to describe one of her coworkers he guessed as long as they were both on the same page it didn't matter anyway.

"Yeah. Him. He's handsome, which is whatever, but he's also really funny and playful and when he jokingly flirts with me it makes thoughts pop into my head that make me hate myself for even letting them enter my head. But I can't stop those thoughts. They just happen sometimes, and they linger despite how much I wish I could exorcise them from my memory. How does that not make me an awful person? I can't just casually make friends with people without forming some pseudo-crush for months at a time."

"Dear, we've talked about this. You think that feeling you have is being attracted to someone when you're just infatuated with them as a person. There's nothing wrong with that."

"How can you be so sure? What if I am a terrible person deep down?"

Elizabeth was silent for a moment before her hand slipped from his.

Immediately Keith's heart sank.

Why did I have to go and say that? She's going to think

the past several years together meant nothing to me. If she breaks up with me I wouldn't even know what to do!

His panic vanished when he felt a kiss land on his cheek.

"Sweetie. I think we're all terrible people then if that's what makes you call yourself that. Everyone has those unwanted thoughts," she finally stated with a casualness that had Keith looking at her shocked. He was so sure she was going to be upset with him. Instead, she seemed like she understood what he was saying.

"No human is free of making mistakes." She continued, choosing her words carefully. "You and I lie all the time, which we know from church is just as terrible a crime as murder. We do it consciously and unconsciously. Our family and friends mess up all the time too, but we love them anyway. You and me, we aren't perfect even if we try to stop ourselves from doing 'bad things'," she air quoted with a bitter laugh. "You feel guilty for having a passing romantic thought about a friend? When Blonde Sarah broke up with her boyfriend of four years a couple of semesters ago I had the sudden thought of breaking up with you so I could be with her. Not that she'd ever be interested in me, of course, but I still thought about it for a split second. I have no idea why I thought that and I never entertained the idea even for a moment, but the 'what if' popped into my head several times that day."

"Like when you're walking down the road and randomly think about jumping in front of a passing car? I hate when that happens."

"That's a good thing! It means you're aware that hurting or killing yourself is a stupid idea. Remember that psychology class I took sophomore year? Intrusive thoughts are to blame. You know, because we aren't always consciously in control of our thoughts or desires? Like when we dream. I'm pretty sure those random, unwanted thoughts are ones all people have. I think there's actually another word for them…"

A quick ten-second Google search later had her showing him her phone triumphantly.

"Aha! See, they're called 'imps' too. They're perfectly normal to have according to him. They help solidify the fact that we're not psychopaths because having them means we know that those thoughts are wrong."

"Okay, so maybe it's not a bad thing to have them if they're out of my subconscious's control, but I still feel terrible when I have them."

"I guess you can't help that, but they're just a part of life, Keith. You can't control your subconscious. However, you are for the most part in control of your actions. You love me, don't you?"

"Elizabeth, I wouldn't be alive right now without you in my life."

"It's the same for me, Keith. You saved me just as much as I saved you. I love you unconditionally and can't wait to spend my entire life with you. Still, I have those random thoughts about kissing a good friend or jumping off the balcony of Tucker and Jared's apartment too. Those spur of the moment urges or thoughts aren't who we are though. Okay? If you're a terrible person for thinking those things then all of humanity is terrible."

"That is a pretty accurate summation of humanity."

She shook her head. "Ugh, why do we always end up in the strangest conversations about life and things?"

"Because we're alive and think."

"I am going to hurt you."

"Will you though? Your punches hurt you more than me."

"I'll still try!"

"Okay. Knowing me I'll like it."

"Keith!"

"Elizabeth!"

"You're so annoying!"

"I could be more annoying, but I reign it in for you, babe."

"You know what? I won't even feel bad when they have you help out in the yard. I'll just laugh from the air-conditioned inside of the house."

"True, but will you be able to laugh while peeling potatoes with your mother? You'll be too busy consoling her about how she's not the reason you're not moving back in after college."

The brunette looked like she wanted to strangle Keith, but after a moment she burst into giggles. Keith merely smiled, almost motivated to laugh but restraining himself because he'd already bared his heart and soul to random strangers sitting nearby them on the train. They didn't need to hear his obnoxious laughter too. Instead, after she worked through her giggles, she grabbed his hand once more and leaned into his side.

"I'm yours and you're mine no matter what. You know that, right?"

Her words made him squeeze her hand back.

"Nope. You'll have to keep reminding me."

For lack of a better word their weekend went by just fine. Other than a wide range of minor inconveniences brought on upon certain people making regular tasks ten times harder than they were supposed to be, Keith knew he'd gotten lucky. The most work he had to do was help Elizabeth's dad take the air conditioners out of their bedroom and living room windows, which wasn't a hard task at all. At most it was a little exhausting due to the units being so heavy.

As for Elizabeth, after helping her mom cook dinner she managed to successfully steer conversation far away from politics as much as she could. The meal had still ended with an awkward amount of tension between her parents about something or another, but they quickly took out whatever negative feelings they had during Uno.

Who knew a card game created to ruin relationships could help mend them too?

On the ride back to campus both of them were in a significantly better mood than either of them thought they would be in.

"We'd better hurry," Elizabeth exclaimed the moment they walked into the terminal after getting off the train. "Our buses come in three and five minutes."

"Who leaves first, me or you?"

"Me."

"I can ride back with you," he offered.

"It's already late though. You teach in the morning too, so you should just head back."

"Are you sure you'll be fine on your own?"

She made a humming noise that sounded like a yes. "Nobody usually messes with me on the bus if I have my headphones in. I'll call you when I'm back at my dorm, okay? And you can text me when you get home since you'll probably beat me."

"Okay," he said. They made it to the bus stop behind the train terminal with a minute to spare. The bus Elizabeth would be taking could be seen turning the corner down the road, and an ache appeared in Keith's chest as he saw it.

Turning to her, he quickly pulled her in for a hug.

"I'm going to miss you."

"I'll see you tomorrow for dinner, silly." Nonetheless she squeezed him so tight he could have sworn he heard something popping in his back. "I did have a nice weekend. It was a good idea; thank you for buying the tickets."

The bus pulled up as she thanked him, and Keith had to fight to keep the smile on his face as she pulled away.

"It was no problem. I'll talk to you later, alright?"

"Yep! Bye-bye!"

With that she followed a small crowd onto the bus, leaving Keith to wait for his ride.

From there his week slowly began to fall apart.

On Monday afternoon he had been called into work. His dinner plans with Elizabeth had to be canceled because of this, which meant him skipping dinner altogether since he had so little time to work with before and after his impromptu shift at the restaurant. Maybe he could have said no to coming in. Sadly, his conscience wouldn't let him leave his favorite manager to close alone. Instead Elizabeth used the time to get ahead on some of her homework, and Keith made roughly fifty dollars working minimum wage.

In the evening, after climbing into bed mentally drained from a night of working customer service, he got a text from Jacqueline stating they wouldn't be coming back until Wednesday evening. That would have been happy news if not for her sending a text the following morning saying she had changed her mind and that they would be back Tuesday night as planned.

Way to get his hopes up, huh?

That same morning Keith finally noticed the house was a lot warmer than it usually was. When he mentioned it to Elijah over breakfast the younger PA merely shrugged it off saying he'd turned the temperature up the moment the Thompsons left Friday night.

"After the fit she threw Friday you still touched the thermostat?" Keith questioned, amazed he would do it again after the argument that had just taken place a few days prior.

Elijah gave him an apathetic look. "What she doesn't know won't hurt her, and honestly I don't give a shit anymore. After how she acted the other day the dwindling level of respect I've been trying to give her is gone. If she can't act like a proper employer or adult and treat me with respect, then why should I keep trying to please her? You were there on Friday. She's a selfish, uncaring…"

Needless to say, Tuesday morning had been full of Elijah's honest words about his boss (aka Jacqueline bashing), which wasn't negated by the fact they had received an email about the Thompsons not returning to campus until Thursday and that they were feeling much better after days away from campus. With all of their changes in arrival time Elijah was so confident he wouldn't need to change the temperature back until Wednesday at the earliest, which meant when they returned super late Tuesday night all hell broke loose.

The faint sound of the house's security alarm going off while he was getting in the shower made Keith's body go cold. It wasn't because the alarm was being falsely triggered either. No, the water heating up around him felt like ice instead of the steaming hot stream it should have been, because he knew Elijah had just turned in for the night. That meant trailing up the stairs with the sound of the alarm being deactivated was the telltale sound of Jacqueline's voice.

It was only a matter of minutes before she noticed something was off and came racing upstairs. As the sound of her knocking on Elijah's door like she was a cop busting him for drugs ensued, Keith found himself sliding to the tile floor of the shower and plugging his ears.

He didn't know how long he sat there. It could have been five minutes; it might have been half an hour. All he knew was that the water was nearly freezing before the yelling stopped and he could bring himself to stand up. He found himself turning off the water and drying himself off so he could sneak into his room; he listened for Jacqueline's departure down the stairs before even attempting to leave. After what he'd just listened to he was sure she would love to scream at him too.

That night he had gone to bed with wet hair and a minor headache, both of which disappeared overnight until they resurged Wednesday morning.

The moment he stepped into the house after teaching his fitness class, Jacqueline's incessant request for his presence in the kitchen made his anxiety skyrocket once more. He sat down at the kitchen table. His eyes remained fixed on the table even as she offered him some of the fruit she'd sliced for Brandon, who in turn tuned himself out to the conversation like his head was in the clouds.

"Were you aware Elijah adjusted the temperature, Keith?" She had asked him like she was trying to incriminate him of being the accomplice to a crime. Her eyes were watching him sharply which honestly only proved to put him more on edge; what did he do to deserve such treatment?

Keith shrugged, deciding to try to feign innocence.

"I was gone most of Saturday and Sunday," he stated truthfully. "I went to visit my girlfriend's parents with her after cleaning up here Saturday morning, so I didn't notice it feeling off in here after I got back because I've been so busy."

"You were too busy to notice the temperature had gone up four degrees for over four days?"

"I haven't been paying much attention to the thermostat since I moved in," he continued slowly. Why did he feel like he had to defend himself? "I got back late on Friday and went straight to bed after taking a shower. Saturday I cleaned, left campus, and then didn't get back until nearly midnight on Sunday. Monday I had a full day of class and work since I got called in, and yesterday I had a bunch of classes, my double shift at the library, and spend the day doing homework at Elizabeth's dorm room."

"I still find it strange you didn't feel unnaturally warm."

"I'm sorry? After the confrontation that happened on Friday—"

"There's no need for such a strong word. That wasn't a confrontation," she waved off like he was being dramatic for no reason.

"It wasn't?"

"I admit voices were raised, but it was more of a conversation than anything else. It was surprising he would disrespect me like that again though. He must really hate me."

When Keith stayed silent, not wanting to agree with her, she frowned harder.

"As it stands I am trying to come up with an appropriate punishment for him breaking the rules that won't end with him being let go." Her tone became more annoyed as she went on. She crossed her arms before releasing a pent up sigh. "I know you won't be able to take his hours if that were to happen, so I am trying to come up with a solution that will avoid endangering any shift coverage. I merely wanted as much information on his actions before I put together a decision."

"Okay," he responded, mostly because he didn't know what else to say.

"Keith."

"Yes?"

"If you did know Elijah had touched the thermostat, then would you have confronted him? Or told me so I could handle the situation?"

"Probably not." He answered before he could think.

Immediately her eyes widened in surprise and barely concealed rage.

"What?"

He ran a hand through his hair if only to do something to stop it from shaking.

"It's not my business to deal with," was his response. "The whole thing with temperature control is between you and Elijah. Not me. I shouldn't have to babysit my coworker to make sure he's following the rules. If I had seen him messing with the temperature I probably would have ignored it, because he knows the consequences."

"And if the harmonium or violin had been damaged?"

"Like I said, I have a lot of other things going on in my life besides making sure that he isn't breaking the rules."

"That's a bit selfish, isn't it?"

It took all of his self-control to bite his tongue.

"How so?"

"Saying it's not your business to get involved to stop your coworker's failings is selfish, because the amount of effort it would take for you to do anything like alerting me for example is not high. You would have to be pretty lazy to not get involved in the slightest."

At this point he was at a loss for what to say. Keith's patience was dwindling, and his head was beginning to feel the pressure of a headache closing in. He just wanted to go upstairs and do some homework before he went to his next class. Didn't Brandon have class soon anyway?

"Oh, how did Brandon's doctor visit go?" He exclaimed like he just remembered and was super concerned, not just desperate to change the subject.

Jacqueline glanced at her son, her lips in a thin line.

"It was successful despite the doctor being a terrorist with no manners. He had no tact telling Brandon he needed to have part of the cast over his hand regardless of our wishes, and that rushing his recovery might cause long-lasting damage. Unfortunately we'll have to see him again in two and a half weeks when the cast is ready to be taken off. I managed to coerce him into taking it off a few days earlier than recommended at least."

"I see."

She continued to detail every unpleasant thing about the doctor and the medical facility they visited. After about ten minutes Keith had to cut her off, saying he'd be late to class if he didn't start getting ready right then.

All of this had taken place before nine in the morning on Wednesday. Barely halfway through the week.

That didn't mean his week couldn't get worse.

On Thursday evening during dinner Keith saw them.

He had acted natural, not understanding what the marks were until he remembered the loud noises he'd overheard Tuesday night. Could it have happened then?

"Eli," Keith caught him leaving the kitchen after the Thompson's had filed out into the living room. He needed to keep his voice down since they were only a room away.

"Yeah?"

The elder PA swallowed his uncertainly. "Those marks on your arm. When did you get those?"

Elijah's face scrunched up in anger. His cheeks turned pink in something akin to embarrassment, but it was overshadowed by the absolute hatred in his eyes.

Hatred that didn't seem to be directed at him.

"It's none of your business."

With that the younger male tried to exit the kitchen; however, Keith dared to grab onto the other's shirt.

"Wait!"

"Let go of me!"

"Only if you agree to talk about this later," they continued to argue in hushed tones until Elijah finally accepted his fate.

"Fine! Nosy bastard," he swore as he walked out of the room.

Later that night, Keith became even more scared of Jacqueline.

"She grabbed my arm while she was screaming at me," Elijah admitted. He was a lot more vulnerable sitting on his bed without the threat of prying ears. "I told her not to touch me, but she just kept squeezing it tighter. By the time she let go she'd already broken skin with her stupidly large nails. I told her she hurt me. She saw the blood, but she just laughed."

"What the hell?"

Frustrated tears welled up in Elijah's eyes. The crescent-shaped scabs on his forearm stood out even more now that Keith knew who put them there.

"She said no one would believe that they came from her. If I were to go to someone about this she said she'd just say I tried to hurt her first, and that she did that in self-defense or something. Apparently in the eyes of the court a 'strong young male' getting hurt by an out of shape middle-aged woman is pathetic, so I would most likely get in trouble for lying and breaking the 'no slander' rule in the contract. I don't want to go to jail, Keith."

"You won't. If I were to testify too, then maybe we can—"

"No!"

"But Eli."

"I don't want you involved," he hissed. Fear saturated his voice. "If you get in trouble because of me I wouldn't be able to live with myself."

"She hurt you though. That's abuse."

"Abuse? What do you think we've been experiencing the entire time we've been here, Keith? Mental abuse, emotional abuse; a little physical abuse is just the icing on the cake. There's nothing we can do that won't end in us breaking the contract."

"There has to be something," he argued. His words felt feeble. "What if we have student legal services read the contract? Their office is on campus. They're open Monday through Friday, and their services are free to students. I know the contract states we're not allowed to let other people read it, but they're a legal organization, so it shouldn't be a problem. At least I think so."

"I don't know. I'll look into it tonight, I guess. Just… pretend you don't know about this. It'll be better for you if you don't. We both have classes we need to pass or else the mountain of debt we're acquiring will mean nothing."

"I'm sure there's someone you can talk to if this is effecting your grades. Also, you should at least take a picture of your arm so you have proof."

"I already did, but I don't think it'll matter much."

"She can't get away with this."

"I'm scared, Keith." He closed his eyes tightly like it was physically painful to speak. "I'm pretty sure she can."

Facing Jacqueline with a straight face the next day was one of the most challenging things he had to do. It was almost as hard as keeping what he had learned about Elijah from Elizabeth. He knew if he told her she would tell him to screw the other PA's feelings and call the cops on their boss; however, she would also know they couldn't do that if they didn't want to go to court. If they went to court, then Keith might not be able to graduate on time.

Being in college was stressful enough. Running the risk of going to jail due to them losing a court case against their employer? There wasn't a word that could fully grasp how mentally debilitating that would be on the PAs, their friends, and their families.

So he kept quiet.

He told his girlfriend nothing was the matter when she thought he was acting weird on the phone.

He put on his customer service act in front of Jacqueline and Brandon.

He didn't stare at the place on Elijah's arm where he knew the evidence of abuse was.

All of it, he buried it down and tried not to think about it.

When he left on Friday night to catch the bus home with Elizabeth, nobody was any the wiser about what he'd seen on Elijah's arm save for him and the PA himself. He felt horrible leaving the other boy there. Still, he had a funeral to go to. He had to be there for his father.

He just wished he'd gotten to say something to Elijah before heading out. Instead the blue-haired boy wasn't in his room that night after dinner.

He must be with Isaac, Keith thought sadly as he made his way to one of the charter bus stops. *I wonder if he'll tell him what he told me. Ugh, I wish I didn't have to leave him alone! I hope he'll be okay. If something happens to him while I'm gone...*

He didn't want to think about it too hard. Surely Jacqueline wouldn't dare touch him a second time, right? The first time had just been a fluke. She'd just been overcome with emotion and accidentally hurt him. That had to be it.

"I am trying to come up with an appropriate punishment," he recalled her saying a few days prior.

Invisible hands tore holes into his gut. What kind of punishment would she decide to give Elijah?

He was scared to find out.

CHAPTER TWELVE

"Oh, you're a personal assistant? For people with disabilities no less? That's adorable! You were always such a sweet kid, Keith. So kind to anyone you met. It makes sense you would work in a field where you could help people. And you teach a fitness class for the elderly too? You're a saint!"

"Are you going to get your master's degree or what? I heard Kinesiology is a useless major unless you have higher certification than a bachelor's. That's the major people get when they want to be gym teachers. You have more potential than that. I know it might seem expensive, but hear me out. The opportunities that will open up for you if you just continue furthering your education instead of getting a job right after graduation far outweighs the cost of attending college for three more years. If you work hard, then surely you'll find a good job! Anything but a lousy gym teacher."

"How do you not get sad working with people like that? Don't some of those old people die? Like, if I were teaching a class and came in one week to find out ol' Dorothy had passed away I would just straight up quit. Or those students with disabilities; do you have to wash the crippled ones? Oh my God, do you have to help them go to the bathroom? Gross!"

"You'd better be careful not to get burnt out. People who are nice enough or not totally socially inept to work in a field where they deal with people usually become emotionally dead inside, because let's face it, Keith, people suck. Besides, isn't caretaking and fitness a woman's field? Maybe you could use that knowledge to become an EMT or a doctor."

"Wow! I could never have the patience to work with the elderly or the disabled. Old people kind of creep me out. I haven't interacted with many disabled people, but I saw some on TV once."

"You're working three jobs? Isn't that a lot on top of being in school full-time?"

"Only three jobs? Back when I was in college I worked at least five part-time jobs in addition to going to class. I paid off all my loans within months of graduating, I did. You millennials think life is so hard now."

If one more person asks me how school is going, he thought after getting away from his great aunt or cousin or something-in-law, *I am going to lose it.*

One would think the main choice of topic at a funeral would be centered on the deceased. To Keith's growing horror, however, his father's side of the family would rather gossip about each other's lives.

Why? He had no clue. The only thing he was sure about was that what little patience he did possess was thinning fast.

After the seventh ~~stranger~~ relative he'd had the unfortunate pleasure of meeting for the first time since he could remember gave him his or her personal opinion about what he was doing with his life, Keith did his best to avoid anyone outside his immediate family. When family members he couldn't remember the names of or how they were even related approached him in earnest he silently begged for Elizabeth to take the spotlight. Of course this just led to his seemingly endless amount of cousins, uncles, aunts, and more being amazed at her tech skills and asking her how to fix problems with their laptops or phones.

Still, he was grateful to not have to explain to any more

people how college was or how work was going. It was all fake pleasantries anyway. After the funeral none of them would speak again until the next one, if at all.

I should go find my dad, he thought after making a successful lap around the seating area without drawing anyone over for a conversation. In the front row directly in front of the urn he could see his father sitting next to his two brothers. They were speaking to each other calmly, although every once in a while the trio would break out into wild gesticulations that reminded Keith they were definitely all related.

"Want to sit down?"

Elizabeth's voice drew his attention. What also drew his attention was the beautiful black dress she was wearing, but those thoughts were neither appropriate for the time nor place.

He nodded. "Yeah."

Ten minutes later the head of the funeral home was wrangling in everyone throughout the facility. She and a couple of other attendants instructed everyone to sit down for the ceremony. Once that was done she took her place at the front podium and spent several minutes reading aloud some scriptures out of the Bible, following the verses with words written by the deceased's sons.

Hearing what his father had to say about his grandma was tear-inducing to everyone gathered there, especially Keith. He barely had reacted to his grandma's death before now. At his father's heartfelt passage about losing his own mother tears appeared in his eyes faster than he could blink them away. It was like a moment in an animated movie where the beloved main character started crying, and he couldn't stop himself from following suit.

All he could think about was how his father was hurting so badly, and that there was nothing in the world he could do to make that pain go away. He could be there for him, he could grieve with him and try to give him comfort, yet there would always be a chunk of his heart that just wasn't there.

All he could think about was how one day his father's pain would be his, his sister's, and his brother's, but there was nothing he could do within his power to prevent it.

Before he could spiral too far down in his despair he remembered the weight in his hand.

Turning to Elizabeth, he leaned down to whisper in her ear.

"I think I understood what you meant now."

Pulling away, the brunette gave him a soft smile despite both of their faces being wet with tears.

She understood. Nothing else needed to be said.

After the awkward, emotional, and ultimately exhausting funeral the rest of the weekend went by in a flash. The remainder of Saturday was spent with Keith's direct family hosting his father's relatives who didn't leave town as soon as the service was over. This was mainly because Michael was the only one who lived in the area. He had taken care of his aging parents over the past few years; his older brothers both lived in California, so even before their mother's health had taken a turn for the worst he was the one to spend the most time with his parents due to geography alone.

It honestly made interacting with them a bit difficult. Before the funeral Keith definitely would have described his family's relationship estranged even before moving halfway across the country. It still was, sure, but suddenly his uncles were trying to make an effort at forming some sort of bond with him, his little sister, and his two older sisters.

Speaking of his two older sisters…

I guess I'm lucky there are too many people around to cause a scene, Keith thought ten minutes into a forced conversation with his older but not oldest sister. *After the last time we saw each other I'm sure she and her scumbag of a husband would love to kick my ass.*

"When are you guys going to get married?" Charlotte questioned, an arm around said scumbag. Her recently dyed hair hung over her shoulders limply in troves. "You've been together longer than I've even known Josh. Tell me honestly, Elizabeth, are you making him wait, or does he just need to grow a pair?"

Elizabeth smiled politely. Anyone could tell it was out of necessity. Next to her Keith just glared at his sister, who had a shit-eating grin on her face.

"I want to finish college first," she answered. "Keith and I also need to make sure our finances are in order before we get engaged, otherwise we'll end up engaged for years. I don't want to be engaged for more than two years so we might as well wait."

"It's also none of your business," Keith added. "Not everyone can elope on the day before Christmas Eve like you."

Josh's eyes narrowed.

"She was just curious. No need to get pissy."

"I was talking to Charlotte, not you. She can speak for herself."

"Not when her brother is being an asshole."

"Oh, I'm the asshole? Who's the one who beat her black and blue last week?"

Elizabeth suddenly gripped her boyfriend's forearm in warning.

"You promised your mom you'd try to get along today," she reminded in a hushed voice. It hurt her to say it since she hated Josh just as much as Keith did.

Unfortunately the damage was done. Josh stood up, nostrils flaring. After a moment of taking in how many other people were gathered in the house he locked eyes with his wife.

"Say goodbye to your parents. We're leaving now."

"Why? Who cares what he says," she motioned to Keith. "It's not like it matters."

"Do you want to argue with me about it here? Right now?"

The implication of a challenge was obvious in Josh's voice, and it made the blood in Keith's veins boil all the hotter.

After giving him a disappointed look, Charlotte got up and walked over with her husband to the kitchen. There they began saying goodbye to some of her relatives but after the initial departure Keith couldn't bring himself to care less. He was too busy trying to calm himself down.

"I hate him," he spat.

Negative thoughts swirled around his head like a bunch of wasps. They stung him at every opportunity, which didn't help him in quelling his rage. He was so caught up in his own feelings that he didn't realize Elizabeth was staring at him for several moments.

"Sorry," he apologized. "I didn't mean to ignore you or make them leave. Well, I did want Josh to leave, but he never leaves her side so I should have known this would happen."

She ran her fingers across his palm in small circles. "I know, sweetie. It's fine," Elizabeth attempted to soothe.

"No it's not. I shouldn't have let them rile me up."

"Dear, the first thing she brought up was how uptight and prude we are for still never having smoked pot or drinking ourselves into oblivion like she does. Between that and Josh asking me if I'd popped your cherry yet I commend you for not getting pissed right away."

"Oh I was pissed the moment Charlotte had the gall to walk over here with that monster on her arm. Why did they even allow them to be here today? I get it was a funeral, but why couldn't she have just come by herself? Better yet, why did my parents tell her it was fine for her to come? They haven't let her on the property since she ran over my mom's foot."

"You know he wouldn't have let her come without him. As for coming here, your dad's relatives don't come to visit us much anymore. They weren't going to stop her from catching up."

"I guess. I just wish they hadn't allowed Josh in," the complaint remained. "He would be better off dead. I know I'm not supposed to wish that, but I do."

"It's okay, sweetie. Well, it's not, but it's understandable. I'm surprised you lasted the entire funeral without even talking to them. The fact you lasted for ten minutes in closed quarters? That takes a lot of restraint."

He let out a sardonic laugh. After a few seconds of silence he let out a long breath and let his head hang slightly.

"I just don't get how she can be so stupid," he raved under his breath so those mingling nearby couldn't hear. "My parents and Christa know why Charlotte has got the ugliest spray tan of her life. Only painting her skin Trump orange could cover up the bruises all over her. Just because it's a funeral doesn't mean everyone should ignore the fact her husband is a piece of shit monster that believes beating women is justified because he thinks men are the superior sex."

Elizabeth sighed. "I know how mad it makes you, but there is nothing we can do. Your sister has had opportunity after opportunity to press charges on him or get away, but she kept crawling back to him. Sometimes it's an issue of not having help. Sometimes, in your sister's case, it's an issue of not *wanting* help."

"Why is she so stupid?"

"I don't know."

"Christa turned out fine, I turned out fine, and Kassie is turning out fine too. It can't be my parent's fault. They raised all of us the same, and yet she always broke the rules."

"You did tell me a lot of stories. Didn't she start stealing when she was seven years old?"

"Six years old, actually. Stealing candy evolved into stealing someone's purse at a charity event taking place at a bank. Why? Why would she try that? Walking out of the store with a vacuum cleaner and instantly getting caught? Selling her infant's inhaler for drug money? You can't even find this stuff in a poorly written poetry book."

Elizabeth winced. She'd heard all the stories before from Keith and his parents, but it didn't make them any less distasteful.

"Some people just don't learn, Keith." She responded, pulling her hand out of Keith's to take a drink of her water. After she was done she went on. "Didn't your dad say she was in all the correction programs your parents could afford? Going to jail time and time again didn't even scare her either. If she doesn't want to change into a less crappy human being, then she isn't going to."

"It's just depressing at this point. You'd think after two abusive boyfriends she wouldn't have found a third and then marry him the day after she ran over our mom with her car. She never apologized for it either."

"She does seem to be one of a kind…"

A noise of genuine frustration escaped him. "And yet somehow I still care about her wellbeing. I wish I could just… stop."

Hazel eyes stared into his before she quirked an eyebrow.

"Stop caring?"

"Yeah."

She shook her head before smiling. "Dear, don't lie. You wouldn't be you if you stopped caring. Even about those who hurt you."

"She ran over our mom's foot with her car and broke it, Lizzy. On purpose. She should be dead to me. I'm an idiot."

"Hey, your parents still love her too despite all the screwed up things she's done."

"That just makes all of us idiots."

"Perhaps, but I still love you all the same."

He found himself giving her a light hug. As he did so he noticed his other sister approaching looking tired.

"We're going to head out," Christa stated while keeping an eye on her kids from afar. Her daughters were busy hanging off of their grandfather while her husband watched. "Our plane back to Illinois takes off early tomorrow. I wish we could stay longer, but I can't take off work."

Banishing his ill feelings from earlier, Keith nodded in understanding.

"Okay. Travel safely. It was nice seeing you," he stated a bit awkwardly as he stood up. His sister drew him in for a hug which he reciprocated with only some hesitation.

They'd been super close when he was younger. After middle school though, his opinion of her had morphed and a disconnect had opened up. Coupled with her moving to Wisconsin and later Illinois their relationship had become strained and after a boatload of incidents courtesy of her husband it had crashed and burned from there. He would still speak to her and the children in good spirits. When her husband was around? That was another story.

"Thank you. Maybe we'll see you around Christmas time?"

"Probably. I get a couple weeks off from school, so I'll be here."

"Cool."

With that she walked back over to her family.

The moment she was gone Keith turned to Elizabeth.

"Can we go in my room to watch anime yet? Kassie got to skip the family get-together as soon as she came in saying she needed alone time. Can we have alone time now?"

The brunette rolled her eyes.

"Sure, let's go finish that anime we were watching. We only have a couple of episodes left, right?"

"Of season two. Season three comes out next year."

"There's going to be a season three?" Her eyes instantly grew wild, excitement causing her to get up and dance. "I know exactly what chapters of the manga they're going to adapt! Oh my god, they're going to talk about my boy's childhood some more and there are going to be so many feels I just can't even!"

Keith grinned while slowly motioning for Elizabeth to head towards the bedroom. One of his cousins was shooting them a confused look, to which they both ignored.

"Let's finish season two before you go telling me spoilers for season three," he reasoned.

"Sorry! I just get so excited. I'll try not to spoil too many things. Well, I still want to tell you about…"

It took him two minutes to get her to move into the bedroom. By then he'd already learned which character would die within the first few episodes of season three, and he was okay with that.

He couldn't deny that he was happy when he got to spend half of the next day with just his parents, little sister, and girlfriend.

"So how's the job going?" Michael asked once everyone got their food. He was quickly unwrapping his burger and dumping his fries out of their box as he spoke, eagerly anticipating his meal.

Elizabeth was already dipping her chicken nuggets in barbeque sauce and inhaling them whole.

"It's fine." He replied.

"What's that mean? Do you like it, or do you wish you hadn't taken it now?"

"It's usually fine," he corrected as he gathered up his courage. "I mean before the full-time PA got fired and

Jacqueline had to come back things were going very well."

"Wait, what happened?"

His father's shock was similar to his mother's. Her eyes widened in surprise and worry, yet his held more skepticism than anything.

"She fired the full-time PA some weeks ago because she felt he wasn't doing a good enough job," Keith began to explain. As he spoke he munched on a handful of fries absentmindedly in between sentences. "Because he worked most of the hours she moved back in so she can work them. I took on extra hours to help Brandon out, but she's been getting upset that the other part-time PA and I can't cover more hours. She's been really on edge lately and it makes living there more stressful than it needs to be."

"You shouldn't feel bad, dear," Colleen stated. "It's not your fault she fired another worker. You agreed to a set amount of hours before the school year began. Anything more is you being kind."

His father nodded. "Yeah, she shouldn't be pressuring you to work more when you're not obligated to work more than what you agreed to."

"I know, dad. And I haven't been working more than I can handle."

"Good. You have schoolwork you should be focusing on."

"And your mental health," his mother added.

"I know. Elizabeth has been making sure I don't overwork myself."

The brunette smiled widely at that comment, one hand holding a drink and the other a burger.

"Did he tell you about the chicken nugget cake we made him for his birthday last week?"

Colleen laughed. "Kassie showed us the picture he sent her of it. It looked amazing. How many of you did it take to eat it?"

"Like seven of us and we still had leftovers. Everyone

left with a plastic bag of chicken that night."

"He's always loved chicken nuggets. I remember when he was five and he first went to Burger King they had the crown-shaped nuggets, and he…"

Keith's mother and girlfriend devolved into a conversation about his childhood for a short while. After that they switched topics to his sisters' childhoods, to which he tuned out as he started on his burger and nuggets. It was after almost finishing his food that he noticed his father looking him over with an uneasy look.

"What?" He asked just as Kassie got sucked into a conversation with the other women. More like she was telling their mother not to talk about her embarrassing stories as a child.

"Are you making enough money to graduate so far?"

The question took him back for a second. Until recently his biggest worry had been making enough money to pay his tuition on time so he wouldn't get kicked out of school before graduation. He might have forgotten, but his father hadn't.

"I think so," he finally replied. "Not having to pay room and board has saved me so much money it's kind of sad. I guess I should have stopped living in the dorm after freshmen year, because going over how much I owe now versus the last three years the money I'm paying back to the school is ninety percent housing costs."

"Really?"

"Yeah, I don't get it either. You'd think the administration would care more about their students than making money. regret how much money I spent the last three years when I could have paid a fraction of the cost and just stayed in an apartment."

"I think you did alright for none of us knowing how the whole college thing worked. There's no use worrying about what we could have done. But tell me, Keith, are you really happy in the house you're staying in now?"

"It's… I was happy," he admitted. "When it was just us PAs and Brandon we had a routine. Cleaning still sucked, but everyone got along well from what I could tell. I thought things were going great. But then Isaac, the full-time PA, got fired. They were giving him way too many hours and not letting him have much time off. I don't know if that had much to do with it or what; however, ever since Jacqueline moved back in it's just been so stressful to be in the house. It doesn't feel like I live there, you know?"

"You don't feel welcome, or you don't want to live there anymore?"

"Sort of both. It just doesn't feel like it's *my* home. Like, I can't walk into the house without the compulsion to ask permission to do things there. It's like I'm tiptoeing around everywhere."

"That's not a good way to feel about the place you'll be living in until May, Keith."

"I know that. I think once they get this new full-time PA hired things will go back to the way they were before. Jacqueline will leave, and then the house will start feeling like an actual home."

Michael didn't seem particularly thrilled by that solution, but he did perk up a bit at the mention of a new hire.

"Oh, they've almost got a replacement hired?"

"I think so. Last I heard they were working on a start date, which makes me think he's already been hired and they're just negotiating stuff. It was supposed to be sometime this week though."

"Well that's good. The sooner that woman is out of the house the better, it seems."

His lips quirked up in a small smile. Images of shattered coaster shards and crescent-shaped marks on skin flashed through his head.

"Yeah, I agree."

It was nearly nine o'clock when Keith and Elizabeth got off the charter bus. The ride back down south had been fairly quiet, the older reading her book while the younger listened to his mp3 player. By the time they got off the bus though they were starving.

"Want to go to the dining hall really quick? After hours dinner only started an hour ago. I could swipe us in." She suggested while stretching her shoulders. They popped in quick succession.

Keith weighed the pros and cons of eating at the dining hall versus fast food.

"Nah. How about we get Chinese super quick? I'll buy."

"But you need to be saving your money for school. I can just use my credits; it's not a big deal."

"Sweetie, you keep them. You already switched to the lowest plan because the other ones were too pricey."

"I have some extra," she defended half-hearted. "Just... not a lot."

"Uh-huh. I'm feeling rice and vegetables tonight anyway. We can hit up that one Chinese place on the way to your dorm, and then after I walk you over there you can see me off at the bus stop?"

"Fine. But only if you get me teriyaki chicken."

"Done."

With that the next forty-five minutes were spent walking, eating, and then walking some more. By the time Keith was on a bus back home it was a quarter to ten.

At least Brandon will be in bed by now, he thought as he got his key out. He unlocked the door and played with the alarm as usual. *That means Jacqueline will probably be downstairs on her computer. I'd better prepare myself for her to ask me how the funeral was. Maybe I'll fake having to go take a shower or go to the bathroom so she lets me leave.*

When he walked into the kitchen he expected

Jacqueline to be sitting there on her computer. He also expected her to ask him to sit down, her entire demeanor screaming stressed and annoyed. What he didn't expect was for her to tell him Elijah quit.

"He… quit?"

"Yes. Packed up everything yesterday and walked out the door today along with a long list of reasons why he couldn't stay and how terrible my family is."

His mouth was dry. He knew Elijah was better off getting out of here. He knew Jacqueline was a terrible boss, and that she didn't feel remorse for hurting her son, husband, and employees. He knew that the other PA had been looking for a way out, yet in the span of a little over two days he was already packed up and gone as if he'd never even lived here at all?

It hurt. It almost felt like he'd been abandoned.

"Did you know he was going to quit?" She pressed, tone accusatory.

"No."

He felt numb.

"Really? I find that hard to believe considering how close the two of you seemed to be."

"Close? We hardly talked to each other outside of dinner or working together. He was friendlier with Isaac than me. Now that he's left I probably won't see him ever again," was the honest retort.

Jacqueline's eyes bore into his own calculatingly. She drummed her newly painted nails along her arm as she thought, her hair looking like it had been freshly cut since he'd gone home.

"I suppose you might be telling the truth. Be that as it may, I will be bringing Elijah to court. He broke the contract by quitting. He also threatened to call social services on us," she added with a noise similar to a snarl. "That brat thinks he can drag DCFS or CPS into this? What kind of cruel person would put such pressure on my son by involving the government? Talk about selfishness. And to think he picked the weekend you were gone to pull such shit. It's like he didn't even care about your feelings or the fact that your grandma passed away. You went to a funeral and came back to find out your friend had left without saying goodbye. What a terrible person, that boy."

Keith wanted to say something. He wanted to defend Elijah, or refute Jacqueline's accusations. But no words were coming out.

Did Elijah leave me behind on purpose? Did he have this planned before our talk a few days ago, before I gave him the advice to go to the student legal services? Or did he go to them on Friday, and they just gave him the resources he needed to leave that quickly? Maybe he just couldn't handle it here anymore. Perhaps Jacqueline hurt him again, so he couldn't wait until I returned.

Doubt lingered in his mind as he tried to be happy for his friend. After what their boss did to Elijah the boy was smart for getting out before anything else could happen to him; however, Keith was as worried for him as he was happy for him. Was Elijah going to be brought to court? Was he going to be fined or put in jail for breaking the contract?

What if he found a loophole to leave, he asked himself. *That would make sense. The only thing I don't understand is why he didn't say anything to me. What if he didn't say goodbye because he just tolerated me? I was worried about him the entire weekend, terrified that Jacqueline's punishment she had in store for him would be something abusive, but instead he's gone and left me here with her. Was it because I didn't stand up to our boss with him? Is this my fault?*

He had always been insecure. Oftentimes he couldn't decipher the difference between his friends' playful jabs or hurtful comments. It depended on his current mood more than anything. Sometimes he assumed the best when in actuality the worst was what he was being presented with; other times he thought someone was treating him with good intentions only to go behind his back. Once or twice he upset a friend by seeking closure, only to offend him or her with his lack of trust.

It didn't help that the last several weeks had drastically put him on edge. He found himself looking for ill-intent when it often wasn't present due to the twisted words and manipulative actions of his boss.

He hated himself for it.

"On the bright side," the blonde continued unbeknownst of the inner turmoil that was Keith's mind, "we have a new full-time PA starting with us tomorrow evening. His name is Thomas. I'll start training him over the next three days, and by that point he will be taking over most of the shifts Isaac was scheduled with. He was supposed to take all of them, but after much debate with hours I was forced to give him less just so he would take the job." She seemed particularly displeased with this. "Still, some hours are better than none I suppose. At least I'll finally be able to have some time to myself back. As it is, now that Elijah is gone I'll have to fill those shifts myself. Many of them are evening shifts which are far easier than the daylong ones, so it shouldn't be as exhausting, but if you wanted to take any of the open shifts feel free to let me know."

His head started nodding almost on its own. It was like he was in a daze, not really listening to the words that were being said to him.

Isaac had been fired. Elijah had quit. He was the only one left from the three original PAs that had been hired and it was only nearing the end of October. Who was to say Thomas wouldn't be fired or quit just as quickly?

Keith was worried. At the rate things were going Jacqueline would never leave. Brandon would remain miserable, and Keith would end up turning into Larry Jr.

because he was too much of a pussy to stand up to his boss. *How much longer can I live like this?*

CHAPTER THIRTEEN

"If one more customer calls back saying they want a remake I'm going to scream," Eden complained.

Keith nodded in response to the general manager's complaint, having talked to two of the three problem customers of the night. Not that one of the three didn't have a valid excuse, but when more than one reoccurring pizza scammer calls on the same night it just makes the rest of the night sour.

"The thing that makes me mad is that we explicitly tell them that if they want the remake they are not allowed to eat the pizza they said was inedible." She continued. "And then half the time they eat the whole thing anyway, which if it was truly that bad to need a whole new pizza why did they eat it? We let customers keep them if they were being honest and they show that by not eating the 'burnt' or 'raw' or 'too spicy' hot giardiniera pizza when the driver shows up, but when the same customers call back every single week to complain about their food even after we read the order back to them before making it I just— ugh. Whatever. It's not money coming out of my wallet."

"Yeah," he replied. "If the owner wants us to give out free food to make the complainers happy, then I'll do it. He just better not get mad at us for actually doing what he says."

She rolled her eyes. "He always complains about the closing shift report to me during our meetings. I have to put customer issues in the report so we can track customer order numbers, and it's rare that he doesn't tell me to start being firmer with repeat offenders yet still makes me give away stuff to stop people from giving us bad reviews."

"The review system sucks though. He knows over ninety percent of reviewers only get online to give feedback when they have a bad experience or want to crap on the store?"

"Yeah, but he doesn't care."

"That's so dumb. He should be trying to reward people for giving valid reviews or do a promotion to get the non-trouble customers to write reviews. I mean, sometimes we get good ones, but most of the time they complain about not being able to order pizza at eleven fifteen when we close at eleven and I just..." He trailed off, letting out a dramatic groan.

Talking to people. Forming relationships with customers. Answering silly questions and going to the trouble to find information that wasn't in his job description. Keith had enjoyed doing those things until he'd traded his cushy office jobs for restaurant work. Not that the sub shop job had been bad when he still spent summers at home because the customers legitimately watched him put their sandwich together piece by piece, but there were always problem customers with every and any job. Those customers were the ones employees remembered forever because the nice ones faded from memory while the bad ones festered as "one time when I worked at..." stories that got passed around as dinner conversation among their friends.

He felt bad sometimes when he recounted a story to his friends. Especially when he had the person's name ingrained in his head from the trauma of the ordeal.

Then he counted the number of times he'd been obligated to give his name to pissed off customers and gotten his name posted in a bullshit review and thought screw it. If customers could complain about him, sharing his information to the public when he was sure he never signed anything saying he needed to tell people his personal information (especially when he had nothing to do with their bad experience ninety-nine percent of the time), then why couldn't he verbally bash them once every couple months when the story arose?

I need to get a life, he reprimanded himself. *Those kinds of people don't think twice about what they do to random fast food or store workers. Why complain about them? I need to let 'em go.*

"Or you could be petty and complain about them anonymously on Reddit," his boss recommended.

Keith recoiled, horrified. "Oh god. Did I say that out loud?"

"Yep. It's fine though. I thought it was pretty funny, actually. But seriously; Reddit is a great way to let off steam. Or piss you off depending if stories about unanswered injustice get you worked up."

He gave her a blank look, only to have to school his features into an approachable smile when a customer came up to his register.

After he gave the student (he could tell because of the green university shirt) one of the signature slices he turned back to Eden only to see her in the middle of explaining the different crusts they offered. A couple more minutes and after reading the order back to them, she handed a family a small stack of cups and they left to find seats.

"So," she said, putting her elbow on the counter and letting her chin rest on her hand, "how's life been? I only get to see you like once a week now, which is sad because you're my best worker. I can't even get you on the manager schedule since you have to be home before ten."

"I'm sorry. It's all I can do between the PA job and the library."

"Lame."

He shrugged, a frown crossing his face. Should he tell

her about his dilemma?

"Jacqueline was trying to talk me into quitting here entirely."

Eden's head came up, her eyes wide. "What?"

Keith winced. He hadn't expected her to care so much.

"Yeah, uh, she's been trying to talk me into working more hours as a PA instead of working one day a week here since the part-time PA left..."

"But I already put you on one day a week instead of two because the *full-time* PA left. When did the other one leave?"

"Um, almost two weeks ago."

"So you're the only one left?"

"No. A new full-time PA started the weekend after the part-time one quit, but the problem is they both worked almost the same number of hours and this new guy works less than the original full-time PA did. I've been covering some of the shifts or making dinner an extra night of the week because of it."

"That's not your fault though."

"I know."

"Then why take all these extra shifts?"

"I've been trying to say no, but she makes me feel like crap when I do and it's not fair to Brandon. Getting paid to sit next to him as he does homework so he doesn't get yelled at by his mom for no reason isn't that bad of a gig when I have the free time. She just won't leave me alone about it," he confessed. "It's so oppressive over there."

"From what you told me it doesn't sound anything like the last PA job you had. He can't leave the house without his mom's permission and he's almost thirty? I would've gone off on my mom if she tried that with me after eighteen. I get she's taking care of him but running his life is another thing altogether. Wait; you're not thinking of quitting, right? Because I know you're only working one day a week but it helps. I could also put you on more days;

I just haven't because you can't."

"No. Well, I thought about it at one point, but I don't want to just because she thinks it would be better for me. What she's telling me when she says that is that it'd be better for her, because she doesn't like assisting her son on account of her health. But it's not my fault she fired Isaac, and she drove Elijah to quit. This is her fault."

"And you're already being nice enough to work an extra few shifts a week anyway," she agreed. "Does she not care that she's maybe asking you to work too much?"

"I doubt she cares."

"Well to hell with her then. I can't match what you make there, but I can offer the usual free pizza and discount. Also if you leave I would seriously cry." She stated seriously, her eyes tearing up a bit. "You're my most dependable employee."

"Thanks," he accepted the compliment sheepishly, rubbing the back of his neck awkwardly as another group of students entered the restaurant. It was nice to know someone would miss him if he left. He liked most of his coworkers very much, so knowing they liked him in return was great.

I definitely can't quit now, he thought. *Not when they need me and want me here.*

"I'm glad we finally got to do this," Brandon stated after the movie ended. "I can't believe this was the first time I've ever seen a movie not on a TV since I started here seven years ago. All this time I've been missing out. I hope my mom will let us do this again; it was a lot of fun."

Keith held back a grimace. While he was happy Brandon had enjoyed the movie, there were so many things he wished he could say to his Person right then. How the fun he'd had didn't have to be something he only got to experience once in a blue moon. How if he wanted to do something that sounded like something he'd enjoy he should just make plans to do it instead of begging his mother for permission. How most people his age ran his or her own life and had the freedom to manage their time according to what they wanted.

The PA could just imagine Jacqueline reacting to Brandon trying to make his own plans for once. It was enough to hear her yelling at him to practice for over five hours a day every afternoon and evening. If her son dared try to do something other than practice the violin or work on his dissertation she very well might make him skip dinner.

She'd done that once. Keith remembered the feeling of unease at the situation, his ears ringing from the tongue-lashing Brandon had received from his mother all because he only got four hours of practice in the previous day.

Shaking those thoughts away, Keith forced his usual polite customer service smile.

"I'm glad we finally found time to do this, and that you enjoyed it! Now maybe we can go see something more often. How'd you like getting to meet my friends?"

"Your friends are very nice. I hope we can spend more time with them, Elizabeth especially. Maybe we can all get lunch together sometime?"

The PA nodded from where he stood supporting Brandon with an arm. The two were waiting outside the bathrooms where Elizabeth, Blonde Sarah, and Tucker would be coming out shortly.

"I'm glad you like them. I was honestly worried you'd dislike Tucker right off the bat, but it seems he was on his best behavior today."

"Oh yeah. He's the one that makes the jokes that are sometimes not very funny, right?"

"He has particular brands of humor. Self-deprecating, offensive, or Spongebob-related. There's nothing else. Well, he does like to quote memes."

"What's a meme?"

"I'll show you. It's easier than explaining."

He whipped out his phone with one hand, unlocking it and pulling up a few images saved to his phone. A solid minute of scrolling later Brandon merely looked at him in confusion.

"I don't understand some of these. Why is the one with Spongebob looking like a chicken just say the same thing twice, and why does the second line have the letters randomly capitalized? Also why are there so many ones about death? Are you okay?"

"I'm fine. Those are all memes Tucker sent me."

"Is he okay?"

"I told you he's a special guy, didn't I? Dark humor is his favorite. Sometimes it means the memes he looks at are also highly controversial much like some of the things he says from time to time."

"Okay. Well, he didn't say anything I would've been upset with tonight. He mostly talked with Elizabeth since I was too busy talking to Sarah. I had no idea she had a disability too," the older boy confessed. "You can't tell by looking at her."

"No, you can't. But if you hung out with her more you might notice how she avoids the stairs, fried foods, and conditions that would make one of her many allergies go crazy. Once we were walking to class in the rain and by the time we got there she was covered in hives. She's not fragile by any means, and she definitely doesn't let several shots a week or her many medications get in the way of her having a good time. She works with students with physical disabilities doing adaptive exercise," Keith added just as Tucker joined them. "We've been in the same classes since sophomore year. She's been dying to meet you since I got the job, honestly."

"It was very nice to meet her. You and Elizabeth too," Brandon said to Tucker just as the two girls exited the bathroom.

Tucker glanced at him awkwardly from where he stood next to Keith. Talking wasn't his forte.

"Likewise." He finally settled with.

Now that everyone was back together, the five students began talking about the movie as they left. After reaching the other end of the quad Sarah took off, telling everyone she had a great time and to have a good night as she did so.

The remaining four started walking once again. The chatter started back up, but a few seconds in Keith felt the telltale tug on his shoulder.

Deadweight followed.

He landed hard on his knee, his upper body keeping Brandon's limp form from crashing to the ground. From his periphery he noticed Elizabeth's eyes widen while Tucker smoothed his features to feign disinterest. Keith ignored both reactions in favor of quickly letting his Person's knees rest on the ground before expertly positioning him against his side in one languid motion.

"Elizabeth, can you start a timer?"

She responded with a quick "yes" before starting one and adding roughly five seconds to it. At the same time he glanced at his watch before focusing on the fluttering eyes of the boy below him.

This episode was fairly short. Elizabeth's timer had only counted thirty seconds when Brandon truly stirred, mouth forming the usual slurred questions he often asked upon becoming aware of his environment again.

"Why am I on the ground?"

"You had a fall, but you're fine."

"I want to get up."

"Let's wait here for another couple minutes," Keith suggested instead. At the same time he felt Brandon struggling, to which the PA gently counteracted by wrapping a friendly arm around his shoulders.

"I want to get up," Brandon repeated a bit louder this time. However, when he looked up he noticed the patiently standing forms of Elizabeth and Tucker. This seemed to cause him to sober up. Pink dusted his cheeks as he pulled his phone out of his pocket. "Never mind. Did I land on my broken arm? It doesn't feel like I did."

"Your arm never touched the ground."

"Great. What was the time and exactly how long?"

The PA rattled off the time and Elizabeth told him how many seconds it lasted. Brandon thanked both of them as he added the information to his fall tracking journal. A couple of minutes of silence passed before Brandon coughed, shouldering Keith's arm off of him.

"We can probably get going now. Waiting for the full five minutes doesn't seem necessary."

Keith raised an eyebrow. "Are you sure? It's only been two minutes since you technically came to."

"We don't mind waiting." Elizabeth piped in at her boyfriend's question. "Right, Tucker?"

"Yeah."

Shaking his head, the black-haired boy instructed Keith to let him stand up.

"I'm fine. It wasn't that long of an episode so the chance of having another one so soon afterward isn't very high. That and we need to get home soon before my mother has a heart attack," he added while pointing at Keith's watch. "I'm already going to be getting into bed later than usual as it is. Might as well hurry up; I don't want to lose even more sleep."

"Okay."

Slipping his arm back underneath Brandon's armpit, the four of them continued walking for another five or so minutes until Tucker started veering towards the right.

"I'll see you later," Tucker waved as he headed in the direction of his apartment. "It was nice meeting you, Brandon. Hope to see you again."

"Me too," was the polite response.

"Have a nice night!" Elizabeth shouted at him before

turning back to the others with a smile. "I should honestly break off here too."

Keith sadly agreed. As much as he'd like to spend more time with Elizabeth it made more sense for her to go home rather than escorting them back to the other side of campus.

"Yeah, your dorm is in the opposite direction of the house. Text me when you get back?"

"Of course." She turned to Brandon with bright eyes. "I'm so happy I got to meet you! We should hang out again sometime. Maybe I can go to one of your performances you said were coming up this November, or we can meet up for dinner? Either way I hope to see you again soon."

Brandon let himself smile fully, which he hated doing since he'd acquired a few scratches on his face during the fall. He looked terrible in his (and his mother's) opinion. He only drew more attention to them when he smiled.

"Me too! I'll try to talk to my mother about maybe inviting you over for dinner in the future. As long as she's there and as long as I am the one asking to have you over it shouldn't be too hard. You'd just have to make sure you stayed on the first floor."

"That wouldn't be a problem. It sounds like a plan, so I'll wait to hear back about it from Keith here."

With that Elizabeth met eyes with Keith in favor of a hug or kiss. It would have been a little awkward to try to hug him when he was in the middle of working and to kiss him still would have felt weird with Brandon basically attached at his hip.

"Talk to you later tonight, okay? But remember we'll have to make it a quick conversation since my parents are picking me up on the way to visit a relative upstate. They'll be driving through at like seven in the morning so I need all the sleep I can get."

"I know."

"Good. I love you, sweetie. Bye!"

"I love you too. Bye!"

He waved goodbye as she spun around and started down the sidewalk. His eyes could make out her getting headphones out from her pocket she got a bit further away.

"You ready to keep going?" Brandon suddenly asked.

"Oh. Sorry about that. I'm ready to go," he promised while following his person's lead.

They managed to make it two more blocks before the older of the two let out a long breath. At first Keith was wondering if it was because he was switching sides he was escorting Brandon on too often. Then he began wondering if he wasn't doing it often enough, and Brandon trying to drop a hint.

What if now that all my friends are gone he's going to tell me he didn't like them as much as he let on earlier? What if something they said after the movie offended him? Maybe he's angry or embarrassed Elizabeth and Tucker saw him have an episode? No, he knows they've seen their fair share of similar health emergencies before. I don't think that'd bother him too much. Unless he doesn't care for them, and—

"I'm a little jealous of you."

That stopped Keith's thoughts in their tracks. All he could do with reply dumbly.

"Huh?"

"You have so many friends. The ones I met today were only a few, right? And Elizabeth seems like an amazing girlfriend. I can't believe you two have been together for so long."

"I got lucky," was his truthful retort. "She is the first person I ever dated and the only person I ever want to date."

"You two seem perfect for each other."

"In a way I guess we are. We're different in a lot of ways, but because of that we meld pretty well together."

"Oh? Like how?"

"Well, she's more knowledgeable about computers and

STEM stuff for starters. I know more about the arts, biology, sports, and general household stuff. She's more outgoing and likes to try new things while I stick to myself or only shine in my friend group; however, I work a lot of customer service jobs and want to go into a field where I work hands-on with others in a health setting. She would prefer to remain working behind a desk and create things in private. She's the positive one while I'm more pessimistic. I prefer to get things done right away, but she procrastinates. Somehow we work," he finished proudly.

Brandon seemed surprised at that information.

"You guys share so many interests I never imagined you'd be so different personality-wise. How do you not get into fights?"

"We get into disagreements every now and then. Sometimes her procrastination gets on my nerves, and sometimes my busy schedule or pessimism makes her upset. The difference is with us is that we work them out rather quickly. We're honest with each other. Both of us would much rather talk things out right away than let a situation fester until it gets worse, which has led to us getting through many hardships."

"That's pretty remarkable. A lot of people our age seem to prefer breaking up when things get tough. Heck, half the time people don't even date to date. I overhear people in class saying they're looking for casual dating or a friend with benefits sort of thing."

"I don't really get that. I could never date someone and not seek a committed long term relationship. To me dating is a way of finding 'the one', and if two people love each other there is nothing they can't work out. But that's just me. If people find others that want what they want who am I to judge?"

"I guess. I wish my parents had a relationship like yours though," he admitted. The words coming from his mouth were bitter like he'd just taken a bite of dark chocolate. "I can't remember them being happy together ever since I was a kid. My father took me being disabled so well from what I can remember, but from what he's told me my mother drew into herself. She hasn't been the same since."

"I'm sorry."

"There's no need to apologize. It's my fault, y' know? She raised my two older sisters well enough, although one did fly the coop as soon as she turned eighteen… Anyway, my diagnosis is what probably ruined my parent's marriage and caused my mother to become so high-strung. She worries about me more than she does herself."

No she doesn't. How can you not see that?

"If I had been born normal, then they would have been able to move on with their lives. Instead they have to make everything revolve around me because I can't take care of myself."

Wrong. You can take care of yourself; you've just never been allowed to. You've never been shown how.

"I'm just a burden. Sometimes I think they would be better off without me around."

"Stop that."

Keith had heard enough. He slowed them down right there in the middle of the sidewalk, a streetlight giving them just enough light to make out each other's faces. A few students were walking past them, but they either had earbuds in or were too busy talking to their friends to pay any attention to them.

"Don't ever think that," the PA continued with shaking hands. Whether they were shaking due to fury or sadness was anyone's guess. All he knew was they'd grown too close in the past few weeks for him to let Brandon berate himself any longer. "You are not a burden. Whatever stress your parents are dealing with doesn't stem from you; they are the ones who choose how to deal with your diagnosis and day to day routine. You obviously haven't been given a choice on how your own life operates, right? Then how do you know that the way you live now is the best possible outcome?"

"Because I can't function by myself. Without a PA I can't even go to the bathroom."

"Am I in there holding your hand while you pee? No. Am I in there while you shower in the bathtub? No."

"But I can't even stand up safely without your help!"

"Yes, you can!"

To show his point Keith twisted his arm out from underneath Brandon's good elbow. For a moment his Person looked like he was about to scream, but then he stopped himself.

"This… isn't safe."

"Why?"

"Because I could fall and hurt myself."

"Maybe, but you *can* stand up. You *can* go to the bathroom, shower, cook, and sleep on your own. Just because you have unpredictable falls doesn't mean you have to live your life afraid of doing even the simplest of things. People with epilepsy, who have seizures that sometimes can't be tracked, usually don't live this sheltered of lives and they have a higher risk of injury that someone with your condition. Same with people with a deadly case of anemia, which is more similar to your condition anyhow."

Taking a deep breath, Keith resumed their arrangement from earlier. After a brief pause they began walking again.

"I'm sorry for doing that," the younger stated after a couple of steps. "I just don't want you to think your disability is the source of all your problems. You're jealous of my friends and my relationship when you could have more people in your life too. The only reason you don't is that when you're not in class you're at home, and the fact that you can't do anything without asking your mom for permission. At twenty-five doesn't that seem a little odd?"

Somewhere Will is thinking about telling me "I told you

so".

"For you it may be, but this is how it has always been. My mother is selfless enough to do everything for me so I don't have to worry about hiring PAs or applying for my state funding."

"But you could do that. Someone as smart as you could do it easily."

"Maybe."

"And your mother wouldn't have to feel 'burdened' as you put it by taking care of all of this for you."

"This is how she wants it."

"So you're saying she wants to run every aspect of your life? Then why do you think it's your fault she has to take care of you over herself?"

"Because I'm her child. She probably feels obligated to take care of me because she loves me."

Keith bit back a hard sigh. "There's a difference between unconditional love and absolute tyranny. With the way she treats you it's hard to believe she does things the way she does simply because she's worried about injury prevention. Listening to her yell at you while you play the violin, seeing the bruises on your knees because she makes you crawl up and down the stairs, and trying not to say anything when she nitpicks everything you wear and everything you do is hard. She's not treating you right for someone your age. She's not treating you right for being her son."

"She loves me," Brandon retorted, an edge to his voice. "Just because your family operates differently doesn't mean how she shows her love is wrong."

"I'm not doubting her love for you."

"Yes, you are."

"Okay, maybe I am, but maybe it's because she views love differently. She already told me how she grew up domineered by her immediate family. Maybe that has to do with how she treats you and Larry."

As the older between them let out a quiet huff at that, the duo crossed the street. Once they were on the other side they both reminded themselves to hurry the conversation up. The house was barely a block away, and they each knew to discuss Jacqueline in the house with such thin walls was a terrible idea.

"My uncle was pretty cruel to her when she was younger. Before he died even as an adult he didn't respect her. He'd told her not to go to college after high school because being a religious man he believed women were to stay at home while the men worked to support them. She didn't want to do that, so he disowned her. It didn't help that after she met my father his family ended up being pretty crappy people too. They didn't like her. That meant she only had my father for the longest time."

"I get that might have been hard," Keith replied as they reached the driveway. He lowered his voice as they walked up it. "But that's not an excuse for her to treat you and your dad like how they treated her."

Brandon's voice was a whisper as he paused at the door. "You're right."

"I am?"

"You are, but knowing that doesn't change anything. She won't change. I'm not about to risk our relationship by challenging her when she runs every aspect of my life. I can't even get a job; she pays for everything for me. My food, my clothes, my computer, my books, and even upkeep on my violin. Everything."

"The funding you get from the state—"

"That's not enough to support me. All I'd be able to afford would be a crappy apartment and off-brand food. No normal person can live like that."

That struck a nerve.

"You've never been poor, have you?" The PA questioned, humorless. "Or even lower middle class?"

"What are you talking about? Of course not."

"Brandon, there were times growing up where my parents couldn't afford food, the water bill, the electricity bill, or the gas bill. Okay, we usually had at least bread or soup in the house so we could bring something to school and have something at home to eat for dinner, but I remember when eating PB and Js for supper were a blessing. Sometimes hot dogs or ramen were the only things we had to eat each day. My dad would skip meals some days despite working sixty hours a week. Some days my mom would eat ketchup on crackers for a meal."

"That's disgusting…"

Keith rolled his eyes. Some people had no idea what it was like to struggle. They had no idea what sort of things could be taken for granted, like a full fridge or a balanced diet. Or not having to flush a toilet by pouring a gallon of water down it.

"No, it's called living. She would go to the food pantry every month we were allowed to get the bare minimum of what we needed to survive. Heck, my little sister and I's school supplies were from Salvation Army growing up. There were weeks we had to heat water with a pot on an electric stove because we had no hot water to take a shower with since the gas bill ended up being the bill we skipped that month. I washed my hair in the sink with cold water every other day to make sure the water bill wasn't too high."

"That's terrible. Why would your parents put you in that situation?"

"Shit happens sometimes, Brandon. Life isn't all full-course home-cooked dinners at home. God, even when my parents did start making better money in high school there were times I ate fast food for over half my meals because they were too busy to go shopping."

"Ew."

"What, you don't think you could live like that even if it meant being free? It wouldn't even be as bad for you.

You might have to live with other people to afford rent, but you can find places to live here for three-hundred dollars a month. With three-hundred fifty dollars left you can still afford food, clothes, and whatever else you need. PAs would be provided by the state like they are now."

"I wouldn't have full coverage like I do now," he argued back.

"Do you even need full coverage? Once you're in bed the risk of falling out of bed while sleeping is almost nonexistent. The doctor's said so themselves. You even said during training it hasn't happened in years. Or if you're going to be in bed you could have someone on call, but not actively working. Maybe even danger-proofing your environment would be a better alternative to what you do now. There are days where you don't even have an episode, right?"

"Yeah, but there are days I have two or three."

"I understand that, but—"

"What do you expect me to do? Chance not having a PA around hoping it doesn't go wrong until one time it does and I end up in the hospital, or worse?"

"A fall from your bed's height won't kill you, Brandon. At least it's highly unlikely."

"My arm begs to differ."

"You would be in bed during the times without a PA. Surely even if you rolled off somehow there would be a way to make the floor safe."

"So you say. Nowhere is safe for me to just walk around."

"I'm sure there are creative ways around this," he pleaded.

"You can't say that when you're not the one here with the disability," Brandon shot back. Despite getting worked up he was still able to keep his voice down enough not to alert anyone inside the house of their presence.

Keith sighed. Maybe he was going about this all wrong.

How do I convince him that I'm not telling him how to live his life, but that I'm trying to show him the better options available to him? Ugh. Either way I'll just sound like a know-it-all or a dick. I thought having a work background in the field and studying the subject would give my opinions some merit. Maybe that was just wishful thinking.

"I'm not disabled," he finally responded after thinking his words over in his head. "Do able-bodied doctors or other medical professionals have the right to preach to you even though they don't have your disability?"

"They're certified or have studied for years; you're not like them. You're just a PA."

Keith schooled his features so he didn't look as upset as he suddenly became.

"You're just a PA."

The sentence replayed itself several times in his head. Why did it hurt so much to hear? It was the truth. He was nothing more than a personal assistant.

"You're right. I am just a PA as you so eloquently put it. However," some of his self-confidence won out over the bigger, more self-deprecating part of himself, "I've worked with enough people our age who have all sorts of disabilities to be empathetic of your situation as well as think outside of the box based on what others with a similar disability have. For instance, Will has his own apartment, found and hired his own PAs, and works in sports management in New Jersey. The state's funding along with his salary pays for everything and then some. His girlfriend works from home and lives with a friend who helps her three times a day in exchange for free rent. Maybe you could figure out something similar?

"Don't act like you know the solution to everything. How do you know what's good for me?"

Despite the seriousness of the conversation it took every ounce of Keith's willpower not to say: "That's my opinion!"

Ah, Vines. Keith would have to introduce those to Brandon too.

Focus, Keith.

"I'm not trying to say I know what's best for you. I hope that isn't what I'm coming off as doing. I just," he paused, "I just want you to know there are alternatives that have been shown to work. I don't want you to be scared of change."

"I'm not scared."

"Then if you know things need to change around here, then why aren't you trying to change them if you're not afraid?"

Brandon stood there silent. For a long moment he looked like he had something to say, but ultimately he shook his head and began unlocking the door.

"We can talk about this later," was all the older boy said after dragging him inside with him. Even after pretending to be back in the good spirits they were in directly after the movie in front of Jacqueline, who was sitting in the kitchen waiting for them to come home so she could grill them on the details of their night before demanding they hurry to bed, they spoke to each other minimally.

I screwed up, Keith bemoaned as he helped his Person get ready for bed. The two males were silent throughout nearly the entire process. It only made Keith feel more guilty. *I shouldn't have butted in. He's used to living his life a certain way; who am I to say it should change after over a decade of it working for him? It's not like I'm any more to him than a guy he met just a couple months ago. I'm just one of his PAs.*

You're his friend though too, aren't you? Another part of him questioned.

Y— He stopped himself, unsure. *I thought I was. I care about what happens to him. I don't want him to be in pain or get yelled at by his mom. I want him to be happy. But he's not happy here, and he doesn't want me to help him change how things are.*

He's scared.

I know that.

If you had a mother like Jacqueline, wouldn't you be hesitant to try her patience?

If I had a mother like Jacqueline I would have tried to seek legal help before it got this bad.

So you say. The situation is similar to Stockholm syndrome; you wouldn't have any clue things were wrong until you accepted them as normal.

Even so she's not fit to be a mother when she's as prejudiced a person as a person could be. And the fact that she'd harm and threaten her child's personal assistants without even worrying about the repercussions because she's such a good manipulator…

Elijah's anguished ramblings about getting out of the house came to mind. The follow-up memory of his suggestion of breaking the contract suddenly seemed all the more tempting; however, if he stopped being Brandon's PA, then he would be doing exactly what Elijah had done. He would be betraying Brandon.

It's not like he could ask Elijah what he'd found out or didn't find in the span of a day or two to make him leave so fast. Ask again, that is. The blue-haired young adult still hadn't answered his texts from the last three weeks.

Maybe Elijah is refusing to talk to me, but that doesn't mean I can't figure out how to break the contract myself.

But if he started looking into a way of getting out of the contract, then would that make him a bad person? If he left he would be leaving Brandon behind. Could he do that with an empty conscience?

Could he do it at all?

As he asked himself these questions he got ready for bed. While switching into his night boxers he finally realized why his knee felt like it was still stinging after falling so long ago. On the knee he'd landed hard on was a layer of blood where he'd scraped the skin off.

Not again, he thought. It was with a sigh he made the routine of washing out the injury with a wet washcloth and peroxide take barely a minute, exhaustion pulling at his frame. He all but slapped a Band-Aid over the inch and a half wide by two inches scrape. The wound would scab up ugly, he knew. He'd caused himself similar injury falling off his bike or scooter multiple times as a kid. Honestly, though he should have stopped himself from going down the largest hill in the area on a bike with faulty breaks or a scooter with no breaks at all. Somehow he'd thought he could land safely in a grassy ditch each time, yet each time he misjudged the distance and gone sailing into the gravel instead.

Maybe listening to Elizabeth and hoping for the best was a mistake. Back then, when he'd been less the pessimist he was currently, and especially now.

CHAPTER FOURTEEN

"You've been sitting there staring at your sheet music for five minutes. Stop wasting our time and play the damn instrument, Brandon! Can or not you can still try!"

Keith's hands shook as he scrubbed the tile floor of the bathroom. He was nearly done with his usually scheduled Saturday morning house cleaning. Without Elijah there he thought he'd spend half his Saturday cleaning the entire house, but thankfully Larry took time to drive down for the weekend and do Elijah's tasks for him. All that was left for Keith himself to do was scrub the second floor of the house as well as the staircase and he would be free to spend the day as he wished.

"You call that an andante?" The same voice started up again just seconds later. "Slow the hell down or else the pianist is going to fall behind. Seriously, you'd think you just learned how to play the violin. Your father has never touched that damn instrument in his life and I bet he could still play this piece better than you. Did we waste our money putting you through all those music lessons? How you got through the last few years in that quartet of yours playing like this I have no idea. Those students must be tone-deaf."

"Mother, please—"

"Don't give me your excuses!" There was the sound of a slap, and then small sniffles coming through the air vent of the bathroom. "You have one minute to calm down before I add an extra hour onto your practice time today."

Same old, same old, the guilt slammed down on Keith like a hammer to an anvil. It was sharp at first, but after a couple of seconds it dulled down to a mere ache. *Remember what Brandon said about not getting involved? He literally asked for this. If I interfere now, then we'll both get it worse.*

Not that Jacqueline had ever raised her hand to the PA. No, her raising her voice and lashing him with her harsh words hurt enough. She knew how to manipulate him mentally. There was no need for her to physically harm him.

For the past two hours the house was full of her critical voice. The entire time the part-time PA cleaned everybody's room he'd been forced to listen to his boss's grating insults assault his ears as well as her son and husband's.

She had started by yelling at Larry about him not knowing how to mow the lawn in the right fashion the first thing in the morning, effectively waking Keith up at half-past seven. After that she let him know exactly how stupid the bushes in front of the house looked once he'd finished trimming them. She multitasked by acting as her son's music teacher despite the fact she knew nothing about how to play the violin. She knew some of the musical terms, sure, but not enough to warrant her drill sergeant treatment of him all before nine in the morning.

The PA nearly flinched as the woman's voice rose once again after having been lowered for a few minutes.

Self-conscious thoughts appeared in his head, popping up like malevolent weeds in his mind's garden.

Tell her to stop. What are you, a coward?

Maybe he was. How could he tell his boss, a psychotic woman who held his life in the form of his signature in her hands, to shut her damn mouth? Brandon didn't want him to say anything that could upset his mother.

She's hurting him. You can do something about it.

Could he though? Who was he to play hero when he couldn't even stand up for himself? Who was he to think he would be his Person's hero by helping him when help wasn't asked for or even wanted?

He's in a living Hell of his mother's making. When you're trapped in that Hell your entire life it's hard to imagine asking for help, let alone thinking you're someone who deserves it. It's almost funny. Hell and help are only a single letter apart. Maybe that's why being a personal assistant is so hard. All you do is help people, and now look where it has brought you? Into Brandon's personal Hell.

"Run through that part again starting at the change in key signature! You're not stopping until you get it right. For every sharp you miss I'm adding a minute of practice time to every day this week."

Keith had to stop himself from plugging his ears. The woman was downstairs, yet her voice was so loud and carried so far it felt like it was blasting out of the vent by his head. He hated it. Honestly, he found himself hating all loud noises now; they scared him.

When did he start to feel scared of them again? Sure he'd never been pleased by the sheer level of noise fireworks produced or the just a tad bit too loud volume in a movie theatre, but it hadn't caused his heart to race in fear. Why was it only as of late that a sudden crash or an angered voice made him freeze in terror if only for a second?

He shook his head, desperately trying to ignore the arguing voices coming from downstairs. All he needed to do was get through the last ten minutes of cleaning and he had his entire Saturday (minus him having to cook dinner) to goof off and have fun. Jared and Tucker already gave him the go-ahead to spend what time he could at their apartment.

This means I don't need to stay in this God awful house any longer than it takes me to finish wiping the stairs, he thought positively.

Every part of him was dying to spend almost the entire day doing what he wanted regardless of how productive it was. He'd worked hard the last week; he deserved a day where he could read fanfiction or watch anime for no other reason than personal enjoyment. While there was a part of him that missed Elizabeth he knew she'd be back late the next night, so the ache in his chest was nothing more than a small thrum.

Sooner rather than later Keith was wordlessly running the cleaning equipment down to the basement. Just one more trip to put all the dirty rags in the washing machine and he'd be a free man. He already knew exactly which fandom he'd read once he got to Tucker and Jared's.

I haven't caught up on this fandom in months. I'll have to filter out so much smut after the character interaction in the latest season. It's going to be a pain, but—

"Oh, Keith. There you are. I thought I heard you coming up and down the stairs, but I wasn't sure."

His thoughts came to a halt as Jacqueline walked through the dining room to meet him in the kitchen. Her tone was light and suspiciously annoyance-free despite the amount of yelling that had been escaping her throat the past few hours.

"I know you aren't supposed to work until late dinner tonight, but I thought I'd ask if you wanted to watch Brandon this afternoon or perhaps this evening? I'm getting a headache. It'd be safer for you to watch over him. I'll have Larry take over if I must, but you're a much more reliable PA."

"I can't," he replied. "I already made plans for today. Sorry."

This is where one would expect an employer to understand his or her employee. Prior commitments had been made, therefore he couldn't work.

Unfortunately, his employer didn't care much about

that.

"Plans? What plans could you have possibly made that are more important than caring for my son?"

Keith looked away, uneasy. Why should he have to defend himself? "I already told some friends I would spend most of the day with them. There's also some reading I want to get done as well as shows I want to watch; I can't focus on doing either of those activities if I'm working."

The coldness that frosted over Jacqueline's demeanor almost made him take a half-step back. As it was he didn't think he could move at all. Her eyes had thrown daggers pinning him into place.

"That's a bit selfish, don't you think? I'd be willing to pay you extra hours if you were to reconsider. Larry is a lousy PA. I wouldn't be able to let you watch your shows, but reading should be fine. Brandon has a lot of practice to get done so all you'd have to do is sit next to him while he plays.

"I really can't."

She threw the metaphorical ball back into his court again.

"Can't, or don't want to?"

"I—"

"You know what? Forget it," she spat while flipping her hand in the air. The gesture followed into a shooing motion. "You spend time with your friends. I'll sit in the living room nursing a migraine while you have fun; useless people are all that surround me nowadays anyway."

She turned around to leave, but a moment later she turned around to face him once more.

"I forgot. Yesterday I brought some people over to look at the house and when we walked upstairs we smelled something disgusting. I nearly gagged, which looked bad for my guests. I want to remind you it is in the contact that you must do your laundry every fourteen days. While I do not know if it is you or Thomas making the upstairs stink, I thought a reminder would do you good. You work out all the time, correct? Maybe you should be washing your workout clothes daily. I don't want trouble selling the house because of laziness."

With that she stormed away. As she left Keith could only feel a sick feeling churn in his gut. It had been uncomfortable before, but now it physically pained him.

He hurried upstairs, throwing up the leftover pizza he'd eaten for breakfast.

Was that necessary? The upstairs smells like the cleaner I use almost constantly! There's no way she's telling me I smell when I keep all my dirty clothes in the closed closet and wash them every other week like I'm supposed to be. And what she said about me not taking another extra shift...

Am I really that useless of a PA? He wondered as his entire body trembled. It was slow work washing his mouth out and flushing his breakfast down the toilet. *Why is it no matter how much I help out she says stuff like that? It's not like I don't care. I do! I just wanted some time for myself. I've already worked an extra ten hours this week. Am I really that bad of a person because I want some time to myself?*

The answer was quiet, but unwavering.

I'm not. I cut down my two days at the restaurant a week to one for Jacqueline. I shouldn't have even had to do that much. I told myself weeks ago I'd stop letting her guilt me into stuff, but I've caved in multiple times since then. I will not let her have her way this time.

Quickly grabbing his backpack, which had been packed before doing his cleaning, he made sure his keys were in his pocket before heading downstairs. He was leaving the house regardless if his boss was going to be petty with him later on.

And then *it* happened. The final straw.

Just as Keith was making his way around the bend at

the bottom of the stairs Jacqueline began wailing in on her son once more. She couldn't see the PA since her back was to him, but Brandon's wide eyes landed on Keith's narrowed ones almost pleadingly; however, it was obvious by the look on his face that he was pleading for Keith to ignore them once again. It didn't matter that the elder male looked like he was on the verge of being sent into an episode. He wanted his PA to go.

As shameful it would be to admit later, Keith almost did leave. He knew getting involved at that moment would end with both of them being yelled at, Keith to mind his own business and Brandon to stop being such a pansy as Jacqueline liked to put it.

He would have turned around without a second thought if not for his eyes tracking the movement of Jacqueline's hands.

"Why are you staring off into space? Are you even listening to me?"

At Brandon's terrified stare, which seemed to go straight through his mother, Jacqueline raised her arm in anger.

"Pay attention, Brandon!"

"I—"

His attempts at speaking during what seemed to be the beginnings of a minor episode were cut off as his mother roughly grabbed him by his wavy black hair. In half a second she was pulling him out of his chair, permafrost in her eyes as she put her face in her son's.

"Enjoy your episode you useless shit."

Time slowed down.

Reality segmented, because there was no way she had actually said that, right?

Something in Keith snapped. It could have been his patience or his sanity; either way, he still snapped.

"W-what are you doing to him?" He started, stuttering with emotion before fragile confidence took over. "What is wrong with you?"

It seemed Jacqueline had no idea he was there. The moment he hurled the questions at her she immediately released Brandon, turning around to look at him in shock.

She opened her mouth to say something that could only be a load of bull, but Keith beat her to it.

"This isn't right. I am tired of this, do you hear me? The screaming, the way you constantly put Brandon down—and now you're actively trying to make him pass out? Do you hate him that much?"

He wasn't sure where this was coming from, but it felt good to get off his chest.

"No mother should ever treat her kid that way. This needs to stop."

"How dare you!" Her reactionary response came with a hand to the chest and fake tears. "I love my son. It's not up to you on how I discipline him."

"He's catatonic!"

Keith gestured to his Person wildly. He sat limp against the back of the chair with his head tilted to the side. His gaze was fixed far ahead, evidence of a mind that wasn't all there.

"Brandon! Oh, honey, are you okay?" She ran to his side like she hadn't realized he was out of it.

"What the hell are you playing at?" His voice was strained. Disbelief permeated every word, his mind trying to make sense of Jacqueline's ever-changing behavior. Truth be told it would be easier to justify her behavior if she was bipolar; however, something told him she was just a garbage human being who was putting on a show. "You are the one that made him like this."

She looked over her shoulder, eyes glinting with malice.

"That's quite an accusation to make with no proof."

"You literally just said—"

"This is my house, Keith, and this is my family.

Brandon loves me, and I love him. We'd never hurt each other." She stressed while patting Brandon's shoulder comfortingly. The boy had still yet to respond. "Larry is downstairs in the basement. You're the only one who heard me. Now, in a court of law, who would a judge believe? You, or Brandon and I?"

"Court of law? Why would I bring you to court?"

"You wouldn't because that would be a very costly thing to do during your senior year when you already are barely scraping by. However, if you were to make more ignorant claims like that again, then I would have to recognize it as slander against my family. You know what the contract says about slander, don't you?"

The PA felt something gross crawling across his skin.

"You wouldn't seriously drag me to court over me saying something you didn't like hearing."

He made sure not to phrase it as a question; he was scared of the answer.

She smiled. "Perhaps I would. I've brought many PAs to court because they couldn't just do what they were told. You signed the contract, Keith, therefore using any language I might deem threatening warrants me taking you to court. I don't want to have to do that though. It would cause Brandon a lot of unnecessary stress. It also costs me my time, because I wouldn't be able to allow you to work during a court case."

Panic started to build in Keith's mind. He was sure Jacqueline could see it too because he wasn't very good at hiding such an overwhelming feeling.

"You're hurting him," he finally said.

"And how is that?"

Her snarky response was met with an honest answer.

"You made him crawl around the house on his hands and feet. His knees were brown and yellow thanks to you. And just a little bit ago I heard you slap him. He was crying. You're..."

"*Disciplining him.* And for the record there was no way I could have prevented him from hurting his knees. It's for his own safety that he must crawl when no one is around to escort him. Maybe if you cared enough to volunteer more often, then he wouldn't have hurt himself. Maybe you're the one hurting him."

"No, I'm not! You could have at least got him some knee or hand-pads."

"He never asked. I assumed it was a non-issue."

"You yell at him and belittle him constantly!"

"He screws up a lot. It's his own fault I have to raise my voice. Belittling him? That's a matter of perspective," she waved away. "How I raise my child in my own home has nothing to do with you."

"Yes it does, because this is my home too. I may not own it, but the contract states the PAs living here have just as much right to the entire space as the members of the Thompson family living in it. I can't work here any longer if you are going to continue hurting Brandon, or yelling at him and Larry. This isn't a proper work environment for any PA, or a proper living environment for any person. It's no wonder Elijah quit."

That appeared to royally piss her off.

"You're saying these conditions aren't good enough for you?" She shouted, her volume rising with each sentence. "You get free food and living space. You get free laundry access, internet, and TV. You get a nice bed to sleep in, and great Wi-Fi. On top of all of it you still get paid. This is way better than any deal you could have gotten living in the dorms! Are you that greedy?"

"Can you please stop screaming?"

His voice was a decibel away from screaming himself, which was stark in contrast to the near silence that followed.

Suddenly, footsteps sounded from the basement.

"Honey?" Larry's call echoed down the stairs as he

descended them. When he entered the living room he quickly took in the situation: Brandon barely starting to become conscious again, Jacqueline looking at Keith more furious than he'd seen her in weeks, and Keith looking more shaken up than ever. "What's going on?"

"Oh, Larry," Jacqueline started while throwing herself at him. He caught her with a look of surprise before casting a worried glance at his son, who appeared to still be at risk of slipping out of his chair. "Keith overheard me saying something he didn't think was constructive criticism to Brandon and he just started yelling at me! Now he wants to quit. Apparently he can't stand working in these conditions any longer."

Keith couldn't believe what he was hearing.

"Constructive criticism?" He could feel his blood pressure rising. "How is telling your son 'enjoy your episode, you useless shit' anything remotely close to that? Especially after you caused it in the first place!"

"Now, Keith, why don't we all sit down and talk about this like reasonable people?"

"Larry, what is wrong with you? How can you just disregard the fact that your wife is abusing your son as well as yourself?"

The man dared to be confused.

"Her abuse me? She's never laid a hand on me in her life."

"There are far more kinds of abuse than merely physical, Larry. You can't be blind enough to not know it when you see it. And even if she hasn't been abusing you, we both know she's been hurting Brandon. If you truly don't see the harm she's doing to your son, then you're the worst father I know. Well, after one of my brother-in-law."

Just as the older man was about to reply, Brandon straightened up in his chair.

"What's happening?"

Without further prompting Jacqueline and Keith

competed to see who could talk over the other better. As they took turns accusing each other of various things, some true and many untrue, Larry merely watched in silence while Brandon slowly became more and more overwhelmed until he couldn't take it any longer.

"Stop!"

They stopped, the woman frowning as she did so.

Brandon turned to look at Keith, who hoped that this was the moment they'd both been waiting for. This was the moment that he'd finally stand up to his mother. This was the moment he'd take control over his own life, and end the mistreatment he had to deal with for over a decade.

And then reality crushed his rose-tinted outlook on life again.

"I'm not being abused, Keith. My mother loves me."

The PA blinked slowly, trying to rid himself of the image of Brandon saying such lies.

"No, she doesn't," he found himself arguing. "She can't. This is not how a mother should treat her child."

"Shut up!" Suddenly Brandon's face was twisted in a rage he'd never seen before. It was raw and ugly, and the spike in volume nearly made him flinch back in reaction to it. "You don't get to decide the truth. I love my mother— I would do anything for her, and she would do anything for me. She would never intentionally hurt me!"

"But she has! You're not stupid enough to lie about this, are you?"

"You're the stupid one trying to tear my mother and me apart. I hate you!"

Those words hit him like a physical blow. He recovered fairly fast, coming up with a retort despite the pain he could feel in his chest. This is what he got for standing up for what he thought was right? Hatred and false accusations?

"You had to have heard her before you were unresponsive," Keith accused at a much more reasonable volume. "You heard what she said. I know you did. Is that anything a parent should say to his or her child? Is that anything a decent person should say to any person?"

"That's it!"

Everyone turned to the source of the shout, which was the crazy woman who was the source of all of the problems in the first place.

Theatrical tears streaming down her face, much like the real ones starting down her son's face, she went over to her son and helped him stand up despite her "bad knee".

"I'm tired of listening to you blame everyone in my family of such vulgar things. You can have the house for all I care; we'll finish Brandon's schooling from home because this is the last setback I am willing to deal with this semester! Larry, take Brandon and start the car. We're leaving right now."

"Don't you think that's a little rash?"

He was met with a glare that could match a mad bull's. Like the pushover he was he nodded, carefully grabbed Brandon from his wife, and hobbled out of the room with him without another word.

"Are you seriously leaving right now?" Keith asked, disbelieving of the entire situation.

She shot him a glare through her "tears".

"Of course we are. After everything you've had to say, after how you've hurt our feelings—"

"Hurt your feelings? Since when did you care about how anyone in this house felt? Now you're saying me calling you out for hurting your son hurts your goddamn feelings when you crap on everyone here every single day?"

"I have no idea what incidences you're referring to. As it is there is no way I can be in the same house with you."

"Then I'll leave!"

"No, you signed a contract, remember? You get to live in this house until the end of May."

"Then let's just talk this over," he pleaded. "I—I don't

want you all to leave." He definitely did. "I just want the yelling to stop. And for you to stop hurting Brandon. And Larry."

"It's too late for that. You opened your mouth in a far less civil manner than the situation warranted, and now you'll face the consequences like an adult."

A harsh feeling Keith had never experienced before bubbled over. He was just so angry.

"Are you seriously telling me you'd rather pull Brandon out of school right before he gets his masters than just treat him like a human being? Is not screaming at him or touching him that impossible a task for you? Is it?"

As he spoke his boss took a step closer. In response he took a step back, eyes narrowing and shoulders hunched defensively. When she began reaching towards him, maybe under the appearance of calming him down, he jumped back.

"Don't touch me! I know what you did to Eli," he stated fearfully. "If you do anything to me don't think I won't call nine-one-one right away."

"Oh, I don't doubt that. You look like the type that would let his emotions get the better of him and make a foolish mistake like getting the authorities involved. However," she stated while darting forward and grabbing him by the wrist. She made sure to do it just hard enough for him not to be able to wrench his wrist from her grip yet not cause any bruising. "I won't harm you. Elijah was too scared to protect himself even if he did threaten to call DCFS on us, which I believe was all talk by the way. No. You might do something if I left evidence on you."

She grinned like she was so smart. Where her hand gripped him he felt like his skin was burning.

He wanted her to let go of him now. She had no right to grab him after he'd told her not to, but did she care? Of course not. The only person she cared about was herself.

"Injuries are such a pain to explain," she resumed while

not breaking eye contact with him. "No, I don't *need* to hurt you physically. I can tell you're scared enough just by fucking with your head instead. You're just a pussy like Larry, aren't you, Keith?"

"You're insane," he breathed after a sharp intake of air. His head suddenly felt light.

"This is all your fault," was Jacqueline's response as she let go of him. As she turned to leave the room she made sure to screw with him just a bit more for good measure. "You are the one that started this; not me. And here I thought you were a child of God. There must be a dark mark on your soul where the devil touched you for you to be such a cruel, hurtful person."

That was the last thing he heard before listening to her quickly put her shoes on and leave the house. A moment later he heard the telltale noise of their car pulling out of the driveway, and then nothing.

He stood there just standing for what felt like hours. After listening to his heartbeat slowly settle down everything that had just occurred finally started catching up with him. Before he knew it he was climbing back up the stairs and pulling out his phone as he threw himself onto his bed. He could feel panic grip him as he called Tucker, his throat closing up midway through the rings since he couldn't stop himself from crying.

He was so scared.

"Hello?" Tucker's monotone voice answered on the third ring.

Keith tried to steady himself, but it seemed just to make him more choked up.

"Hey, um, Tuck Tuck? Can you pick me up, please?"

"Why? I thought you were going to walk or take the bus?"

Of course he can't tell something is wrong, the PA thought exasperatedly. *He's never been great with people; even more so when strong emotions are involved. That makes this even more embarrassing on my part.*

"I— something happened with the Thompsons just now and I... They— everything that could go wrong sort of did."

"What does that mean? What did they do?"

"I saw Jacqueline do something terrible to Brandon," he said between hiccups. His heart thrummed painfully in his chest. "She— she induced him to lose consciousness on purpose, and she was grabbing him by his hair and I just couldn't stand there so I told her to stop and I lost it."

"Keith, I'll come to get you. Let me just—"

"Tucker, they flipped their shit and just took off and that was after screaming at me for trying to stop Jacqueline from hurting Brandon but it didn't matter because he hates me now and she threatened to take me to court because she thinks they would believe her and Brandon over me and now I'm freaking out and I just want to get out of this house. Please?"

After his rant he had to hold back a sob. His hand gripped the phone tightly despite everywhere else along his body trembling, waiting for Tucker's response.

"I'll be over there in ten," was the answer. "Let me just get my shoes on."

"Thank you. I'll be waiting outside."

"Okay."

Numb, Keith hung up on Tucker and pulled up Elizabeth's number. Ten minutes was long enough to tell her what happened and ask her what he should do, right?

CHAPTER FIFTEEN

As soon as they arrived at the apartment complex, Tucker not so discreetly told his brother to talk to Keith. Between the two brothers the elder was far better with people in general. The PA had immediately holed himself up in Jared's room with barely an uttered "hi" to the older brother upon entering; due to Jared having lent him his bed to rest on prior occasions, he didn't feel the need to ask.

"What happened?" Jared questioned Tucker after noticing his friend's appearance. "You took off pretty quick after his phone call. I paused our game while you were gone too, by the way."

"Thanks. I guess the psychos he works for finally made him snap, and they didn't take him speaking up too well. Can you maybe talk to him? He's pretty upset. I sort of tried talking to him in the car, but I don't know if I said anything right. You're better at comforting people."

The curly-haired boy smiled in response to his brother's praise. "Thanks, bro. I'm proud you tried. I know how awkward you get around crying people."

"I can't control it, okay?"

"I know, I know! Chill. I'll go talk to him now."

"Cool. Thanks."

After gently closing his laptop, Jared steeled himself before cautiously walking over to the propped open door of his room. The lights were off and the curtain was drawn.

"Hey, buddy. You okay in there?"

A groan answered him from underneath a blanket.

"Let me guess; you have a headache?"

"Yeah…"

"Do you want some Tylenol?"

"No. I hate pills. If it gets bad enough, then I'll take you up on it. Thank you though."

"Fair enough. Can I get you anything at all?"

"I could use some water, but I can get it myself in a minute."

"Nope!" Jared stated while running out of the doorway and into the kitchen. Within thirty seconds he was back in his room holding a cold glass of water out to Keith, who now sat up in bed holding the blanket around him like a shawl.

Keith glared at his friend with pink eyes. "You're not good at listening."

"Funny, that's what my last two ex-girlfriends told me. Now drink this before you make your headache worse from dehydration."

A sigh came from the bundled up figure. Once he'd grabbed the glass, drained half the contents of it, and propped it against one of the pillows in the corner of the bed he spoke again.

"Thanks, Jared."

"You're welcome. Can I sit?"

The PA let out a small laugh. "It's your bed."

"True, but you're using it right now. If you don't want me here, then all you have to do is tell me. I won't be upset or annoyed."

"Sit down," Keith instructed with an eye roll while patting the spot next to him. A moment later the two males were close enough that their knees were touching.

Jared grinned before mock cuddling up to Keith. "No homo, right?"

"All of the homo."

"Oh *yeah*," he said in a deep voice, causing both of them to laugh a little bit. The smile on Jared's face stayed for a few moments, while somewhere during the first few seconds of chuckling Keith's face fell. "Hey. Sorry for deflecting; I just thought I'd try to cheer you up before we talked about the heavy stuff. If you want to, that is."

"I want to, but after loading it all onto Elizabeth over the phone I think I need a little while. I feel horrible for doing that as it is. She's upset now because she's hours north of here and won't be back until tomorrow, and I'm here. She thinks she needs to be here because of what happened."

"That's really sweet, Keith. She knows you're hurting and wants to be here to comfort you. That's love."

"I know she loves me, but that's exactly why I feel bad for making her feel like she has to be here when she can't be. It's driving her crazy that she can't see me until tomorrow and it's my fault."

"I'm sure she's still happier that you told her instead of putting it off until she's back."

"Yeah, I guess."

They sat in silence for a couple of minutes. After about thirty seconds Jared began tapping his fingers against the headboard in a rhythmic pattern. Finally, once more than enough time had gone by without Keith attempting to reinitiate conversation, the owner of the room cleared his throat.

"Well, if you're sure you don't want to talk about what happened I'll leave you alone. I'll be at the kitchen table gaming with Tucker most of the day, so if you need anything just let one of us know. We're doing dinner with my family tonight though. They're wanting to go to get pizza if that's cool with you?"

"I… do I have to go?"

"Oh, no. Sorry. You don't have to go, but it might be a good idea to get everything that happened off your mind? Feel free to stay here. I'm sure we'll have plenty of leftovers. You can also help yourself to anything here. *Mi casa es su casa*, bro.”

Keith nodded, his heartwarming with gratitude the longer his friend went on.

“Thanks, Jared. It means a lot. Tell Tucker thanks again too; I really didn’t want to walk all the way here looking like the emotional wreck that I am. Knowing me I’d have started bawling all over again on the walk over like I did in the car with Tuck.”

“Ah, so that’s why he looked so out of place when he stepped in the door after you.”

“Yeah. He’s not very good at interacting with crying people,” he said with a small laugh.

“No he is not, but he did say he tried comforting you, which is a huge amount of effort on his part.”

“He told you he tried to comfort me, huh?”

“Yeah. Why?”

“He offered to spray the Thompson’s flower garden with weed killer to get revenge,” he admitted. “As much as Jacqueline deserves something to happen that would royally screw up her day, she’d probably just blame her husband and then become even more unbearable to be around after getting pissed off beyond belief. When I told Tuck this much he flat out offered to kill the entire family, and as much as the idea of murdering my boss is tempting Tuck would never survive in prison.”

“Nope. He’d be a bottom for sure, but not by choice.”

They shared a smile before Jared reached an arm around his friend. What started as a one-armed hug turned into a full-on embrace as Keith pulled the other in tightly. Jared returned the hug just as tight, no feelings of awkwardness present between the two. They were too good of friends to *not* be able to hug each other.

Okay, they secretly did feel a bit gay. But Keith was bisexual and Jared was mistaken for gay at least twice once a month due to his love of fashion, so in the end they weren’t all that concerned.

"It's going to be alright, man." The elder of the two stated once they pulled away. "It might not seem like it now, but it will be. You know working at that place wasn't good for you. You can crash here as long as you need to, and there are plenty of places to sublease if you—"

"Jared, I can't leave. I signed a contract, remember? I have to sleep there at least three nights a week no matter what. Regardless of that if the Thompson's are so done with me that they're seriously going to make Brandon finish his schooling from their own house, then I can stay in the house without them there until graduation. When they're not there I feel like I can breathe. I'm just worried Jacqueline was being dramatic."

"She is a very dramatic woman from what you've told me. Didn't she start crying during dinner one night because you forgot to place your drink on a coaster?"

"Yes. She started going on and on about the condensation staining the table, which would make the house harder to sell, and—whatever. I'm *terrified* I'm going to wake up tomorrow and they'll be back. I don't think I can face them again after what happened today."

"You're that scared to go back?"

"I guess I am."

The other boy hummed in thought. "That sounds like another word for help if I ever heard one."

"Maybe it is," Keith whispered back.

Jared opened his mouth, wanting to ask again if Keith was ready to talk about the incident, but he held back.

"That's a tomorrow morning problem. For now I think you should work on trying to nurse your headache, hydrate, eat some of our well-stocked snacks, or take a nap. Maybe talk to Elizabeth some more. Or call your parents. I know you might not feel up to talking to anyone about what happened now, but if there's anyone you should tell at some point it would be your mom and dad."

"I know. I've been thinking about lying down in the

dark and talking to my mom. I'll call her in a little while. If I talk about what happened I'm bound to break down again, and my head is already killing me. God, I'm such a loser."

He couldn't help the edge in his voice. Self-deprecation was common when it came to his friend group, yet even he knew Jared could tell his words weren't meant to be joking.

"You're not a loser," the engineer argued, suddenly very serious. "I think it's a ridiculous notion that men aren't allowed to cry without perceiving themselves as weak. Some people get stressed to a point where a chipped nail will make them burst into sobs, but a guy who has been living in a mental hellhole isn't allowed to have a day where he can just not care about how much of a pansy he is for crying? To heck with that. You're allowed to feel, Keith. You're allowed to cry."

Somewhere in the middle of his speech Keith's eyes threatened to fill with water again, but he held them back with a deep breath.

"All I've been doing is crying. I'm so done with it," he responded with a drained voice. His shoulders slumped in fatigue. "I feel like a complete wreck now, Jared. I've been getting more emotional than ever, having panic attacks because I can hear Jacqueline saying cruel things about Elijah, Thomas, and I from the basement where she thinks we can't hear her. Half the time when we eat together I can barely get any food down because the atmosphere at meals is so damn oppressive. I hear screaming from downstairs so often I can't even go to the bathroom without hearing it at max volume since the vents line up so that it just carries the sound right next to where I'm trying to take a crap. Some nights I lie there for an extra hour because Jacqueline is on the phone until two in the morning talking to Larry about how much she hates being in that house and how they need to get their hot tub at home working or something else. Sometimes," he hesitated, "when I'm walking home from class I spend way too long crossing the crosswalk."

"Why?"

He let out a bitter laugh.

"Because I wonder if getting hit by oncoming traffic would injure me enough to get me out of the job, and not just kill me."

"Keith, buddy, please don't—"

"I'm not going to do it, Jared! I just think about it all the time. Don't tell Elizabeth about it. She'll freak out and think it's more serious than it is."

"It sounds pretty serious."

"I'm not going to do it. It's just the fact that the idea of it sounds great to me scares me. It scares me so much, because other people have it much worse off and here I am fantasizing about hurting myself to get out of a legal contract and…"

He had to stop. Not only because his train of thought has been lost, but because between the mucus in his throat threatening to get way out of hand and his sudden excessive amount of talking his lungs were screaming for air. After some shaky breaths he broke out into coughing, only stopping after Jared had run out of the room to refill the glass that had been drained previously.

"Thanks again," Keith responded after drinking half of the glass in about two gulps.

"No problem. I feel for you, man. I really do. Thoughts like that can be terrifying. And as for what you were saying, you need to know that it's not crazy for you to be dealing with so many emotions or issues when you're living somewhere where you're being forced to listen to someone be abused. Any decent person in your situation would be a little messed up. Forget about being stressed out; you're getting so bent out of shape from an abusive boss and living situation that they're causing you to have panic attacks. You need to get out of there, man. Contract or not you're not going to feel any better until you're gone."

"You're right, but that means breaking the contract and I don't know how to unless I become unable to physically do the job. I tried calling and texting Elijah and Isaac but neither of them is answering me. I don't know what to do."

"You don't know what to do yet, but I do know what you can do right now. How about you do what I told you earlier and take a couple of hours to just relax? Lie down, drink water, take some Tylenol or Advil for your headache. Just close your eyes and try not to let the thoughts of the worst possible outcomes get you more worked up. It will be okay, Keith. You know why?"

"Why?"

"Because if you believe it will all work out in the end, the chances everything will get better skyrocket. Also, this is you we're talking about. Between Elizabeth and how smart you are you will be able to get out of your situation. Trust me. There's nothing you can't do."

The amount of confidence Jared had in Keith nearly made the PA start crying for the twelfth time in the past hour. What did he do to deserve such amazing friends?

What did he do to deserve such bad luck?

"Elizabeth," he whispered as he hid underneath his blanket, "they're back. They said they wouldn't be back but I heard them downstairs and now outside my room in the hallway most likely bringing Brandon to his room or the bathroom I'm not sure which. I guess I should have stayed at Jared and Tucker's last night after all. I can't go out there— not after yesterday. What am I going to do?"

He was talking way too fast, his chest heaving for breath and he rambled on about not being able to face them. A blood pressure cuff wouldn't have been necessary to notice his heart was suddenly working overtime.

On the other end of the phone, his girlfriend was wide awake after hearing the panic in Keith's voice at barely nine in the morning.

"Sweetie, just take a second to take some deep breaths. Your door is closed, right?"

"Of course."

"Okay, so they don't know if you're there or not, right? Just don't make a lot of noise and maybe within the next few hours they'll leave. It's Sunday; maybe they'll go to church?"

"I don't know. They usually get up to go to the early morning mass, which they'd be late for if they left now, but they might go to the noon or evening one later. I can't wait too long though. I'm supposed to meet my bio-lab group at the library at noon so we can work on our poster presentation."

Elizabeth made a frustrated noise. "Well this sucks. I freaking knew they were over-exaggerating yesterday. Wait, don't you work for them tonight at four anyway?"

Keith's heart dropped like it was suddenly made of stone.

"You're right. Oh my God, I can't work tonight. Brandon hates me now. I was getting closer to getting through him about taking charge of his situation, but I doubt he'll listen to what I have to say anymore."

"Are you sure he didn't just say he hated you because he was overwhelmed? Maybe after having a day to think the situation over he'll realize you were defending him."

"Maybe. You didn't see the way he looked at me yesterday though; he was angrier than I've ever seen him, Elizabeth. I called his parents out and there's no going back on that and—"

"Hey," she cut him off gently yet firmly. "Stop panicking. If you keep this up you'll make yourself sick."

"I know, I'm sorry, I just can't..."

"I know, dear. We're going to fix this. Right now just pretend to be asleep or not there at all. Read stuff on your phone for a couple of hours, listen for if they leave, and if they do then get out of there. If they don't leave by the time you need to go to the library just try to act natural I guess? Like just leave as if you don't even acknowledge their existence. You have somewhere to be, so act like you have somewhere to be."

He took a deep breath.

"I can try that," he relented. From underneath the blanket it was getting harder to breathe, so he pulled it off his face. There was still a churning feeling in his stomach as he continued. "Thanks, Lizzy. I don't know what I'd do without you."

"You'd be a lot better off, probably. I'm the lucky one who somehow fooled you into loving me back. I still don't understand it."

"I'm the lucky one." He was too exhausted to argue, so his words came out tired. On the other hand Elizabeth had enough energy to be cheeky.

"Nuh-uh. I'm the lucky one. You could do so much better."

"I doubt it. No one else that liked me would have had the patience to deal with me. Too hyperactive, too nerdy, too nice, too weird. How you put up with me I have no idea."

"I love you, silly."

"I know. And I love you too."

"I'm really glad you called me," Elizabeth stated. He could hear movement from across the line. "My parents are bugging me to get off the phone though. I've been gesturing at them to back off for a few minutes now, but they're getting upset. I need to go. Are you going to be okay for a while? Should I call you later when I'm free, or will you text me? I don't want to bother you if you're dealing with group stuff."

"I'll call you on the way to the library later, or on the way home from there. I'm just going to read for a while. I didn't get anything read or watched last night because of that migraine I had. It didn't go away until some point in the night."

"I'm sorry, sweetie. Try to stay hydrated today to prevent another one, okay? I'll talk to you later."

"I will. Talk to you later, dear."

The moment she hung up he felt hollow inside. How was it all his optimism disappeared when it didn't feel like Elizabeth was still there with him?

I'm such a mess. It feels like I can't even function properly anymore. Since when did I wake up anxious, feeling too scared to just get up in the morning? I've read about signs of depression; am I starting to show those? I don't think I'm depressed. It's not like the numb loneliness Lizzy and I experienced in high school. Killing myself doesn't strike me as tempting. Though if I broke my leg I wouldn't have to work, right? Would I be willing to run into traffic just to not work here? Maybe jump off a second story building... I definitely wouldn't die. I might break something, but that would be a better alternative than staying here. It would be my ticket out.

Something was definitely wrong with him. He had to be going crazy.

No. I told Jared he didn't have to worry about me hurting myself. We're going to work through this problem for a solution. Between my friends and me there's got to be a way out of this.

He pulled up some reading material before his thoughts could spiral into something that would make him even more miserable. For the next two hours he stayed in his room listening to the sounds within the house. His muscles remained tense for minutes on end every time he heard a voice, and he was on edge nearly the entire time he read. For the duration of the two hours he desperately hoped to hear the sound of the alarm system going off to signal their departure.

When the time came for him to get dressed so he could meet his lab group at the library he was pretty sure the

Thompsons had yet to leave.

What am I going to do? Just walk out and act like everything is normal? Maybe I can sneak out. Wait! I forgot about the freaking security system. They're going to hear it.

So what?

Deciding he'd just have to do his best at being stealthy, Keith shoved everything he'd need to work on the project into his backpack and swung it onto his shoulders. Putting his ear against his door he listened for signs of activity. There was nothing.

I thought I heard them downstairs the last I heard them. But were they in the living room, or the kitchen? I can go out the front door if they're in the kitchen and the back door if they're in the living room. Wait, no, I need my shoes and they're near the back door. Ugh. Maybe I can just grab my flip-flops if I hear them in the kitchen? Hopefully the stairs won't give me away.

Opening his door was a slow task to make sure it didn't creak. Going down the stairs was even slower as to not cause a floorboard to groan. Halfway down the stairs his heart skipped a beat when he heard the sharp voice of his boss from the living room.

"Can you stop typing so hard? It's getting on my damn nerves. You're going to break your computer at this rate too, and then I'll have to buy you another one."

"Yes, mother."

Brandon's voice sounded so meek it made Keith want to punch a wall.

I hate that woman. I hate her so much.

An ugly feeling mixed with the fear coursing through his heart. It made limbs ache like he'd just been through some high-intensity interval training.

Calm down, he coached himself. *Just get out of here.*

He descended the rest of the steps quickly yet quietly until he was safe at the inside steps of the back door. All but shoving his shoes on, he felt his heart nearly burst in his chest as he gathered his courage to press the buttons on the security program.

They're going to hear. They're going to know I was here the whole time unless they assume it was Thomas leaving. They will also see me from the windows walking by unless I turn right and walk around the block instead of going past the house. It'll take some extra time since it's out of my way, but I think it's worth it.

Similar to ripping off a Band-Aid, Keith disabled and reactivated the security system as fast as he could. Within twenty seconds he was out the door and near the end of the driveway. His heart rate had almost settled when he began walking down the sidewalk away from the house. He was so sure they would assume it was just Thomas. The older man was usually a bit louder when he walked around, but he would be as antisocial to leave without saying anything. That meant the coast was clear, right?

I still have to come home later for work. How am I going to deal with that? It makes me sick just thinking about having to be in the same room as any of them anymore. How can I—

The sound of his phone ringing interrupted his thoughts. Confused, he pulled it out of his pocket only to almost drop it.

Jacqueline was calling.

No. No, I don't have to answer it. I have somewhere to be. She can leave a voicemail or whatever; I'll be home for work like I'm required to be. She can't make me answer my phone.

Keith was wrong. Five unanswered calls and five voicemails simply saying "return my call" in a bland tone of voice later, his frustration with the situation boiled over.

Pushing away his dread and answering the sixth call, he couldn't hold back the anger leaking through his words as he spoke.

"Hello? I'm a little busy at the moment."

"Ah, finally." Jacqueline's saccharine voice only made him more aggravated. "I thought I heard you leave a bit ago. I understand you might have somewhere to be, but unfortunately I'm calling a mandatory meeting. Can you come back to the house, please?"

"Why are you asking if it's mandatory? Never mind, don't answer that. I have to meet my classmates for a group project right now. I can be back early for work to talk to you if we must."

"Are you saying you refuse to come back?"

"You do realize you don't own me, right?"

"Are you refusing to come back?" She repeated, her tone growing colder.

"On such short notice? I'm pretty sure I shouldn't have to, especially considering what I just said about me needing to meet up for a group project for one of my classes."

"I see. Well, Larry needs to get back on the road and he can't leave until we've had this meeting. Are you okay with making him wait hours for you to do your homework instead of just coming back here for a short, civil conversation?"

"If you needed to talk to me so badly this morning you could have just texted me like a normal person."

"I've sent you three emails about it since we arrived back at the house this morning. If you had simply checked your email like a normal person, as you put it, would, then we wouldn't be making you late. We gave you plenty of notice."

Don't scream, he thought. *Don't let her get to you. You're better than this.*

"You know what? Fine," he bit out, making a one-eighty as he did so. If she wanted to threaten him to come back then so be it. "I'll be back at the house in a couple of minutes. I don't want to make Larry suffer any longer than he has to."

"I have no idea what that could mean," she snapped, "but I'm glad you've chosen to listen. See you soon."

She hung up, leaving Keith to shut his eyes tightly as a headache began forming behind his temples.

CHAPTER SIXTEEN

Five minutes later he was sitting in the living room with Larry and Jacqueline. The atmosphere was tense, thick with so many mixed emotions that a feather could cut through the mess. He wanted nothing more than to get the hell out of there.

"Where's Brandon?"

Larry pointed up. "He's upstairs in his room. We didn't want to stress him out by being here for a conversation he didn't need to partake in."

"Okay." When no one said anything else, he shifted uncomfortably in the armchair he was in. "What did you two want to talk about then? I'm going to be late for the meeting as it is, but I want to be as least late as I can be."

His question was met with Larry giving a sidelong glance at his wife, who emotionlessly reached into a computer case and pulled out a small black device. She set it on the table along with a blank notebook and pen. Next, she pulled out a notebook he recognized as her own along with a pencil.

"Here," she handed the PA the notebook and pencil. Then she did something to the black device on the table before continuing. "That notebook is for you to take notes of our conversation if you wish to do so. While we talk I do want to let you know I will be recording."

"Why?"

The question was out before he could stop himself, his entire aura suddenly exuding confusion, terror, and fury.

What the hell? I'm being recorded?

The woman just raised an eyebrow, her next sentence more than a little condescending. "Because I can, Keith, for possible legal purposes. You're free to record as well if you wish."

Even if he had a phone capable of recording such a large amount of information, his device didn't have enough storage space to hold anything more than a few ringtones. He also didn't have a recorder some students had for recording lecture, because he preferred handwritten notes.

Basically, her proposition meant nothing.

"That's kind of weird," he stated while attempting to calm his breathing. Panicking was something he was very close to doing despite needing to keep a level head.

His body didn't want to cooperate though; being in the Thompson's presence made him more uncomfortable than he'd ever felt in anyone's presence before. The overwhelming fear that was trying to surge up and drive him into a panic attack was involuntary. No matter how much he rationalized staying calm there wouldn't be much he could do if they drove him over the edge.

Jacqueline made a face that convened confusion, but there was something else in her expression that Keith couldn't read.

"Weird? People record interactions all the time for the sake of evidence, Keith."

"Well I'm not very comfortable being recorded."

"That's unfortunate. I'm not comfortable not being recorded."

"Why would you need evidence anyway?"

"In case you take action at a later time that might force our hands."

"Which means what? You'll sue me?"

"If you break the contract, then yes we will."

"This whole conversation feels like you're threatening me," he accused.

Moving a strand of blonde hair out of her face, she began writing something down in her notebook.

"What are you writing down?"

"Just that you find me stating facts about the situation threatening, and that the wording I used was indeed not a threat but simply me restating already known information."

"What?"

She shook her head in pity. "Pay attention, Keith. Me telling you if you break the contract that we will sue you is not a threat; it is a fact. Therefore your opinion on the matter is mere dramatics."

Keith could feel his head start to throb even harder than it had been.

"Okay, whatever. What did you make me come here today to talk to you about?"

"We didn't make you come here at all, Keith."

"Yes, you did. You guilted me into coming saying it would inconvenience Larry."

"That is from your perspective. I told you he needed to leave soon, so your arrival here was your own choice."

"Oh my God. What are we meeting here about?"

"Such impatience," she commented while writing something else in her notes. The more scribbling the PA heard the more unsettled he was becoming. Maybe it was all part of her plan? "I wanted to ask some questions, because after yesterday's incident I no longer feel completely at ease with the idea of leaving Brandon in your care. He feels the same way."

Hope fluttered in his chest.

"If you don't want me to be his PA anymore, then just fire me."

"I wish we could. Sadly, we can't do that without finding another PA to replace you first. Thomas is okay, but he can't cover making meals half the week. I can manage half the week on my own but without you here I'd have to cook all the meals, and that is just far too time-consuming."

"Then what do you want me to do?"

"I want you to tell me what we can do to make you feel more comfortable here from now on."

"You're serious?"

"Of course. Why would I lie?"

He could think of several reasons, but he pushed away his suspicion and surprise at the question. Maybe he could give her the benefit of the doubt just one time. Maybe, just maybe, they were finally willing to hear him out.

"Okay," Keith began with some confidence. He could do this. "I want there to be zero screaming in the house. There's honestly no reason for it unless someone is hurt, or there is an emergency. Also less negativity. I'm constantly hearing insults from you directed at Brandon and Larry, and it's starting to make me depressed listening to it constantly. I don't like that every time we cross paths you try to drag me into a conversation when most times I am in a rush, or giving you many clues that I'm too busy to keep talking. Stop asking me to take on more shifts. I was doing the amount of work required of me when I signed the contract; making me feel bad when I don't want to work more or saying rude things to me when I say no has started to make me extremely stressed out. It's not my fault there are open hours."

A deep breath later, he continued.

"I don't like the idea of you making Brandon crawl around on the floor. I get that he isn't allowed to walk around, but he's getting bruises on his knees and hands from it. Get him pads, please. I don't like seeing him hurt. Speaking of which," he curled his fists instinctively as if bracing for a rebound, "I don't want anyone punishing Brandon ever again. No slapping him, or grabbing his arm way harder than necessary. No grabbing his hair. No making him go without a meal. No verbally telling him all his mistakes in a non-constructive way, or degrading him because of his mannerisms. It's been driving me crazy since I got here. It's all abuse, and it needs to stop if you want me to keep working here."

There was a long moment where the only noises in the room were those of Larry and Keith breathing as well as the sound of a pen running across paper. After roughly a page of notes on Jacqueline's account she looked up, locking eyes with the PA.

"Well. That's certainly a lot."

When she didn't continue, opting to simply stare at Keith, the boy tentatively answered.

"I guess it does sound like a lot," he agreed, "but none of what I asked for is that hard, so it shouldn't be a problem, right?"

"On the contrary, it will be very hard. Do you want to know why?"

Keith was bewildered at the sudden animosity coming through as she spoke.

"Why?"

"You're asking me to change who I am as a person, Keith."

You have got to be shitting me right now. God, give me patience!

"What do you—"

"You demand I stop yelling when I hardly ever raise my voice." *Liar.* "You think I'm too negative a person to be around, which is a downright hurtful thing to say. I'm sorry my stories and opinions may come off as depressing," she sneered. "However, any harsh comments you're referring to aimed at my family aren't really of your concern. Changing how I talk to my husband and son is such a silly thing for you to ask me to do. As long as I'm talking to you in a 'positive' manner from now on why should I limit how I interact with members of my own family? Speaking of interactions, I suppose I can shut off my chatterbox personality when you enter the room.

Ignorant old me never realized saying hello to you or asking you how you were doing was taking valuable time away from your day. I must be such a terrible person."

She dramatically wiped away a tear before going on, not a trace of actual hurt in her voice as she spoke. All Keith could hear as he listened to her speak was a load of garbage for the recorder.

"I won't ever ask you to work an extra shift again. I had no idea that offering you more hours would be such a burden to you. I hadn't meant to come off as overly demanding of you." *Liar.* "As for the idea about getting Brandon pads to prevent injury, I will look into it. The solution hadn't occurred to me until you proposed it." *Liar.* "Also, despite how alarmed I am that you would accuse me of abusing my disabled son, I promise I will not allow any unjust physical harm to come to him. While I cannot take away punishment entirely I will make sure to reprimand him in a way that won't offend your sensibilities." *Liar!*

"What is that supposed to mean? Sounds like a loophole if I ever heard one."

"I have no idea what you're talking about. Anyway, now that we've discussed what we need to change, I will be telling you how I believe you should adjust for the remainder of your time here as well."

He glanced at Larry just to break eye contact with Jacqueline and wasn't surprised to find he was zoning out of the entire conversation.

So much for needing you to be here. What kind of peacekeeper are you?

"For the remainder of your time here I no longer wish to engage in conversation with you. Furthermore, I will refrain from being in the same room as you entirely. You of course get higher privilege seeing as you live here whereas I am just here until all positions are filled."

"What about during meals?"

"I suppose I'll eat by myself in the guest dining room. It

would be preferable for me, and I know it would make you happier not to have to listen to me talk."

Keith blinked dumbly.

"You're kidding, right?"

"What do you mean? It's completely understandable for me to be upset after my entire personality was attacked. I think it will be better for our already estranged relationship for us to limit our interactions with each other. I no longer wish to engage in unnecessary conversation with you. From now on Brandon can be our liaison if emails don't suffice. Although," she added as if an afterthought, "I doubt he'll have much to say to you anymore either."

He knew that should have made him happy. Not the part about Brandon not wanting to talk to him anymore, but the part where Jacqueline would finally leave him alone. No more thirty-plus minute conversations. No more her pressuring him to take on more shifts or her asking him to quit his other jobs. No more even having to be in the same room as her.

He should have been happy. But he wasn't.

"If you hate me so much as to not want to be in the same room as me any longer," he started with a shaky breath, "then maybe I should just leave. From what you told me and what Brandon screamed at me yesterday he hates me now anyway. I'm not sure I can handle living here and working for people I know hate me."

"I don't like living in the same house as a child who insulted me, but for Brandon I am willing to make sacrifices."

"C'mon. You obviously wouldn't want me here if you had another option."

"While that might be true from your perspective," she argued while writing something else down. It was driving him crazy. "I must remind you that you signed a contract. Simply quitting will create more legal problems than you can afford."

"But you don't want me here. It's so obvious."

Jacqueline brought a hand to her face, a snarky smile hiding behind it.

"I think that maybe you no longer desire to be here, Keith. You seem awfully concerned about getting me to say I wish you no longer worked here."

"I enjoyed working here," he defended. "Everything was going great the week you were gone. Isaac, Elijah, Brandon, and I got along fine! Maybe they weren't the best PAs, but Brandon was safer and happier then than he is now. The environment only started getting insufferable when you moved back in and started finding fault in every little thing we did. I've heard you on the phone complaining endlessly about how much we all sucked at our jobs on the nightly. It's no wonder Elijah left. It's no wonder I no longer can stomach working here, let alone living in this house."

"Oh, do say more. You haven't offended me enough today."

"I'm not trying to offend you! I'm recounting the truth, as you would put it."

"The only thing you're recounting right now is your opinion on how much I've wronged you since moving in."

"Every problem coming to light in this house is your fault," he said.

"A matter of perspective," she gestured to the recorder, "that perhaps a third party would need to get the full details on before believing a concerned mother could drive so many young men to psychological instability. You know, Keith, you might think I'm the one in the wrong here, but did you ever think you were the one jumping to conclusions and bullying me with your hurtful words? Have you gotten feedback from a neutral party that you're the one in the right and we're the crazy ones? Maybe you should see a doctor."

She's trying to trick you, a part of his mind shouted in

warning, *into saying you broke the contract by talking about what has happened in the house to other people. Don't let her know you have! If you do, you're screwed.*

"It's against the contract to talk about what happens in this house to other people, especially if it could have negative connotations on your family's character. So no. I haven't been able to get any input if I'm the one that's being ignorant or rude, because there is absolutely no one I am allowed to talk to. Unless you're giving me permission to talk to Elizabeth or my mom about it now?"

"While I find it hard to believe you haven't blabbed to your girlfriend or parents yet, I am willing to allow you to talk to a school psychologist." She glared at him distrustfully as she said this. "It's free to students. After everything you've said in the past twenty-four hours I imagine seeing a mental specialist is something you desperately need at this time."

His lips tightened into a thin line.

She's calling me crazy now? Maybe I am, but if I am it's because of her!

"Fine. I'll make an appointment with the counseling center right away then. What do you want me to do if they tell me I shouldn't work here anymore?"

"Why would they tell you that?"

"Because after I tell them how you treated Elijah and how you continue to treat your son and husband they'll probably advise me to get away from any stressors causing me distress. I'm not going to lie to them. If they tell me you're affecting my mental health in a bad way, then I'll need to leave."

Jacqueline rolled her eyes. "If it comes to that I'll need to make you an appointment with a professional doctor for a second opinion. You're not getting out of the contract, Keith."

"That's not really up to you though."

"Why do you insist on arguing with me?"

"I'm not trying to argue with you," he said pleadingly. "I just want everyone to treat each other right. Is that so much to ask?"

"You're asking me to change who I am, so yes it is. You're attacking my unique personality. My autonomy. Such a hypocrite. You act like you're so innocent and smart when you go out of your way to insult everyone in my family's flaws, yet you don't think there is anything wrong with how you're acting."

"What are you talking about?"

She shook her head, eyes half-lidded as she gazed at him with contempt. He was so focused on the way she was looking at him that he didn't notice her turn off the recorder before she started talking.

"You're such an ignorant boy. You think everything you do is an act of kindness, that you're helping someone. You thought you could help Brandon by turning him against me? You'll never turn him or my husband against me when I'm the one holding this family together. They would be lost without me."

"I don't think so. They'd probably be better off without you running their lives for them."

He'd said that in a moment of courageousness which faded the second Jacqueline's face lit up in unconcealed anger.

"You're just the hired help! You don't get to disrespect me by talking shit to me like that!"

Finally, as if the yelling had woken Larry out of his daze, the older man intervened.

"Honey, please. The recorder is—"

"I turned it off a few seconds ago, so shut the hell up and stay out of our damn conversation!" She whirled on him before facing Keith again. "As for you, this meeting is over. Go work on your school project for all I care. I expect you home tonight to take care of Brandon at six."

"How can I take care of Brandon after all of this?" He

questioned, getting more worked up. "Just thinking about working tonight makes me want to throw up!"

"I have no idea why. It's not like I'll be bothering you anymore."

"That doesn't matter! What matters is that I don't feel comfortable working with or for people who are verbally abusive to me and physically abusive to Elijah and Brandon!"

"We've already discussed this; what you perceive as abusive is inaccurate. You're misguided on several subjects. Now I'll deal with your cruelty for—"

"My cruelty?" He scoffed. "Are you serious?"

Larry cleared his throat, putting his hands in the air and sending a placating look towards his wife. "This is getting a little out of hand."

"Oh, now you want to say something?"

"Excuse me," the older man continued, "Keith, but if I may propose something. I understand you have some strong feelings when it comes to Jacqueline, but maybe you need to withhold your judgment?"

"Withhold my judgment?"

Jacqueline snorted. "What are you now, a cowardly parrot?"

"I'm not the one who turned off the recorder because I was scared of something incriminating being recorded!"

"I turned it off because I thought we were done with this conversation."

"Even though I had asked a question before you messed with it? Yeah, that doesn't seem suspicious or anything."

"You truly hate me, don't you?"

"Yes!" He spat before backtracking. "I mean, no! A little. Ugh, you terrify me! So many things you do are just not normal and after what you did yesterday I can't live in a place like this, let alone sleep here any longer! I don't want to be here anymore."

"Really? I don't understand how you could possibly be

scared of me." She said this with a self-satisfied smile that would appear in Keith's nightmares. "It's a shame really. But very well, I'll give you a week off of work to deal with your mental issues. I didn't want it to come to this, but I suppose it has to. Go see a doctor, a psychologist, whoever you want. Larry and I will manage until then. I assume you have somewhere to sleep this week since you said you would be unable to rest here? I wouldn't want you to become exhausted or ill because you can't sleep."

He nodded stiffly. "Yes, I'll have somewhere to go."

"Great. You can go then."

With that she got up, collecting her things before leaving the room and heading towards the basement. Larry followed her after giving a tiny nod to Keith in parting. Once the PA was the only one in the room he found himself cradling his head in his hands.

What have I done? He thought despite his now throbbing headache threatening to split his head apart. *I never should have said anything. I can't come back from this. I can't.*

What felt like half an hour but was barely a minute passed before he gathered the strength to stand up. On the way out of the house he nearly went to grab a glass of ice water, but he stopped himself. The ice maker was incredibly loud, which was something he hated about it. He also knew if he dirtied a glass and put it in the dishwasher that Jacqueline would complain about having to put away "unnecessary dishes" as she called them. It was for the same reason he'd taken to eating fast food for lunch instead of cooking stuff at home. She'd nagged at him for making dishes even if he washed them himself (because he didn't clean them right either), so he'd stopped making them altogether.

He decided he would just visit the drinking fountain when he got to the library. Later, when he was sure the Thompsons would be in the living room listening to

Brandon practice the violin, he would come back to grab what belongings he needed. He didn't want to stay in the house any longer than he had to.

"Hey, Keith, what's up? We were getting worried about you," one of his classmates greeted him upon arrival.

"Yeah. You're usually the first one here."

Another one looked him over critically. "Did something happen at your job?"

As he sat down he managed a small smile. Shalyn, the one who asked the most recent question, kept typing something on her computer as he replied.

"More of the same old, same old. My boss did something way worse than she usually does yesterday and I confronted her."

"Good job!" Jessica grinned. "From what little you've told us that bitch deserves to be told off. What happened? Is she going to stop so you don't report her, or what?"

Beside her his other two group mates were on their laptops while she drew some reference lines on a tri-fold presentation board. She already had the graphs and pictures for the poster printed out by her computer as well. It seemed they picked back up on what they'd started during the lab pretty quickly for only being there for roughly thirty minutes.

He looked away sheepishly, a hand running across the back of his neck out of sheer nervousness. His group mates didn't know much about the situation other than he was a live-in PA with a terrible boss. Not only were there legal reasons he didn't go spouting names or conditions, but he didn't know his group mates that well to trust them with the full details. Sure they exchanged some "juicy" pieces of info about their lives seeing as this was the second out of three classes they shared together. Jessica was having trouble raising money for an equestrian club because of poor club management, Shalyn was trying to find a job for the summer while dealing with a classmate that seemed to be stalking her, and Alex was having frequent disagreements with his girlfriend. They were all great people who Keith would miss seeing when he graduated in May. Still, even after weekly study sessions, snacks, and story-times he couldn't tell them everything.

"Uh, well, she's threatening me with the contract. She said if I try to call DCFS like one of the former PAs did she'll sue me."

Alex, a biology major like Keith's other two group members, raised an eyebrow.

"No way. I'm pretty sure places like that are legally sanctioned to cover you in cases like this. It'd be like if she said you can't talk to a medical professional about it or call the police; I'm pretty sure that's illegal. Maybe star-sixty-nine them?"

"I would, but I'm afraid some of the examples I'd use will point to me and they could prove I called them in."

"Go to student legal services," Jessica advised. "I had to go there once over an apartment lease. A lot of times people write contracts using language that sounds scary but isn't covered by the state or government. Like there was a clause in my lease about the security deposit that isn't something they can legally charge me for in this state. I wouldn't have known that if I hadn't sought out a professional. The lawyers are free too. I'd definitely have them look at that contract to see how much of what that lady's been spouting off is just talk."

Shalyn nodded in agreement. "You should. Your boss sounds like she's just trying to scare you."

"Yeah. I guess I'll stop by tomorrow morning then to see about making a walk-in appointment."

"Awesome! Let us know how it went on Tuesday during class, okay?"

"Thanks, Jess. You and Alex as well," he directed at Shalyn. "Anyway, how's the project going?"

"Oh boy! Shalyn and I had an idea that Alex is skeptical about, but you know how our professors love *Beyoncé?* I was thinking we could incorporate her into the presentation by…"

Keith listened to her gush about a great idea connecting the famous singer' liking of blueberries to the part of their project that relied heavily upon anthocyanin levels like a pro. He knew their professors would be thrilled if that were thrown in their presentation.

I'm going to miss these guys, he thought with a bittersweet smile. *More time with them is the only reason graduation can take its time getting here.*

CHAPTER SEVENTEEN

Elizabeth squeezed his hand before letting go.

"You're sure I can't go in there with you?" She asked from where she sat outside the student legal services office in one of the many chairs stationed in the hall. "I know you're capable of talking to them on your own, but…"

"I'll be fine. Honestly I don't even know if I'll get an appointment today anyway. I might just schedule mine today, and have to come back later. And if I did get to talk to one of the lawyers today you definitely wouldn't be allowed to overhear anything because of legal reasons I'm sure."

She pushed out her lips in a pout. "Fine," the word stretched over the span of two seconds. "You're probably right, but that doesn't mean I'm happy about it."

"I know. I'm going to go in now though, okay? If I get an appointment I'll come back out really quick to let you know. If I just get it scheduled, then I'll be out in a little bit."

"Okie dokie. I'll just be here watching YouTube videos."

His smile grew as she flashed him a smile of her own. After hearing about how he was going to check out the student legal services this morning she hadn't hesitated to skip class. While he'd initially felt bad, she explained there were no attendance points and the lectures would be posted online after class anyway.

"And even if I did have things to worry about", she'd

told him last night after getting ultra-rare permission from her roommate for him to sleep at their dorm, *"I'd still prioritize being here with you over anything. Work, classes, homework— those can wait. I've already felt like I haven't been doing enough to help you with your situation. I've been such a failure of a girlfriend! I just want to tell this lady off. I get that I can't because of legal reasons, but still. I have to at least support you now."*

He'd never wanted to make her feel useless. She was his other half, and to know she felt like a failure because he put himself (no matter if he had been ignorant) in a situation she was helpless to take much action in made him feel like the shittiest boyfriend ever.

And maybe he was.

Even so, she was still there for him and it meant the world to him. He'd spend every day making sure she knew that.

Steeling himself, Keith finally gathered his courage and went to push open the door to his office only to stop. On the door he noticed a note card taped onto it stating to knock before entering. It seemed a bit unprofessional, but with a mental shrug he did as the paper said. Immediately a woman's voice came from the other side of the door.

"You can come in!"

He shot a glance at Elizabeth, but she'd already put her earbuds in and was listening to a video. Facing the door again he pushed it open and slipped inside.

The first thing he noticed was that the front desk was directly in front of the doorway, which made more sense as to why visitors were to knock before entering. How small the main office was the next detail he noticed, the room being cramped with other desks as well as four doorways to rooms the size of walk-in closets. Above those doors were signs with peoples' names on them who he assumed were the lawyers.

"Hello, young man." The middle-aged woman at the

desk greeted him. The moment he'd shut the door she smiled at him, handing him a clipboard. "If you could please sign in for me."

"Okay."

Once that was done, she offered him a seat while she did something on the computer. A minute later she walked around from the front desk and prompted him to stand.

"It seems you don't have an appointment with us. Did you come today to see about a walk-in appointment? Because unfortunately the only one that was offered today is in the evening and someone already booked it online to secure their spot."

Keith flushed, embarrassed. He hadn't thought about booking an appointment online, or to even check online for anything more than their hours. He probably should have searched their website more thoroughly.

"I'm sorry. I just needed an appointment as soon as possible, and I thought it'd be faster to come in person to book it."

Her features softened at his honest response. "It's fine, sweetie. We have exactly two open slots for tomorrow if you'd like to pick one. Come with me."

They both walked back over to another desk where she pulled out a small whiteboard with the dates of the week and time slots. There were three times for tomorrow each with a different lawyer.

"Oh, before you pick I should tell you they all have different specialties. Most of them have experience with apartment contracts, but depending on what you need a lawyer for it will impact which one I'd personally recommend. You don't have to and shouldn't disclose much to me, but what is the nature of your visit?"

"I need a contract reviewed to see if I can get out of it without legal repercussions," he began hesitantly. "I guess that's not very specific... Without saying too much, um, I work as a live-in PA for someone with a disability and his mom, who is my boss, is abusive and I can't work there anymore, but she keeps threatening to sue me and…"

He trailed off when the woman looked at him with dawning horror in her eyes. Was he not supposed to say that much?

"Oh, you poor thing! I think I know exactly what family you're talking about. The last name starts with a T or something, right? You're sadly not the first PA in the past four years to come to us for help with getting out of that nasty contract."

Whatever he was preparing to say left his mind in an instant.

"What?"

"I believe Dr. Sime was the one to deal with the last nine cases," she continued as if she hadn't entirely heard him. He watched as she preemptively wrote his name in a spot on the whiteboard. "He's got a free half-hour tomorrow at noon. Does that work for you?"

"Yes, of course. But can we back up just a second? You're telling me I'm the tenth PA to come here for help in getting out of this contract?"

"Technically I can neither confirm nor deny that statement, seeing as I'm just the secretary and much of what we handle here at Student Legal Services is confidential information. I can only say I've heard of nine or so very similar cases in the past few years and recommend Dr. Sime as your preferred lawyer due to his history in dealing with such cases; however, you should not feel obligated to pick him as your lawyer simply due to my discretion. You can choose whoever you would like."

The woman said this with such practiced ease that it was obvious she was used to having to backpedal when she slipped up. She must use this particular language often.

"I understand." And he did. Keith knew what it was like to be in the predicament of not being able to necessarily speak freely lest she get in trouble, but it didn't make him feel any less upset about the news she'd initially given him. "But what about the university?"

"What about them?"

"If multiple students came here due to a job that was posted on the job board, then shouldn't you guys have made them take the job down after the fact? There shouldn't have been any more cases after the first student came here to get help."

She nodded, quickly understanding what he was getting at. The sad look on her face told him she's heard this before though.

"Trust me, sweetie, we've appealed to the department in charge of the university's job board to take down jobs we believe put students at risk in the past. In certain cases they are taken down. In others, hypothetically ones similar to your issue, the issuer of the job post can fight back about their job posting being taken down. Due to case confidentiality we are not allowed to tell another university entity or person a reason other than our professional opinion of the job being unfit for students."

"So they did take it down."

"Yes."

"But they allowed it to be put back up. What the hell?"

Instantly, he felt bad for cursing, but he was just so disappointed.

The woman made a small noise of discontent.

"I agree with you completely, dear. I wish the university had more of a backbone when it comes to these issues. Unfortunately, push can come to shove and the person fighting the job board on putting the job posting back up could easily pull disability services into the mix. He or she can rally to get the disability office to force the office in control of the job board to put a job posting back up despite our warnings, and continued threats to sue the university may overrule our professional advice permanently. My educated guess is whoever would do that has a lot of money, and unfortunately, even in a university as prestigious as ours money, as well as the possibility of a scandal involving disability rights, talks more than it should."

"But she said they didn't have money," he argued weakly. "She said that they barely have enough to pay medical bills."

"I'm sorry, Keith, but perhaps you were lied to. Perhaps the person who made the job posting lied to everyone who applied to work there to suck them in, and then slowly sucked them dry. Or so I would guess."

He didn't know what to say next. He'd known he was being played for some time, but the truth still stung. It was like a knife had been planted in his back since he'd accepted the job, and ever so slowly it was getting pushed in inch by inch. Only now was he realizing the copper taste in his mouth was blood, not his imagination.

Suddenly he felt even angrier than he had over the past few days. How had he been so stupid? How had he let this go on for so long? Why had the university not issued some sort of warning at least, something that could have prevented him from even getting involved in such a situation?

It's their fault, a bitter train of thought fought to the forefront of his mind. *You only found the job because it was on the university job board. If someone had prevented the Thompsons from putting up their ad, then you wouldn't have even applied in the first place. You wouldn't have bent over backward during the application process to secure the position at all if university housing had gotten ahold of you about being a residential advisor. Instead they hire a druggy that sleeps with anyone who breathes, and her friend who's had three abortions in the past year alone.*

The university doesn't know everything about the students they hire just like they don't know why the job was flagged on the job board in the first place, he defended. He wished he didn't feel obligated to do so.

Excuses.

But they don't! How can they protect their students from harm if they don't know what is hurting their students in the first place? They couldn't have known how many PAs were leaving, right?

It doesn't matter. If they have rules or laws in place that allow their students to be introduced to an unsafe environment again and again without any sort of checks, then maybe they should take some time and effort into enacting some clauses that allow for them to monitor the safety of their students. You can't tell me a top ten university doesn't have the resources to begin looking for a change. Oh wait, this is the same university allowing their disability resources supervisors to forbid any of the students living with disabilities in the dorms from using the accessible kitchen. For some reason the university doesn't think it strange it can be used by disability resources' staff members, but not the students it was built for. Tell me again how they're so innocent?

Okay, there is some change necessary. They aren't perfect. But they're better than almost all of the other universities in the world!

That's rich. That's like saying a man who beats his wife is the better option because the rest of the men kill their wives.

That's some dark imagery I didn't need right now.

But it's true. What is the point of being a great university if it has no real drive to be the best? Complacency is poison. Having problems and refusing to fix them because other places have worse problems is even more poisonous.

"Keith, dear?"

He snapped out of his daze, bringing his gaze up from the floor to the woman looking at him in concern.

"Sorry, I was just thinking. Tomorrow at noon will

work for me. Is there anything specific I should bring?"

"Just your student ID and a copy of the contract you want looked at. If you want us to print it out for you just send it to Dr. Sime's email and he will print it out beforehand," she instructed while giving him the lawyer's business card.

"Thank you so much."

"No problem. We're just doing our jobs. Oh, but I will recommend one thing!"

He tilted his head, interested in what she had to possibly add.

"If you have time today I would suggest you go to the student counseling center. In many of our previous cases seeing a professional there and having them write you a note can help your chances of getting out of a physically or mentally unsafe situation. You would still probably need a second opinion and note from a doctor in your insurance network, but the counseling center has walk-in hours every day. Maybe after you leave here you can pop in really quick?"

Nodding, he took the hand she was offering him to shake.

"You've been so helpful. I'll go there right away," he promised. "See you tomorrow morning then?"

"Absolutely. Try to hang in there."

"I will. Have a great day. Thanks again."

With that he left the room, feeling lighter than he had in months. All he had to do now was see a counselor, a lawyer, and another doctor and he'd be free. He could do this.

"Tell me about yourself."

Keith sat there with what must have been a blank look on his face.

I can't do this, he thought as his usual nervousness kicked in. *I've never had to talk to a counselor before. I don't know what I should or shouldn't say to them, or how much is relevant and how much is useless information. What if they diagnose me with something and it stops me from getting a job in the future? I don't want to be labeled as depressed or crazy just to get out of this job.*

Part of him knew that wasn't quite true though. When he spent more than a couple minutes of his time trying to figure out a way to break his leg for Jacqueline to let him go he knew that maybe having something written down on a piece of paper about his mental state was a better alternative.

"I'm sorry," he said after a minute of complete silence. "I don't know what to tell you. I mean, I'm a student with a problem obviously, but..."

He looked up at the man expecting to see a raised eyebrow or at least some sort of judgment in his gaze. Other than a small upward quirk of his lip though, the man seemed unfazed. He radiated patience and an aura of understanding.

"This is your first time seeing a counselor, correct?"

"Yes."

Dr. Oxner, a clean-shaven man with one of the nicest smiles Keith had ever seen, hummed sympathetically. He put away the recording device he'd set out initially, something he had noticed made Keith stiffen up in discomfort. He also set the pen and paper in his lap off to the side as well.

"I apologize for not giving you something to go off of. Counseling sessions can be whatever you want them to be. You can talk as much or as little as you want, or if you'd rather I ask you something else I can do that too. This is all about you, Keith. I'm here to listen to you as well as help you in any way that I can."

"I— okay. I just... I'm not sure what I can and can't say."

"That's understandable. A lot of those who come in

worry about saying something quote on quote 'wrong', but I should tell you that you truly can speak freely here. Everything you say here is completely confidential. Since you are above the age of eighteen you also do not need to worry about your parents or legal guardians being contacted for any reason."

"What about the authorities? I'm sure you've heard some pretty bad stuff, right?"

"It depends on the level of danger I believe an individual is at. The only reason I would contact anyone about what was said here today is if I was completely convinced you might commit suicide or harm another person after our session here. In those cases I would call the hospital though; no police involved, usually."

"Oh. Okay. So I can talk about anything even if a legal contract states I'm not allowed to talk to a doctor or the police about it?"

This time the psychologist did raise an eyebrow.

"I'm not sure what kind of contract you are referring to, but you are *always* allowed to talk to a medical professional or member of the police. There are rare exceptions having to do with government operations such as military veterans being under strict rules of silence, but unless that applies here you can tell me whatever you feel comfortable telling me."

Keith swallowed hard. After a few seconds of processing time, he found himself relaxing against the back of the chair he was in.

"Okay. I think I can talk now. Um, can you remind me what the question was again?"

Dr. Oxner smiled, his blue eyes reflecting honesty and genuine passion of helping those he spoke to.

"Sure, Keith. I asked if you would like to tell me about yourself."

"I can."

He started small, stating the basics such as his year in

college, his major, and how he was from a small town on the state border.

"I chose this school because my girlfriend of almost six years came here for computer engineering…"

After consolidating half a decade of information on the love of his life into a couple of minutes, he was finally ready to broach the topic of why he was there in the first place.

Keith told him about Will. He told him how he'd applied and accepted a job to be a personal assistant in desperation for college funding but ended up loving it so much he transferred from Biology to Kinesiology. He shared that the last semester working with Will upset him so much because he knew the chances of them seeing each other again were slimmer than most since Will lived in New Jersey. Of course, they promised to visit each other at one point. People always did that though. They came and went, putting those always in their lives or closer to home first while slowly letting strong friendships fade due to distance.

"It hurts a lot sometimes," he admitted. "I know why people drift apart. It just happens. Someone moves while someone else stays, there's not a lot of time in a year, and money or transportation just isn't there. I messed up a relationship with a friend back home simply because I forgot to stay in contact with her for so long that when I finally remembered I was too scared to contact her. I haven't talked to her in years now; I doubt I'd have the courage to speak to her unless she found me."

"Would you invite her to your wedding whenever it occurs?"

A wince. "I'd have to think about it. In my heart I still feel like we are close like we once were, but my head tells me she hates me for not keeping contact with her. I feel like I betrayed her by dropping off the face of the Earth. I know it got busy here with school and multiple jobs and all sorts of other problems but those are just excuses." He blew out a stream of air. "Sorry. I'm getting off-topic."

"It's fine. Take your time."

"But don't we only have a half-hour?"

"Unless I get a notification that another walk in signed up for my next appointment in the next ten minutes, then we can go for another forty minutes. I'll sign you up for a second slot for today regardless. You need to talk, so I'm here to listen."

Keith suddenly felt like crying. For weeks he had been so afraid of talking to someone other than his close friends about what was going on in his life. It had felt like a noose had been wrapped around his neck with Jacqueline holding onto the rope. Now, however, he felt like someone had untied him from said noose.

With newfound courage, the PA opened up about his financial struggles. He stressed how last semester he was crunching numbers for the upcoming year and realized he wasn't going to be able to afford living in university housing as well as pay for college. Panicking, which looking back on wasn't the smartest thing to do at the time, he scoured multiple job boards resigning himself to working sixty-hour weeks during the summer and simply not sleeping during the school year.

And then he saw it. The ad for a live-in PA: on campus, free full room and board, meals every day, as well as being paid for hours after the first ten. He wouldn't have to pay over ten thousand dollars to live in a mediocre dorm with a hit or miss roommate and eat dorm food for every meal. It was like a godsend.

So he applied, and he fought tooth and nail to be the one out of five PAs that got chosen for the last spot in the house. There were nights he prayed to God that he would get the position. That was saying something since he wasn't the best Christian and only prayed when he got really worried about something or someone. That and he was extremely forgetful. Back when he used to make praying before bed a routine he went over a month without doing it before he'd even noticed.

Either way, when he got offered the position he'd nearly cried tears of joy.

"I was so happy," he stated somewhat bitterly. "I finally felt like everything was going my way. I wouldn't have to work myself to death; I would get to form another relationship similar to the one with Will too. It was a win-win."

Until it wasn't.

Those words didn't make it out of his mouth, but it was a close thing.

Dr. Oxner listened as Keith slowly began to tell him about his first impressions of the Thompsons. How Jacqueline had been just a tad bit domineering over Brandon, how Brandon seemed to have lived a life more uptight and sheltered than Keith thought was healthy, and how Larry seemed to bend over backward without asking questions as a devoted husband should.

But he'd thought nothing of any of it. Who would, honestly? Every family had their quirks and way of doing things. Who was he to judge based on a couple of meetings? He didn't know them. So he did what he felt like he should do.

He assumed the best in people like he always did, something Tucker and Elizabeth had been adamant would bite him in the butt one day.

"My parents tried to tell me something was off about them the day they helped move me in, but I was too optimistic to see that maybe something was off about the way they did things. No, wait, that's wrong." He heaved a sigh. "I don't even think it's because I didn't notice. I just don't think I cared enough at the time. I guess I was just willing to deal with whatever I had to deal with to get through school."

"But then it became too much?" The older man surmised.

Keith nodded and then told him *everything*.

"At this point I get nauseous just from being around them. It's like the moment I enter the house their energy just, like, makes me sick. I don't know if it's because I'm afraid of Jacqueline, or if this is just my anxiety acting up again."

"She assaulted another PA as well as her son. If I were in your shoes, then I would be fearful too. I might even have trouble eating and sleeping."

"I haven't been able to eat as much at meals with them in the past couple weeks," he admitted. "She made offhand comments about the amount of food Elijah and I used to eat, which made me self-conscious during meals, and half the time I have to listen to her berate her son or husband at the table and it makes me lose my appetite. Most nights I have trouble sleeping too. Either I'm so anxious about everything going on in my life, or I'm kept awake by Jacqueline complaining about other people on the phone all night. Brandon, Larry, Isaac, Elijah. Strangers, acquaintances, and friends too. Sometimes," he could feel a lump well up in his throat, "she talked about me."

The psychologist didn't ask Keith to divulge anything more. Still, the PA felt like he needed Dr. Oxner to understand why he was so messed up.

"She called me so many things behind my back, and I still don't get why. She's probably doing it right now too." He raved, suddenly blinking back tears of frustration. "I was used to her calling me useless or selfish to my face, but to hear her tell Larry that she thought I was an idiot for staying at the restaurant because I liked the staff there, or that she was so sure the entire second floor was starting to smell because I wasn't doing laundry or showering enough on account of my exercise classes was just mean. And it wasn't just once or twice. It was almost every night."

"That must have been hard to listen to."

"It was. When she talked about other people it just made it difficult to sleep since it was hard to ignore her yelling, but when she brought up my name I would be wide awake. I'd listen to her talk about me and wonder if she was right. Were my opinions childish or unrealistic? Did my mannerisms make me weak? Were my life goals unobtainable because I am a complete pushover?"

He let his head drop into his hands. "I seriously still wonder if I'm not the crazy one, making things a bigger deal than they are. Like, maybe it was me all along. Maybe she was ranting about me because I *am* a filthy moron who doesn't have the backbone to go anywhere in life. Maybe what she said about me being selfish, ignorant, optimistic to a fault, and everything else was right. What if I'm the crazy one, Dr. Oxner?" Keith asked, voice raw and vulnerable.

"You're not crazy."

"Are you sure? Maybe I'm not crazy, but even I know I'm screwed up. I can't eat, sleep, go to the bathroom, shower, or even just sit in that house without being paralyzed with anxiety. What if it's because of guilt? I hurt their feelings. Maybe I'm the one in the wrong. Maybe I should go back to apologize and try to fix things."

There was a moment of silence, and then the psychologist let out a small hum.

"Keith, may I ask you something?"

"Of course."

"You mentioned earlier that you have entertained the idea of seriously injuring yourself to get out of this job on several occasions. Is that right?"

"Yeah," he answered shamefully.

"And you said you not only witnessed your employer harm her disabled son but also learned that she physically assaulted your coworker?"

"I— yeah."

"Do those seem like reasonable situations to have been placed in? To be put in a contract with no way out, threatened with legal repercussions that sound falsified, and to be forced to live in an abusive home with a racist and xenophobic employer is not helping your mental or physical health. Listen, Keith, one thing I've learned over the years as a psychologist is that truly mentally unstable people trick others into believing they are the crazy ones. I know you told me this family showed you several acts of kindness as well, which probably has you a bit confused about their natures, but that is a common tactic in abusive situations. Punishment versus award. Perhaps they weren't even aware they were doing it. Maybe they do truly care for you in some regard, but that doesn't negate the fact that your job is not a safe environment for you."

"I'm going to write you a letter similar to a doctor's note recommending you leave your place of employment right away in case that contract calls for something like that," he continued while writing something on his clipboard hurriedly. "I do hope the student legal services can find the loophole that got those other PAs out of your situation."

The younger man nodded numbly, emotionally exhausted from the roller coaster of a day he had.

God give me strength. He thought as he watched Dr. Oxner finish up writing some notes.

Honestly, he just wanted this all over with. It was hard to focus on his schoolwork when he had to worry about getting fast food for meals and crashing at his girlfriend's dorm.

Sadly, he still had a test to take the next morning.

CHAPTER EIGHTEEN

Metaphorical as well as literal clouds hung over his head.

The sky had been a sheet of gray since the sun had risen, but the air of sadness that hovered over him was more recent due to his academic failings. He'd known to go into the biology test that he obviously wasn't prepared for like he usually was, was a mistake. What he hadn't known was how terrible a night's sleep he was going to have the night prior, tossing and turning after a wonky nightmare about Elijah freezing to death in his room because there was a lock on the thermostat.

Stupid, he knew. That didn't make waking up to Elizabeth asking him what was wrong any easier. It also meant he had a slight headache from not getting a restful night of sleep. Well, that and the fact he hadn't gotten a long night's sleep in a while.

Maybe I didn't fail, he mused as he walked towards his favorite Subway to get a quick sandwich before lunch. There was just enough time for him to walk halfway across campus to get it and eat it on the walk back to the quad where the student union was. From there it was just a trip up the stairs to the student legal services office. A sandwich from this particular Subway was well worth the walk when he knew his favorite manager was working.

"Long time no see!" Said manager called across the store as soon as Keith entered.

The PA pushed away his shyness and waved at the

large dark-skinned man with a huge grin on his face.

"What're you talkin' about? I see you every night I work down the street because you're here all day every day, man."

"Gotta work to support the family," he responded. He went back to helping the customer he was currently working with. The entire time it bugged Keith he was not wearing a nametag.

I wish I knew his name, but he only introduced himself that one time and I can't remember what his name is for the life of me. It's been months now though. Maybe it was Victor? But what if I'm wrong? I can't risk calling him the wrong name! I can't ask him what it is at this point either; what's worse is that he knows my name somehow despite having so many customers. What a guy.

After another minute passed and the woman he was ringing up walked away from the counter, the large man planted himself on the other side of the counter at the beginning of the line.

"What'cha want today, Keith? Oh, wait, let me guess. Steak, cheese, and barbeque on flatbread."

The younger man glared with no real malice behind it.

"I dunno. I think I'm feeling rotisserie chicken today."

"What a change. Want a little bit of spinach on it today to spice it up?"

"You know what? Sure. Throw on some green peppers and onion before you toast it too. I'm feeling adventurous today."

"Whatever you want, kid. I still think the green pepper may be a bit too spicy for you from what Edgar, Gerardo, and Gabe told me down at your pizza joint."

"They put red pepper on my popcorn when I wasn't looking. My *popcorn*. Not to mention they put hot barbeque on my wings instead of regular barbeque; I only realized when my lips started swelling up."

"You really can't handle heat, huh?" The sandwich

artist asked while popping the sub into the oven to toast. "Anyway, how are your classes going?"

Keith shrugged. "Well enough."

"And those jobs of yours? Not at the restaurant. The library one and I think the caretaker one?"

"Stuff at the library is going fine. The personal assistant one," he hesitated, "not well at all. My Person's family situation is a lot more complicated than I anticipated. There's also a lot of drama going on in the house. I tried intervening, but I just made it worse."

Humming in understanding, the older man took the sub out of the toaster oven and began pouring on barbeque sauce without even asking. He knew exactly what Keith liked.

"That's rough, buddy. All I can tell you is to try to keep a level head. You're a smart, hardworking kid. Whatever is going on over there will pass, or maybe getting out of the situation would be a better option. You're intelligent enough to know if staying will help more, or if it is best to get out of there to help yourself."

"That's some solid advice. Thank you."

"No problem. Oh, but if you're as indecisive when it comes to important stuff as you are when picking out what type of sandwich you want I'll tell you right now..." He paused while wrapping his sandwich to point at Keith sternly. "Don't do that. Whatever decision you make is the best one. Try not to be too hard on yourself. Okay, kid?"

"I'll try," he promised, paying with card before grabbing the bag with his sandwich in it. To his surprise there was a chocolate chip cookie in there as well, something he usually got as a stand-alone on the way home from work some nights.

Instantly, the figurative clouds that had been hovering around him cleared up. Even though it was drizzling outside he felt warmer all of a sudden.

He stood in front of the door to student legal services once more. It took him nearly a full minute to bring himself to knock, his brain telling him he was too early but his watch telling him he was nearly late.

Ugh, I'm starting to feel like a mess again.

"Come in!"

The same middle-aged woman from the day before greeted him as soon as he entered, telling him to sign in again with a smile while his designated lawyer finished up with the person he was seeing. Keith sat down in one of the only two chairs they had in the tight space they called a waiting area. He killed time by meaninglessly scrolling through fandom-related content on Instagram, liking posts almost carelessly if they were about something he liked. It felt like his brain was on autopilot. He was looking, but not seeing. It was strange because the involuntary task of just breathing seemed like it was taking more effort and focus than usual.

Suddenly, the sound of a door opening caught his attention. It came from the direction of his lawyer's office which was the only reason he particularly cared if a door opened in the first place.

He swung his head around to see a girl shaking the hand of a brown-haired man who appeared to be in his fifties. His hair was slicked back like he'd done it on the way out the door, golden tanned skin a contrast to the black of the suit he was wearing. The girl thanked him before making her way out of the office, leaving the man to lock his eyes on Keith's.

"You must be my next appointment," he stated as a way of greeting. The skin around his eyes crinkled as he smiled slightly, reaching a hand out to shake Keith's own. "My name is Dr. Sime. You must be Mr. Sloan, correct?"

"Um, yes."

The student quickly stood up and shook the man's hand, his nerves settling slightly at his approachable demeanor. There was something else in the man's eyes that he couldn't help but notice. How to place it though was the question. Was it mischievousness? Or was it playfulness?

Dr. Sime inclined his head before he could figure it out.

"It's a pleasure to meet you. Now how about we go into my office and discuss that contract?"

Nodding, Keith followed the lawyer a total of two yards until he was asked to take a seat in front of his desk. Dr. Sime closed the door behind them, grabbing a couple of papers from a filing cabinet near his desk before taking a seat in front of his computer. There were several seconds of shuffling as he pulled what Keith recognized was a print out of the contract but with certain sections highlighted and a few parts circled in red ink.

"Okay," he began while sliding a second copy in front of the student. "Let's get started, shall we? I looked over the contract you emailed to me yesterday and noticed it is the same one the Thompson family has used the previous two years. This, lucky for you, means I already know what advice to give you for getting out of this crappy stack of paper those psychos call a legally binding contract. Ha! Any first-semester law school student would be able to tell the whole thing's a sham."

Keith stared at the still pleasantly smiling man in awe.

"I... what?"

"Oh, sorry about that. I sort of just started ranting, didn't I? I always get like this when I see this contract. It's like a joke that only get's funnier every time you hear it. Their contract is full of shit, kid. They had some big-shot Jewish lawyer from New York write this list of reasons to kill yourself in fancy terminology just to scare everyone who works for them into following their rules without question. Jacqueline, if I remember correctly, hates it when people think for themselves. She wrote dozens of rules because she didn't like her son's personal assistants getting distracted while working or blabbing about how tight a lease she keeps on her kid. She also would have an aneurysm if something in that house got damaged or wasn't kept clean enough to eat off of any surface. That woman is a terror, Keith. You honestly couldn't have picked a worse person to PA for. I will commend you though. The longest I've known a PA to last is four weeks; however, you beat that record by a long-shot. How is that?"

"I needed housing," he answered honestly. He pushed the tidbit about him lasting the longest of all the PAs away for the time being. That was something he would be annoyed about later. "I also had no idea the situation would have turned into what it did, so when it kept getting worse I thought it would eventually get better? But since the other PAs got fired or quit Jacqueline had to stay at the house. And she's so…"

He trailed off, looking up at the older man meaningfully.

Dr. Sime's eyes shown with empathy. "I understand exactly what you mean, Mr. Sloan."

"Just Keith is fine."

"Sure, Keith. Now let me ask you a follow-up question. You didn't find, at any point, the fact she made you sign a contract that wouldn't allow you to talk about your job outside of those you work with a bit strange?"

"Well, a little, but I thought it was more for medical disclosure reasons."

"It also didn't occur to you to get the contract looked over by a professional before signing it? Contracts are usually legally binding. Well, in most cases."

The PA let a bit of his frustration show when he answered.

"Look, I didn't know about student legal services until I needed help. I also probably wouldn't have used you guys to look into the contract beforehand, because when I went over to their house to sign paperwork she said the contract could not leave the home and I would only get an electronic copy once I signed it."

"She lied to you about that, Keith. You have always had the right to legal services before signing such a binding document."

"Well I wouldn't have known that," he sighed, exasperated. "I really needed the job at the time. I wasn't going to question my future employer too much, since in past experience that ended with me just not getting the job at all. My financial situation is too tight to have risked that. I'm barely affording my final year of college as it is."

"And that's exactly the kind of situation she looks for in potential employees."

"You have *got* to be kidding."

"I'm afraid I'm not. Seven of the last nine PAs that came in here seeking help, and they mentioned having put off trying to leave because they needed the money and housing. It makes sense though. Those with a surplus of money so to speak have an easier time leaving because they don't have to worry about not having somewhere to go or earning money to pay for college. Or, well, anything really."

"That's crazy. And there's no way to stop them from putting up the ad? The receptionist, I mean, someone said you guys tried to have the job board people take it down but the Thompsons threw a fit and threatened to sue them because of discrimination..."

Dr. Sime shook his head, a stream of air leaving his lips harshly as he heaved a great sigh.

"It's amazing these days what people can get away with by whining and crying. The people who run the virtual job board are pansies who let the word discrimination scare them into bending over like they dropped the soap in a prison shower. They don't understand that the Thompsons are all talk and no bite. At least not after the first time they tried bringing someone to court."

"What do you mean? Jacqueline keeps telling me she's

in the process of suing the last PA that left."

"Did they leave with a doctor's note?"

"I'm… not sure. I tried texting and calling him but he's had no contact with me after he quit."

"What was his name?"

"Elijah."

A spark of recognition flashed in his eyes, but when he went to speak it was with an air of whimsy.

"That's very unfortunate. All I can say is that I saw *someone* within the last several weeks and gave them the same advice I'm going to give you. The Thompsons cannot sue you for leaving if you have a doctor's note stating the environment is not a safe one to live in, be it damaging to you physically or psychologically, or if the job as a PA has caused you injury and your doctor gives you a note stating you must stop working in order to get better. Heck, get two notes if you can. Otherwise she might try to say you have to see her recommended doctor for a second opinion. And I've heard he's friends with her lawyer."

"You... you're saying all I need are two doctors' notes? And then I can leave?"

"Yep. If they try telling you anything else or show you some clauses in the contract that make what I said look untrue, then they are lying. Their lawyer wrote so many illegal things in that contract that often get overlooked unless brought in to a professional. Most of what is in there will not hold up in court. For example," he raved while pointing to a section on a page circled in red, "when they say you cannot talk about what happens in the house with anyone, medical professionals, the police, and legal staff included. That's outright against national as well as state law. They cannot tell you that you aren't allowed to talk about your living situation to professional staff or otherwise. You can't technically disclose their son's disability, but anything else is fair game. Slander? Libel? To hell with that. Unless you publish their personal information on paper or online using their names or close physical likenesses in a factual piece they can't sue you for a penny."

"You're positive?"

"Like a teen girl's pregnancy test after prom night. One hundred percent." When he saw the skeptical look on Keith's face the lawyer smirked. "Don't worry about it, kid. They won't bring you to court."

"But how do you know? You're so sure."

"Keith, the Thompsons have only ever brought one PA to court. It was the first PA that ever saw me deal with that family, and let me tell you that I have never had an easier time defending someone in my life. First of all, the jury realized within the first session that the family was not all there in the head. You could just tell all of the excuses for her actions towards the PA as well as her son wasn't going to fly. Honestly the jury would have reached a verdict in the first session if not for her and her lawyer being a pain in the ass and dragging it out as long as possible. Ever since then they haven't brought anyone who sees me to court. Probably because my daughter as the same disability as her son, and she wasn't going to risk going on trial against me again. Oh does that woman hate my guts."

He laughed, which would have been contagious if not for the fact Keith was mind blown. All this time Jacqueline had been using fear-mongering and lies to keep him under her perfectly manicured thumb. She'd been doing that to everyone who ever worked for her too, and he doubted she even felt bad for it.

"How could someone like her get away with this over and over again?"

"She's rich. People with money can get away with murder. Literally. It's happened in the past, it's happening now, and it will keep happening because that's just how the world works. And I am sorry you had to go through this. Maybe it's a good learning experience for you though."

"I guess."

A minute passed without either of them speaking. Dr. Sime pulled out a sheet of paper and began writing something down on it during that time, only speaking once he was done.

"Okay. I wrote a list of recommended psychologists who are also doctors in the area that will be able to write you a catch-all doctor's note. Of course you can also get a note from the counseling center as well as your primary doctor; those two will work just fine. I usually recommend these people," he circled two names of the four recommended, "simply because I went to school with them and know that they know their stuff. Personal bias, I know, but the three PAs that went to either of them sent me a follow-up email confirming they were a great help."

Keith nodded. "I'll look into it. Um, do you mind me asking about your daughter?"

"Sure thing. What about her?"

"You said she has the same disability as the person I'm assisting. Is it the same exact disability? Could she collapse at any time because of blood irregularities, or does she have some form of epilepsy?"

Dr. Sime raised an eyebrow. "She has anemia, Keith. The Thompson boy has something along those lines from my medical understanding but seems to have been brought up to think his condition is so much worse than what everyone else with any disability has. Not that some forms of it aren't more severe than others. His mother has drilled it into his head that he can't even walk on his own," he said while gesticulating wildly. "Not to mention the fact he's probably nearing thirty and doesn't even have his own bank account, and from what I heard last time I was in court with them his mother even looks at his text and call log. What sort of parent does that to their child? And don't even get me started on their daughters. Well, the one that didn't cut ties with their family."

"Chelsee? Huh. I've never met her. She's studying abroad or something right now, so..."

"Well aren't you lucky."

"Is she that bad?"

"Imagine the spitting image of Jacqueline, but with black hair and raise the level of pettiness to having sex with someone, regretting it a day later, and then claiming assault."

"I— you're joking, right?"

The lawyer responded with a half eye-roll, which Keith couldn't tell meant yes or no.

"Anyway, you know what you have to do now. Go see whatever plethora of medical professionals you need to get the notes you need. Also, if you haven't already because that woman has you scared into silence with her so-called gag order, talk to somebody for God's sake. Tell your girlfriend, your parents, your friends, or even a stranger. As long as you don't use names or disclose the disability you are allowed to talk about what's happening in that house as much as you want. The clause in their contract won't hold up in court even if hell froze over and they pressed charges against you."

"But they won't, right? You said they only did that with the first PA."

"Correct. Every other student who has seen me tells me Jacqueline threatens to bring them into court, but she never did."

"What if she waits until they're out of school and can't have you defend them?"

"That wouldn't help her out, because cases started here while you're a student last a lifetime. She could drag you to court ten years from now and someone from the university would defend you. Hopefully me if I'm still around."

Keith blinked stupidly.

"Really?"

"Yep."

"That's pretty awesome."

"Well you pay enough to go here. The university better have some good benefits for students other than free food and bag clips."

That actually did make Keith chuckle, his nerves giving way from wound tighter than boa constrictor to a loose rubber band. The tension was still there, but he was feeling much better after hearing what he had. He was still beyond angry at Jacqueline of course. His situation, however, seemed much less damning now that he knew a way to get out of it.

That was something, right?

"I really can't thank you enough," he decided to go with as he took a stack of papers from Dr. Sime and put them in his drawstring bag. "You have no idea how much you've helped me out. I've been sick over this for days. I was starting to wonder if I was the one blowing everything out of proportion; I thought maybe I just needed to grow up, or that I was crazy."

The lawyer's lip quirked up in a half-smile as he stood up and shook Keith's hand once more.

"Nope," he stated reassuringly, "it's not you. The problem is crazy people usually drive other people crazy, which either makes non-crazies think they're losing their minds or actually does cause them to lose their minds. And it's a damn shame too. The world loses too many good people that way. But not you," he reassured with a smile.

Keith nodded, the lawyer's confidence rubbing off on him as he was escorted out of the office. "I'm going to call my doctor right after this and book an appointment. I already saw someone from the counseling center yesterday and he's going to email me a note any day now."

"Perfect. Good luck getting out of there, Keith. Shoot me an email if you need any more help or advice."

"I will. Thank you again!"

"You're welcome."

With that Keith told the nice secretary lady to have a good day as he left, pulling out his cell phone all the while.

He had a couple of calls to make.

CHAPTER NINETEEN

Two days later, Keith's mother was picking him up from class and driving him to his doctor's appointment.

"Thank you for coming down here all of a sudden." He thanked from the bottom of his heart. He knew they didn't have a lot of money right now, and two four hour drives by herself was a lot for her in a day. "Is Kassie mad I made her skip school today so you could come? Is dad mad he had to get a ride home from work?"

"They're both crabby as usual, but who cares. After what you told me I had to be here to get you out of that hellhole. You're my baby."

He looked out the window. There was a blush on his face, but his mother didn't need to know that.

After seeing Dr. Sime, the first person he had called was his mother. He's told her everything. Within minutes she had been telling him to call her after he'd booked a doctor's appointment. She needed to know what time to be there to quote-unquote "save her baby", something that both warmed Keith's heart as much as he wished she didn't have to come to his rescue at all.

"I'll pay you for gas."

"Thank you, sweetie. As much as I don't want to have to take you up on that I might have to since your father doesn't get paid for another day."

"It's not a problem. I can spare twenty dollars for gas, especially since you'll be helping me move out today if stuff at the doctor goes well."

"I don't like borrowing money from my child. A parent should be the one you're borrowing money from; not the other way around. And I'm sure you'll get that second doctor's note," she said optimistically. "You already have the other one from the school psychologist printed out and ready to go, right?"

"Yep. Elizabeth printed it out for me yesterday."

She smiled, her voice growing fond. "Lizzy's such a sweet girl. I'm so glad you two found each other, and that you're both such a good match for one another. If only your sister could've found someone like that instead of all the losers she winds up with."

"Yeah, we all wish that."

After a couple more minutes of driving and idle talk, they arrived at the clinic Keith had discovered the day of making his appointment. It wasn't one of the giant facilities that existed on or close to campus, which he was thankful for since that meant he had less of a chance of getting turned around, but a comfortable two-story convenient care center with a Walgreens and CVS attached.

Upon entering, they did end up going to the wrong desk because there were apparently three of them. It took nearly all the extra time they had to determine the one they needed to be at was upstairs. Once he'd checked in though, Keith and his mom took a seat next to the ever-present fish tank near the wall marked "family care".

"Why is it always fish?" He asked, leg bouncing uncontrollably. As his eyes wandered around the room taking note of everyone else around them the urge to talk rose. "I get that some of them are nice to look at, and they're pretty low maintenance, but wouldn't a dog or a lizard be so much cooler? Oh, or a cat."

His mom gave him a look. "A lot of people are allergic to dogs and cats, and lizards need a lot of care. Too many kids would tap on the glass and annoy the poor thing."

"Kids tap on the glass of fish tanks all the time."

"Maybe, but still lizards aren't as cute as fish to most people."

"To most people. They could get a snake and only have to feed it once a week."

"Keith, some adults are terrified of snakes. Imagine how many children would be scared before even entering their doctor's office."

"Snakes are cute though! It's not like it'd escape."

"Sweetie, no."

"Okay, but what about a therapy pet? A dog or cat would be so popular. It could help with anxious patients and entertain bored kids."

"Too many people are allergic."

"I get that, but what's to stop someone with a registered therapy pet coming in here anyway? Nothing. So the doctor's office having one wouldn't be an issue especially in a building as huge as this one."

"I guess you're right about that. But the animal would have to belong to someone. It wouldn't just be able to live here," she said.

"Well duh. If it belonged to an employee—"

The sound of his name getting called by a nurse made him shut up. Suddenly he felt sick like he could throw up at any second.

"Do you want me to come with you?"

Keith stood up, nodding without doing more than glancing at his mom to make sure she followed. He loved his mom, yet he wished Elizabeth was there right now. She had a quiz though. She wouldn't be available for another half an hour at the earliest; however, part of him was thankful she couldn't come. There were a couple of details he hadn't told her that his mom and doctor would soon find out that he felt were best left unsaid. It would only make her more upset about the situation.

Her unbridled rage was scary too.

"Right this way," the nurse instructed him after introducing herself. "Since it's your first time at this location we'll take the usual height and weight measurements. After that I'll get some information from you concerning this visit, and then I'll have you sit in the waiting room until your doctor is ready to see you."

"Okay."

Measurements were taken, a sinking feeling hitting him at learning he'd lost over ten pounds in the past several weeks. He knew he hadn't been eating as much, sure, but enough to account for nearly ten pounds? Maybe part of it was because of the extra exercise he was getting from his classes. That had to be it.

The nurse showed them over to a room once the measurements were taken in the hall.

"Now that that's over with, would you mind telling me the reason for your visit? Let me know if you are in any pain as well according to the scale shown here," she stated, her pointer finger indicating the classic one through ten number chart ranging from a happy face to a crying face.

Keith looked at his mom, then looked at his hands.

"Um, I'm here because I started assisting a student with a disability over a month ago, and after weeks of working as a live-in PA for him I've been having more and more health problems. I started having panic attacks because of the environment, which I've never had in my life. I can barely eat or go to the bathroom anymore without being sick with anxiety, and I can't focus on my studies because I'm worried those I'm living with will hurt me. I haven't slept for more than a few hours a night due to the nightmares I've been having recently concerning the job. I talked to a few people because I thought I might be going crazy, but after visiting a psychologist we determined the toxic work environment is what is causing all of these issues. I was told if I got two notes from medical professionals I can and should leave that job because of how badly it's affecting me. I already got a note from the university psychologist. I was hoping Dr. Aleman could write me one too because if he doesn't I won't be able to leave and I don't know what I'd do if I can't get out of there today."

At this point his steady voice began to wobble, so he just decided not to divulge anything else. He didn't trust himself to talk further without losing his composure.

I'm so pathetic, he thought as the nurse gave him a look full of pity. She was writing something extensive on the clipboard. *I should have just stayed quiet. I've caused so much trouble for everybody all because I couldn't suck it up. Elizabeth, Tucker, Jared, and my mother are having to take important time out of their daily lives to support me when I should have been able to deal with things myself. And all these professionals I've been visiting are listening to my sob story like they haven't heard worse ones before. God, I'm so selfish.*

No you're not! Another part of him argued. It almost sounded like Elizabeth. *Your friends and your family want to help you because they love you. Your parents love you unconditionally, and your friends wouldn't be your friends if they didn't care about your wellbeing when you're sad or going through something like this shitty situation. And who cares if others have had it worse than you. That doesn't mean you should use that as an excuse to stay miserable.*

I don't deserve their kindness. I'm just a burden.

Like hell you are!

His internal struggle was broken when he heard the nurse say she'd send the doctor in as soon as he was ready. The moment she shut the door behind her he looked at his mother, who had tears in her eyes.

Look what you did. Look at what you did to her, you asshole. You made her cry. Why couldn't you man up and see the doctor on your own? Mom has enough of her own worries and health problems without you—

Once again his thoughts stopped short, this time because his mom was offering her hand to him. In an instant he was holding it, a tiny part feeling ashamed for being so hard on himself and another, bigger part of him feeling so damn grateful for having a mother who loved him. He'd never take her for granted again.

Finally, after a couple more minutes of silence, the door rattled. In walked Dr. Aleman.

"Hello," he greeted jovially yet without much of an expression on his face. His clipboard clattered on the table where he haphazardly dropped it on the way to sit in front of the computer monitor. He began typing a few things before bringing his attention to his patient. "Keith, correct?"

"Yes, sir."

The man ran a palm across his bald head before going straight to the point.

"I read over what you told my colleague. From the symptoms presented and the timeframe specified it is apparent to me your new position as a live-in PA isn't good for your psychological or physical health. My professional advice is to quit this job for the sake of your wellbeing. I understand I will need to write you a doctor's note in order to legally quit, is that right? Your employer won't accept your word for it?"

"No, she won't. As for the doctor's note technically I need two to leave without repercussions. I got one note from the school psychologist saying the place I work now is not good for my mental state and his professional opinion was to terminate my employment, but the school's lawyer said my employer might make me go to her recommended doctor for a second opinion if I don't get a second note myself. I don't trust her doctor to not twist my words into saying it's all in my head or convince me into staying a PA."

"That's unfortunate. Well, you won't need to worry

about something like that happening. I'll gladly write down whatever you need to get out of that situation."

"I— what?"

Colleen gaped openly. "Are you serious?"

Dr. Aleman raised an eyebrow at the mother. "Of course I am. I'm not going to write any falsehoods, but I will write down what truths need to be documented for your son to get out of such a horrid-sounding situation."

"Thank you so much," she told him sincerely.

Keith was full of the same gratitude.

"I can't thank you enough either. You have no idea how much this means to me. If I wasn't able to get another note I would have had to go back to work in two days and honestly breaking an arm or a leg sounded better than having to do that."

"There's no need to hurt yourself. I will write you what you need. Now, you told the nurse you've lost your usual appetite?"

"I, yes. I mean being around the Thompsons makes me nauseous on account of the anxiety, so I can't keep much down. They also restrict what and when I can eat for dinner. It's hard to just sit down and eat when I feel like it. I can't bring snacks to my room, and I have to sneak water to my room even though I get super dehydrated at night."

He nodded. "Okay, and have you hurt yourself while assisting this person?"

"I've scraped my knees a couple of times. Um, and my lower back aches after I catch him since the sudden deadweight is a lot all at once. I try to use my legs, but since it happens without warning it's nearly impossible."

"And has the stress of the job caused you to lose sleep?"

"Yes. Between the mother's gossiping at all hours of the night on the phone and how I feel like I can't relax since I'm in the same house with people I don't feel safe around I get maybe four hours a night."

"Okay. That should be everything I need."

A minute passed where he typed some things on his computer. After another minute filled with mouse clicking he stood up, telling them he'd be back in a moment. Sure enough he was back within ten seconds holding a sheet of paper.

"Read this over," Dr. Aleman instructed while handing it to Keith.

"Okay."

As he read over the official-looking document his eyes widened. There were only a couple sentences, hardly over a hundred words, and yet the finality of what his doctor had written was there.

"Thank you. This will work."

Dr. Aleman finally allowed himself to smile. It was small, but it was still there.

"Good luck with your situation, Keith. If for some reason that note is not enough then feel free to give this family you're working for my card," he said while handing a business card to him as well. "I love arguing with people on my patient's behalf."

"I'll be sure to give this to them." The student nodded while hanging onto the note and card for dear life.

This was it. He was finally going to be free.

"Do you want us to come in with you?"

"I think we should. They might try to not let him leave."

"They can't do that, can they?"

"Those people are crazy."

"Well if they try to make my baby stay or not let him grab his stuff then I'll call the cops."

"Guys," Keith broke in before Elizabeth and his mother could get too worked up, "they have to let me leave. If they try to say I can't, then I'll call the cops myself. But it shouldn't come to that. They want to avoid trouble as much they can. The lawyer told me it puts the money the Thompsons get from the state in danger because they already get audited yearly once the state noticed the turnover rate of the PAs. The more trouble they get in the more likely the state is to cut off funding."

"And that woman wouldn't like that at all," Colleen guessed.

"Exactly."

"I feel sorry for Brandon. That poor boy."

Elizabeth rolled her eyes. "Poor boy? He's old enough to make his own decisions. I get that his family more or less brainwashed him when he was younger, but there's a point where he realized something wasn't right. He could have tried to fight back. If not in high school, then at least sometime in the last several years. Too many PAs left for him to not get that something about his family is messed up. I'm sure Keith wasn't the first person to try and help him."

"The problem is he doesn't want help," Keith said in between bites of his cookie dough donut. God, he was starving. Between his morning classes and the doctor visit he hadn't eaten yet; therefore, before picking up Elizabeth from her class he'd begged his mother to stop somewhere to grab something to eat. Lucky for him his favorite donut shop was on the way.

"He doesn't want help because he's too scared to take a risk. He's not willing to give up his lavish lifestyle in favor of controlling his own life."

"Lizzy…"

"I'm sorry, but I don't have any empathy for a guy his age taking out his anger on you for trying to stop his mother from hurting him. It's not your fault his mother is a psycho. She was hurting him, and you intervened, so excuse me if I'm still pissed he would turn on you for being a decent human being."

From in the front passenger seat of the car Keith moved

his arm so that he could wind it behind the seat. A moment later he was squeezing Lizzy's hand from where she sat in the back, looking energized and ready to fight his boss if the situation called for it.

"I know you're mad at him, sweetie, but he's had a rough life."

"He's going to keep having one too if he doesn't stand up for himself. Disability or not working with Will the past three years showed us that needing help does not have to stop anyone from taking charge of his or her own life."

"Maybe he doesn't want people to think he's weak for needing help?" Colleen wondered out loud as they got closer to the house.

Elizabeth let out a frustrated noise.

"I seriously don't get it. Too many good people have gone through unnecessary pain because they think asking for a bit of help is bad, that it makes them look weak or pathetic. That doesn't make any sense."

"It's hard to ask for help," Keith defended.

"I know. That's why being able to ask for help means someone who does it is strong, not weak, because they aren't trying to go it alone. Getting the help you need means you cared enough about yourself to overcome that barrier of fear or embarrassment or extra work and put self-care and love before all that."

She squeezed his hand meaningfully, making him feel self-conscious.

I wasn't brave, he wanted to say. *I waited too long. I only asked for help because the situation escalated into something I couldn't handle.*

Colleen looked between her son and her future daughter-in-law in the rearview mirror. She wanted to agree with Elizabeth, but before she could she realized they were there. Parking on the other side of the street for the time being she turned off the car.

"So are we coming in or not?"

The almost-former PA took a deep breath as he let go of his girlfriend's hand.

"You guys can stay out here. As much as I'd like for you to come in she probably wouldn't let you, and honestly I probably need to just deal with this myself. I'll call or text you if I need anything."

He grabbed the notes he'd need as well as his phone, the latter of which he slipped into his pocket after getting out of the car. After shutting the door he walked with purpose across the street and up the driveway. His heart pounded harder the closer to the front door he got; he didn't need to look over his shoulder to feel the worried gazes of his mother and girlfriend as he reached it either.

Bringing out his key to the house, his hands shook as he unlocked it and ran in to deactivate the alarm.

Once inside he heard movement from the kitchen. He ignored the overwhelming urge to vomit as he slipped his shoes off and prepared to go up the steps; however, just as he was about to do so his courage gave out. Suddenly he found his arms tensing up so quickly it was painful. A cold sweat broke over him, and he could feel his breaths coming out faster one after the other.

I'm scared. I can't do this. I can't handle getting yelled at today. She's going to call me things and tell me I'm crazy, and I know Dr. Sime told me this is what she does and I know that but it's so hard to ignore when she's so loud. Brandon is going to hate me even more now. What if he cries? I don't want to make his life worse than it already is. But I can't stay here any longer. I can't. They all hate me. I need to leave.

If not because of them, then for myself.

Forcing one foot in front of the other, he pushed himself to go up the steps and into the kitchen.

CHAPTER TWENTY

Immediately he noticed Thomas sitting next to Brandon. His Person had a couple more bites of a sandwich as well as a single cookie left on his plate. From the other side of the room he noticed Jacqueline, her blonde hair standing out like a beacon, making her way out of the kitchen like he had the plague. It hurt. He knew she said she would avoid him, but literally running out of the room was a bit much, wasn't it?

"Um, hi." Keith greeted lamely as he continued through the room. He got an indifferent "hello" back from the PA and complete silence from Brandon.

Once out of the kitchen, he looked past the second dining room to the living room to see Jacqueline standing in the middle of the doorway looking as unhappy as usual. The moment she met his eyes her lip curled. In an instant she was off, nearly jogging out of the room and heading towards the staircase.

This is ridiculous.

He did not want to have to spend any more time chasing his boss around. This meant he'd have to shout, which was something he really hated doing.

"Excuse me, but can you please stop running away from me? I need to talk to you!"

In an instant she pivoted mid-step, stomping her way back into the room with a sneer on her face.

"What do you want, Keith?"

"I need to talk to you."

"Oh, is it about you finally returning to work? Did you get your mental state properly assessed?"

She said this in the most condescending way, which meant he felt less guilty when he handed her the doctor notes.

"I did. I went to one of the free counselors provided by the school. The psychologist I saw deemed this position and environment to have a negative effect on my mental, emotional, and physical state. Keeping my wellbeing as the top priority, he advised me to resign from my position and move out of the house."

The way her face went from conceited to shook to absolutely pissed would have been almost funny if not for her anger being directed at him.

"Are you serious?" She spat, taking a step closer and putting her finger right in his face. He leaned away slightly. "You would leave Brandon after knowing how little coverage he'd have? He'll be devastated. You must know that. He probably won't even finish his paper on time, because he'll be too stressed out with his living situation to get anything else done. You would leave knowing that you caused him to not get his masters on time?"

"Doctor's orders."

Somehow he said that without stuttering, something he did when he was extremely nervous like he was now. In the back of his head he was chanting "ignore her" over and over again if just to remind him she would say anything to guilt him into staying.

"I demand a second opinion," she threw the sheets she'd snatched out of his hand earlier onto a nearby chair. "I'll have you see one of my recommended doctors. He'll give you a proper evaluation in case the person who saw you was incompetent."

He pointed at the papers.

"I *did* get a second opinion. My doctor agreed that since living here my overall health has deteriorated, and he wrote that I would sadly need to stop working as a PA in order to get better. He also gave me his card," he explained while pulling it out of his pocket. "He said if you wanted to chat with him about the prognosis that he would be happy to take a call or email."

She doesn't need to know I only started seeing the doctor today.

If looks could kill, then Keith would've been dead.

Jacqueline picked the papers up and read them with venom dripping from her eyes. She scoffed at each one after reading them, but even she couldn't deny they were legitimate.

"Well, this is very unfortunate. I suppose you're going to break the contract and quit then?"

The fear he'd felt when he was being threatened flared up. Had Dr. Sime been wrong?

"I'm not quitting. I'm resigning for medical reasons, which is not breaking the contract."

"Who told you that?" She laughed, borderline hysterical. "Leaving unless you're fired you're going against the contract, which means there will be legal repercussions."

She's lying, he told himself. *Dr. Sime told me she'd try to tell me I couldn't leave even with the notes. So just ignore her threats. She's trying to do what she had been this entire time: scare me into doing what she wants when guilt-tripping me doesn't work.*

"That's unfortunate," he bit out, "but regardless I need to put myself first."

"I see. Well, I'll call Larry to let him know he'll need to drive down this weekend to help you move out."

"Actually, my mom is waiting outside in the car. Elizabeth is there too. They'll help pack stuff in the car once I bring it down."

He was wrong. He'd thought he'd seen Jacqueline at her angriest already, but now he knew that her face turned red when she wanted her gaze to incinerate him on the spot.

"You aren't allowed to bring stuff up and down the stairs!" She shrieked. "It's against the contract! Only Larry and I can move things, and I have a bad knee. I could injure it further by doing this today!"

"That's fine. I can call the non-emergency police and have them move my things instead."

"You're a cruel, selfish child. Bringing your shitty girlfriend and dragging your mother down here to 'rescue' you. How pathetic. You know you're going to Hell for everything you've done to my family, right?"

A confident smile split his face as he gathered up the courage to play her game.

"I hope not. But maybe others will agree with you should I ever need to give this recording to a lawyer," he stated coolly while pulling out his phone. It was all a bluff, but she didn't need to know. "The more people that know what a terrible person I am the better it looks for you, right?"

"You little—"

She cut herself off, her face quickly going from red to white. All at once her demeanor changed so that she was meek and on the verge of tears.

"Fine. Go upstairs and start packing. I doubt you have much to put your belongings into, but I'll grab your suitcases from the basement. Anything else you can store in garbage bags. Before I go grab those, however, you need to tell Brandon you're quitting."

His heart sank. She saw it on his face and took that as a sign to continue.

"Oh, so you have the balls to quit, but not to tell the person you're affecting most what you're doing to him?"

Keith frowned, the guilt that had been festering just under the surface coming back up to choke him. Technically he wasn't obligated to tell Brandon anything since his mother was designated as his boss. Listening to her by telling Brandon would only prove to upset both of the males more, which was probably what Jacqueline wanted. She loved making him feel miserable.

He inhaled sharply. Standing his ground, he told her he was going to start packing up what he could.

"Fine! I'll go break the news to him since you're a quitter and a coward."

He nodded, pulling out his phone again as a silent reminder that everything she called him could be recorded.

The next forty minutes were filled with rapid packing. Part of him regretted not discretely packing up his belongings before quitting because Jacqueline watched him in the doorway the entire time he did so. She's stationed her quietly sobbing son and Thomas out in the hall to be "witnesses" in case something was to happen.

She said she no longer felt safe being around Keith alone.

Go figure, he thought when he heard that. He wanted to scoff at her openly, but he didn't want to start anything else. She was already driving him crazy with her constant gaze and biting remarks.

"You know I'm pretty sure the wicker bedpost wasn't damaged here," she picked at a part critically.

"It was like that when I moved in. It's on the move-in sheet I filled out."

"I'll be sure to fact check that statement."

Silence, and then:

"Once you leave I'll have to air out the room. There's a foul odor coming from somewhere in here…"

He ignored her. It wasn't long though before she interrupted him stuffing his school supplies into a garbage bag to point out a stain on the rug.

"Larry specifically told me to write that on the move in sheet when I first got here."

"Hmm, did he? It just seems bigger than it was."

"I assure you I didn't spill something right over the spot

of a stain. I never ate or drank anything up here, and none of my school supplies are purple."

"So you say. Regardless, if I do find anything out of order I will have to bill you for damages."

"I hear you," he ground out. As if having to put all of his stuff in garbage bags wasn't humiliating enough, especially since he knew they had boxes in the basement (some of which were his), listening to Jacqueline run her mouth was giving him a headache. It didn't help that he could still hear Brandon crying occasionally from where he sat in the hallway.

"You know I still need a resignation letter from you."

Stopping what he was doing, Keith whirled around to face Jacqueline.

"A resignation letter?"

"Yes. Do you not know what one is?"

"I know what it is. It's just that the past five jobs I had I never had to write one."

"How lucky you've been until now," she faked a congratulatory tone. "I still am going to need one from you in case the state needs one from us due to your sudden departure. You understand such a hasty absence is seen as strange, right? Two weeks is what decent people usually put in when leaving a job."

Like he'd been doing for nearly an hour, Keith held his tongue.

"I'll get it done after I'm done packing, which I could do faster if you weren't talking to me."

"Oh, am I distracting you? I'll shut up then." She took a step back into the hallway, relaying the fact that she was told to not talk to him to her son and the PA.

He rolled his eyes once he turned around, one-hundred percent done with her shit.

Except he was two-hundred percent done with her shit when she started taking his stuff down the stairs. Mostly because as soon as she picked up a bag containing clothes she started crying within seconds.

"I'm not allowed to carry anything over twenty pounds without causing my knee further problems," she explained to the full-time PA who for the entirety of the last hour hadn't said a word. He was completely impassive. "I hurt it during my time at the middle school I taught at years back. It causes me pain from time to time. Moving all this is going to leave me unable to walk for days."

To her surprise the full-time PA raised an eyebrow.

"You could always let Keith, the people outside waiting for him, or myself move his things instead?"

"It's against the contract. You know that."

"I know it's in the contract that no one else but you and your husband can do it because of the stairs or whatever, but you made the contract. If it was causing you that much pain to pick up a bag of toiletries then maybe you can just allow him to carry it down? Hurting yourself unnecessarily seems a bit silly."

Keith hid a smile as he heard Jacqueline huff and stomp down the stairs. It wasn't until after she'd carried a few bags down, crying and groaning theatrically all the while, that he realized he'd been hearing the alarm at the front door activate and deactivate like crazy.

"Are you putting my stuff outside?" He asked only once she'd taken most of his stuff.

"Of course. I didn't want your mother and girlfriend to get bored outside. Waiting in the car for an hour must have been dreadful, especially since it started raining not too long ago."

"It's raining, and you put my stuff outside?"

She rolled her eyes. "Most of it's in bags anyway; it's not like anything is being damaged."

"My dress clothes and my corkboard weren't in bags."

"I assure you if anything is ruined we'll gladly reimburse you for a replacement. We've given you enough free money as it is since I submitted your regular hours for next week. What's a little more?"

"Why would you do that?"

"Larry and I made a mistake believing you'd come to your senses. Brandon was the only one worried you'd do such a rash thing like quitting like this."

Keith knew she threw in that tidbit about Brandon in just to bother him, and it stung.

"Well it's not my fault you submitted my hours preemptively."

Ignoring his retort, she refrained from speaking to him until after she'd taken all of his stuff save one bag.

"Before you leave I will need that resignation letter," she reminded him as she picked up the bag, one arm clutching her back dramatically as she did so.

Just. Tell. Her. NO.

"I'll email it to you."

Son of a bitch, he thought.

"No, you can't. I need it in my hand before you leave."

"Am I legally obligated to give you one in the first place? I'm pretty sure jobs don't require a resignation letter to leave."

"They don't, but it's about professionalism, Keith. It's also caring enough about Brandon to give us something that won't look bad to those assessing our family."

Something about the way she said that made him irrationally angry. He didn't want to make Brandon's life worse or make his situation more complicated than it already was, but all Jacqueline cared about was how good her family looked on paper and it just made him see red.

I'll write a freaking letter alright, he thought angrily. *But I am not sugar-coating anything.*

"Okay," he said aloud in a much calmer manner than he was feeling. "I'll write one if it makes you happy. I need a pencil and paper then. All of my school supplies are packed up."

"Of course. I'll go get them."

He was glad to have her away from him so he could text Elizabeth without watchful eyes. She let him know that Jacqueline had just started putting his stuff out on the driveway haphazardly and that his mother had to quickly pull onto the driveway to grab everything before it got too wet. Elizabeth sent several angry texts saying "what a witch" and "how rude". If he wasn't already done with his soon to be former boss's antics he would have brought it up to her.

Instead, he put his anger into his resignation letter. Screw sounding professional. He would never put this on his resume anyway.

Ten minutes and a quick Google search on formatting the letter, he handed a crude-looking piece of paper to Jacqueline with a smile.

"Since all my stuff is gone I will be leaving now," he told her after parting with the paper.

"Not until I read over this really quick. I need to make sure you wrote it correctly."

"No."

She ignored him completely, not letting him past her as her eyes roamed the top of the sheet. Sure enough, within seconds she told him he had to write an address down in case she had mail to forward (which she wouldn't). He wrote down his home address like the resignation letter outline said only for her to snap at him that it must be a local address.

"You're not moving back home, are you? It would be pretty hard to keep taking on-campus courses from nearly seven hours away. It's not like you have a driver's license or a car to commute with."

"You said you needed my address for forwarding mail. It shouldn't have to be a local address," he challenged. She didn't need to know he'd gotten permission from his girlfriend's roommate as well as Jared and Tucker to crash with any of them for the next few weeks. He'd find a place for next semester soon.

She took a deep breath like she was dealing with a toddler who knew too much for his own good.

"I need a local address," she stated again slowly.

"I don't think you do."

When his response was as slow as hers, she growled at him and shoved the paper to his chest roughly.

"Just write an address down, Keith!"

"Fine. No need to get physical," he said loudly enough that he was sure Thomas and Brandon heard.

Neither of them said a word as he hastily wrote down Jared and Tucker's address.

"Here. Now I'm going if that's all?"

"We can all move downstairs while I read through the entire letter," she corrected while moving out into the hallway. Her eyes were already scanning the sheet thoroughly.

"Uh-huh..."

He avoided Brandon's gaze as he went downstairs, the others close behind him. As he turned into the kitchen and began walking towards the back door Jacqueline hissed for him to stay in the kitchen until she said so. He listened if only to speed the whole ordeal up.

Brandon and his PA went into the living room at Jacqueline's request, which made him nervous since she also closed the doors behind them. He made a show of pulling out his phone like he was making sure it was still recording. She paid no attention to him though. She was too busy looking more and more upset as she read what he'd written. Finally, once she was done she looked up at him with more fake tears in her eyes.

"Are you fucking kidding me? You can live with yourself calling this job bad for your mental and physical health?"

"That's what it says on my doctor notes."

"That doesn't mean you have to include it in your

resignation letter!"

He held strong at her screaming from only a few inches away from him. If his mother wasn't outside she was sure she'd have tried to claw him like she did Elijah.

"You told me I had to write one, so I did. If someone reading it takes certain things negatively then that sucks for you. I could have written a lot more factual things about why I no longer feel comfortable living or working here, perhaps what I witnessed last Saturday, but I didn't because I *do* care about Brandon. I won't lie for him though. Withholding what little information you might not be happy about would just be plain wrong. I'm not doing that."

"You won't change the wording at all?"

"No."

Her lips a thin line, she closed her eyes and squeezed a few tears out for good measure. It sort of made Keith want to laugh.

"Fine."

"I'll just be leaving then," he said. They had to be done now, right?

"You're not going to say goodbye to Brandon?"

He stood there for a moment as if contemplating it. After a moment he walked past Jacqueline, who violently jerked away from him as he passed. Within seconds he was in the living room with a splotchy-faced Brandon looking at him like he'd killed his sister.

"Goodbye, Brandon. Good luck with your paper. If you ever decide to move out on your own I'll be the first person to apply as your PA."

With that he turned around, taking a good guess that the boy wouldn't have said anything to him anyway. He did take a mini pack of candy out of his pants pocket though. He made sure to set it on one of the tables as he walked out, hoping that leaving it would make the other college student understand that he did care about him. Even the little things like his favorite candy.

"You think getting him sweets is a good apology for leaving?" Jacqueline criticized before he'd made it out of the room.

"It's not an apology. If anyone needs to tell him sorry it's you. Seriously, if I had you as a mother I would have killed myself years ago."

To his surprise Thomas started laughing, which only made their boss angrily demand what he thought was funny while he made his way to the back door.

When he got to the back door, however, there was one problem.

"Have you seen my shoes?"

"Of course I haven't," was the instant reply.

"Okay, but I know I was wearing them when I came in. I put them where all the other shoes are stored."

"That's unfortunate."

Keith looked at her incredulously. It was raining outside, and he would rather not get his socks wet. She didn't seem like she was going to budge or admit to anything though. Shaking his head, which was already throbbing at this point, he deactivated the door and stepped out onto the place-mat only to find his mother and girlfriend standing there waiting for him.

"Finally! Hurry, put on your shoes," Elizabeth said while handing them to him. "They were the first thing she put outside for some reason."

Of course they were.

As he slipped them on he watched his mother from the corner of his eye.

"It's sad this arrangement didn't work out." She said casually, a glint in her eye as she held her gaze with the blonde.

"It is. With the amount of stress this situation has caused Brandon I doubt he will be able to finish college on time. He'll probably have to drop out until he's mentally available to finish his classes. I hope you understand that his failure will be much do to your son."

"What situation? I've been asking Keith about his job for weeks but he said that he can't say anything about what he does. Can you tell me what's been going on?"

"No, I can't."

"Really? No explanation as to why I was called here to help him move out because multiple medical professionals deemed this job to be bad for his health?"

The blonde's face was as hard as stone. "I am under no obligation to say anything. And according to the contract he can't talk about anything that happens in the house that might be taken as slanderous."

"Slander? I see. So bad things *have* been happening in the house since he hasn't been able to talk to me about anything." Jacqueline opened her mouth, but Colleen was faster. And more petty. "Obviously as his mother I've been extremely concerned because it seems like over the past several weeks he hasn't been as happy as he usually is at school. Either way, I'm glad he's following the doctor's advice and doing what is best for his health. It's his senior year, after all. And my boy's future is what I care about. Tell Brandon good luck, I suppose. From what little pleasure I've had speaking with you just now I believe he'll need it."

She smiled at Jacqueline with the amount of excessive bullshit happiness the situation warranted.

Jacqueline didn't think it was very funny, going back in the house and slamming the door without even saying a fake goodbye. Not that any of them cared.

Immediately the three of them went back to the car, Keith's chest feeling lighter than it had since he'd first arrived at the home.

"She really dragged that out, huh?" Elizabeth stated.

Colleen agreed. "It's been nearly two hours since you went inside. She also threw your stuff on the driveway just after it started to rain. What a bitch.”

Elizabeth broke out into giggles.

“Mom!”

“I can swear every now and then, sweetie. You just can't because I'm your mother and I said so.”

CHAPTER TWENTY-ONE

To say he avoided certain areas of campus was an understatement.

"Let's go this way instead," he told Elizabeth. She squeezed his hand just a little bit tighter as they changed course, neither of them minding the two-block detour in order to go around the liberal arts and sciences building instead of walking past it. He didn't need to add the fact it was around the time Brandon would usually be walked to one of his history classes.

They didn't go anywhere near the southeast corner of campus at all. Every time he got closer to *that* house he started feeling this strange tingling feeling throughout his body like his blood was burning him from the inside out. In addition to feeling like it physically hurt him; his breathing became more forced and his mind panicked about what would happen if he ran into any of the Thompsons. It drove him crazy because he couldn't *squash* the feelings. He refused to acknowledge that he couldn't do a simple thing like walk past a house just because he had some bad memories there.

Elizabeth told him it was understandable, but his pride was already damaged. He felt ruined by the whole ordeal.

It didn't help that he still couldn't get a hold of Elijah. Keith had texted him about getting doctors' notes and leaving, hoping that would coax him to respond, yet there was still no sign he'd gotten the texts in the first place. Maybe his number had been blocked? He left a voicemail too for good measure just in case that was the problem.

He texted Isaac once, but there was no word from him either.

As for the Thompsons, Keith kept Brandon as a contact on his phone. Despite how badly he wanted to get rid of Jacqueline and Larry's numbers he left them if by chance they contacted him about something involving the contract. He did archive all of the texts and emails though, that way they were saved yet hidden. Seeing her name pop up on his phone or in his email left him in a bad mood.

"What do you want for dinner tonight?"

Keith hummed, guilt racking him even as he thought over the cheaper options.

"A burger and fries are fine. I don't want you spending all your credits on me."

"Sweetie, I get enough buffet meals a week from the dining hall that spending my credits at the shop won't put a dent in my eating habits. You know that. Stop choosing the cheapest thing on the menu or else I'll order you chicken wings and a milkshake."

He pouted. "I don't want that. Also, I grew up on fast food. Do you think eating the same thing every day is going to bother me? It isn't. We only have three weeks left until Thanksgiving break anyway, and barely two weeks after that until the end of the semester. Once the spring semester starts I'll move into an apartment. I can cook to my heart's content there."

"Have you found any good apartments yet? All the ones I see advertisements for are the fancy ones that are almost two-thousand dollars a month for rent."

"I found a couple for five-hundred and six-hundred a month. I'm going to check them out."

Elizabeth nodded, her mouth in a line before asking a question that was weighing on her.

"Will you be moving in by yourself or with a roommate?"

"Well, if I move in with a stranger the rent will be way cheaper. Apartments or a space in a housing complex for a single person are usually closer to a thousand dollars. It's less expensive for me to rent a two-bedroom apartment than it is for me to rent a studio."

"That's dumb. You'll end up having to use almost all of your money on rent and food. Will you be able to finish paying off the college in time to attend the graduation ceremony?"

"I might need to get a credit card to pay for the last installment. My parents and I don't have good enough credit to get a loan, so…"

"What if we moved into an apartment together?"

Keith was confused. "Didn't you take out a one-year housing contract? You know the college is a stickler for making money; they won't let you out of it unless you drop out, graduate, or die."

"You forgot I technically have enough credits to graduate with a bachelor's degree early due to the dual undergraduate-graduate level courses I've been taking the past three semesters. I can submit that I'm graduating to the housing office and they should let me move out early with no problem. I can officially start as a graduate student next semester when I move in with you."

She said "when" she moves in with me. This would be our first time living in an actual apartment together instead of cramming ourselves in the same dorm room for convenience's sake. We'd need to pay bills and upkeep the place and make food for each other. We could get a cat.

It sounded amazing to him.

"What about your parents? You know they won't approve of us living together unless we're married, and right now isn't a great time for me to pop the question. Not to mention if people from church found out they might be disappointed in us."

"Keith, my parents got married at sixteen after knowing

each other for maybe two years tops. My sister moved in with her boyfriend after going out for a year and lived together for two before they got married; they weren't treated any differently by their church friends. I'm sure our friends and family will understand why it's finally necessary to get a place together. Not only to save money, but we're going on dating for four years now. It'll be fine."

"You really want to?"

"Yep! Living with you sounds like a lot of fun. We could even find a place that allows pets and get a cat! It'll be like having a baby but it'll be self-sufficient and so much cuter!"

"You just really want to be able to get a cat, don't you?"

"No! Well, a cat would be nice, and living together also means me having access to a kitchen and that means I can cook all of the time so…"

"I see. A cat *and* food are your main motivators for this."

"You're twisting my words," she whined as she poked him in the stomach playfully. When he retaliated by poking her back she poked him again even harder. Luckily for him her jabs didn't bother him in the slightest. This just meant he could keep the game going until she finally gave up, which she did moments later when they got to a crowded crosswalk.

Keith smiled at her brightly after the crowds dispersed again.

"I'll start looking for places that allow pets in the six-hundred dollar range. Anything cheaper and we'll be stuck in one of those towers that have tiny rooms, shared laundry, and a bunch of restrictions."

"Shared laundry? I hate that about the dorms. People always touch my stuff."

"I know. I'll try to make sure no one steals your *Fullmetal Alchemist* shirts, okay?"

"You better!"

Approximately one week later, he got a message from Elijah.

Are you free tomorrow night?

Keith had never texted back faster in his life.

Yep. What's up?

Elizabeth looked over his shoulder from where she sat on her bed as they made plans to go to the campus observatory. There was a free stargazing event happening tomorrow where students or people from the community could look through telescopes as well as walk around the planetarium. It sounded like a good time; however, Keith knew the other PA couldn't be inviting him merely to look at the stars.

"I'm going to invite Tucker to come with us tomorrow too," she told her boyfriend. "That way if you need time to talk to Elijah alone Tuck and I can go look around but still be close by in case you need anything."

"Good idea. Thanks, Lizzy."

With a plan set he tried to get his mind off of all the ways tomorrow could go wrong. It was only when Elizabeth got him talking about the latest fanfiction he'd been reading that his mind let go of worrying about the future and instead focused on the present.

The walk to the observatory the next evening was a whole other story.

"Isn't Elijah the PA that likes Spongebob?" Tucker asked when he noticed the serious look on his friend's face. "Why are you so worried about talking to him? He seems cool to me."

"He is cool, which is exactly why I'm embarrassed to talk to him face to face again. Eli was the only one who ever stood up to Jacqueline. He didn't give a shit about her crazy rules or lectures, which is why she hurt him and why he left must have left so suddenly. I don't really blame him anymore for not texting me back. If I were him, then I might ignore me too. I was a pushover like Larry nearly the entire time I lived there."

Tucker seemed confused. "But you thought if you did anything you'd get brought to court or thrown in jail. It's not your fault Brandon has a bad home life; you were scared those people would ruin your life too if you tried to get them in trouble."

"He's not going to listen to you, Tuck." Elizabeth sighed. "He's set on thinking he was selfish for leaving without doing more to get Brandon out of his situation. I think he's been reading too much *My Hero Academia* fanfiction."

"Wow, Elizabeth. You're usually the more forgiving half."

"I don't want to give that woman the satisfaction of making the love of my life feel like shit because of *her* deplorable actions. The sooner he distances himself from everything that happened with the Thompsons the better, I say."

"I get that you don't want what happened to be a sore spot on my life," her boyfriend said, "but I can't forget about what happened that quickly."

"It's not about forgetting about it. It's about learning from it and moving on. Dwelling on what you could or should have done won't help unless you plan to do something despite the trouble it could cause for us in the future. And if you want to do something, then I'll support you the best I can."

Keith brought his hands to his face and began massaging his temples.

"Trying to help him without being sure he wants my support will put more than my own wellbeing in jeopardy. It could potentially affect everyone that I care about. Maybe I'll text him after graduation just to make sure he finished school okay."

"That works for me too. Getting involved in other people's business against their wishes works in television shows and movies, but in real like sometimes it's best to put yourself first."

"I don't know. I guess that makes sense. Still, I'm always going to remember Brandon and think I failed him."

"But Elizabeth is right. There's nothing you can do right now that wouldn't harm Brandon or yourself more in the long run," Tucker pressed as the neared the observatory. They were only one more block away. "Forcibly pushing his situation to light by calling DCFS on his family would stress him out too much to focus on his classes. Maybe he'll try to get away from them after he graduates? I think texting him after things die down is a better route."

"I wish I could text him now, but the last we spoke he made it clear he hated my guts. He might show anything I message him to his mother, which with how she rationalizes things she will see as harassment or something equally misleading."

"I wouldn't worry about him then. Maybe in a couple of months he'll have cooled down enough to realize his PAs cared more about him than his parents."

"Maybe."

They were now standing outside a small dome-topped building painted a solid white color. Outside of it along a stretch of open grass there were at least a dozen telescopes pointed at the quickly darkening November sky, wooden signs staked in the ground next to each of them with the name of the star or planet the telescope was trained on. The doors to the observatory were wide open as the visitors went in and out.

Keith pulled out his phone to text Elijah that he was outside by the telescopes when Elizabeth stopped him.

"No way. Keith, Brandon is here."

Upon hearing her words a spike of fear went through his chest. His anxiety skyrocketed as he followed her pointer finger to a telescope on the far side of the crowds. Sure enough Brandon was gazing through one of the devices with his cast close to his body. But he was standing without someone holding onto his good arm. What was more surprising was the person standing beside him, which quelled the rising anxiousness he was feeling somewhat: Elijah.

"I don't understand. I thought Brandon didn't like Elijah?" Tucker asked.

"I thought he wasn't allowed to stand without someone attached to his hip," Elizabeth added.

Keith was more confused than the two of them combined.

"I'm going to talk to them. I don't see Jacqueline, so you guys enjoy yourselves for a little bit. I read they are having a short lecture inside about the possibility of extraterrestrial life. Maybe you guys can check that out if I end up taking forever?"

Elizabeth grabbed Tucker's arm and gave him a thumbs up. "Don't worry about us! You do your thing, and we'll be around learning about aliens."

With that she steered Tucker towards the observatory, leaving Keith to make his way over to Brandon and Elijah by himself.

When he walked up to the two of them Brandon was peering through another telescope while his blue-haired companion watched over him. It was after tapping on Elijah's shoulder that he noticed Keith, his eyes widening upon seeing him.

"Keith!"

To the older PA's surprise Elijah squeezed the life out of him in a bone-crushing hug. Keith barely had time to hug him back before the younger pulled away and Brandon stood up to face him. He seemed to shrink in on himself as they met eyes. To be fair, Keith was just as scared to face his former Person. He was sure Brandon at least disliked him, and that Brandon believed Keith was upset with him.

"Hi," Keith finally said after a few seconds of silence. Brandon managed a small wave before the trio was forced to migrate away from the telescopes mid-greeting due to some eager children running to the one beside them. "You're… standing on your own."

The graduate student nodded at the stellar observation. He shifted from foot to foot awkwardly like he wasn't sure how to stand still without an arm in his.

"I thought I'd try a night-out living the way you thought I could live. I told my mother I was tutoring someone in my history class for an hour, and Thomas was kind enough to 'volunteer' to work extra hours tonight."

"The old guy walked him over here a little while ago," Elijah explained. "I need to have him back around nine, but Thomas said he'd keep quiet about this. I don't think he cares much for Jacqueline or her rules. No offense, Brandon."

"None taken. I mean, I always sort of knew why so many of my PAs quit. It was never solely because of me."

For as much as that cleared some things up Keith was still lost.

"Okay, so I get why you're here," he motioned to Brandon. "But why is Eli here with you? You and your mother made it sound like you disliked him even before he left. And why didn't you ever answer any of my texts before yesterday?" He asked Elijah, who looked like he'd expected those questions.

"I was having trouble finding somewhere to live short notice. Sorry I took so long to get back to you, but having a roof over my head while also attending classes was my main concern for a while. I also didn't want to get you in trouble with Jacqueline if she found out we were talking. I was worried she'd drag me to court despite what the lawyer said. As it was I had to crash on Isaac's floor for a couple weeks until I subleased someone else's apartment with a couple of roommates. It wasn't until like a week and a half ago that I couldn't ignore the situation I'd left anymore and started pulling some resources together."

"Elijah sent me links to some legal information on Facebook," Brandon cut in. "My mother doesn't mess with my apps the way she does my messages. If you ever need to message me that's the safest way to do it without her reading whatever you send. Anyway, he only sent me that stuff a day or two before you quit. At first, I ignored it because I was convinced neither of you cared about me, but after some time alone I started… reflecting on things."

"Yeah?"

"Yeah. I wrote down a list of things my mother does for me and says to me and then I looked up everything online to see how other people reacted to similar treatment. Turns out a lot of the things were not normal. Ugh, I hate that word, but you know what I mean. Anyway, I was hoping you would come back so I could talk with you in person about the incident that led to you leaving, and apologize for saying I hated you, but you were already prepared to leave and I didn't want my mother to know what I was truly feeling at the time..."

Keith held up a hand.

"Wait a second. You don't hate me?"

"No. I was so angry when I said that," he confessed, "but I didn't mean it. I understand if you don't accept my apology. I am sorry though."

"You're sorry? I'm sorry for leaving you behind."

Elijah rolled his eyes. "Dude, I left both of you behind. If anyone should be sorry it's me."

Brandon frowned. "Neither of you should feel bad for leaving. My mother hurt you, Elijah. You sent me the pictures. And Keith, she went out of her way to terrorize you. You should have seen her the days you were gone.

She was restless in a way I'd never seen her before; she was actively looking up tactics for keeping employees in line. You both stood up to her before quitting, which is more than any of my former PAs have ever done for me. Don't say sorry when I'm the reason you both ended up involved in my situation."

"It's not your fault either," the blue-haired PA pointed out. "Your mother was the one that put up the job, connived us, and made all of our lives a living hell."

"I'm an adult though. I should have done something before it got as bad as it was."

Keith shook his head. "Brandon, you are not at fault for anything she did to you. She controlled your life as a child and kept doing it even when you were old enough to grow up. There was no way you could have known some of the things she did were toxic."

"Maybe, but I did know when she started going out of her way to hurt me. Even when I saw she enjoyed doing it I was convinced it was my punishment for ruining her life. But I understand now," he forged on when he noticed both of his former PAs open their mouths to interject. "I didn't choose to have this disability; however, instead of living in spite of it I want to live with it. I want to learn what it's like to be surrounded by friends like yours, Keith, and experience fun things like you get to, Elijah. I'm so tired of being told my fate is to forever get taken care of by the same person who hates doing exactly that.

"I've started looking into my rights as a person living with a disability. I think, after Christmas break, that I might be able to find somewhere to live in a state-assisted living program. I qualify due to being unemployed while in school, so after I graduate I will need to find at least a part-time job to pay a reduced housing rate. All utilities would be included. I would also still get my disability check to pay for anything else I might need starting out."

"And I told him if his mother tries to stop him from

taking his belongings he can threaten to call the police. Brandon buys everything on Amazon, so he has electronic receipts for nearly all of his belongings," Elijah continued energetically.

"Well, there are a lot of things that were gifts, but I think the threat of me calling the cops called on her will have her letting me take what I want. Elijah said he and Isaac would be able to help me move when the time comes."

Keith grinned. "Elizabeth and I can help too! All of my friends would be thrilled to help you out if I asked. Jared, Tucker, and Jose have cars as well."

"That would make relocating a lot easier. I'll message you on Facebook when I have more details. The bigger question is did you mean what you said to me before you left last week?"

"You mean about me being your first PA? I don't know. I feel like Elijah deserves that job more than anyone. He stuck up for you way more than I did."

"As humbled as I am," the younger PA cut in, "I am fine with being hired second. You need to make enough money to graduate on time, don't you? You wouldn't have known this but my tuition and housing are covered by a scholarship. My mom was a veteran. I only worked so many hours because I like having spending money. It's not like I need as badly as you."

"Oh. Well, if that's the case, then I would love to be your first PA," he told Brandon. "It won't be a live-in job though, will it? Because I think Elizabeth and I will be moving in together next semester."

Brandon raised an eyebrow as if that were the most scandalous thing he'd ever heard. Or perhaps he was messing with him; Keith wasn't sure.

"I would need one live-in PA, but I think I might be able to talk Thomas into that role. I can split regular hours between you two though. I was going to see if I could spare any for Isaac, but Elijah told me he got a job as a foreign language tutor."

"He did. He tutors Italian," Elijah said.

"Isn't he Italian?"

"That's what makes him a great tutor."

They laughed for a few seconds before sobering up. Above them the sky had darkened considerably during their heartfelt conversation, and even more people were showing up at the observatory.

"Want to take a look inside?" Keith asked after a long bout of silence. "There's a lecture on alien life going on. Elizabeth and Tucker are already there."

Brandon, with Elijah right by his side, smiled.

"That sounds like fun."

EPILOGUE

"Is the food ready yet?"

"I don't know. It's probably close to being done though."

"Can I go check?"

"Nope. They already have the tray to put the kabobs on when they're done."

"But I wanna look at the food."

"Elizabeth, I love you, but the last time you went to just 'look' at the food you turned the temperature up when no one was looking and burned the burgers *and* the potatoes."

"That was just one time…"

"The one time you did it without anyone knowing. The time before that you convinced Sarah to take the chicken legs off before they were fully cooked."

"We put them back on! And no one got sick, so it wasn't that big of a deal, was it? Besides, Tuck wouldn't let me mess up dinner again! Elijah's also out there. He loves food too much to let anyone ruin it."

Keith shook his head even in the face of her pouting adorably.

"You promised us you would stay away from the food today."

"I was joking! I was the one that bought and cut up the

food in the first place."

"I know, and you did a great job at that! Now let the rest of them do their jobs. Besides, you really need to learn patience."

"Hey, I know patience. It's been over six years and I still haven't bothered you about marriage yet!"

"You definitely have. It's just other people tend to bring it up more, so you don't have to."

"True… But still, that shows I'm patient."

"Not when it comes to food."

"Well, maybe, but that's because I'm starving!"

He rolled his eyes. "So is Jared, but you don't see him—"

Keith was cut off by the back door slamming open, an annoyed Blonde Sarah dragging Jared in by the collar of his shirt.

"Hi guys," he greeted with an impish smile. As Sarah released him he fixed the messed up curls of his hair. "I think I'm in trouble."

"Yes you are!" Sarah stated with a glare before rounding on Keith. "Keep him inside until the food is done, you hear? I'm having enough trouble babysitting Jose, Elijah, and Brandon while Tucker grills without Jared constantly trying to mess with the propane tank. With his clumsiness he'll get us all killed. He's also distracting his brother," she added for good measure. "I'm too hungry for the food to be under or overcooked, so keep him inside."

With that she went back outside. Elizabeth merely grinned at her boyfriend, who looked appropriately disappointed.

"So can I—"

"*No.*"

"Not fair," she pouted. Pacing around for several seconds, obviously bored, she busied herself with grabbing plates and silverware. Anything to make the time go faster. When she was hungry it was like time slowed down.

At least she's not so hungry she's getting irritable. She's worse than Jared when that happens.

As for Jared he stared out the window of the back door dramatically, making faces at the friends that were outside at the grill more or less ignoring him after having a quick laugh. Once he was done being silly he turned around and smiled at Keith.

"So what's the plan for after dinner?"

The shorter of the two shrugged.

"We were going to watch *A Silent Voice*. Sarah and I are doing a project on deaf culture, so I thought it'd be a great movie for us to watch since it's one of the best movies out there with a deaf protagonist. Elizabeth has wanted to watch it for a while, and Jose and Elijah love anime so they want to see it too. Brandon doesn't mind because he said it won a bunch of awards, so he's interested to see why."

"Sounds good to me! Tuck will probably be the only one not excited at the choice, but that's because he doesn't like movies in general unless there's a dog in it."

"Trust me, I know. At least I found a version in English. I know he hates subtitles."

"Oh he does! Which is funny because he doesn't mind them in video games. Anyway, the new place is treating you well then? I think this is the first time we've grilled out here. We usually pick my place to entertain people."

Keith fought off a blush. "I wanted to host for once," he stated sheepishly. "Elizabeth thought it'd be nice since we almost always go to your place. I thought it'd be a nice change? That and I figured since its the first apartment we've ever had it would be good to break it in with some fun."

"I get ya, bro. It's a nice place. I'd say it's small, but knowing it's just the two of you living here there's no real reason other than luxury to have a bigger place. And you said the rent is only five-seventy-five a month? That's what

Tucker and I pay each to stay at our place. What a deal."

"You're welcome!" Elizabeth hollered from the other end of the house. She might have been in the bathroom now, but the vents in the house carried sound well and Jared was a loud talker.

"Elizabeth handled finding us this place," Keith explained, "since she's good at searching for things and comparing prices. Other than the whole mess of babysitting the past tenant's dog I like the place. We're both happy with it. We're looking into adopting a cat within the next week too, just to liven it up a bit."

"That sounds awesome. You'll have to invite us over again when that happens."

"Of course."

They were both quiet for a moment. Keith was comfortable in the silence, but it was obvious Jared wanted to say something.

"Hey, Keith?"

"Yeah?"

"Elizabeth told me you're looking at a job at some hotels here in the area. Did you like your summer job at the conference center that much?"

"I don't know. I guess I did like it a lot, looking back on it. Elizabeth is going to attend and work for the university for a few more years, and we like the area, so I know I need to get a job around here. I'd need to get a few more certifications to do group exercise classes or personal training though. Just having a degree and two times as many hours as I need doesn't count, I guess."

"That sucks, but I thought you were going to keep working as a PA? You can work more hours once you're out of school."

"I know. I just... I thought working with Brandon this semester would be enough for me to get over what happened last semester. But I was looking at some job postings for PAs and looking at them was enough to make me sick. I feel so bad too because I'm sure those people need help and hopefully aren't in a situation like he was, yet at the same time there's no reason for me to have to go find a job right away since I have the restaurant until August. A hotel seems like a better position for me for the time being, I guess. The people there can't be as manipulative or two-faced as Jacqueline was, surely?"

"Hopefully not. She hasn't tried to contact you or anything since you left, right?"

"Nope. I haven't heard a thing from her just like Dr. Sime told me. Of course Brandon has to deal with her all the time, but as far as she knows I'm out of the picture."

"Well, good for you man. I'm happy for you."

Keith smiled warmly. He hoped Jared knew he was one of the kindest souls he had the pleasure of knowing.

"Thanks, Jared. It means a lot. Your one of the best friends a guy could ask for. You'll make an awesome best man once I get my crap together."

"Aw, man. You're gonna make me cry."

"Please don't. The food should be ready any second, and Tucker added enough salt as it is."

Soon after their chat Jose raced in the house carrying a platter of beef and chicken kabobs. Like the finicky eater he was he pulled off the potatoes that were on them, trading them to Elizabeth in exchange for her pineapple and tomatoes. Somehow the two of them were just fine eating onions and bell peppers though? Keith didn't care that much, instead eating his share while he listened to Jared compliment his brother's cooking only for Tucker to berate his brother's. He pretended not to notice Elijah and Brandon holding hands under the table.

Once they were done eating they squished themselves onto the two couches: Elijah, Brandon, Jose, and Sarah on the long couch while the other four got up close and personal on the love seat.

Half an hour later, all of them heavily invested in the

movie, Keith took a moment to appreciate those around him. Even with Jared's elbow digging into his side and Elizabeth occasionally putting her freezing hands to his leg to warm them up he was content.

Just another day closer to graduation.

ABOUT THE AUTHOR

K. E. Marlow makes her debut with the support of her high school sweetheart as well as two furry felines. She hopes *Another Word for Help* can show that seeking help, while sometimes a difficult or painful task, is something people shouldn't be afraid of.

www.ingramcontent.com/pod-product-compliance
Lightning Source LLC
Chambersburg PA
CBHW062022190726
48284CB00014B/1667